LAND OF DREAMS

OTHER TITLES BY GIAN SARDAR

When the World Goes Quiet

Take What You Can Carry

You Were Here

LAND OF DREAMS

A Novel

GIAN SARDAR

This is a work of fiction. Names, characters, organizations, places, events, and incidents are either products of the author's imagination or are used fictitiously.

Published by Lake Union Publishing, Seattle

www.apub.com

EU product safety contact:
Amazon Media EU S. à r.l.
38, avenue John F. Kennedy, L-1855 Luxembourg
amazonpublishing-gpsr@amazon.com

ISBN-13: 9781662526800 (paperback)
ISBN-13: 9781662526817 (digital)

Cover design by Faceout Studio, Addie Lutzo
Cover image: © Sudha Peravali / ArcAngel Images; © juanma hache, © Jiojio, © Jose A. Bernat Bacete / Getty; © Angel DiBilio, © Brocreative, © TWINS DESIGN STUDIO, © Ava Peattie / Shutterstock

Printed in the United States of America

For Joe, who made the dreams possible

CHAPTER 1

Do What You Gotta Do

December 1930
New York City

A city full of people with no place to go. They walk just to walk, move to not stand still; they do anything they can to not feel where they are or, worse, *who* they are. Up and down Mott Street, cars crawl and horns make almost comic protests while signs blink on and off, on and off. At the corner, a newsie, a boy no older than ten, stands on a crate and waves a newspaper, bundles tied with twine at his feet, and a movie palace's marquee is missing half its bulbs, the entire *a* in *theatre* dark. But it doesn't matter; the line to the box office stretches the length of the building, everyone shifting and restless. Though no one should be spending the thirty-five cents for a movie, all are desperate for the warmth and the escape. Sit back, look up, and leave your life behind. Though nobody has enough money, all have plenty to forget.

Frankie's the only one not moving, struck still by the racing of her heart. A block over, there's a job interview taking place, but the line was around the corner when she went to drop off her application, and if she doesn't make it uptown within the hour, she'll miss the only other opening she knows about. Yesterday she found the man she's been working for hanging from a rafter. Today she is unemployed. She told herself to not feel or think, to not even consider her situation, but instead to jump right in and find something new, but the line threw her, sapping her resolve.

She's twenty-three years old and worn thin. She knows the exact shade the ceiling gets during every hour of every night, because she's there, studying the cracks. Her mother died just months ago, and even though Frankie has worked almost her whole life, she has done so mostly at the whims of others. The laundress who broke a wrist: *I'll need help this week, and maybe next.* The dressmaker who was fighting with her cousin: *Until she says sorry, the work is all yours*. Nothing steady. Nothing under her control. The one thing she's done for years is cook for the landlord's frail wife, but without Frankie's mother's income, it's not enough.

"Only a penny!" the newsboy shouts, slicing the air with the paper, back and forth. "Special deal for a special day!"

She catches the date on the page. The kid's hawking last night's edition, hoping no one notices. Most likely he took whatever the *New York Times* tossed into an alley this morning. Most likely he's got a mother who always claims she ate just before dinner. *Honestly, I'm full. You have that.*

"Only a penny?" Frankie manages to say as a man turns the corner. "That's a deal." Without looking, the man hands over a penny and grabs a paper and keeps moving. Frankie winks at the kid, who gives her a grateful smile.

Still, her heart hammers. So fast, it's made its way into her ears, the sound relentless, and she realizes she might be having a heart attack.

It's actually this thought that calms her. If she died now, struck down by her grieving and worn-out heart, there would be no blame, no failure. *Never give up,* her mother, Fiona, used to say. Essentially, *endure*. Bend but don't break. *It is better to be strong than to be loved,* Fiona also used to say, but only after years and years of falling in love with men who lifted her high into cloudy adoration, who made promises and assurances that proved to be nothing more than mist.

But Frankie is tired and doesn't want to be strong. She doesn't want to keep going. In this moment, she only wants to stop; she wants to disappear and somehow leave her life, if only for a break or a chance to start over.

Suddenly, the kid hawking papers looks above her head. And it's the expression on his face that makes her turn.

Above her, the sky has broken open.

A crack. A beam of light has somehow pierced the gray and white, sifting into something like a rainbow. A slice of color. *A wonder,* a romantic might think. Frankie, however, is not a romantic. All the faith she had in miracles died with her mother, because when Fiona was gone, there were no signs, no messages, no chills on her shoulder from a ghostly touch. And while some might see this beautiful rift as a sign or a miracle, Frankie jumps to suspicion, wondering how someone managed to pull this prank. But then she sees that everyone has stopped, and is looking up. Whatever it is, it's real, and the whole depressed world is caught up in its strange beauty.

And that's when Frankie looks down and sees that the line for the job interview has scattered, all the women stepping beyond the restaurant's green awning and into the street, raising their hands to shield their eyes as they look and point at the sky.

Life, Frankie's mother always said, *is a web of choices.* Every decision, every moment, branches off and leads to the next. Sometimes you actually feel the moment of change, the exact instant your path turns, but more often than not, the real shift was earlier, unannounced and overlooked. Something small that's only apparent in hindsight. Identifying those moments became a game Frankie and Fiona used to play. *If your shoelace hadn't come untied, you'd have been right there when the dog came loose,* or *if my stomach didn't start hurting, I never would have stopped and seen that job sign.* The idea that something little could be essential to something big was comforting to people who lived in a small corner of a small apartment, who were lost in the haze and shuffle of a big city, and who worried that when push came to shove they would slip from the earth unnoticed.

Now it feels as though an entire city is looking up at the sky, and Frankie understands that this is one of those moments. A shift she can feel while it's happening.

Within seconds she's there, and while the manager's pressed against the window, Frankie slips her application on top of the pile. Nearby, a man in a double-breasted pinstripe suit sees this and sits back, lowering his paper as if he understands a better entertainment is about to commence. On the plate before him are four dark-purple figs and a scoop of ricotta, and the sight of the fruit—during winter—throws her.

There's talk among the customers—a *sundog*, someone calls the occurrence, which hooks into one of the few memories Frankie has of her birth family, whom she last saw when she was five. Her memories of them are threadbare, worn thin over the years, but one that's clear was of their dog, who was black and liked to sit on the bricks behind the house and soak up the sun. Heat radiated off him when he went inside, and Frankie remembers resting her head on his rib cage when he lay down. Hot, like something left inches from a flame. Dusty, like dry earth.

By the time the manager's returned, Frankie's standing near the bathroom, casual, as he picks up the top application. Beside her, the wall is covered with postcards from Italy and newspaper clippings and a map of the boot with hearts drawn around certain cities and villages. She's often assumed to be Italian, someone from the north with olive skin and dark hair but blue eyes, and that, along with the name she was born with, Francesca, could be enough if the man doesn't fixate on her adoptive mother's last name.

"Francesca Donnelly," the manager calls, looking expectantly at the first woman in line.

Frankie steps forward, wiping her hands on her skirt as if she's just been in the restroom, and tells him to call her Frankie. Out of the corner of her eye, she sees the man in the pinstripe suit smiling as he cuts a fig in half and smothers it with a dollop of ricotta.

"Whoa," the first woman in line says, a blonde with finger-waved hair, smooth and sculpted like something straight out of a film. "I didn't see you here."

"There's a *line*," someone else says.

All the women turn. Disapproving, annoyed, but waiting for Frankie to speak, because, despite the fact that they clearly need jobs as well, part of them must still hope there'd be a reason someone would cut in front of them. That in the face of everything, kindness and order have not been forgotten. And this thought breaks Frankie's heart—or it would, if she had time to let it. But a glance at the clock on the wall tells her she needs to start the journey uptown in ten minutes if she's to make it.

She smiles at the first woman. "Honestly, *you're* why I left the line."

At this, the man in the pinstripe suit lowers his paper, abandoning all pretense of not listening in.

"Your hair," Frankie continues. The woman touches the crown of her own head. "It's flawless. My mother used to help with mine, but she's gone and I'm hopeless. Seeing yours made me want to try."

The woman's eyes cut to Frankie's hair, which is chin length and waved naturally and, she's heard, energetically. "Well—" the woman starts to say, but the manager cuts her off.

"Come on, now. You see what we got here. You think it's time to talk about hair?"

Down the line, someone says, "*And* I was just at the restroom, and I did *not* see her."

The blonde glances over her shoulder. "Edith, you were outside with the rest of us."

"Not before that, I wasn't."

"I was in the alley," Frankie says. "The restroom was occupied. I figured it would be a while, and I have a mirror in my compact." To the manager, she says, "I know this is wasting your time. I'm sorry. I just wanted to do what I could."

He softens, then shakes the page in his hand. "This you?"

"It is. But I can get back in line. I don't want to upset anyone."

Frankie thinks she hears a laugh from Pinstripe, but won't look his way.

"No," the blonde says. "You'll be fast, I'm sure. You go."

And though all Frankie intends to do is tell the woman *thank you*, instead she hugs her. A full hug, with her arms wrapped around the woman's shoulders. The embrace catches even Frankie off guard, and she feels the woman stiffen and then relax. At last, she whispers into Frankie's ear, "You just need a good brilliantine. And a brush."

Before the protests get too loud, Frankie follows the manager to a corner, where he takes a seat. When he flips over her application, she quickly starts to explain. "The charges were—"

"You got an *arrest* on your record?"

"You see, my mother—"

"That lady was right, this is gonna be fast." He turns in his seat, yelling to a man near the kitchen, "I thought you got the bad ones out!"

Frankie stays seated. "You *want* someone like me to work for you. Someone not afraid to get their hands dirty. Someone who will do what it takes to get the job done."

There's a second when he pauses, when she knows he's actually considering her words. But then there's a smirk. "The job's waiting tables. I'd prefer hands that are clean."

"I know how to cook every Italian dish. *Ribollita*, *puttanesca*, *crostata*, I can make a Bolognese that will make your heart sing—"

"Don't need it, don't need it, don't need it. And what makes my heart sing is someone without a record. *Please.* Do what you gotta do in life, but you can't do it here."

~

Tall buildings hunker over the street, casting shadows. Frankie stands in a wedge of cold outside the restaurant, watching three feathers flutter slowly to the ground, before she looks up, tracing the fire escape all the way to the top, where a group of kids hang their arms over the railing, watching the plumage drift. She closes her eyes. Just barely, existing somewhere behind the noise of everything, she thinks she hears a chicken scream. Then silence.

She's tired. Though a wood partition separates her from the family who shares her small apartment, in one spot they ran out of wood, and so the wall is improvised with a hanging sheet. Late at night, when the man's wife and child are sleeping, he cries. And though he retreats to the corner farthest from them, he forgets, or doesn't have the luxury to care, that Frankie's right there, just beyond the tattered cotton, sleepless and living both his sorrow and her own. If she traded sides with them, she could tuck herself into an alcove and spare herself some sound, but many of her best memories with her mother took place at the window on her side. It was there they carved hearts in the wood, there her mother taught her a wordless code for *I love you*—three taps in the center of her palm, a silent promise in the night—and there her mother strung up a plastic morning glory vine, the purple petals now dusty but beautiful if Frankie squints.

"Never lead with the word *honestly*," someone says. "It's like a megaphone announcing you're about to lie."

The man in the pinstripe suit. Italian, forties. Pants with the perfect pleat. A side part and slicked-back hair. He has the appearance of something polished to a dangerous shine, and yet the laugh lines at his eyes and the set of his mouth convey a sense of humor, a slight undoing to his composure. "But you got one thing right: Pay someone a compliment, and you win 'em over. That was fun."

"Was it, now?" she asks, peering back up at a sky that's mended. Seam of light sewn shut, the colors gone.

"More fun for me than you. I get that. But listen, I didn't come out here to proposition you. Or maybe I did." Now she looks at him sharply, and he laughs, a laugh that seems to gather momentum. "Here's what I'm saying. I could use someone like you. For work. Someone who thinks on their feet." He smiles. "Someone not afraid to get their hands dirty."

She stands straight. Can almost feel the ruler along her spine, the sisters' way of making sure she didn't slouch. "Done. I'm your girl. When do I start?"

Again, a laugh that gets bigger as if he's retelling a joke in his mind. "You probably shouldn't ask *when* but *where*."

She stays silent, waiting.

"Fine. The answer's five days and two trains away from here. But you get yourself there, show me you want it, and the job's yours."

In a little over two years, on a mockingly clear and beautiful March afternoon, she will think of this day while attending a funeral at Hollywood Memorial Park. As knives of sunlight glint on the pond near the mausoleum and fans push against barricades, ripples of grief overtaking them now and then, Frankie will hide in the corner, guilt tugging at her heart as her mind traces the breadcrumbs of events back to this day in New York, this afternoon when the sky broke open.

What would've happened if she never looked up? Or if that boy didn't decide to sell newspapers on that specific corner, that corner where her heart started beating and her mind went loud and the world stopped, just for a bit, to peer at a crack in the sky? If that moment didn't occur, would the gun have gone off, years later?

The link in the chain. The breath before the sentence. That's how she will think of this moment, right here, when the man hands her his business card.

Nico Marconi. Head of Publicity. RCO Studios. Hollywood, California.

CHAPTER 2

Everyone Holds the Cards to Their Downfall

Sunday, February 19, 1933
Hollywood, CA

An English village with half-timbered houses and climbing roses that reach and stretch in a never-ending bloom.

The Sphinx, steady and silent.

The Eiffel Tower, swooping upright, elegant and pristine.

At RCO Studios, circling the globe is a snap—a slight consolation to Frankie, who's never left the country and whose only travel experience involved train stations and clouded windows, a downtrodden country and long, dusty roads that snaked empty and endless. But here, here, she can see the world with the pedal of a bike.

When she takes a quick detour through the Wild West ghost town, she searches for one of the studio cats that lives there, black with a white-tipped tail and six toes on each foot. But the planked wooden sidewalks are bare. Only dust and a few streamers left over from a recent wrap party. A pause by a saloon's facade, the spot of the second kiss she shared with the man she's been seeing for seven months. Her boyfriend—a title she's only lately and reluctantly admitted to—whose eyes are the same blue as a giant butterfly she saw when she was a child during her one and only time in a museum. Pinned to a board, the turquoise-blue wings were edged in black. *A Ulysses!* a boy beside her said, and she was struck silent because she'd never met a child who had time to learn the names of butterflies.

Ulysses. At first she joked and called her boyfriend *Ulysses S. Grant*, but soon the nickname became *Grant*, as she latched on to a portion of the name that was much more fitting for someone whose voice still sends shivers all through her body. She tells herself that the fact that they have no future doesn't matter; after all, people flash in and out of this world so fast that the only thing that matters is *now*, and the truth is, he is only meant to exist between what should matter in her life—herself and her job—because she learned from her mother what *not* to do with men. The problem is that Frankie's been breaking her own rules. For the first time ever, she's been having fun, and fun is not something she's used to having, or even wanting. Fun and happiness, lust and craving; all of it is problematic to someone who understands just how easily she could lose everything, and how crucial it is to cherish a job that often feels like hitting the jackpot. Even if she's only Nico's girl Friday, the one whose chance to learn and whose studio perks offset the measly paychecks, she's part of a world that used to entrance her and her mother, and every day she walks among the stars, witnessing the magic that will spill from a film reel. Most importantly, though, soon Frankie will be Nico's associate—a fixer like him—once he can convince the studio that a woman can do the job.

Prop rooms with ceilings crowded with glimmering chandeliers and heavy wrought iron light fixtures. Walls of oil paintings and shelves of swords. Rows and rows of statues and tables and sets of fancy china. There is even a section of taxidermized animals, and a wolf that wears a hat. The studio has it all, and nothing is as it seems. Normal offices are disguised by all-American-town-square fronts and red, white, and blue bunting, and even the soundstages at the studio are like giant geodes, gray and tan on the outside, while inside they're bright shocks of ancient kingdoms or cityscapes or even the Grand Canyon. In one corner there might be stuffed Siberian tigers lit with tripod lamps and, in another, a swimming pool that gleams turquoise under Fresnel lights. *Doesn't matter how fancy we get, nothing we do will ever beat golden hour,* Nico has told her, referring to the time just before the sun sets or after it rises. Everything is an attempt to emulate what's real. In most cases, they do it even better. Recently, the studio's scenic artists sculpted the *Venus de Milo*, but added her missing arms. A joke, a gag gift for Nico, who now keeps her in his office, fully clothed. *Everyone's got a strict morals clause,* he said, laughing.

It's a weekend, so only a fraction of the usual crowd is here, and those present attend to a promotional shoot for their upcoming release *Desert Son*. Frankie abandons the search for the cat and decides to take the last minutes of her break in her favorite location: the New York City back lot, streets with fake brick buildings and stoops and fire escapes that were actually brought in from New York. It's where she goes to think, and it clears her mind in a way that only *home* can.

Nico, I work sixty hours a week and still live in an apartment with two other girls, and my towel is always, always *covered in pink lipstick, and you know I hate pink.*

Nico, I appreciate that the studio pays for my rent and car, but I need a raise.

Nico, I'm not a secretary, but I'm also not your associate. I do the work and don't get credit.

Nico, I deserve *a promotion. I've* earned *it.*

Has she been fooling herself that this will happen? *You have to know when a dream is just a dream,* her mother once said, when they were looking at Christmas window displays and Frankie wanted to go inside the store. Is that what this job is? A dream that's just beyond the glass?

She leans her bike against a light pole, and faces a restaurant. *The* restaurant, in fact. Nico's cousin's New York restaurant, the spot where Frankie and Nico met, a restaurant the cousin eventually lost in a card game. All it took was Nico showing the studio's scenic designers a photo, and now it's a chance to visit the past. *Do you see what I see?* Nico asked when he first brought her here. And she'd taken in the green awning and the big bold red lettering and even the brick, which was dirtied to the exact shade of that faraway building, and she saw herself outside the window in a moment of *before*. Embarrassed, she swiped at her eyes, feeling memories of her mother and her past and everything she'd turned her back on when she went West. With a quick squeeze of her shoulder, he looked away, letting her cry, just a little, before they got back to work.

People need to be saved from themselves, he often says. *Everyone holds the cards to their own downfall.*

Maybe she shouldn't push it. Maybe this isn't the week, not so close to the *Desert Son* premiere. This film release has him tenser than usual, and Frankie suspects it's because the final film they released in '32, *The Last Chance*, was what some called a *passion project*, something June Finney—their biggest star—wanted to do because the role was intense and challenging and rewarding, but something that made no money. Jack Sawyer—the studio's other top name—went along with it because he claimed the script sank its teeth into him, but *The Last Chance* was a drama and one of the few movies the studio did that didn't end on a happy note, so while it was critically acclaimed, audiences wanted no part of a story that reflected their own world too precisely. *Next time she gets a craving to act,* the head of the studio said about June, *make her do a play. I'll even pay for it myself. Lord knows it would be cheaper, and at least no one would see it.* Irony was thick in that June's contract mandates that she only do RCO productions, which excludes plays, and that June, in fact, has no interest in the theatre—Jack is the one aching to get back on the stage.

"I knew you'd be here," a production assistant says, rounding the corner on his bike, the handlebars a chrome glare of sunlight. He stops by the newsstand, shellacked newspapers glued in place. "They said you'd be in Egypt, and I said no, she goes home whenever she gets a chance."

Frankie makes a mental note to find a new spot. "What do you need?"

"Aren't you uncomfortable? There's a chair over there," he says, motioning toward a corner café. "So you don't have to sit on the floor."

Uncomfortable is trying to sleep wearing all the clothing you own, because it's that cold. It's never having a pillow and sitting on boxes when the chairs get sold and only having cold baths with water that also has to wash the clothes and other people. Frankie wants to say all that and more, but what she says is "I'm not on the floor. I'm on a step."

He whistles, as if her logic is too much. "Nico wants you in his office. Now. Or, ten minutes ago, but they sent me to Egypt—"

She doesn't wait for him to finish. In seconds, she's rounding a corner by the commissary, startling two women from the photo shoot who are sneaking cigarettes, each in a white blouse and long skirt, their hair tousled as if they've just been riding horses. One is an *option girl*—someone the studio has under contract for six months with an option to renew—a young woman who's been planting herself in Nico's path. Frankie stands on the bike's pedals to go faster and is flying past when suddenly someone steps from behind a Ford Model B and right into her path.

She swerves hard to the left. Wobbles and starts to fall. Miraculously, somehow, she rights the bike just in time. When she comes to a stop, she searches for the person she almost crashed into, but whoever it was must have run off.

Jack and June stand by a wagon, watching her as if she's fallen from the sky until Jack realizes what happened and scans the street as well. Jack, famous not just for his acting but also his heavy right hook, is thirty-four years old, with a bio that waxes poetic about his rustic start on a ranch, a past that left him rough around the edges. *That man came into the world swinging at the doctor,* Magda Lockwood, the studio's favorite tabloid reporter, has written more than once. Regardless, men still want to end their days on the barstool beside him, and women still want to start their nights in his bed. Even now, Frankie notices the option girl getting closer, gaze fixed on him as he takes off his hat and runs his hand through the flop of his dark-blond hair.

Beside him, June pretends not to notice. A couple for three years now, they increase ticket sales simply by holding hands in public. It's their movie, *Desert Son*, that's about to premiere. A Western that fell behind schedule when the director discovered that June was afraid of horses. *What's next,* Nico asked, *an island romance so we can find out she's scared of water and coconuts?*

For some reason, Jack's carrying a fishing pole. Frankie squints at it. "There's no fishing in this movie. Is there?"

"I'll tell you what there's not," he says loudly. "There's no *marlin in a river*." The property master, standing beside a wagon, shakes his head. "Even *baby* marlin," Jack continues, eyeing the man, "which, believe it or not, are *still* marlin."

June's production assistant hands her a glass of water, but from the slow sip and the new-fawn wobble in June's step, Frankie knows it's not water. To Hollywood, Prohibition only means hidden doors and hidden flasks, covert fun and tunnels that provide party guests with routes out in case of a raid.

June winces as she takes another sip, and Frankie decides she'll mention this to Nico. June, though only twenty-six, is more famous than royalty and tends to leave pandemonium in her wake, the result of an inexplicable insecurity and a mood that too often swerves from bright optimism to dark despondency. *There is a wilted flower at her core,* Nico's said.

"Marlin are saltwater," Jack explains to Frankie. "Saltwater fish are different than freshwater."

Another sip, another wince, and June says, "We know *all* about marlin now. It's been a captivating half an hour."

Frankie catches the option girl shifting over a few feet—so she's directly in Jack's line of vision—as she lifts her dress to adjust her stocking. With every second, Frankie's resolve to talk to Nico is slipping. "I've never fished."

When she looks back up, Jack's eyes are wide. "You've *never* fished?"

"From Montana," she hears the option girl say to her friend, about Jack. "And he plays tennis and boxes."

"I stole a fish at the Fulton Fish Market," Frankie says.

"That's not fishing."

She shrugs. "I went home with a fish." He laughs. But she won't let him distract her, so gets back on her bike. "Sorry, have to see Nico."

"There a problem?"

Suddenly June's all attention as well. There's a twitch in her eyelid. *Watch her eyes,* Nico's said. *You wouldn't think an actress would have a tic, but it's how you know she's not acting.*

"No problem, I just wanted to talk to him," Frankie says, but then she remembers that *he* wanted to talk to *her*. "Or maybe there is a problem? I don't know."

"Would you please take this?" June says, unclasping a barrette from her own hair and handing it to Frankie. "I swear, Frankie, it's as if your hair is at war with itself."

While all around her are perfectly sculpted finger waves, Frankie doesn't have the time or patience. Despite her lack of extensive grooming, she's still heard people say she's beautiful, a claim that catches her off guard. *She's actually quite beautiful,* she heard recently, a statement that rose at the end with bewilderment, as if maybe Frankie had done her best to hide this fact. *But a bit feral, I'd say.* That was the part Frankie loved.

Now, without any idea of what she's doing, she fastens the barrette and tries not to look at Jack, who she knows will start laughing.

"Mr. Sawyer," a man says, approaching. "I'm with Acqua di Parma. You might know our fragrance, Colonia. If you have a minute, Mr. Marconi was saying—"

"Sorry, all I endorse is a bar of soap."

"Sure, sure. But I do come bearing gifts. My wife tells me you've got one hell of a sweet tooth."

The man holds out a box of chocolates, and Frankie pauses, always confused by this world in which rich people are handed so much for free. Jack, however, doesn't care that it's free—only that it's chocolate—and Frankie uses the moment to escape, rehearsing her speech.

Nico, it's time.

She parks her bike in front of their office building, which is two stories, the first level dressed up with fake storefronts. Across the street is a town square with a quaint center park and water fountain, the kind of life most of the people here have filmed but not lived.

Inside, Nico's secretary, Betty, spots her and holds up her hand like a traffic cop. Glasses and short hair. She smells like expensive perfume, like the crushed petals of a thousand French roses. She nods toward Nico's office, and whispers, "The powers that be."

Frankie falls silent, listening. *The powers that be* is Nico's term for the top brass at the studio, men who could decide on a whim to fire everyone in their line of vision, men who could destroy an actor's career in such a variety of ways that Betty once joked they had a card catalog of options: *A* for *audition*—put a significant chip into an actor's confidence by holding auditions for the role they were set to star in; *B* for *budget*—allocate such a low budget that the entire film looks cheap and tanks overnight; *C* for *character*—force the actor to play a character that audiences are meant to hate. *Page seven! Page seven, he kills the family dog!* one of their former stars screamed when he read a rewrite on the film he was doing, a rewrite ordered the day after someone spotted the actor talking with a competing studio.

"Are they," Frankie whispers about the top executives, "*in* there?"

Betty makes a face. "I don't think they've *ever* gone to someone else's office. No, they're on the phone."

Quietly, so she might catch part of the conversation, Frankie moves to the side of the room with the parrots. Romeo and Juliet: two red-crowned Amazons, lime green with red foreheads, an irony in their names since they're forever forced together. On one side of the office bullpen is what started off as a massive birdhouse in the same *style moderne* as the new Chrysler Building in New York City, complete with steel spire, sunburst motifs, and geometric patterns. But despite how much money the head of the studio paid for the birds from an exotic animal dealer in Mexico, he quickly decided they were too loud, and since then producer after producer has schlepped the parrots around until, at last, they landed with Nico. Nico, who enlisted the help of the studio's metalworkers to open up one side of the cage and build what he calls *the addition*—a giant floor-to-ceiling enclosure stocked with tropical plants and a wall that the studio artists shaped and painted to look like lava rock, complete with ferns that require biweekly misting.

Betty, not a fan of the noise, must've decided to let the birds sleep for as long as possible, and so Frankie draws up the curtain that covers them. It kills Frankie that they're inside like this, but no one could release them without incurring the studio head's wrath. *This is better than being in the wild,* Nico has said. *Here, their only predator is Betty, and if I'm a betting man, I got the birds to win that one.*

"You eat?" Betty asks. "This working-on-a-Sunday bit has thrown off my schedule."

Frankie nods, though she forgot to eat lunch, too consumed with all she needs to say to Nico. "A sandwich the size of my arm."

"I can never tell when you're lying." A laugh. "Nico's trained you well."

Frankie smiles. "Or maybe I trained him."

Betty tilts her head as if considering. "I might actually believe that."

Though she shouldn't take it as a compliment, Frankie does.

"Did I tell you I saw one of them outside the window?" Betty asks.

It takes Frankie a second to realize she's talking about the parrots. Frankie looks at Juliet, a bit fainter with her colors, who edges back and forth on her perch. "One got out?"

"Oh no, I mean there was a third. It was outside the window. Juliet, or maybe it was Romeo, I don't know who's who, and I don't care, but one of them was going crazy. Drove *me* crazy."

These birds are not native to the United States. They don't live here, and so what Betty saw—if indeed the same species—must have been an anomaly, an escapee perhaps, and now Frankie's picturing a lone, solitary bird. What would it do upon finding two of its friends behind the glass? Would it want to join them and no longer be alone? Or would it prize its freedom, no matter the expense? Frankie doesn't know who she feels worse for—their birds that are caged or the one who lives by itself, its calls unanswered.

"I hear Nico took you to see a house," Betty says. "Is it just for the studio to have? Because we've got the bungalows if someone's coming to town. I can arrange to have one cleaned. Is someone coming to town?"

"Not that I know of."

"Did you like it?"

"It was tiny. In Edendale." The Edendale district, home to the original studios, Mack Sennett, Keystone, and Disney. All hills and steep streets and wooded secrecy. Frankie's favorite part of town. Where she lives now is just on its edge, in a fourplex.

"Iffy won't like a small house," Betty says about June's older sister, Ida Finney, referred to as *Iffy* behind her back. Iffy, entitled and prim and proper, but an ally when push comes to shove. Then Betty laughs. "That's my guess who the house is for."

"No. It wouldn't be for Iffy. It's too small, too secluded. Honestly, no one would want to live there."

It was Frankie's dream house. The ultimate goal for someone raised in a tenement: a small, quiet home, far enough away from the hustle and bustle that one could pretend nothing else existed. A place to live alone and to indulge in silence. Barn red with wide wooden planked floors and a small, shaded garden surrounded by trees. There was even a fig tree without leaves that Nico immediately spotted. *I'll have to ask the neighbors if it fruits. Most wild fig trees don't,* he explained to the woman showing them the house. The woman nodded and said, *How truly interesting*, boredom slowing her words.

Betty unwraps a mint and pops it in her mouth. "If the house isn't for Iffy, we still need to find her something, don't we? She can't just live with June, can she? I feel like that's not so great for June?" And then a smile. "*Though* I keep hearing there's going to be a wedding."

The long-standing rumor, one the studio started, after conjuring the entire Jack-and-June relationship with a wave of its wand, back when June needed to repair the dent an ex had put in her reputation and Jack was an unapologetic bachelor whose career needed a bump. Both with years left on their contracts with the studio, neither with a say in the matter.

"No way," Frankie says. "If there was a wedding, I'd know."

Betty, chastened, starts straightening papers on her desk. The mint bulges in her cheek.

Frankie's made a mistake. Betty, often underestimated, is the gatekeeper, the one who's always listening and is the key to almost everything Nico-related. Because of this, those in the know have her at the top of their Christmas lists, and the office fills with flowers on her birthday. Frankie leans in. "You're right, though. Iffy needs a place to live. Between me and you, I think that place should be Detroit."

Now Betty smiles. "I know we need her, but that woman is a nightmare. And it kills me that June doesn't see it. I'll never understand how the strongest people are simply undone by love."

Loving or being loved—all of it can be a downfall, a lesson driven home with Frankie's mother's mistakes, culminating in the time Fiona left the one decent job she had to work for a man who brought her bunches of sweet peas from his garden every Thursday. A man whose wife came into the office only one week into Fiona's new employment, recognized the flowers she herself had grown, and put an end to everything. Fiona: long dark-red hair and arctic-blue eyes and freckles that she hated but men found charming. *She's too pretty for her own good,* Frankie once overheard about her mother. *That kind of pretty makes you dream stupid dreams.*

Nico opens his office door. "You find the cat?"

"It's gone."

"It's not gone," he says, and steps aside as she enters the room. As the door closes, Frankie catches a glimpse of Betty's face, watching as she always does, with open curiosity. Not many women make it past the desks outside the offices, and though Frankie's desk is out there as well, the fact that she's invited inside so often—without ever being asked to take notes—has sparked more than just curiosity. "Every starlet in town feeds that cat. No way it's leaving."

"Is everything all right with . . ." Frankie stops, and motions to the phone, referring to the studio brass.

"Head of production is getting his walking papers."

Frankie's eyes widen. "But they love him."

"Love*d*. Someone's always gotta take the fall. But it's not out yet, so mum's the word. Anyhow, the reason you're here. Magda's not happy that you gave Dottie a scoop."

Dottie is Magda's competition. "Because I told Dottie that Joan Crawford didn't like her name? Come on, if a studio named me *Crawford*, I'd think *crawfish* too. It was nothing, just a morsel to keep Dottie close. I didn't intend for it to be a scoop."

"I'd be a rich man if intentions counted—what matters is that Magda got touchy. I had to settle her down. So make sure she knows it was a morsel, not a meal. Oh, on that, Angela's cooking something special tonight. Come hungry. Really hungry, or she'll be mad."

Sunday dinner. Every week. Six p.m., on the dot.

"But," Nico continues, "what I really wanted to say is this: You're almost there."

"Where?"

"What do you mean *where*? You're almost my *associate*. I got the green light from the powers that be." When she says nothing, he raises his hands. "Hello?"

But Frankie's thrown. Being given what she's worked for is not something she's used to, and these days, in this economy, there's no correlation between hard work and reward. In her mind, she thought she'd have to fight forever. After a moment she realizes she's nodding, though she's not sure what she's agreeing to. "I got it?"

"First, a two-month probation—"

"What about a *two-year* probation? Isn't that what I just did?"

"Ah, there you are."

"*Nico*, no one can say I haven't proven myself—"

"*Frankie*, I get it. I know that. But the men in the clouds here, they don't see a woman doing what I do."

"Well, they wouldn't until I *did* it. Then they'd see it."

"*Exactly.* Exactly what I told them. So two months—a *provisionary promotion*, you might say. But that gives you a title, clout, even more money. Listen, though, you gotta tread carefully. You're good at your job, way better than I'd even hoped. But you're fearless. And fearless people take too many risks."

A pause as he lifts a jade paperweight from his desk, glancing at the phone message beneath it. Frankie's mind races. What does he know? She's gotten sloppy, has forgotten her own rules, has started enjoying life more than is wise. *Don't say it,* she told her boyfriend a few months ago, when it sounded like he was about to tell her he loved her. Though no one had ever told her that before, and it wasn't as if she had practice in these matters, she'd felt the approach of the line as if the words themselves were swarming around them. *You feel it too, don't you?* he'd said, and he was happy. There were a few reasons she chose to not believe that he loved her, but in that moment she only knew that she was slipping and needed a handle on her life. Love, as she'd learned, was the great derailer, the crusher of plans, the water doused on the fire of ambition. So again, she cut him off, irritated. *You're used to getting what you want, but I'm not. Take it from a pro: It only hurts when you realize you* wanted *what you couldn't have. So don't say it, and whatever you do, don't make me believe it.*

"To start you off," Nico continues, "I'm giving you something big, something that will help you prove yourself right out the gate."

Wordlessly, she nods, and he sets the messages down.

"What I'm going to tell you is the scoop you'll give to Magda. You ready? Jack and June are engaged."

Frankie smiles at the joke. Rumors of an engagement have riveted the nation. But that's all they are—rumors. "Funny."

But Nico's shaking his head. "In about a month they're getting married."

Now, a subtle, faint spike of panic. "A new rumor—"

"Not a rumor. Or it won't be, once you tell Magda. Because *you* get to give her the scoop, while I tell Jack."

"I don't understand. This is real?" Her skin's gone hot, her heartbeat in her ears, because even as she says the word, she knows that this is real. Or maybe not *real* but *happening*. "He doesn't want this. Neither of them does."

"She does."

"No, she doesn't. She *hates* him."

"Frankie, June is with child."

Struck silent, Frankie can feel her mind racing. At last, she manages to say, "But it's not his."

And to this, Nico laughs. "*Of course* it's not. Can you imagine? No, those two—no. But they'll be fine. No one's asking them to pledge love and be faithful—"

"Aren't they?"

"In technical terms only. But we gotta get ahead of this. June's not saying *whose* it is, but what she *is* saying is that she wants this baby. Who better to marry her than the man she's been with for years? The man the country *wants* her with? Anyone else would be a disaster. Not exaggerating, it would destroy her if another man stepped in and said he was the father. Naturally we won't bring up the baby till after the wedding. But you know how it goes: Everything comes to the surface eventually. It's *when*, not *if*. So they need to be engaged *now*."

"And Jack raises another man's child?"

"Just because it's someone else's child doesn't mean you can't love it. You know that."

"My mother had a *choice* when she adopted me." Even as she says this, she knows Nico's patience is wearing thin, so she changes the subject. "June was drinking today. I could tell."

He shrugs, but there's a flicker of concern on his face. "I don't imagine much will change in that regard. Or with the other stuff."

The other stuff: inhalers, broken in half, split apart like shucked beans, with the cotton Benzedrine-soaked strip insides removed. To make impossible deadlines, actors need to work in impossibly long shifts, and if the contents of a perfectly legal inhaler make the difference, so be it. Roll up bits of the bitter-tasting strip, swallow with coffee or alcohol, and strap in for a spike of productivity. Then, when necessary, there's a pill that's like a pin in a balloon. And another to take you further down. Sleep, wake up in four hours, repeat. There's an entire room with broken inhalers. *Once on that ride, you don't get off,* Nico's said disdainfully. Jack, at least, won't touch the doctors' offerings, and is notorious for getting the sleep he needs by simply becoming tired and useless. The studio, aware his altered states can be a liability, lets him get away with this.

"Is it safe?" Frankie asks.

"Doctors know what's safe, and they'll keep an eye on her."

"Jack's going to hate this fix."

"Which is why you're lucky you don't have to be the one to tell him." A deep breath, and he says, "The studio needs this. I won't get into how badly they need this, but after *The Last Chance* tanked, and with Paramount making truckloads on *The Sign of the Cross* and everything MGM touches turning to gold, RCO needs *Desert Son* to be a smash. This wedding builds the Jack-and-June frenzy, and that drives people to the theatre." Then, slowly, he adds, "Jack Sawyer is *not* in a position to argue. Not with what we cover up for him. Not with his past. The last thing he wants is for the studio to be on his bad side. You understand?"

She nods. The threat barely veiled.

"This is what we do, me and you: *We* see the big picture. We make them take their medicine because it's good for them. The country's favorite couple has a baby? That's *great* for them. That's not in magazines, it's the cover. Every cover."

The reality of this is settling in.

"Great. Good," Nico continues. He stands, shrugging on his coat. "So you'll tell Magda, who will put it on her evening show."

"When? *Tonight?*"

"No time like the present. Magda's in the lobby."

Frankie glances toward the lobby. From the outside, it looks like an ice-cream parlor. "I don't know what to say."

"The beach one, remember?"

The beach proposal. Over a year ago, June's mother, an older woman with an unstable and eroding mind, managed to send June a confusing letter before passing away. The note was a jumbled scrawl of accusations involving a death and names no one recognized, a mishmash of her life, perhaps, or even tales she'd heard at the salon long ago; who knew what she was talking about. Whatever the case, the letter was no longer harmless when it fell into the hands of a disloyal maid who wanted to make some extra money. Frankie and Nico thought an engagement would be a perfect distraction from the story, should it hit. For an entire day, they invented proposals, throwing out options as if trying on new shirts.

"Yeah. Do the beach one," he continues. "With the food on the hood of the car. Plaid blankets, whatever, the whole thing. Lobster from Murry's Malibu. Just make it good, and then tell us all so we know. And listen, *you* got the easy job. You hear me earlier? I get to tell Jack. So, next step is batten down the hatches because, with his temper, there's gonna be blowback. It's a hell of a way to promote you, isn't it? Straight into the fire. Hand me that script there, would you?"

Frankie forces a smile and watches her hand as she picks up the script, surprised when her fingers work. Bodies, treacherous with instinct, continuing on even while the heart breaks.

"By the end of this day," he continues, "Jack Sawyer fan clubs all over the country will cover their mirrors in black. Millions of tears will spill into pillows, those poor girls who go to sleep dreaming of him. But, Frankie," he continues, "remember the deal. No missteps. This is probation. The eyes of the studio are on you, kid." A smile. "And if I didn't already say it, *congratulations*."

She feels caught off-balance, a sucker punch when she didn't have both feet on the ground. There is pain to this, a voiceless agony. Though not because she's in Jack Sawyer's fan club, or goes to bed dreaming of him—but because she goes to bed dreaming *beside* him. She's brokenhearted because Jack Sawyer is her boyfriend.

Though they had no future, they still weren't supposed to end. Not like this.

"Oh," Nico says, waiting. "You had something you were going to tell me?"

"I was going to tell you I was ready. That I deserved to be promoted."

"Well, look at that. Guess all you gotta do now is not blow it." He smiles. "Kidding. You'll be great. Hey, you happy?"

"I'm happy," she says, thankful no one can tell when she's lying.

CHAPTER 3

One Lucky, Lucky Man

The rest of the afternoon, thoughts of Jack swamp her, heavy and insistent. Even as Frankie tells Magda about the engagement, she's consumed with Jack—*her* Jack, not the public's Jack. There is a difference, not just in the details but in the very fact that what the studio's deemed unfit for the public is exactly what she likes, because Frankie's drawn to interesting over polished, to unique over perfect. That Jack is so good-looking is a strike against him. *Her* Jack is real with flaws and fears, and is beautiful *because* of them. And though he might propose on a beach, he would never stage a message in a bottle—*will you marry me?*—and would never follow it up with dinner in a fancy convertible, or lobster on porcelain, or champagne in crystal. Her Jack is honest with her about why he doesn't drink often, and it isn't from some sense of right or wrong or adherence to a barely respected law; it's because when he drinks, his time in the Great War rises around him, thick and insistent and confusing. Her Jack is already a restless sleeper with bouts of sleep talking, but add in alcohol, and he's told her that everything heightens, the past shot to the surface and real.

So her Jack would plan on NuGrape soda, his favorite, and a simple blanket, with simple food. He would be barefoot on the sand, and would lay her back, and together they would face the sky, the stars and everything above, as waves beat the shore. Her Jack would simply roll over and breathe the question into her ear.

"It was a late night?" Magda asks, and at first Frankie's confused until she remembers she said she was there to set up the table and to strike it at the end. It's a trick Nico taught her: Looping in others helps sell a story. Assistants, secretaries, producers, friends, there are all sorts of people who will lend their names to the charade. If Magda's aware that elements—or the whole thing—are fiction, she doesn't let on. It's tit for tat. They give her exclusives, not just as payment for the favorable stories she prints but also for the stories she *doesn't* print. Silence can express more support than words.

Late-afternoon sun scatters through leaves. They're in the small "park" in front of the office, alongside an empty and still carousel, horses caught in frozen leaps. Already it feels as though a year has passed since Nico told her about this new plan, since her career began to rise while her love life got shut down.

"So when's the date?" Magda asks.

"To quote Jack: *On March 25, I become Mr. Jack Finney.*"

Magda laughs, appreciating Jack's elbow nudge to the fact that June's fame eclipses his own. Jack, who's the most confident, secure person Frankie's ever met. Though the quote is one they invented, it's actually something he'd say.

Then Magda turns serious. "That's soon. Any word on bridesmaids? Maid of honor?"

Frankie watches the still carousel. One of the horse's mouths is open, frozen in a laugh or a scream against its bit. "Ida, her sister. And Jack asked Milton Ewing."

"Ida, RCO family, and Milton, a writer at RCO. I see the studio's keeping it all close." Off Frankie's silence, Magda smiles and refers to her notes. "And June will move into Jack's Pasadena house? That big Spanish-style one?"

Frankie nods. *It's got all the cozy charm of the Spanish Inquisition,* June's said of the mansion. The Pasadena house belongs to the public.

Her Jack prefers his cottage in Venice Beach with chipped paint and cheap trim, built-in cabinets and mismatched glasses and piles of old scripts—a house no one knows about because flashy holiday gifts silence the immediate neighbors. Her Jack is, in fact, embarrassed of his wealth, aware that it's unearned, while the public practically insists on price tags.

The Venice cottage, she thinks. That's how they could still see each other. Their world as a couple would be narrowed to one location, but that's not such a far cry from how it's been.

"No chance of them moving to Beverly Hills? I heard June has her sights set on living near Pickfair."

"Jack likes being where everybody *isn't*."

"You know there *is* a postcard of his Pasadena mansion."

Periodically, there are people in front of his gate. A few times in the alley behind his house, hoping to find souvenirs in his trash.

"There's something June's neighbor told me," Magda continues.

Frankie tenses, understanding they're veering into dangerous, unsanctioned territory. *Never fill the silences,* Nico's told her. *If you do, you won't hear what you need to.*

Magda continues. "The one who lives across the street from June? It was about a month ago."

A month ago. A month ago, Jack wanted to come clean about their relationship. *Not yet,* Frankie told him, and let him think that she was stalling because she wanted the promotion first, because she was confident and determined and knew she could have it all. The truth was she knew just how easily she could have nothing. The truth was she wasn't sure she was willing to risk everything she had for everything she wanted.

"The neighbor said that a man was watching June's house. That she had her lights on, and he was watching. The neighbor said he'd seen the man before. Could've been two months ago."

Immediately Frankie thinks of Tank Adams, June's ex, a giant man who always seemed a bit clumsy, a bit lost in the confines of his body as if somehow mismatched with himself. Years back he stole from the warehouse where he worked and cashed forged checks, and the two broke up, but Tank never seemed to grasp that no means no and still sees nothing wrong with sleeping in June's driveway to surprise her or renting hotel rooms in whatever place she's staying on publicity tours so he can ambush her. Frankie would bet money that it was him outside her house.

"I didn't ask when I heard about it," Magda continues. "*Last Chance* wasn't doing so hot, so I didn't bring it up. I guess I wanted to let you know I didn't."

Frankie recognizes the favor. "Thanks." Then she remembers something Nico told her. "Why tabloids, Magda? Nico said that for a long time you were . . ." She pauses, looking for a way to phrase it.

"A real journalist?"

She nods.

"You won't like my answer."

"Try me."

"This is easier. It's easier to fall asleep at night after a day watching movies and talking about who's dating whom and who's wearing what designer." Then, with a smile, she adds, "What can I say, the hungry kids were wearing on me." She tucks her pencil into the spiral of her notebook. "You know I wasn't really mad at you, for the Joan Crawford bit."

"I know." Again, Frankie faces the empty park. She considers the manipulative moves Magda pulled to get this scoop. Truthfully, Frankie would've done the same. "It's all part of it, isn't it?"

Magda pats the top of her hand. "We make a good team, Frankie Donnelly." She stands, gathering her things. "If you see Jack again, tell him congratulations. He is one lucky, lucky man."

CHAPTER 4

JUSTICE AND A HAPPY ENDING

HOLLYWOO LAND. The *D* has fallen again. Dusk holds the world in a tight grip, and the white letters are pink-tinged, appearing to undulate atop the darkened terrain. Made of flimsy wood panels and held in place by telephone poles, the housing development sign is anything but sturdy. Just last year, a discouraged theatre actress from New York climbed a fifty-foot workman's ladder to the top of the *H* and jumped off. The day after her death, a letter arrived with an offer of acting work. That was the detail that Frankie knew would pulse steady in the hearts of actors everywhere. *Keep going, the next day could be the answer.* June was the one who gave Frankie the news when it happened, and as she spoke, she cried. *Did you know her?* Frankie asked. June nodded, but then confused the moment by saying, *Didn't we all?*

Maybe they did. Settled deep within Frankie's core is still someone afraid to hope that a new day is a new chance. Someone who felt none of the promised comfort of an afterlife when her mother died and who, since, has felt nothing but alone and tired of fending for herself against a troubled world. Though she is excellent at sequestering her feelings—a survival tactic, a way to move forward without the past's determined grab—she is also someone who would never admit to finding comfort in the height of the *H*.

The bottom line is no matter how worried she is about what will happen with Jack and how things will change and if it will work, she doesn't feel entitled to sadness, not with all she has. Most of the people she knows back home are stuck in windowless rooms, living in spaces no bigger than half a subway car. People on an entire floor share one toilet and steal electricity and wear flour-sack dresses and eat lard-and-bread sandwiches, if lucky. It's a life lived between the cracks, a world of scraps. Now, somehow beyond logic, Frankie has a job that she loves and a room that sometimes feels like just her own, with walls that aren't strung-up sheets. Now there is no ice on the inside of the windows, and she can drain the bathwater without thinking, and the mirror on the medicine cabinet steams from the heat. All of it, a miracle. So this sadness, this feeling that she's missing out, it's shameful, and she knows she has no right to it.

Instead of trying to stop for a light, she floors it and a horn trails after her. The studio owns her car, a '31 DeSoto Deluxe convertible, but since she's on call day and night and often made to transport actors who can't be seen in anything rusted or clunky, the vehicle is with her at all times, and is considered part of her compensation. Two-tone mint green with a tan interior and white-walled tires. The trunk is actually a foldout rumble seat, and just the sight of the car conjures picnics with wicker baskets and scarves trailing in the wind. Nico took her to pick it out, right before he realized she didn't know how to drive. Not legally, at least.

The beautiful car. An apartment that's bigger than anything she's ever dreamed of. Still, the numbers in her bank account don't match the outward image of her life, and what she's managed to save wouldn't get her very far. Soon, though, her income will catch up. Thankfully. But then she thinks of Jack's engagement. What will they have to do to make their own relationship work? If things were difficult before, how will they be now?

As usual, she's in her apartment only the minimum amount of time.

"Off to Grant's after Sunday dinner?" Virginia, one of her roommates, a secretary at the studio, asks. Her other roommate, another secretary, Susan, gives Virginia a knowing look. *I couldn't say my name,* Jack told Frankie the first time he donned a New York accent and left a message at the apartment. *So Grant I am.* Grant, her roommates claim, is a creep, because he's never once picked her up for their dates. Meanwhile, Virginia has a framed headshot of Jack on her nightstand.

"I'm not sure yet," Frankie says. They don't often see each other on Sunday nights, due to his usual early-Monday-morning call times. But this week he's not filming.

"You make yourself too available," Susan says. "If he hasn't planned a date by now, I'd let him know he missed his chance."

Missed his chance. She and Jack spent so much time fixated on what they didn't have that they never fully appreciated what they *did* have—or understood just how quickly they could lose it all.

She waits till both roommates have left and then goes to the phone in the living room to try Jack at his Pasadena house, where if necessary she can leave a message with his valet, O'Shea. A butler, an assistant, a driver, and sometimes also a bouncer, he is a man Jack trusts with his life, and though she's pretty sure O'Shea knows what's going on between them, she still casts her calls and visits in appropriate lights.

"He's on the court, miss," O'Shea says.

The tennis court, at the bottom of his property. Tennis is Jack's chance to work out whatever anger he might feel, and more than once Frankie has watched him play, shocked at his intensity. It's all she can do to not stare at his arms or the sweat that darkens his shirt, and though she knows he's strong, there seems to be an underlying fury that drives him. The only person he's been able to play against in any satisfying way is a professional he hires to hit with, a man who has claimed that any time Jack wanted to leave acting, he'd have a career waiting for him. But Jack—despite his stature and his strength—has no interest in taking tennis any further. To him, it's simply a way to unleash.

"How long has he been on the court?" she asks. In her mind, she sees him playing, the shine of anger on his skin.

"Two hours now—since he got home from the studio. He's got to be almost done. At least, that fellow he's hitting against looks to be almost done."

"Could you ask him to call Frankie? It's about an interview tomorrow."

"Yes, miss. If he comes up before I leave."

"Leave?"

Though operators are generally forbidden from eavesdropping, some calls are just too tempting. In the silence she can almost feel O'Shea weighing the options of what's safe to say.

"He's given me three nights off. Told me to visit my sister. I was about to walk out the door."

Three nights off. Jack's done this so he can be alone, which doesn't bode well. She needs to see him in person. They'll both feel better when they've addressed what's going on and come up with a plan.

When she hangs up the phone, Virginia is standing there. "I forgot my pocketbook," she says. "Was that Jack Sawyer you were talking about? Was he the one playing tennis?"

But Virginia doesn't give her time to respond.

"You said, *Ask him to call Frankie*. I heard that. Not even *from the studio*. Which means he knows who you are."

"He's not *blindfolded* when I come in the room. I would hope he knows who I am."

Virginia lowers herself into the nearest chair. "I always figured Nico dealt with the stars directly."

"Nico doesn't want to deal with *anybody* directly. That's why he has me."

Slowly, Virginia smiles. "You said he was on the court. He's supposed to be amazing. A natural."

"Who's amazing?" Susan says, appearing in the door. "We're late."

"Frankie just called Jack Sawyer's house, and he was playing tennis."

"I'm *working,*" Frankie explains.

Susan shrugs. "When is Frankie *not* working?"

"But with *Jack Sawyer.*" Virginia turns to Frankie. "Just tell me one thing no one else knows. One thing, and I'll leave."

He notices everything and leaves a full glass of water on my bedside table because he knows I get thirsty. "Let me think." *He waits to shave till I'm there, because he knows I love to watch.* "There's not much." *When he rolls up his sleeves, there are golden hairs and a pulse in his forearm.* Now she's thinking about his forearms. "He's actually annoying."

Susan's eyes are wide. "Frankie, do you have a crush on Jack Sawyer?" She turns to Virginia. "She's blushing."

Virginia looks almost upset. "You don't, do you, Frankie?"

Frankie stands to go back to her room. "I just said he was annoying."

"Good," Virginia says with something like relief. "Because no one could beat out June."

"I've seen their chemistry on-screen," Susan says, "so I won't argue."

They're on the ride, Nico's said about audiences swept along in the Jack-and-June story. Because a lie is one thing. A movie is a lie, a screenplay a lie. But provide the illusion that there is truth just beyond that lie, just beyond the lens of the camera or in the hand that holds the script, and it's a different beast. With the myth of Jack and June, they've given people the ability to watch them on the screen and see another layer, something that enhances every look, every glimpse, every kiss. The whole country is involved, a part of their romance. *They're on the ride. Buckled in and captive, watching it play out thirty feet high.*

An hour later, she's on the way to Nico's house. Night deepens the upper part of the sky, the horizon still bright with lights from the city. *Jack Sawyer is not in the position to argue,* Nico said. *Not with what we cover up for him. Not with his past.* As Frankie drives, she imagines telling Virginia the truth. Would she still like Jack, if she knew?

Soon the houses grow bigger, the lawns steeper. Then the sidewalks become bare, clean, and the roads free of potholes and old cobble. It's been cold for Los Angeles, and Frankie wears a motoring coat in the car, which she takes off as soon as she's parked in Nico's driveway, an arc around a pristine expanse of grass. Right at the height of the arc, there's a fountain with a statue of what looks like three fish holding a shell, and drops of water shimmer like crystals in their moonlit fall. By the door is Nico's orange-and-black Bugatti coupe, a sophisticated but sinister-looking car. *Halloween for the rich and famous,* Frankie's always thought.

At the last second she remembers to grab a few plates that she has to return from the back seat, and heads up the path to the front door, where Angela, Nico's wife, appears before Frankie's even pressed the bell. The apron Angela wears is blue and white checked and punctuated with red felt tomatoes in the lower corner, and the sight is a familiar anchor to every week.

Angela leans in, a waft of Chanel and shallots. A kiss on each cheek, and she takes the plates. "He's with his juveniles," she says before turning back to the kitchen. "Dinner's soon."

Bing Crosby croons into empty rooms. Past French doors is the garden, which, to someone who didn't know better, would appear filled with an army of skeletons. Rows and rows of bare trees, their naked arms white against the night. These are *the juveniles*, as Angela's termed them. Young fig trees. And in the middle stands Nico.

Maybe he sees her shadow on the ground, but without turning, he says, "I have a few cuttings inside that are leafing out."

She's learned to let Nico lead conversations. And though all she wants to do is demand to know about Jack, instead she says, "Already? You'll have figs by Easter."

He smiles to his trees. Almost all are from cuttings, collected from places of significance or even from wild trees he's spotted in California. *Cuttings are the only way to get an identical fig,* he's told her. *A fig from a seed is new, with one unknown parent and questionable traits, not unlike most people I know. And, sure, a seedling could be mediocre or bad, but it also might be the next best thing.* Once, Frankie had to wait in the car late at night, after a premiere, while Nico climbed a hillside against the road to take a fig and a cutting from a tree that was growing wild. *This might be the one. Taste this,* he'd said, his eyes bright.

Now his finger glides on the branch in front of him. "This is from my grandmother's house in Puglia. Dark-red figs, almost black on the outside. We'd pile them in our shirts and run down this path, down her hill to the water, tripping over grapevines. I'm telling you, grapevines are everywhere, and they'll take over, like figs. Never plant grapes unless you want to cut them back every year with a machete."

"I won't," she says, though she will. The second she gets a house. She'll dare the vine to become a monster. Free grapes, shade. She'll welcome its dominance.

"We'd run to the water and sit on the sand, and stuff our faces with figs hot from the sun. Like strawberry jam inside. Then jump in the Adriatic, which is warm and turquoise and nothing like the Pacific, I'll tell you that. Then swim till we needed to eat again."

Frankie traces an X with her foot on the ground. "We stole apples from a cart on Hester and ran all the way to the hydrant on Canal. I like your childhood better."

"No. Yours is good too." He lowers his arm. "They lost that house. I just found out. My grandmother's house. The bank took it. I didn't know."

She looks up. "Nico. I'm sorry."

"A hundred and sixty-three years it was in my family. Couple years back there was a quake in Irpinia, not even near the house, more in the middle, on the way to Naples. But my cousin was there for it and wanted nothing to do with Italy after that. He wanted to move *here* actually, but I said no, California gets earthquakes like the best of them, so he stayed put." He looks up, at bark that's white against the sky. "What no one told me is he was hurt in that quake, and couldn't work. If they'd told me, I'd have sent money. He wouldn't need to work. And we'd still have the house." He looks over his shoulder. "This whole row is from Italy." Quickly, he glances at each tree as if speeding down the Italian coast. "So, Jack."

"Jack," she repeats. Waiting.

"He's not happy, but he understands."

"He does?"

"He knew it was coming. You don't date someone for years and not move forward. Fictionally or not. But at least June's happy. Or, happi*er*, I should say. I tell you what she had in her handbag? A derringer."

A gun.

In time, this conversation will be something of a bookmark, the memory she keeps flipping to. But now, the change of topic is only an indication that Jack is not as upset as she thought he'd be, which is both disturbing and a relief. Could it be that he'd always figured this would happen, that he long ago made peace with their relationship being temporary? It's a miserable thought, and she tells herself to stop. She just needs to go to him, to see where his mind really is. Then she can worry.

"I thought June hated guns," Frankie says. After June's ex, Tank Adams, surprised her outside a diner, Nico tried to convince her to carry a firearm. At the time, though she was rattled, June refused. *I'll master the slingshot.*

"She got spooked a couple weeks ago. Some couple asking for money on the street; they got a bit aggressive and she got scared. I don't even think they knew who she was, just saw she was dressed nice. I told her, keep one on you if you're by yourself—but you know what it really took? She saw some movie where the heroine had a gun that was pearl-gripped and pretty. See? Westerns and mob films. Everybody wants them. *The lowly man makes something of himself,*" he says in an announcer voice. "You know why people love those films? I'll tell you: justice and a happy ending. That's all anybody ever needs, since the beginning of time. Why do you think people like religion? Justice and a happy ending."

"There's something Magda said today that you should know about. She mentioned that about a couple months ago, June's neighbor saw a man watching June's house. Watching her *in* the house, I mean."

Nico nods, taking this in. "Tank."

"She needs a house that's gated."

"She'll have one soon."

Jack's house. "Right."

"Speaking of Jack," Nico says, "Diego from the Cocoanut Grove called. Our groom of the hour sat down for a bourbon."

"I thought you said he took it well."

"To my face, he took it well. Because he had no choice. But he's out drinking, so we need to listen for the phone."

On studio payroll are those they call *helpers*, people on the lookout who will call them at the first sign of trouble. Sometimes just for a heads-up that someone's on their first drink, while other times it's more than a heads-up; it's a full-on call for help, like a flare shot into the sky. Waiters, bartenders, valets—the list of helpers is endless. Usually, the second a helper makes a call, Nico sends *the troops*: a nurse, an ambulance driver, and two heavies who can stop fights or carry someone out. Whatever's needed.

"You send in the troops?" she asks.

A shaft of light widens at the back of the house as a door opens, and Nico's daughter tells them dinner's ready.

"Of course I did. Anything goes wrong tonight, it sets the tone. We can't afford to mess this engagement up."

~

Dinner looks like a cake, a fragrant pastry crust that hides a meal, a dome that Angela cuts into carefully, releasing steam and a heady scent of mushroom and meat. Baked tubes of pasta twist like little tunnels. Frankie watches Angela tip a slice onto Nico's plate, and she quickly swallows down a full glass of water—a trick her mother taught her to do before each meal. *We just need a head start, that's all.* That fear of ending a meal still hungry never goes away. Taking that last bite and still being consumed by a hollow ache . . . Sometimes Frankie thinks it was worse than not having the meal to begin with.

Now she sets her empty water glass on the table, and Nico launches into a story about his father's family in Calabria, the side that used to make the dish, *timballo di maccheroni*, as Gabriella, his daughter, tries to talk about the wedding.

"My cousin Beatrice called," Gabriella says to Frankie. Twelve years old, Gabriella's got a pink fade from lipstick that she must have wiped off before her father got home. "All the way from *New York*. Even *she* heard. It was on the radio in Brooklyn. They said it was in *a month*. That's soon!"

Nico turns to the girl. "And did your cousin have a theory on why?"

Angela's eyes widen.

Without missing a beat, Nico continues. "It's so they can vacation in Italy without the summer crowds. With *nonno e nonna*."

Now it's Gabriella's eyes that widen.

Nico laughs. "Or maybe they'll just have dinner with them."

"I wouldn't care if it was a snack," Gabriella says. "Jack Sawyer is perfect."

Angela laughs. "I must say, I'm surprised June's *unofficial* husband is letting her get married." She says this looking straight at Nico. When he turns to her, she winks.

"Not even letting," Nico says quietly. *"Insisting."*

Gabriella puts her napkin on the table. "A wedding that fast. It's impossible."

Nico shakes his head. "That word's not in our vocabulary. We built an English village in a week, the Statue of Liberty in three days."

Subtly, Angela leans in to Frankie and whispers, "She's expecting, isn't she?"

Frankie pretends to consider the question. Nico's always said he keeps his wife out of studio business, and clearly this is the case. But the omission feels fragile, something Frankie doesn't trust herself with.

"I know her morals clause is tight," Angela adds as Nico turns, perhaps sensing his attention is needed.

But before he can speak, Gabriella chimes in. "Imagine Jack Sawyer as a husband. In pajamas."

"Gabriella Marconi."

She looks confused. "Or flipping burgers. I mean husband things."

And though the comment draws a laugh, Frankie's food catches in her throat. Jack standing outside at a grill, flipping burgers. A common, mundane thing they never did because they could never be outside if there was a chance the neighbors could see. She takes a sip of water, which shoots cold at a tooth that's gone nervy.

Gabriella continues. "I heard he got a medal in the war. Is that true?"

"A lot of people got medals," Nico says.

"Maybe you should make a movie about that."

He shakes his head. "We need happy stories right now. And no one who went through it wants to relive it." A glance at Frankie. They both know that even loud noises can be tricky with Jack.

Just then, Nico's private line rings, a shrill sound that cuts through the house. *Loud enough to wake the dead,* Angela often jokes about the phone in his office that the helpers call, usually in the middle of the night. The number's not listed in phone books, and operators can't find that number attached to Nico's name—so if someone's calling it, it's because they're part of the inner circle, and there's a problem. Quickly, Frankie stands, thankful for the interruption, even though it means dinner will be cut short. Angela watches her as she goes.

~

Attached to Nico's den, which he uses as an office at home, is a small bathroom converted into something of a makeshift greenhouse. Against the window, there is a table that takes up half the room, and on it are dozens of little pots, some with fig cuttings and others that are waiting, prefilled with his special soil mix. Every so often, Nico runs the shower to give them humidity, and now, as he hangs up the phone, Frankie notes the ghostly trace of a heart someone drew on the mirror.

Almost immediately, the phone rings again.

"Christ," he says into the mouthpiece. "Five? I'm on it."

Once he hangs up, he appears in the doorframe. "You want to take your dessert to go?"

Without being told, she knows Jack's involved but waits to hear how bad it is.

Instead, he says the name of their top director. "Little bit ago, Olivier Monteleon hit on someone's wife, and apologized by throwing an ice cube at the husband, who returned the favor with a punch. So I sent in the troops."

Olivier, a flirt, but not usually a troublemaker.

"But now I get a call from the Cocoanut Grove, and guess who's on his fifth?"

"His fifth?" Frankie repeats. Jack doesn't drink. Or when he does, it's one glass. Maybe two. "I'll head to Jack. Got it."

She won't bring up their relationship to him tonight. Not when he's already upset. The priority is to get him away from the bar with the fewest eyes on them.

As she leaves, she stops in the kitchen to take some cannoli with her. Right by the tray of dessert is one of the plates she returned, along with a napkin.

Angela appears, leaning against the doorframe. "Just bring it back next time."

"You had it ready."

"Hope for the best but prepare for the worst." Angela smiles. "You're not the only one who's learned from Nico."

CHAPTER 5

People Can Surprise You

Night hovers just past the city's aura, that faded line of lights. Despite Nico's hints that the studio needs a financial hit, the film industry in general has benefited from an increased need to run from reality and crawl into the fantasies of movies. But the rest of the city suffers with the rest of the country. Shantytowns, or *Hoovervilles*, as some call them—a nod to their outgoing president, Herbert Hoover—are common in most major cities, and despite Los Angeles's efforts to clean up before hosting last summer's Olympics, there are many; one of them has more than seven hundred people. Houses made of tar paper, tents, and discarded boards. Stoves made of car gasoline tanks. In New York there are also shantytowns, such as Hoover Valley in Central Park, Packing Box City on Houston Street, and the one that was closest to Frankie, Hard Luck Town in the East Village, between Eighth Street and Tenth Street. The tenement where she and her mother lived was bad enough, but Hard Luck Town loomed at the edge of her life. The fact that Frankie didn't end up someplace like it was strictly a result of the job she got with Nico. Though the truth is, she's still only a couple of paychecks away from that same fate, with an apartment paid for by the studio, a car that's not hers, not much in savings, and a job she suspects only Nico would hire her for, since she's a woman and even has an arrest on her record that Nico actually seems to *approve* of. As different as her life looks, that difference is only a front.

On the way to get Jack, she passes well-to-do neighborhoods smack against slums. Sometimes it's only blocks that make the difference, the houses suddenly becoming smaller and crowded before again becoming wider and bigger, streets seeming to expand like boa constrictors that swell in certain spots. Once, she heard, Wilshire Boulevard was a twenty-foot-wide dirt road with a peppering of oil wells and a smattering of barley fields. Now, the whole city feels under construction, like a child who keeps growing.

When she's stopped at a light, she spots a hot dog vendor on the corner. Near the studio, there's a former silent film star who now sells hot dogs, thanks to the advent of talkies and a thick Swedish accent that hurled through the screen like a sack of rocks, dragging him down from a celebrated star to a no one. That's how drastically life can change. How swift the fall can be when the perch you're on was built precariously. Nico and plenty of others have tried to make a study of it, adhering to the words of Edward Bernays, the father of public relations, who warned about the public's standards and demands, and the risk in going against them. While Nico tried to argue that the silent film star should've expected it, that anyone with an accent should've seen the tide changing with the coming of sound, Frankie sees it differently: The public wants what it wants, ruthlessly, and what seems like an endless stream of love can run bone dry, just like that.

The Ambassador Hotel stretches across twenty-four acres of manicured land and is a new height of luxury, the host site of the Academy Awards and the home of the Cocoanut Grove, a Mediterranean- and Moorish-style club that serves alcohol despite Prohibition. Papier-mâché palm trees stand tall, taken from the set of one of Frankie's mother's favorite films, Valentino's 1921 *The Sheik*. Illuminated stars dot the dark ceiling, and when John Barrymore is present, so is his monkey, Clementine, often perched by life-size mechanical monkeys, each with glowing amber eyes. The sight of Clementine spotting other monkeys and eagerly racing to join them only to be confused by the lie has broken Frankie's heart over and over, so now if she spots Mr. Barrymore's Murphy body L-29 Town Car with its long, extended front, she knows not to go inside.

When she parks at the Ambassador, she's so lost in thought that she doesn't see Dottie, Magda's rival, approaching from between the cars. Suddenly Dottie's walking alongside her, matching her pace, a lit cigarette trailing smoke.

"You gave me fluff."

Frankie doesn't stop. If Dottie's been inside, that means she probably saw Jack or, worse, spoke to him. There's no telling what mess Frankie will have to clean up. "I didn't give you fluff."

"You gave me fluff. But by the way, I appreciate fluff, when it's true."

"So now I'm a liar? Joan Crawford really said that. I'm sure of it."

"Tell me this then, to make up for it: Is it true that June Finney submitted herself for that same beauty contest that Clara Bow won, back in '21? The one for *Motion Picture* magazine?"

Frankie glances at her. Two red rhinestone barrettes hold Dottie's short hair back, and flash in the night like warnings. "What, when she was a kid? Come on."

Dottie quickly brings the cigarette to her mouth, and smoke fills her words. "June was a working actress at fifteen."

"Sounds like you know more than I do. I should be asking you."

Frankie walks faster, but Dottie matches her pace. "But you don't know if they competed, even back then?"

Even back then, implying they compete now. It's dangerous territory, to speak of June competing with any actress, but with Clara Bow especially—because it's true. Though Clara's fame is undeniable—the actress gets forty-five hundred fan letters a month—and she and June are close to the same age, Clara's nowhere near June's popularity, yet for some reason June keeps a close eye on her, tracking her success and box office receipts and movie announcements even more than she does those of bigger names such as Joan Crawford or Greta Garbo. Frankie's never understood the competition, as they're in no way the same. June was from a small Midwestern town, the shining hope in a family that struggled to make ends meet but got food on the table. Clara lived destitute in a Brooklyn tenement, and wasn't anyone's hope, an existence that was real and raw and would never fit neatly into a studio bio. *She can cry on cue,* Nico once said of Clara Bow, *and we won't talk about* why.

"What I know is Clara's been through enough," Frankie says, referring to the lawsuit the actress became embroiled in when her best friend and secretary stole money and personal correspondence, which she then leaked to the gossip magazines. "Now I have someplace to be."

"You mean in there, rescuing Jack Sawyer?"

Frankie's steps slow. Dottie must see this, because she comes out firing.

"The night his *engagement* is announced," she says dramatically, "and he's out drinking and chatting with the ladies—methinks this spells trouble."

Chatting with the ladies. Dottie's younger than Magda, hungrier, and lacks the finesse of someone who's established. Frankie stops walking, tired. "Today was the announcement, like you said. *Not* the day he proposed. He's allowed to be out without his fiancée. For all you know, he just had dinner and is waiting to meet a director. Don't you have something better to look into?"

Dottie laughs. "*The nature of celebrity centers on the stars' lives.* Your own boss said that. It's not just about their work, it's about *them*."

"He also said *know when to quit*. What is it you want?"

The red heart of the cigarette zigzags as Dottie speaks. "I do like how direct you are."

"Then return the favor and tell me what you need."

"Tell me what I have to do, to be the one. Magda gets all the good stuff."

Frankie watches a couple leave the hotel, the man's hand on the woman's back. "It's not me who decides. Though accusing me of lying when all I want is a drink—"

"You don't drink."

Now Frankie smiles.

"See?" Dottie says. "I pay attention. We could be good for each other. Both of us coming up in the world. Are you a Dry? Is that why you don't drink?"

"I don't drink because I don't drink. And I just got promoted. So I don't need help. I'm as high as I go."

"For a woman, you mean."

"For what I do. There's no going past Nico."

But Dottie must hear it differently than Frankie intended, because her eyes narrow. "You wouldn't go against him, even if something was wrong?"

"I have no idea what you're talking about."

"The truth means nothing?"

Later, Frankie will replay these words, hearing them as both meaningful and hollow, that strange dichotomy their lives are composed of. But now, she only laughs and starts toward the building, stepping over a curb. "If you want the truth, Dottie, I'd say you're in the wrong business."

~

Jack is six foot three and the tallest person at the bar. Above him, chandeliers with white alabaster shells blaze like suns. As she approaches, Frankie sees the top of his head until he turns, smiling at something the bartender's said. The fact that he's smiling is a relief, and she slows her pace, no longer feeling each second as one that might spiral out of control. But then she gets close enough to hear him speak, and hears a Southern accent coming through, which runs contrary to the studio bio and means she's arrived just in time.

"I thought you were from Montana?"

A woman's asked this, and now Frankie spots three blondes and a brunette at his side. The brunette arches her back, leaning against the bar to expose more of her cleavage. With a few steps, Frankie presses herself behind Jack, her mouth right at his ear. Soap, tobacco, and leather, that scent that makes her want to fold herself against him. "Jack," she says, and notices the woman against the bar straighten, confusion on her face that soon turns to possessiveness as she looks Frankie up and down.

Quietly, Frankie whispers into his ear, "What happened to your two-drink maximum?"

The sides of his cheeks bunch with a smile. And with this, the woman's expression shifts to surprise. Surprise and shock that someone like Frankie would make Jack Sawyer smile. Frankie, in pants, with only ChapStick glossing her lips. When he turns to her, he meets her gaze and doesn't look away. *He observes everything,* Nico once said about Jack. *You think he's staring, but he's studying. The guy'll meet you once and know exactly what you do with your hands when you talk.*

"Ladies," Jack finally says. "The studio's reeling me in. This is good night."

Heads turn as Frankie leads the way. More and more. Quick, furtive glances, along with blatant stares. And Dottie, she realizes, is no doubt perched by the entrance, ready to pounce and ask why he'd be here and not with his betrothed.

As they pass the kitchen, Frankie says, "I thought you don't like yourself when you're drunk."

"One: Who says I like myself right now? And two: I'm not drunk. Out of five drinks, I had one and dumped the rest. Fine, I had two."

A pause in her step as she glances over her shoulder. "You did this so Nico'd send me?"

He smiles. "I kept watering a palm tree with Old Staggs so I could keep going and Nico'd get the call. A waste of bourbon, but it did the trick."

"Well, you almost got the troops, not me. If it weren't for Olivier—"

"Olivier hitting on a married woman at the Canteen, just down the street from here? Who do you think was *at* the Canteen, telling him all night just how much that woman was making eyes at him?"

She smiles as she searches for the best, least noticeable way out. "All that to get me out of Sunday dinner?"

"Nico took enough from me today; I at least wanted you for the evening."

They can't talk about this now. Not yet. "I heard your accent back there."

"I said I wasn't drunk. I didn't say I was sober. Take the side entrance, through that hall."

She veers off, taking the hallway. They've almost made it to the side exit and are passing a man who's leaned heavily against a pay phone, when suddenly that man sees Frankie and steps forward and pinches her butt. Without thinking, she wheels around and slugs him. Not a slap. Not a sweet scolding, but a full-on punch. All her anger at the situation landing on the man's jaw.

There is a moment when no one does anything. Each thrown by the sudden course of events. The man holds his face, confused and staring at Jack as if sure *he* is the one who threw the punch. Then Frankie snaps to and is pulling on Jack's arm, and the two are running through the hall when the man starts to yell. In seconds they've burst into the night.

Outside, Jack stops, doubled over. Unafraid and laughing.

"Don't stop! Move!" She spots her car and grabs his elbow, and they've just made it to the next row of cars when she hears the door to the club sigh as it opens. Quickly, she yanks on him to duck. They crouch by someone's tire.

Jack's eyes flash. "Nico teach you to punch like that?"

Just barely, she raises her head enough to see the man turning back inside. "I'm from New York. We don't slap."

"I'll say you don't." A pause. "I liked it."

She ignores him, focused on the side entrance. For a bit longer, they stay crouched, then hurry to the car.

"The guy's not following," Jack says, getting in the passenger seat. "You're fine."

But her heart won't stop racing—even as she drives, she checks the mirrors.

"Cop-spotter," he says, motioning to the side mirror. "That's what they used to call them. And why they put them in cars, so you could see if you were being trailed. Are you?"

"No."

"See? We're fine." He gives a short laugh and puts his arm on the door, relaxed wherever he goes. "Maybe your dad was a boxer."

"Not my mom?" She grins, but calling anyone but Fiona her mom feels wrong, and she quickly loses the smile. She's always been curious about the people who raised her for five years before deciding she wasn't worth the effort, and even the curiosity feels like a betrayal. When she thinks of them, she sees a large Italian family, but that could just be a result of people assuming that, with her first name and dark hair and olive skin, she's Italian.

When she nears Westlake Park, the night air is cold, and feels like a reprieve, a separation from what just happened. Palm trees splay like fireworks against the stars. The implications of tonight's events are hitting her. Jack Sawyer, in a private hall with a woman who's not his fiancée, a woman who's throwing punches. Nico sent her to keep him out of trouble, yet she caused it. On the night he promoted her. "Did that man see it was you?"

Jack shrugs. "He didn't yell out my name, so here's hoping."

Frankie debates over where to go. Where they are now seems to be in the middle of everything. Though they're somewhat close to the studio, which isn't too far from Frankie's apartment, Jack's houses are either in Venice—west from here and on the coast—or Pasadena, which is east from here and farther inland. Even without traffic at this time, the drive, with so much unsaid, seems torturous. Then she thinks of the bungalows, two little houses that the studio owns, one behind the other on a long and secluded lot. They're near her own building and not far from where they currently are. "I could take you to the bungalows."

"We having an engagement party?"

He laughs, and she shoots him a look. Stars go to the bungalows for privacy or parties, a place for either seclusion or secretive intemperance. Rumor has it bootlegging tunnels exist beneath the lush grounds, and Frankie knows of one that's closed off, a sign on the door with a drawing of a gorilla with an *X* through it, as if everything else is allowed. *Just a bunch of spiders,* Nico told her about what's in the tunnel, *but you go through it, and you end up on the street behind the property, so take note if the cops ever arrive. They shouldn't bother us, but now and then you get a Boy Scout who's new on the job and doesn't know better.*

"I'm kidding," Jack says. "June's at the bungalows. Maybe she's there with the father of my child." He adds a laugh at the end, but it falls flat.

"June likes the first bungalow. We could put you in number two."

"Frankie, you make things really hard sometimes, you know that? I need you at my house because I have something for you there. A surprise."

She tightens her hands on the steering wheel. "You just got engaged."

"But I'm not going to do it."

Quickly, she glances at him. "They'll call your bluff. Jack, I've seen what they can do. Remember what the sound guys did to that actor in *Let It Lay*? Raising his voice? People laughed the entire movie, and it *wasn't* a comedy. Really, you don't want to mess with them. You've got *years* left on your contract, that's years till you—"

"It's not a bluff. I'm not getting married. I'll work it out, but it's not happening. Where there's a will, there's a way. But tonight, tonight we don't talk about it."

Her job, of course, is to force this. To convince him. To *make him take his medicine*, as Nico said. But that objective is directly opposed to what *she* wants. And what she wants is for there to be a way. Finding time together would be harder than before, but could be possible.

Then she thinks of what the studio knows, of why the strong arm of their protection could easily turn against him. Jack never had the life they painted for him in his bio. There was no ranch in Montana, no doting parents who have since passed. Instead, there was a more-than-rocky existence in Louisiana, and a wife he left high and dry. Donna. She's the person the studio has dealt with, the reason for the subterfuge and stories. Jack claimed she never loved him and only married him because it got her out of her family's house, and that when he went to war—a war that battered him with incessant, nerve-racking noise and blasts of fear—he realized that if he survived, he needed to be more than just a paycheck to someone and to lead a life that was more than just a ticket out. But he did it the wrong way. He took the coward's exit and simply never returned to Louisiana, abandoning Donna to do what, he wasn't sure. Deplorable. Shameful. A regretful move he most likely wouldn't have made had he been of sound mind, but at the time he only knew that acting made him happy, the one production he'd done in school, and so he moved to New York, where the theatre saved him. By the time he found his sense of right and wrong, it was too late to contact her. There was no going back. And when the studio discovered him and lured him to Los Angeles, Donna saw him on the big screen and did what any scorned person with no love in their heart would do: She promised to destroy him. So the studio stepped in with a divorce attorney and Nico, who took care of the rest.

People abandon people all the time. But not Hollywood's leading man. Not like that.

"So," Jack continues. "My house. O'Shea isn't there. I gave him three nights off."

"I thought that was so you could . . ." She pauses, looking for the word.

"Break down?"

She smiles. "Maybe."

"Just goes to show you, Frankie, sometimes people can surprise you."

~

The foothills rise in the distance. Houses in his neighborhood are mansions, many shrouded and tucked deep into greenery, set apart from each other with massive trees and expensive landscaping, tropical jungles and English gardens. A pause at the gatehouse—a small building the same Spanish Mediterranean style as the main house, but with only one room—and Louis, Jack's groundskeeper, hears the sound of the car and appears in the window, a slow blink as he clears his vision. Recognizing Frankie, he starts to let her in, but then spots Jack in the passenger seat and hurries. The imposing metal frames creak open, and the car's headlights bring patches of the yard to life as they wind up the hill.

The mansion is pure opulence. Sprawling and three stories, it's white stucco with dark-brown trim, Moorish-style light fixtures, and tiled stairs. Terraces jut from several locations, each with stunning views of the tennis court and the Arroyo and the Colorado Street Bridge. On either side of the house, bright-fuchsia bougainvillea grows against the white walls in a brilliant grip. There are seven bedrooms, eight bathrooms, marble doorframes, and painted wood ceilings. Off the kitchen, there is yet another little tiled patio surrounded by a wood fence with a gate that leads to an alley. The alley was Frankie's escape route on the occasions when she accidentally fell asleep with O'Shea still in the house. Once, she even startled a trophy hunter, a little man who was rifling through Jack's trash looking for mementos or scripts or anything he could sell. *I get reporters out there too,* Jack admitted when she relayed what happened. After that, they deemed it safest to stay together in Venice.

His Venice cottage. Already, it's become a symbol of what they shared, a common loved ground, their haven where nothing else mattered. Yet even there she snuck in the back gate and waited till the coast was clear. At first the effort was fun, but eventually she began to wonder if part of her appeal was her willingness to play the game and not question the rules. How much of why he likes her is because she accepts his situation?

Though O'Shea is gone, he readied the house before he left. Windows glow, amber tinted and warm. "Follow me," Jack says at the front door before leading her straight through the house and out to the back patio. Beyond is a path that snakes through twists of oak trees to a small pond, around which are boulders and a few Adirondack chairs. Past that is the western lip of the Arroyo, with views of the Rose Bowl and mountains and streams and gullies and even the massive and opulent Vista del Arroyo Hotel, which sits directly across the way. At six stories tall, the resort often hosts guests who stay for months at a time, and has so far survived the Depression, known even now as the seat of high-society events and a top spot for fine dining. Beyond the hotel is Colorado Boulevard, chock-full of people and businesses: a bowling alley and clothing stores and restaurants and Dad & Ernie's Gas Station, where O'Shea fills up, and Vroman's Bookstore, where Jack spends as much time as he can reading and browsing and relishing in the fact that the people around him are too consumed in their stories to notice the star in their midst.

When they reach the pond, Frankie spots two fishing poles leaned against the chairs. She turns to him, questioning, and he smiles.

"I made a call after you said you never fished. Catfish. They're nocturnal. Now's our chance."

There are two pails nearby: one on the ground packed with dirt and another on a small wooden table filled with mostly melted ice and bottles of NuGrape soda. "So we catch them?"

"Only if we want to eat 'em. I do spicy and spicier blackened catfish."

Frankie reaches for a bottle of soda. "If you can handle it, I can handle it."

"That's what I figured."

The water is all dark moonlit reflection. With Jack, her world continually cracks open, and so much is a stark contrast to her past that she feels guilty, as if somehow she is betraying who she used to be. Trying not to think about it, she uses the bottle opener O'Shea left to pry off the soda's cap. The shape of the NuGrape bottle reminds her of a top-heavy woman, bulbous but with a cinched waist, and as she hands the soda to Jack, she's thinking of the bottles she collected with her mother. For vases, for water, for decoration, or to sell. They would've cherished this one, and even that thought undoes her, just a little.

When Jack lights a lantern, a circle of brightness surrounds him. "You look like you're on a stage," she says.

"I wish I was on a stage."

An owl calls into the night, and the sound is so real that for a second she assumes it must have been a sound effect. She searches the treetops, studying the shadows.

"The first time I did a play," he says, "everything made sense. All the escaping and pretending I'd done. Everything felt right. Like trying on clothes that fit for the first time."

Though they've been together for a while, she still conceals how much Nico's told her about Jack's life. Jack had a mother who died in childbirth and a father who let a whiskey-strong grief pour through his fists, fighting on the job and on the streets and against walls and barstools and his own son. To account for the injuries, Jack had to get creative. That's the acting class he owes everything to, the part of the acceptance speech no one will ever hear. *He made me into the actor that I am.*

What she also knows is that it's in his contract that he can only do RCO productions, which means no plays. Frankie understands she should direct them away from what can be a sensitive topic. "I don't deserve this," she says.

He sets his soda bottle between two rocks. "Everyone should fish."

"But not on a whim, because someone made a call and had their pond stocked with fish."

"Probably no one should do that." Now he edges closer to the water, then leans down to touch its surface. Ripples of light spread from his fingers. *"Today I brushed my teeth with champagne because it was there, and I spit my soul into the sink."*

"What's that from?"

"June said it to me. A couple months ago. The champagne was by the bathroom sink, and she just did it because she could, because it was there, and then she curled up on the bed and didn't talk to anyone for two days."

Frankie thinks back, remembering a weekend when June disappeared.

Jack continues, standing and looking up at the moon. "Sometimes I think we hate each other because we're stuck together in this. But it's also why we understand each other."

"Oh good, I'm glad you two can talk about all the hardships of wealth and fortune."

"That's *exactly* it. Everyone sees it the way you do. Everyone but her. Our lives are amazing, but they're not ours. Not the way we'd want to lead them."

Frankie glances back at the mansion. "When your suffering looks like that—"

"*Which is why I don't feel right questioning it.* Which is why I do what I'm told, because I'm lucky, and I know it. I don't expect sympathy, and I'm not asking for it. I'm saying she's the one I can talk to because she feels the same; it's why she called after the morning with the champagne. We get what a horrible wonder this all is. Everything good we have—it's like the ugly beauty. A woman who's so beautiful that her beauty loses all meaning."

"When you talk, it gets worse."

Again, he smiles. Charming, even now. "But it could be a man too."

"That's good to know."

"Anyone that's just too perfect," he says. "Or has it too good, maybe that's it. Because if all you get are perfect apples, you don't think twice.

You forget to appreciate them. And pretty soon you forget there was something to appreciate to begin with."

"Maybe the perfect apple's just not as interesting as one with curly, frizzy hair, let's say."

He watches her, steady. "To me, the curly, frizzy-haired apple *is* perfect."

The way he looks at her, sometimes it takes her breath away. But now an idea is forming, a new tactic. "You and June have that in common."

He takes a swig of his soda. "We spend most of our time hating each other. But we know what it's like to belong to the world, and not belong to ourselves. We'll always have that."

Ignoring the chairs, she takes a seat on a large boulder at the water's edge as Jack picks up the old aluminum pail by the fishing poles. Tentatively, Frankie says, "So maybe you'd consider helping her? Since you understand her—"

"No," he says firmly. "I want my life. But I know June, and I know she'll understand why. And I know she'd make the same choice. But that was a nice try, Frankie Donnelly." He gives a grin before sifting through dirt in the pail. "Night crawlers. Look away if you don't want to see this." Which, of course, makes her look. Jack notices, and smiles as he hooks a worm. "Fishing is how you eat. It's not a luxury—at least not the fishing I've done."

She studies him—the flop of his hair against his forehead, the trees behind him, lit up and haunting—and wishes she hadn't stopped him from talking about doing plays. "So you'd really prefer theatre and all that struggling?"

"It's not a struggle if you love it. Theatre is *acting*. Real acting. At least for me it is."

"I never did a play, but I got good with being somewhere else. We didn't have money for books or movies. But the movie posters—those you can look at for free. And my mother practically hunted them down.

Every time there was a new one, she'd take me to it to show me, and later she'd have an entire story ready to go with it."

"She could've been a writer."

"In a way, she was, just nobody knew it. Nobody but me. And she got me doing it too, with the posters. That's what kept me going while I worked."

He watches her. "My fellow dreamer."

The owl calls again, its question emerging from deep within an oak tree. Jack turns toward the sound. "With my dad, the second I saw the whisky come out, I had my stories ready to go. They were always about someone I pretended was in the other room, someone I was protecting. Maybe it gave me a purpose, I don't know. My black eye would always be one some imaginary person didn't get." He takes another swig. "So. Who should we be so there's no house, no studio, nothing but a pond and fishing poles and us?"

"Can I be someone named Bertha?"

"Only if you want me fishing on the other side of the pond. Bertha was my first-grade teacher, and she was awful."

"How's Annie?"

"Annie," he says, watching her take off her shoes and touch the water with her toe. "Annie goes barefoot and eats apples down to the core. She hates snakes but can charm bees."

"Bee charming? That's possible?"

"I thought I didn't need to explain the rules of imagination. Because there's one rule. And that's that there are no rules. So yes, Annie, you're a bee charmer. And I'm some guy named Grant."

She smiles. "Are we a couple, Grant?"

"You know we are." He hands her a fishing pole. "Like this," he says, casting the line into the water. "I forgot the music."

For a moment, each falls silent, listening. Often, music's drifted across the ravine from the Vista del Arroyo Hotel, and they've danced beneath the treetops. Tonight, there's nothing, so she conjures a song in her mind. She starts to hum. A swinging melody.

He smiles as he places the tune: "We Just Couldn't Say Goodbye" by Guy Lombardo. "Well, Annie," he says, taking a seat behind her. "My thought is maybe we don't have to."

She leans back against his chest, breathing in the smell of water and oak and sage and him, and lets him say this. Why correct him? Life will do that on its own when he realizes that the studio will not cave and that she's accepted a promotion for a job that she's wanted and worked hard for, but that the job's goal is to protect him and save his reputation and, in truth, will mean warning him off a relationship with someone like her. Because if he gets out of this engagement and people find out about her, they will assume she's the reason, and they will hate her, and hate him for what he's done, especially when June starts to show. The public doesn't want Jack to be happy as much as they want to be happy *for* him, in their own way.

So she lets him say what he wants to, because tonight is a night for pretend.

CHAPTER 6

A Coil Wound Too Tight

Monday, February 27, 1933

A frenzy of wedding plans. Talk of designers and dresses, of color schemes and bridesmaids. Throughout it all, Frankie keeps an eye on Nico's door, wondering if Jack will indeed try to call everything off. Now and then, she reminds him: *Get out of marrying June if you want, but if my name comes up, I lose my job, guaranteed.*

On Monday, after a week has passed, she decides Jack probably thought better about derailing the studio's plan until Betty patches through a call and Frankie hears Nico's voice rise. Subtly she goes to the parrots' addition, which is slightly closer to Nico's door.

"Who's he on with?" she asks Betty.

"Milton Ewing," Betty says of Jack's closest friend, a writer who's in London. "Last-minute changes to the script. A transatlantic call, do you believe it? Sounds like Nico doesn't—he's yelling loud enough that Milton and all of London could hear him without a phone. Oh, your *cookies*," Betty adds, and holds out a cookie tin.

Inside are telegrams. Everything coming in to the studio's stars, and everything going out. *We can't fix something we don't know about,* Nico's said about the practice of reading words that were intended to be private. Once a week, Frankie or Nico pore over everything, determined to head off disaster. Doing this was how they learned that one of their stars had a heart condition he'd kept secret, and so they knew to have a doctor on standby during rough shoots. It's how they found out an ex-girlfriend was blackmailing another actor for a child he claimed wasn't his, and how they discovered someone else was cheating on her husband with a director who wasn't trustworthy. From potential sex scandals to stars flirting with other studios or trying to break their contracts, being in the know is what makes the difference.

"Frankie."

Nico's at his door. Quickly she goes to her desk to shove the tin into her bag and then follows him into his office. As she does, Romeo or Juliet lets out a shrieking squawk. Nico clears his throat. "So, Milton asked me, *What do you call a month's worth of rain*?" A pause. *"England."*

She smiles. "Funny."

"Before I forget, you'll want to take out money from the bank before they close."

She glances at her watch. "Don't they close soon?"

"No, close as in shut down. As in not just for the day. New York Reserve Bank's gold reserve is about to fall below the legal limit, and when that happens, it's trouble. So, get your money, because they *will* shut down, and then you'll be up a creek."

In her mind, she sees the measly sum from when she last made a deposit. She can't think about that now. "Anything with the wedding? Jack or June? Cold feet?"

"Cold feet we've got in spades. Lucky we've got Ida on our side, because just this morning June's telling me she can be a single mother and maybe she's done acting. *Done acting.* Lord help me. And Jack. When has Jack Sawyer made my life easy? I said that when he called. *From day one I've been cleaning up your messes,* I said. *From day one.*"

"He called?"

"Right before Milton. But, Frankie, *this* is about you."

This *is about you.*

In a flash, she sees the world she's about to lose. Everything. Her apartment, her car, her job, this life on the West Coast without real winters, this place where dreams come true and where who you were doesn't dictate who you'll become—everything, all of it, gone. Her heart pounds in her ears as she sees her mother the day she left the one job she loved for that man who brought her flowers. The stupid happiness on her face. "Nico—"

"That house in Edendale? You liked it?"

Frankie's sweating. Can he tell? She understands he said something about a house, but she lost the train of thought. "The house?"

"Yeah, that house I took you to, I took you there to make sure *you* liked it. The studio'll own it, of course, no way around that, but you can live there."

"The house?" she says again.

"Eventually, when they get past this financial bump, the studio wants that whole hill. And then they'll tear down whatever houses are on it, but until then, it would be yours." When she says nothing, stunned, he continues. "You were looking a little down, so I thought I'd tell you now. But you're still looking down."

"The whole house?"

"Whole house. No roommates. The middle of March—you can plan on that for a move-in date." And then he considers something. "But we're not kidding. This is a probation. You gotta be good. You've worked hard. It'd be a shame to not make it." Then, a smile. "Not that I think that will happen. I'm just saying that now, of all times, is when you tread carefully. I think I said that before, but I wanted to be sure you heard it."

With this, she understands: He knows. He knows, and he's telling her she will have nothing if she strays outside the line of what's allowed with Jack. But here, right now, is her chance for correction. He gives her a small smile, and she realizes he's aware of what he's taken with this wedding, and he's giving her this house in return. A dangled carrot. A consolation prize.

"Thank you."

"Don't thank me. It's work. It's sacrifice. But reward too. If you want it."

Anything she thought she could get away with is no longer an option. She needs to choose.

"I think," he continues slowly, "Jack could use some hand-holding on this. The cold-feet thing. I'll just say it—he was upset when we spoke. This is the eternal bachelor we're talking about, the one with a girl on each arm—that's his true nature, you ask me. So an engagement, even a fake engagement, it's doing a number on him. The man's probably at his house beating the hell out of a tennis ball. So go earn your raise and your house and show us what you got. Do some convincing."

Jack is sliding out of reach before she's ready. "But, Nico, if he really doesn't want it—"

"Frankie, before you get started, let me tell you what he really doesn't want: He doesn't want the studio as his enemy. But he *wins* in this. *Wins.* The love of the country and the ability to keep working. And you know what else? It's not just him: If June's not married, she can't have the baby. You want to tell her she can't keep her baby? I don't. But this is where we're at: The country will *not* let her be an unwed mother, and the studio won't let her destroy herself. God knows she tries. Now. The hand-holding. This is part of the job. Go fix."

~

Jack's house looks empty, and it's this difference, this emptiness, that drives everything home: It's over, and they both know it. This isn't an idea, it isn't something in the future—it's real, and it's happening now.

Louis lets her past the gate, and as she winds up the drive, she catches glimpses of the house above, windows dark. To her right is the empty tennis court. She keeps going, noticing one light on in what could be the kitchen. Still, at the house, there is no sign of Jack—or O'Shea, for that matter, who usually parks his truck on the far right of the driveway. He had three days off last week, but for him to be gone again means Jack purposefully got rid of him. She tucks her car on the side of the garage, alongside ropes of hanging ivy, and makes her way to the front door.

When she knocks, another light goes on deep within the house.

Minutes later, Jack opens the door, and she smells the bourbon on him. She starts to turn around. "We can talk later."

But he steps aside, ushering her in. As she goes with him to the kitchen, she tells herself this is not a breakup with her boyfriend, it is simply her doing her job, but all she wants to do is cry. "Where's O'Shea?"

"Sister's."

"More time off?"

"Do I not get to have my own house to myself when I need it?"

They're diving in, she sees. "There's the issue of the wedding and the issue of us. Which do you want to talk about first?"

He shakes his head. "So logical."

"It's not logical, it's *sober*."

He shoots her a look. "Fine, let's talk about us."

"We couldn't have done it for much longer," she says firmly. She needs to believe her own words. "Me sneaking through your yard at night, never being able to call you my boyfriend, never being able to even *call* you just to say hi without making up a story."

"I could've kept going."

She tosses her tote bag onto the built-in kitchen table. "Sure, because *you* get your fame and reputation, while I sneak around and settle for scraps."

Suddenly he looks completely sober. "That's a hell of a thing to say, coming from someone who didn't even try to stop Nico."

She glares at him, incredulous. Angry that he'd ask her to risk everything when he knows how close to the edge she lives. "What difference would *I* make? I'm no one."

"You're like a daughter to him. Maybe if he knew the truth—"

"The truth? That their big plan, their moneymaking headline and the story that'll drive people to the theatre, can't happen? The studio *needs* this, and you want me to tell them that one of their top stars wants to call it quits with their other top star, to hang her out to dry in her time of need, all to be with a *no one*? That sounds like a good plan? And the public, forget it. They would *not* love you for that."

"I don't care about being loved."

"You would if they stopped loving you."

"Maybe I finally want to live my life."

Frustrated, she calls his bluff. "*Then do it.* Tell them you're done and you don't care."

He raises a brow. "I know you're not serious."

"*You're* the one who's not serious. If it were really what you wanted, and you were willing to risk everything, then I would help you."

And that is the truth. But so is the fact that though he grew up impoverished, that former life is such a far cry from where he is now that it's a reality he must not fully remember. She thinks of Rudolph Valentino, who spent unwisely but also ended up on the losing end of contract disputes with his studios, disputes that rendered him unable to work. Though he'd made a fortune, he died penniless. Even his resting spot at the cemetery is a loan from a friend who took pity on him.

"What I worry about, Jack, is that when you have people looking out for you all the time, you don't deal with repercussions. But what happens when they stop fixing things?"

Angrily, he takes a bottle of bourbon from beside the toaster and refills his glass. "God, that one fucking choice. Leaving Donna like I did. And the irony, the real irony of it all, is that I just wanted my own life, I just wanted to start over, and now I'm handcuffed to her forever." He gives a small laugh. "On our wedding night, she told me she never loved me. That we'd have two separate rooms. And then she convinced me to go to war—widower's payments dancing in her eyes, no doubt. I was practically a child. I didn't know. Maybe if I could remind her that *I* wanted *her*, but she didn't want me, maybe it would help. I don't know. But she skips town. She doesn't want to be found."

Don't blame us, Nico told Frankie when she first started working for him, when he explained how Jack and other stars were and would always be beholden. *We can only fix what's already broken. And remember,* we *didn't do the breaking.* While that's true, and all the arguments about how this is actually good for Jack's career are true, it's more than this now. It's June. Because Nico's right: This marriage is the only way she can have her baby. But saying this to Jack, who already clashes with June, would only make things worse.

Carefully, she says, "I know you don't want to hear this, but whether Donna loved you or not doesn't matter. You still left a wife who made it very clear she needed you, and you left her high and dry after she waited faithfully for you to return from war. That's how it would look."

He doesn't take well to the comment. "She's not high and dry anymore, is she? And I doubt the faithful part. Hell, I should've stayed with her in Louisiana and done theatre. I'd be happier."

Frankie tries to ignore the sting of this comment. "If you go against the studio, and they're not there to protect you, you could lose acting too."

Saying nothing, he goes through the kitchen and outside to the little table on the patio. But he leaves the door open as if hoping she'll follow, which she does, rubbing her arms against the cold.

A coyote howls. One, and then another, and another. Cries that break into a furious yipping that takes over the night, filling the ravines and bouncing from the hills, until again their sounds go long and solid and haunting. A hunt. The excitement of the kill.

"*I* tried to fight for us," he finally says.

"Don't put this on me. It wasn't *us*; it was your life you were fighting for. And that's fine. I'd do the same thing."

"No," Jack says. "It wasn't just my life I was fighting for." Quietly, he turns to the trees, the sound. "They've left me no way to prove how much I want to be with you, have they?"

He downs the entire contents of his glass. Where she grew up, someone slinging back booze like that was just the beginning; the end involved rent money spent in an evening and fathers on stoops outside of buildings, morning dawn on their faces as mothers scooted their children past. There's a beat of regret on Jack's face as he says, "Don't watch if you don't want to, but I'm having another one. And one after that."

With that, she goes into the living room. Thankfully, the coyotes seem to have stopped, and the silence is a relief. She doesn't want to leave him like this, so when he still doesn't emerge from the kitchen, she sits in the chair by the giant arched window that overlooks the Arroyo. The view is stunning, even at night, capturing the winding, lit-up beauty of the Colorado Street Bridge, a Beaux Arts arching expanse over the Arroyo seco, which runs with water every winter. Here, at the window, was where they had their first kiss—after a long day of interviews, when the last reporter had left and the bridge was lit up, its globe lights like little moons. For months there'd been chemistry—a stupid word, she'd always thought, to describe attraction, but with him, she understood because when they stood beside each other it felt like the air sparked, charged and reactive. Each of them tended to look away, always finding an excuse to stand apart as if needing the space between them. And they were never alone. Until they were. It was late July, a day that held on to the heat, and when all the interviews were over, and O'Shea was escorting the last reporter down the long driveway, Jack needed help with a right cuff link. Unwisely, he asked her, and foolishly she went to him. The air grew hotter with every step, then hotter still, almost excruciating, as the space between them closed. She felt his gaze on her face, even as she worked to unjam the clasp. Her hand on his wrist. Their feet were almost touching. She knew all she had to do was look up and he would kiss her.

And he did.

His hand in her hair, the cuff link caught for a moment as the front door closed loudly. Nervous laughter, racing hearts. Logically, she knew that, before the studio set him up with June, he'd dated a new woman almost every other week, and that gave her comfort, because he wasn't the type to want anything serious. That, combined with the ruse of his relationship with June, meant this could go nowhere. There was nothing to fear. But even as those rational thoughts aligned themselves within her mind, she felt it like a draft slipped under a door: This was different.

Seven months ago. A lifetime. She knew it would end, but never like this. When neither of them wants it to.

When he eventually emerges from the kitchen, he's surprised to find her still here. In his hand is a full drink, the liquid an amber glimmer.

"Thought you'd left." His words seem caught on a slide. Then he sees the bridge through the window. "Someone jumped last week."

Suicide Bridge, people have started calling it. "Were you here?"

He watches the bridge steadily, as if it might try to get away. "Raining that night. A man, no coat, no umbrella. I knew."

He's drunk.

Without looking at her, he continues. "Guy climbed to the ledge and I'm screaming and O'Shea ran in, thought it was me, that I was hurt. Then he saw. Wasn't a damn thing we could do. Not a damn thing. Man couldn't hear us."

"Even if he could—"

"What? I couldn't help?" He's looking at her now, a swirl of anger in his eyes. "What the hell good is any of this if I couldn't help? Of course I could."

You don't grow up as she did, around men whose sweat stank of whiskey, and not know to be quiet in a situation like this. Someone drunk, who's let booze light the fire of their anger, you walk away. You leave words unsaid. There is no pride, there is no being right at a moment like this; there is only saving yourself. And she knows this, but she also knows that Jack struggles with the idea that all he is to people is a dollar sign. She remembers when it rained last week, and how she didn't hear from him at all that night, and the next day when they met in Venice Beach, he'd seemed still stuck within a storm, his eyes dark though the day blared with sun. Now she knows why. "Jack. It's not always about money."

He gives her a knowing look, his eyes red. "You break my heart." Then he takes a deep, wobbly breath, lifts the glass to his lips, and slings back the rest. A wince, and he returns his gaze to the bridge. "It's never about money until it is. And it always is. A quote I gave Milton."

"What are you talking about?"

"For his script. I could've fixed things for that man. *And* his whole family."

"Now you're talking about the man on the bridge."

He nods dramatically as if his head has grown heavy. She gets up and goes back to the kitchen, smelling the bite of bourbon on him as she passes. "I think it's time for you to go to bed," she says, grabbing her tote bag off the kitchen table. "And for me to go."

"No, come on, Frankie," he says, and somehow, in his mind, it must be that the bag is the deciding factor, because he tries to take it from her and pulls too hard. The cotton strap breaks, and the entire thing spills onto the built-in kitchen table and the floor below.

"Damn it, Jack!"

She's got her coin purse and her keys on the table when they hear the noise. Outside the kitchen door and just beyond the patio. Coming from the alleyway where he keeps his trash.

The moment is like a coil wound too tight. In a flash, it comes undone. He says the word *reporters* and is gone, then back with a shotgun. She chases after him, yelling at him to stop, but already he's outside, and from the way he's got the gun hoisted against his shoulder, she knows he's no longer seeing his yard, that his mind has caught in a crevasse of the past, and he's banging open the gate and lifting the gun as Frankie catches up and sees the muzzle pointed at a woman going through his trash.

"Stop! Jack, stop! That's a woman!"

He blinks. Once, twice, three times—clearing what's before him. The woman is frozen and pale from fear, and there's a whimpering sound, but Frankie won't look away from Jack until he lowers the shotgun—and then she sees the little boy who clings to his mother's leg, maybe four years old. On the ground is a piece of cardboard, on top of which are two browned bananas, a half-eaten slice of carrot cake, and a torn box of crackers.

Frankie turns toward Jack and hisses the word *Go*. He's staring at the kid, then stumbling back through the gate, as Frankie faces the woman. "I'm sorry. We have food. I'll bring you food. Stay. Please stay."

The woman either doesn't understand or is still too shocked to hear what Frankie's saying, but Frankie motions to the food and indicates the house, and the child is still crying when Frankie runs back inside, into the kitchen, headlines flashing through her mind as she quickly takes her empty tote bag that still works but now doesn't have a handle and puts as much food in it as possible. Chicken legs still in a small glass Pyrex, fresh oranges, an unopened box of crackers and a tin of Ovaltine, and whatever else she can grab, she doesn't even know, and as she runs back outside, she knows the woman will be gone, that the alley will be empty, and then she will have to work with Nico to head this off, and what are the odds that this woman didn't recognize Jack, whose face is on multiple billboards throughout the city?

The gate is still unlocked, and she pauses before pushing it open, afraid to startle the woman if she's still there, yet even more afraid to find her gone. But the woman is there. Still at the trash can, eyes shining with tears. It's clear that though she is terrified, her son is hungry, and Frankie knows that a mother will face anything to feed her child. Just then, somewhere not far enough away, the coyotes' howling starts up again, and Frankie understands that the hunt never stopped, it simply went silent. The woman, as well, turns to the sound, and her son draws closer to her legs.

Trying to ignore the noise, the chaos of this evening that she can't seem to control, Frankie holds the bag from the bottom and indicates the broken strap. But the woman just nods, tears now streaking, and hugs the bag in her arms carefully as if holding on to someone she's afraid to lose. When she turns to head back down the alley, her son is at her side, his small fist around the fabric of her skirt.

CHAPTER 7

Don't Yell at a Swarm of Bees

Tuesday, February 28, 1933

The next morning, Frankie wakes in the guest room and checks on Jack before she leaves. Spread out on top of his bed, he's got his right arm flung over a pillow. Meanwhile, the shotgun—minus its bullets—is on the chair against the wall, so he can put it wherever it belongs when he wakes. She takes in the dark gleam of the gun and Jack's closed eyelids, the slight part of his lips and the slow-paced rise and fall of his rib cage. *Wake me,* her mother used to say, between shifts of work, when Frankie had to guard her so she could steal a nap: at a bus station, in a park, in the far back booth at a café. Sleep, Frankie decided during those hours of watchful protection, was a design flaw. That something so necessary would require the body to be so exposed, so defenseless, made no sense. Such irony in that the only way to be strong is to first be so weak.

Today there is a long stretch of interviews, all leading up to the *Desert Son* premiere tomorrow night. At work, Frankie immediately orders the studio doctor to visit Jack, claiming that something he ate had him up all night, knowing she'll get a quote from the man later to give to the press to explain Jack's absence. Then she asks June to do what she can alone. June, who looks pale and as though she didn't sleep last night either and who, at times, is held upright by her sister, who walks with a steadying hand on her elbow.

"June, June," a male reporter says, sidling up to them. His Adam's apple bobs up and down. "I heard you've started the eighteen-day diet, is that true?"

The eighteen-day diet—otherwise known as the Hollywood Diet—consists of a grapefruit at each meal, and severe restrictions, which is the last thing June needs.

Frankie steps in front of the man. "Questions happen in a few minutes, and they'll be about the film, not food." She stands firm, waiting till he's gone. When she turns back to June, June looks as though she's struggling to process what he just said.

"Yesterday I wanted a grapefruit."

Ida smooths a finger down a wave of her sister's blond hair. She's only three years older than June but looks much older, her features harsh, lines honed with a sort of fierceness. Coffee-brown eyes, hair that's bluntly cut and raven dark. *While my mother entered me in beauty contests,* June once told Frankie, *Ida got stuck working in the kitchen at Rick's Easy Morning Café, and trust me, there was nothing easy about Rick.*

Now June looks down at the floor. "I didn't know anyone was watching." Her thin shoulders drop. "It was just a grapefruit."

"It's when they stop watching that you need to worry," Ida says before taking June's hand in hers. Discreetly, she presses something into the center of her sister's palm. "Go to the couch and relax a minute."

Frankie tries not to look as June raises her hand to her mouth, then swallows dry what appears to be a rolled-up Benzedrine strip.

When June's out of earshot, Ida turns to Frankie. "We're doing our part. You make sure Nico knows that. Jack's the one not here."

She never got what she wanted in life, June also said to Frankie about her sister. *She sacrificed. I can't tell you how much, but trust me when I say I owe her.*

When Frankie repeated it to Nico, he nodded as if it made perfect sense. *True. But Ida's seen a significant return on her investment, so at this point, they might be even.* He left it at that.

"I'll make sure he knows," Frankie now says to Ida.

"Dede Domenico's nipping at June's heels."

Dede Domenico, the studio's newest find. Fifteen years old but tall enough that people mistake her for an adult. Long legs and dark hair and dark eyes and one eyebrow that's arched more than the other, making her appear as though she's constantly entertained by the world. Any role that June turns down falls to Dede, despite the age difference. *A small tweak in the script,* Frankie once heard a director say, *and the role was practically made for her.*

An hour later, and June still looks sick but is awake enough to be angry that Jack's not pulling his weight.

"She's too upset," the makeup artist says quietly to Nico. "I can barely get her lipstick on."

"Do her eyes, then, her cheeks, I don't know. We'll be there in a second." When they're alone again, Nico turns to Frankie. "What do you do when someone's mad?"

You don't yell at a swarm of bees, you throw flowers in their path. When Nico first told her that, she laughed and replied that he'd clearly never made a swarm of bees mad. To that, he shook his head. *You get my point. Distract with something good.* "We're throwing flowers at bees."

Sure enough, moments later, he's standing beside June in the makeup chair. "How 'bout some good news?"

June looks up at the ceiling lights so the makeup artist can work. "Are we going to be graced with his presence? Because I know I'd like to sleep all day too."

Ignoring that, Nico charges forth. "Magda says she's heard from *several* voting members of the Academy of Motion Pictures Arts and Sciences that you're a shoo-in for an Oscar for *Last Chance*."

Now June's mouth drops. Even the makeup artist knows to pause, taking a step back. The award, though only a few years old, is already considered a top honor.

"You're not serious."

"June. Would I lie?"

Frankie's never seen June smile so big. *"Yes."* And then, more seriously: "What about Clara Bow?"

Nico shakes his head. "For *Call Her Savage*? No. She's not getting nominated for anything. She's retiring. Moving to that ranch in Nevada. She was meant for silent films anyhow."

Maybe it's the shared tenement experience, or the fact that Clara does what everyone else does but doesn't try to hide it, but Frankie's always liked Clara Bow. "She's only twenty-eight," Frankie says. "Maybe she's just taking time off?"

But Nico shakes his head. "No. She's done."

June holds her cherry-red lipstick, the cap discarded on the top of a script. Absentmindedly, she swipes the pad of her finger on the lipstick.

Nico watches her, curious. "That doesn't make you happy? You, who's always keeping tabs on her?"

With one slender finger, June smears the lipstick on the script. "They won."

There is a drop to June's words, like an end that's reached. Frankie glances at Nico, who takes it in stride.

"Who?" Nico asks. "The press?" June doesn't look up but nods slightly, and he continues. "They've been ruthless to her, I know. But she made it easy for them, the way she lives her life."

Sharply, June glares at him.

He raises his hands. "I only mean she flaunts the rules. Does what she wants. I don't mean they're right to crucify her, but she's given them the material, hasn't she?" When June doesn't respond, he shrugs. "Now she's on a ranch with her husband and never has to work again. Pretty sure she didn't lose."

"She doesn't get to do what she loves. How can you say she didn't lose?" With that, she swipes her finger once more on the page. Another red line, faded this time. Outside the room, someone's shrieks settle into laughter.

"Chin up," the makeup artist says, and June obeys. Frankie watches as the woman sweeps ivory shimmer onto June's lids, instantly making her look alive and hopeful.

Frankie thinks of Clara's last role. "Her Brooklyn accent wasn't a problem."

Now June opens her eyes and looks at Frankie. The makeup artist surrenders, and starts to gather brushes at the next table. June blinks heavily as if to clear her vision. "You're right. It wasn't. They didn't *want* her to succeed."

"Neither did you." Nico laughs. "At least I thought you didn't. But there's a reason the woman negotiated to *not* have a morals clause with Paramount—I think she's had a good run."

Somewhere in the room, a set of lights around a mirror flickers off. Frankie turns toward the darkness, but no one's there. Then she excuses herself to go back to the office to call Jack.

"I'm sorry," the operator says eventually. "There doesn't seem to be an answer."

"Keep trying."

The operator does as told, and after six more rings, Jack answers, apologizing.

"Sorry," he says. "I forgot O'Shea's not here. I kept waiting for him to get the phone."

She's standing at her desk, and speaks as quietly as she can. "I put everything off till three, but we need you then."

"Three," he repeats.

She waits for him to say more, and slides open her desk drawer, where she keeps an apple. Beneath it is the final script for *The Last Chance*, with each of the cast members' inscriptions and signatures on the title page. Jack's reads: *Frankie, It's always a good day for a beach day! —Jack* A reference to their life together in Venice. An easier time that seems impossibly long ago. Below that is June's happier, buoyant cursive: *Frankie, don't worry, it's not your last chance . . . it's all just beginning!* ❤ *June*

She takes a bite of her apple.

"I think I need to eat," Jack says.

"Eat, then."

"That him?" Nico says.

He's standing behind her, for how long, she's not sure. She nods, and covers the mouthpiece as Nico speaks. "I need him here *in good form*. Food, hair of the dog, whatever he needs—I don't care."

She tells Jack she's on her way with food, and slowly, he replies, "Frankie, something that's usually in the butler's pantry was on a chair."

The gun. "Right."

"But I'm not sure why."

She feels herself nod, and presses the phone's handset tight against her ear as if to contain his words. She can feel Nico's gaze from across the room. "You're not?"

Silence.

This is good, she thinks. She'll tell him what happened, and it will scare him enough to pay attention, to never again ignore his two-drink rule. "I'll tell you when I see you."

She takes another bite of her apple, tosses it into the trash, and promises she's on her way.

Once off the phone, Nico stops her. "Make sure he's showered. Get his hair combed. Betty's got the kitchen making him *spaghetti aglio, olio, e pepperoncino*—don't question it, just make him eat it. Whatever you have to do, *make him presentable.* He cannot mess this up. I've got Magda, I've got Dottie, I've got every outlet you can think of, everybody lined up. We can't have him looking like he just tied one on."

Frankie agrees, but Nico must see something on her face, because he continues.

"Drinking too much is *not* something he does. You hear me, Frankie? He smells like booze, looks like he has a hangover, any of it, that's us waving a giant red flag. You remember what Bernays said about details? Nothing is too trivial."

"I know. Got it."

Two years ago, Jack dropped to the floor of a limousine. Waiting in the line of cars at a premiere, one backfired. Frankie remembers the grip of his hands on the back of his head, his fingers white. At the time, she was new, and it didn't occur to her that the sound had cannonballed the past into the present, but June, who'd been in the seat alongside him, simply leaned forward and calmly tapped the driver, telling him to go around the block. There, she instructed the driver to drop off Frankie and Jack behind the building, then to drop her off at the premiere before circling back to take them home. Not once was there surprise in her voice, or even disappointment. Instead, there was a strange mix of protectiveness and frustration, like an older, annoyed sister who must step in to defend a sibling.

"Thank God we weren't out of the car yet," June said to Frankie. She glanced at Jack. "And don't even *think* about taking him to the premiere. Not unless you want a scene, because here's the order, in case you need to know, which you do. First, panic. Second, confusion. *Where am I?* Third, embarrassment, because the war was how long ago? Then the anger—"

"My old neighbor's son was a veteran," Frankie said, even then protective of Jack. "And he still doesn't speak, to this day. Or, I guess to the day I left New York."

"It's a weakness is what it is. I had family who fought. Don't think I'm unsympathetic. My uncle lost a leg, and I felt bad, we all did, but he *chose* to be helpless because he could be. My mother had to drop out of school to take care of him. She didn't get anything she wanted out of life because he couldn't snap out of it."

Sure enough, all the phases June listed off came to pass, and soon his confusion flipped to a silent embarrassment before frustration rocketed into anger. Anger at the war all those years ago. Anger at his mind, still so capable of yanking him under. Anger at himself, for not being strong enough to resist it. And anger at June, for seeing it all, and for being right.

Now Frankie knows that if she tells him what really happened last night with the shotgun, he'll find that same shame and anger. As she drives to his house in Pasadena, she decides she'll see what he remembers, and if he doesn't remember what happened, she'll take it as a blessing and keep it that way. She can't risk going down that same road, not when he's about to go in front of the press.

O'Shea answers the door. "More time with your sister?" she asks him, and he takes a deep breath, then motions to the kitchen.

Jack is standing at the pantry, and turns when she walks in. "Finally." His hair is still wet, and he watches her like a patient eyeing a doctor entering the room. Quickly she gets the food ready, notes the time, and hands him the plate.

He sets it on the counter. "I need to know. Was there an intruder outside?"

She stays silent to let him continue, to see what more he offers.

"I remember holding the gun. I remember there was something bad outside."

Something bad. She thinks of the little boy, the woman with her wet eyes. She thinks of Nico and then Jack, who just needs to make it through the day without making things worse, who has the rest of his life to be good but now just needs to be good enough.

"We heard something," she finally says. "I think someone was trying to break in, but you scared them off."

He nods just slightly, as if he's tasting forgiveness, allowing himself a hint that it might be all right. But then it builds, and he seems to be in full agreement, clinging to this new narrative, perhaps even seeing the scene play out in his mind. Then a cloud, a shift. "You were breaking up with me, before everything. I remember that."

"Jack, I didn't say that. Just eat—"

"And what? Everything will get better?"

"Let's just get through today."

He shakes his head. "You've got your priorities, don't you?"

"That's not fair. You always knew I didn't want to jeopardize my job."

"Thank you, yes. And you continually make that clear." Then he narrows his eyes as if having spotted something from a distance, something not right. "Was someone crying? A dog?"

The whimpering. The child. "No," Frankie lies. "There were coyotes. Maybe that's what you're remembering."

And he lets her say this, perhaps believing her, perhaps just wanting to believe.

Frankie, soothing and accommodating and convincing. Jack, wanting to be good. Later she will think of this day, how he went to the studio and did the interviews and smiled and laughed and played his role, and how for all intents and purposes, it appeared that she had done her job because she helped. She fixed. But did she? Sometimes she will wonder. Perhaps she should've told him what really happened in the alley, because maybe, just maybe, things would've turned out differently if he realized just how close he was to the edge.

CHAPTER 8

Some Things Can't Be Faked

Through the wall, she hears a neighbor run a bath, the pipe's clang and pulse. It's a daily ritual Frankie could set a clock to, and it means it's still early evening. There are *hours* left before the day is over and she can escape with sleep—far too much time for second-guessing and regret. She opens the book on her nightstand. Inside is an old note from her roommate Susan that she used as a bookmark. *Grant said to tell you "What do you say to a beach day?" He said to write it down exactly like that. What a* weirdo.

What do you say to a beach day? Code for *meet me in Venice.*

Nights with both of them crammed into a little porcelain tub, sweating bottles of sodas hanging loose in their hands, a Jelly Roll Morton recording swinging music into the room while Jack told stories of seeing the jazz pianist and composer back in New Orleans. Then walks on the beach, when it was late enough that everyone else seemed to have slid from the planet, the sand left glistening and empty. Back then, the worst that would've happened had someone seen them was a slight scandal, most likely something they could've contained. Now, everything's changed. After the interviews, she tried to talk to him. *Let's just get through today,* he said stiffly, turning her earlier statement against her before walking away.

"We're seeing a movie," Susan says, grabbing her purse from atop the dresser. She's about to walk out again when she turns to Frankie. "You're not interested, are you, in *The Mayor of Hell*."

It's not said as a question. Maybe she's upset that Frankie's moving out in a couple of weeks. Maybe she figures Frankie's already in bed or isn't interested in a film put out by competing studio Warner Brothers—known for tougher gangster and mob flicks, as well as animated short films—but there's a note of presumption in her tone that, to Frankie's ears, sounds like a gauntlet being thrown.

Frankie, always the first to accept a challenge, sits up. "I love James Cagney. Wish we'd gotten him."

In the hall, Virginia laughs and appears in the doorway. "RCO does *romance*."

"We don't *only* do romance."

"Fine. RCO's *known* for romance, how's that? Cagney's weirdness is *not* sexy. At least not to me. I'll stick to Jack Sawyer, thank you very much." Virginia, who's engaged to a man named Fred, and has the framed photo of Jack on her nightstand, adds the last part with a smile.

Frankie's already standing, but it's the mention of Jack that seals the deal. "I'll go."

The theatre has orange-and-red awnings and a marquee that glows purple in the dark. The second they pull in front, however, Virginia starts frantically pointing down the street to where RCO plays its films, the word Theatre a bright-yellow promise in the night.

"*The Last Chance*!" she's saying. "I never saw it! Go, go, go!"

Susan, who's driving, hits the gas—before Frankie can say she's seen it or doesn't want to see it or maybe can't see it tonight of all nights, because it stars her soon-to-be-ex-boyfriend and the woman he's set to marry, and this is really, truly, the last thing she wants to do. All she can do is look over her shoulder as they pull away from the theatre with the movie that's safe, that would've been a true escape, and head toward one that will promptly hurl her into the very pit she's trying to avoid.

With a jerk to the curb, they're parked, and are getting out of the car when suddenly they're lit up by spotlights. Frankie faces the white glare. "I think we just got pulled over."

"We're already parked," Susan says as if this is a rule the police should obey. "We're even out of the car."

"Just be polite," Frankie tells her. The three of them stand on the sidewalk, on the terrazzo sunray pattern that bursts from the theatre doors. As if lit from this low sun, their car is bright in the squad car's spotlight.

The police officer who approaches holds back a laugh. He's in his fifties, padded around the middle, and has a scar on his cheek. The fingers on his right hand look bent, arthritic, and painful. But it's the laugh that gets Frankie, as if they're three girls who got caught trying on their mother's clothes.

"Something funny, Officer?"

Beside her, Virginia shoots her a look.

"Never seen someone change their mind about a movie that fast, that's all."

"Was I speeding?" Susan asks, going for the innocent approach. Head lowered, she peers at the man from under her lashes. Frankie wants to kick her.

The officer scoffs. Everything about the man tells Frankie that he works hard and gets paid little and has no patience for Hollywood. *Some cops are old school and by the book,* Nico once said, *and they blame Hollywood for their forces' corruption, and the fact that their bosses are in our pockets. Not much we can do but watch out for them.*

"Honestly, Officer," Frankie says. *Never lead with the word* honestly, Nico likes to say. *I'll always know you're lying.* "I'm a writer and am working on a story about how Hollywood is just ruining this town. This movie, in particular, I've heard terrible things about it."

He glances over his shoulder at the marquee. "Too many actors here. For one thing."

Frankie nods as Susan watches her curiously and Virginia stares safely at the ground. "A dime a dozen. The whole article's about how wrong it is that the people who make the most do the least."

A laugh. He's nodding. Agreeing with her. Telling them they need to pull away from the curb carefully before he wishes her luck with the article.

"*You* work with the people who make the most and do the least." Susan laughs, when he's gone and they're safely standing in line.

Frankie opens her coin purse to find her money. "Doesn't mean it's not true."

"The way your mind works," Virginia says. "I don't know if it's admirable or frightening."

Susan smiles. "Is *scrappy* a compliment?"

Twice Frankie started fights with a bully when she knew someone bigger and stronger was about to walk past and would get involved. Once, she hid canned peaches and peas in her skirt pocket when the grocer was distracted by the front bell—and, in fact, she had arranged for the person to enter the store at that moment. Many times, she's cut in lines or trespassed or even figured out where to sit in class in order to catch the window's reflection of the smartest kid's test papers. Being called scrappy *is* a compliment, as far as Frankie's concerned. *Scrappy* means she's here, now, despite everything.

Frankie moves forward in line. "Surviving, when you have nothing, means getting creative. I'm not ashamed. But it's not like I'd hurt someone."

Walking past them, an older man catches this and shoots Frankie a dirty look.

"Unless they asked for it," Frankie adds with a smile.

Ahead of them in line is a boy with thickly cuffed pants as if he's rolled up a good six inches. Politely, he says to the cashier, "One, please."

The ticket-taker leans forward as far as he can in his booth, attempting to look in both directions for anyone the kid might be with. Frankie can see farther than the cashier can, and spots a group of older school-age children who wait until the boy in line has his ticket before disappearing around the corner.

"Quit your dreaming there," Susan says, "and pay up."

Inside, they settle into the middle of the theatre, and Frankie leans back, studying a ceiling that is plain but for crown moldings. With so many working-class people seeking the escape of a movie, theatres have begun to shed their opulence, like an overdressed woman at a party who realizes the effort was unnecessary. Now theatres exist in neighborhoods, and are intended for everyone. Eighty million Americans see a movie each week, which, Nico has informed her, is the most ever, and translates to 65 percent of the American population. In a world ravaged by economic despair, people find the money for a movie.

Or, Frankie knows, they find a way in.

Sure enough, the second the lights go down and the trailers—once trailing at the end of the movie, hence the word—begin, a wedge of light breaks into a corner of the theatre. Frankie's been waiting for this, for the kid who bought the ticket to prop open the door that leads to the alley. In a bright flash, a tide of his friends rushes in, kids who have probably never left these immediate blocks, who've never been in the mountains or been ice-skating or even boarded a train, who will probably never do those things or claw past the boundaries of their lives. Thanks to movies, however, they can. Briefly, these kids will lift above themselves and imagine and experience. At least this is how it was for Frankie, the times she managed to scrounge up enough money or sneak into a theatre. The first time she saw a farm was in a movie. The first time she saw a giraffe, or a forest, or the inside of a boat. To live a different life, it was worth every effort.

An usher storms down the aisle, but the room darkens as another trailer starts up, and as fast as the kids came in, they disperse and meld into the audience. They had their timing right.

The usher stands a few feet from Frankie, scanning the crowd.

"You reacted so fast," she says, pointing to the other aisle. "They ran that way and out. I think you scared 'em." *Pay someone a compliment, and you win 'em over.*

Beside her, Virginia stares straight ahead. Virginia, who confesses every time she eats food that belongs to one of her roommates, and cannot pull pranks. The usher, satisfied, walks backward up the aisle, keeping his eye on the screen. The corner of his mouth tricks into a smile right as the audience laughs, and with that, he surveys the crowd, pleased, as if he, personally, is responsible for their joy.

"Shoot. Powder room," Virginia says, standing up. "Don't let it start without me."

When she's gone, Susan whispers to Frankie, "Fred wouldn't see this with her. I don't know if it's because *she's* in love with Jack Sawyer, or because he is."

"Fred?" Virginia's fiancé, a quiet man with a receding hairline. He's a middle manager at the studio and someone always looking for a way up. Virginia, who works for one of the top executives at the studio, could be the closest he'll come to a promotion, is the way Frankie sees it.

Susan raises a brow. "You never heard her complain when she doesn't hear from him, sometimes for days? It happens a lot, Frankie. Nights he claims he didn't hear the phone or went to bed early. And that group of guys from his college that he's close with—something doesn't sit right there. But don't get me wrong, I think Fred loves Virginia, and I think he'll always be good to her and she'll have the life she wants, but I'm guessing he bats for the other team. So, if that's important—"

"If?" Frankie asks.

"There's not just *one* way to lead a good life. Not everyone gets handed a house to live in all by themselves." Before Frankie can protest and inform her that she *earned* the house, Susan continues. "And really, being alone isn't everyone's goal."

"The goal *isn't* to be alone. It's to be *able* to be alone."

Susan smiles. "I'm not sure you've helped your case."

Virginia makes it back just in time, and the audience cheers as the opening credits roll.

First on screen is June, radiant with blond hair so light it looks white, like spun sugar. "She's practically *transparent*," Susan whispers to Frankie.

But Frankie's bracing to see Jack, and when he appears, it feels as though a hole has opened up in the center of her chest. Because she remembers when he filmed this, remembers him learning the lines. She mouths one along with him—*She's one of those gals who holds your hand while she stomps on your heart*—and as she does, they're back in his kitchen in Venice, twirling spaghetti around their forks. The night was hot and the windows were open, the scent of seaweed and salt in the air.

But then he stops being Jack. His talent catches even her off guard, and at one point she realizes she managed to forget him, that for a whole chunk of the movie she's watched a man whose obsession with a married woman grows and grows, a married woman who will end up dead. The victim's husband will wake on Christmas morning to find a present from his dead wife that leads to the arrest of Jack's character, Charles. Love, or obsession? Either way, Charles couldn't handle her with someone else. Truly, Jack is phenomenal, everything about him transformed. Even his breathing is different—faster, more panicked inhalations, something Frankie wonders if anyone else has noticed. Curious, she looks around the theatre, at faces that shine with the shifting light, entranced.

Then the Christmas-morning scene begins. Frankie takes in the giant tree and flickering candles, all the presents and the garlands, and instead sees a family her mother worked for when Frankie was eight years old, a rich family who lived on Lexington Avenue in a house with crimson damask-silk walls and domed ceilings. Christmas Day, Fiona had to work, to clean up after the morning chaos and ready the family for a dinner they were hosting that night. As she often did, Frankie went along, the two entering the house through the service entrance in the back. Though usually she trailed her mother, this time she saw something in the foyer: the Christmas tree. While her mother bent over a stain in the rug—*Cranberries? Is that what this is?*—Frankie stood before the grand fir, looking up. It was the most beautiful thing she'd ever seen. As tall as street signs, as tall as the double-faced cast-iron sidewalk clock on Fifth. A tree like this should not be in a house, but there it was, draped in red velvet ribbons, dotted with candles on its boughs. It smelled cold and warm all at once.

"Santa brought me Kewpie dolls and Crayola crayons so I can draw," a girl said, "and a wagon and a tricycle, but Mother says that's for when I'm bigger." She was a couple of years younger than Frankie, and had a blue-and-purple stain on the corner of her mouth as if she'd been sucking on a colorful lollipop.

Frankie didn't see what was under the tree until that moment: crumpled-up wrapping paper, discarded ribbons, and presents. So many presents.

"You mean your parents," Frankie said. That morning, she'd unwrapped her present from Santa: two Clark candy bars, wrapped in silver foil. "Santa brings one present."

The second she spoke, Frankie knew she was in trouble. Not only was she correcting someone, but that someone *lived* in this house. And more than that, Frankie wasn't supposed to leave her mother's side. Everything about this was forbidden.

The girl didn't seem to care about any of that, though. She shook her head and said no, she meant *Santa*, because she holds their dog's leash and she made up her bed and held the door open for this lady at church who smells. "Santa writes it all down," the girl informed Frankie. "If you only got one present, it's because you weren't good. You didn't deserve as much."

Frankie never saw her mother enter the room. All at once, she was jerked away, and in that moment, Frankie knew it was true: She was not good. She'd wandered where she shouldn't have, and she'd spoken out of turn. But somehow Fiona was pushing Frankie behind her, and facing the little girl. Leaning down, her mother let her voice drop to a low hiss. "Not one thing under that tree is because you're good, and you're certainly not better than my daughter. What you are is spoiled. All of that is from your parents, because *there's no such thing as Santa*."

In that second, the day blazed into gold. Later, Frankie realized there wasn't even a moment when she considered or cared about Santa, nor did it occur to her that this exchange was an axe to her mother's job. All that mattered was the look on the girl's face, the surprise and shock, and the feeling of her mother's hand in hers as they raced down the street and through Gramercy Park, laughing, *faster, faster*. It was the first time she'd ever run with her mother. It was the last time she'd ever run with her mother.

"Frankie," Virginia is saying. "Frankie, the lights are on. It's over."

She tries to leave her mother in the park, to not think about when they slowed down and reality caught up. The look on her mother's face: someone trying to be brave. Fiona, who'd taken on an unnecessary expense by adopting Frankie, who worked hard and got nothing in return. Nothing but an overworked heart that would one day stop as if it had simply reached a limit.

The lobby is bright and blaring. Frankie passes the concession stand in a daze, and in the car, she barely hears Susan, who won't stop rehashing scenes, starting almost every sentence with: *And then.* Beside her, Virginia is strangely quiet.

"And then, when he realized he could frame the husband—oh my God, I never knew I could hate Jack Sawyer, but wow, so believable as a creep who just couldn't let someone else have the woman he loved. And then, and then, when the husband opened the present? It was like a message from the grave. And you know what? I don't know that I'd kick Jack Sawyer to the curb, even if he was guilty. That scene with him and the punching bag, my God, his muscles. Imagine loving someone so much that you can't let anyone else have them and you'd rather they be *dead* than with someone else."

Frankie, finally emerging from her own past, from missing her mother, says, "You mean Jack Sawyer's character, Charles. You wouldn't kick Charles to the curb."

Susan laughs. "Sure, that's what I mean."

"Virginia," Frankie says, noticing her other roommate's silence. "You didn't like it?"

Now even Susan quiets, both hands on the steering wheel, concentrated. Because Virginia's one of Jack's biggest fans, and should be raving about the film.

"I loved it," Virginia says.

Frankie's confused. "Then—"

"Fred doesn't look at me like that. The way Jack looks at June."

Again, not the way Jack's character looked at June's character, but they, themselves. *For people to love them, they need to feel that they* know *them,* Nico's said. *It's part of celebrity, that false familiarity.*

"You just don't see the way Fred looks at you," Susan says, and Frankie meets her gaze in the rearview mirror.

Even the thought of Jack looking at her makes Frankie's skin warm. The way he observes her. How he anticipates everything. And then she remembers his bitter words: *You've got your priorities, don't you?*

Virginia twists around in her seat. "Frankie, when *you* don't say anything, alarm bells go off."

I'm guessing he bats for the other team. "All that matters is how *you* feel about it."

"He's my best friend. But we've been together for so long. I don't get chills anymore. When he touches me? You can *see* the electricity between Jack and June. They can't hide it."

"They're *acting*," Frankie says, aware there's an almost defensive note in her voice.

But Virginia shakes her head. "Some things can't be faked." Then she's back to looking out the window, headlights streaking her face.

CHAPTER 9

The Beast We Work For

Wednesday, March 1, 1933

In the morning, Frankie wakes, unsettled. Everything thick with a sense of *wrong*. She didn't expect Jack to call last night, not after how they left things, but it was only as she was drifting off that she realized she'd still held out hope. She needs to get through tonight's premiere and tackle everything tomorrow, but it feels as though she's driving in the dark and can only see what's in front of her; what's just beyond could be a drop, a free fall in the dark.

And indeed, the danger is close. At the studio, Frankie spots the head of production, the man Nico mentioned was going to lose his job. Two secretaries flank him, struggling with boxes, while a security guard ambles slightly behind. The executive walks slowly, defiant. *Feared and revered,* Nico always said about him, *a perfect combination.* For six years his name was linked with the studio's success, but now here he is, a scapegoat. *Someone's always gotta take the fall.*

When the man turns in her direction, she studies the pavement and quickens her pace.

The second she gets into the office, Betty's at her side. "Oh-this-day-oh-this-day-oh-this-day. Thank God you're here. Tell me you've got it."

Frankie opens the curtain that covers Romeo and Juliet's addition. Romeo, a larger splash of lilac blue, twists his head to look at her before stretching one long wing. Green feathers splay, tipped in black. "Got what?"

"*The cookie tin.* The telegrams? I spoke to your roommate this morning."

The cookie tin. A relic from a different world. How could that have been just the other day? What did she do with it? She hears herself saying she left the house while her roommate was in the shower and must have missed the message, while in her mind she retraces her steps. The tin, it hits her, was in her bag that broke at Jack's house. It must have fallen out. Right now it would be under his table, waiting to be discovered. But then a worse thought: Was it still in the bag when she filled it with food to give to the woman? No. She'd have noticed, wouldn't she? She remembers retrieving her coin purse and essentials from on top of the kitchen table but forgot she'd even *had* the tin in her bag.

"I'll get it," she says, praying she can. "Why? What's going on?"

Betty eyes her. "Clearly you didn't read those telegrams. If you did, you wouldn't leave them anywhere."

Never admit, Nico's said. *Always deflect.* "Betty, what you did isn't that bad. He'll understand."

"He'll understand once we get them back. I really thought his stack was on my desk, but I must have put them with the bunch."

Telegrams to *Nico*, Frankie realizes.

From their addition, one of the parrots lets out a screech. Calmly, Frankie leans toward Betty, whose breathing is coming up short. "Put your head down." The woman does as told, dropping her chin to her chest. "Has he asked for them?"

Keeping her head down, Betty nods. "When he called in this morning. That's when I realized what I'd done. So I was honest and I told him and said you were coming in soon and I'd get them from you right away." Now she looks up. "You having them, that's not such a big deal. You know everything. But them being *away* and where other people could get them, especially that one, that won't go over well. They need to be *here* or in his home safe with the others, but under lock and key, right?"

Nico's safe. Emergency money should she ever need it, the title to cars and houses and who knows what. *You ever need to get in there,* he once told her, *just ask Angela for our anniversary, and then let me know what it is, because I'm always a day off.*

"I'll go now." Frankie looks at her watch. *Especially that one,* Betty said. Frankie replays her words. Then calmly, leadingly, says, "Especially that one, you're right. Can you imagine?"

"*No.* Anything to do with Jack's former"—she turns her voice to a whisper—"*life* can't be out there where anyone can see. But imagine if Jack read it? Whew. Thanks, Frankie. You're a peach. I owe you."

~

Whatever's in the telegram isn't something Jack should read, and yet best-case scenario is it's *at* Jack's house. If she weren't terrified, she'd laugh—or even just fixate on the actual content of the message, versus the message itself. But all she can think of is that she needs to locate it, *now.*

What would the woman from the alley do if she found it? Frankie accelerates through an intersection, keeping an eye out for the police. Getting pulled over would mean name-dropping the chief of police, who's also head of the studio's security, but Frankie doesn't have *time* to be pulled over. She remembers when June's maid found private correspondence; no amount of loyalty could've matched the lure of those dollar signs. *It's never about money until it is. And it always is.*

White clouds thread the sky, though there is a knot of gray by the mountain, a storm either about to slide past or almost here. At the gatehouse, she tells herself the cookie tin most likely just fell out, and is hopefully under the table. Winding up the driveway, she squints at the house. All the curtains are open, and the outside lights are switched off, which means that Jack's housekeeper is there. Yet another person who might've found the tin.

When she knocks on the door, Frankie prays to see anyone but Jack so she can beeline to the kitchen.

O'Shea answers, and looks relieved. "He's outside." He nods toward the French doors in the living room, beyond which is the terrace.

Sycamore and white alder and cottonwood and oak. Chaparral and sage. Frequently Jack sits outside, reading scripts and searching treetops for red-tailed hawks and woodpeckers, so when she sees him at the huge wrought iron patio table, the pewter clouds bunched above the mountains in the background, she's thankful. He's just enjoying the last moments of sun. Until she gets closer, and spots the telegrams spread out on the table.

For a split second she's relieved—they're *here*, her worst fear dodged. But then he turns to look at her, and she sees the heartbreak on his face, and that's when she realizes that he doesn't understand *why* they do this to begin with. To him, it must seem horrible. An unforgivable invasion of privacy.

Quickly, she explains. "Not everyone tells us what they're mixed in with. We can't fix something we don't know about, so we read these to head off disaster—"

"You *knew* she was remarried and in Akron?"

"Who?"

"Donna. My ex."

"I didn't know."

"Well, this guy did." He holds up a telegram. "A private investigator, giving Nico the update. *Still married to Holden Bussfield and living in Akron.* 'Still' living there means Nico's known where she is this entire time. He told me she was skipping from town to town."

Frankie takes a seat. "What would it have changed?"

"I would've talked to her! I would've *done* something."

"Don't you think that's what Nico was afraid of?"

Now Jack looks at her, surprised. "You think I would've *hurt* her?"

"I didn't say that."

"Jesus, Frankie. I meant talk to her. Convince her to leave me alone, take her claws out of my life. If she's fine now, she doesn't need me."

"You really think she'd just back off? With all the money she gets?"

"I could've done something. At least I could've apologized. It might've been a start."

"You can't just show up, Jack. In any town, or at any house—you do that, it's news. It gets out."

"But it's *my* life." With this, he stands, shoving the chair back. Metal scrapes against the stone floor. Then he's at the edge of the terrace, braced by the darkened sky, a drop before him. "I deserve the information. I deserve a chance to handle *my own life*."

Even as she speaks, she knows she should stop, but frustration pushes against her. "*You* walked out. You left a mess. You did that. And this whole time, the studio's been cleaning it up and protecting you from someone who's *blackmailing* you, but you see *the studio* as the enemy? At least let me talk to Nico about it. Let me get the full story. There's always more to it."

He turns to her with a strange calm. "You're right. I am angry at them, not just because they've hijacked my life but because this wedding means I can never openly be with who I *want* to be with. The real question is, why aren't *you* angry?"

You have to know when a dream is just a dream.

"This is my job." With that, she starts gathering the telegrams, putting them back in the tin.

"Your job is not your *life*."

Neither are you. Though she stops herself from saying it, he must catch the momentum of her thoughts.

Coldly, he says, "Well, I guess we have something in common: the beast we work for."

Frustration spills over. Anger that her job and her personal life have collided, that one demands she fail at the other. And then there's what he's asking her to risk. What he expects her to jeopardize, after she's come so far.

"Do you know what it's like watching your mother not eat? Wanting to believe her when she says she's full, because you're that hungry? She was thirty-nine when she died. She hadn't eaten a proper meal in I don't know how long, just so I could have something in my stomach, and she died for it." These words compose a fear she's always shied away from. Even speaking it out loud seems to give it life, and now she wishes she could take it back.

"Frankie, you don't know that—"

"What I know is that you think you understand me because you once lived on the edge, but the edge would've been miles up from where I was. Now you want me to go against the studio and my boss, who's the only reason I can take care of myself. But you and I worked *because* I would never do that." His silence seems to push her closer to where she doesn't want to go. "And you *knew* that, didn't you? Was that part of my appeal? That I would never force your hand? Until now, when it works better if I speak up and risk everything."

At her words, he turns his back, facing the Arroyo. She watches his shoulders rise with a deep breath. Already her regret is bitter, and she's about to try and lessen her words' sting, but he turns and his expression makes her stop.

"Betty told me you'd been promoted. They really doubled down, didn't they? Congratulations, Frankie; they bought you too."

Always know when to leave, Nico has said. Without giving Jack a chance to say more, she takes the tin, turns, and walks away.

CHAPTER 10

Admission to the Battle

Grauman's Chinese Theatre is chaos. Lush and tropical but frenzied and packed. A gray and menacing sky appears to be on the verge of bursting, a dark background for the towering queen palms that line the entryway. The pagoda, with its roof of oxidized copper, appears slick in the humid air.

Frankie stands near the three sets of double doors, by a flame made of punched-out metal that Nico said represents *the enduring spirit of creativity*. Voices surge, commands are barked, people hurry with cameras and reflectors, crates of bottles and boxes of glasses and trays of food. A long canopy leads from the street to the door, and dragons are stenciled on its side. Usually Frankie loves chaos and the subsequent thrill of ordering the disordered, but this is different. The hectic frenzy of anticipation, which often feels like that moment a magician reveals the woman he's just cut in half is, in fact, fine, has changed. Tonight it feels as though the magician has other plans.

She messed up. She was careless with the telegrams and reckless with their star, fighting with him on the worst day possible, essentially sending him into an important night with even more reason to be mad. *Whew,* Betty said when Frankie returned earlier with the tin. *We squeaked by that one, didn't we?*

The wind picks up, scraping leaves against the sidewalk. Elaborately dressed ushering staff hurry past her, and a man with a broom stands on a ladder, sweeping off the top of the canopy. Frankie stops just in time before walking into a billow of dust that clouds like smoke from the stenciled dragon's mouth. Above, the sky is a cold fist.

She will admit it: Though Jack is the one who made the mess in the first place, the studio should never have filtered what he knows of his own life. She needs to talk to Nico and get the details. There must be something she can say to Jack to calm him down.

"This is a cave," she says to a man setting up for interviews. "Face them that way. *Use* the diffused light, don't work against it."

Behind him, a woman Frankie doesn't know waves to her. "Nico's been looking for you. In the lobby."

"Finally," Nico says when he sees her, as if she's just arrived. *A boss is like a three-year-old who believes a room doesn't exist until they're standing in it,* her mother once said. "I don't know what's going on, but Ida and June are fighting, and June's in a foul mood, and for all I know Jack's gone off the rails, and holy Christ, we need this movie, Frankie, we need it to do well."

Always catch a person off guard, Nico has told her, *before they can rehearse.* "Nico. The telegram. From the PI. Why didn't you tell Jack you knew where Donna was?"

He tilts his head, studying her. "It's nothing to worry about. But what *I'm* curious about is why you think this moment is the right time to bring it up."

He's turned it around on her. "I know there's a reason for everything you do. You're always ten steps ahead. But right now, all I can think of is you lied to him about his own life, and I don't want that to be true."

"Fine, fine. Let's go somewhere quiet."

Somewhere quiet is Mr. Grauman's private box on the balcony level. From here, the projector room is on their left, the source of banging and whirring and a loud voice swearing. Below them, the empty seats curve like ripples from a stone.

The moment they sit, Nico dives right in. "We're not monsters. The wedding, I know you don't agree with it, but Jack was a bachelor who didn't *want* a real relationship when we set him up with June. He didn't *lose* anything. It was the opposite. His career soared. And it's only going higher with this wedding, which also happens to solve a million other problems."

"For the studio."

He looks at her steadily. "For the studio, yes. And for June. After everything we've done for Jack, all we're asking for is a modicum of discretion, and then, after a while, when it's safe, the two of them can explore other options. If they need to."

She feels herself blush, and quickly says, "So Donna."

"Donna. When Donna first saw Jack on screen, she reached out to him at the studio, and he was upset but took it in stride. He owed her. He knew that. Lots of guilt. So we arranged for their divorce, made it official, kept it quiet, and paid her a nice sum. A divorce settlement—for what was apparently the most expensive marriage ever, because she keeps getting more and more. Every time she's in a bad mood or wants a new toy, she fires off another threat."

"That's blackmail."

"Sure is. And the money's not even the kicker. After Jack made headlines for dating June, Donna claimed she had *more* expenses and needed to hock her wedding ring if he didn't bump up the payments. Jack flew off the handle. Not about the money, mind you, but the ring. It was his mother's, and Donna made some promise way back when to keep it safe. So Jack was not happy. Even threatened to come out publicly if he had to, just to be done with her. Imagine that scandal—America's most desired bachelor left a wife high and dry? A bride who waited faithfully for her husband to return from war, only to be ditched? No. This was an impoverished woman when he left her—and he's got houses, plural. We talked sense into him, but he was *furious*. So when he demanded to know where she was, we lied. Seemed safest. We told him we send money to her, care of whatever post office or bank she asks us to, because she moves around. All in all, she's got him by the balls, excuse my language."

Frankie shrugs, and Nico continues.

"But I'm not an idiot. I hired a private investigator so I know what I'm up against. My guy's got someone in records; marriage, birth, whatever we need, he can get. And lo and behold, she's remarried. Lives in a nice house. I mean, a *nice* house. She never needed to sell his mother's ring. She's bleeding him because she can."

"That's horrible."

"Right. And you want him to know that? And know where she is? I don't. He'd flip out. So we lie about where she is, and we pay—I mean, the studio pays. Not even just him. And we do it because *you don't piss off a bull.*"

"Jack's the bull?"

"No, she is. She calls the shots. Make her mad, and she could destroy him. And hey, like I said, I'm not done with her. At some point I'll catch her on something—I've got her letters, telegrams. I've got everything in my safe because *everyone slips up*. Give them enough time, they slip. And when she does, the tide will turn. And I'll get Jack free."

Frankie absorbs this. "You didn't tell me."

"Maybe I should've."

As soon as she can, Frankie will explain this to Jack. Let him know that he's confused his enemies. Then she thinks about what Nico said, that his PI knows someone in records. "Birth certificates list your parents, right? And adoption records, your guy can get those too?"

He smiles. "Adoption records are usually private, but my guy's good. And failing that, *if* you had a birth certificate, then they list whatever parent they know about. But not many people had birth certificates then." A pause, then he continues. "This might be one of those times."

"One of what times?"

"I don't know what you've told yourself over the years about your birth parents—that they didn't have money or that they got sick or whatever it is that made it feel better—but I can almost guarantee that it's not that. And once you know, you can't unknow. Sometimes the truth hurts worse than the lie."

While everyone else exists on solid ground, roots strong and definitive, Frankie's felt as though her life floats on a current. A sense of connection always missing. She remembers an older sister, an older brother too. Maybe a younger sibling as well. Rainy days and being happy inside, never once eyeing the ceiling for stains or shoving newspapers or old rags at windowsills. The dinner table was an impossibly shiny oval where they all sat and held hands before they ate, and not once was anyone instructed to drink a glass of water first. She has no memory of leaving. Were they sad? There is an entire stretch of time that her heart blotted out.

She tells him she still wants to know, and he smiles sympathetically. *Once you know, you can't unknow.*

~

The red carpet is swept and spotless, the marquee blazes, and searchlights sweep the sky. Miraculously, even the rain has held off. Frankie stands with Nico at the sidewalk, watching the crowd push against barricades, when Jack and June arrive.

Nico's gaze focuses on the line of limos. "Banks are heading to a shutdown."

She forgot to take out money but lies so he won't lecture her. "I didn't get much."

"All you need is enough for groceries and gas. Your car and rent are covered, so you're good there. And you know we've got you, if you need anything."

Frankie watches a dark-burgundy limousine pull up. She can't think about this.

"I mean it."

Now she glances at him.

"If you had to move in," he continues, "you know you could. We're there for you. Not just for Sunday dinner."

She's never had this before, someone who holds a net beneath her should she need it. Suddenly she wants to cry—an infuriating feeling. As she thanks him, she hears the emotion in her voice.

He only looks at her a second before turning away, as if needing a moment for himself as well. "Here we go," he says.

June starts to emerge from the limo, bent over as she ducks out. When she straightens, Frankie's breath catches.

"A beauty, ain't it?" Nico says.

Diamonds shine, an emerald the size of a child's fist at June's throat. Frankie's never seen anything like it. When June turns, the necklace flashes like stars bursting from existence.

"We could charge admission just to look at her," Nico says.

Every move beams light. The jewels, the shimmer of her green satin dress. When June waves to the crowd, the necklace flares even brighter, as if sparked by the shock of its audience. "That's from the guy in New York?" Frankie asks, referring to the necklace and a new jeweler who's taken the world by storm.

Nico nods, watching the car now, because Jack should be getting out too, but he's not. "Harry Winston. You know how he started? Pawnshop. Twelve years old, and he bought a ring for twenty-five cents that turned out to be a real diamond. He had the eye, even then. He got married the week I talked him into this. Must've been distracted by the big day or he'd never have let something like that out of his sight."

"At least without a security guard. We sure we want to send her home with that thing?" Frankie tries to laugh as she watches Jack slowly swing his legs out of the car.

Nico pushes in closer, glancing at the people nearby. *"Frankie."*

It was stupid to say and not even true—O'Shea always carries a gun, and June has security and a safe at home. Frankie was trying to make light of a situation that's grown heavy with Jack's arrival, and she starts to offer the correction when she sees that Jack has frozen. It happened once before; the flashing lights suddenly bothered him, and he had to slip into a premiere through a back door, both the crisis and the chance for publicity missed.

"Come on, Jack," Frankie says.

"Goddamn it."

The expression is so uncharacteristic of Nico that Frankie whips toward him, alarmed, only to see him staring not at Jack but across the street, where a huge man stands, watching June. Tank Adams, June's ex. Smiling almost proudly.

"I got it," Frankie says, but Nico's shaking his head.

"No, *I* got this. I'm not sending you over to deal with that lunatic. Just make sure Jack gets out of the damn car."

The second he leaves, there is a flash. And then another. Frankie blinks as a barrage of lights stuns her, all the reporters turned her direction as June approaches. Voices clamor for attention, but June ignores them all. "Frankie. My sister said she was going to look for you. Can you find her?"

Nico mentioned June was in a bad mood, so Frankie leads with something pleasant. "Of course. Did you tell her about the rumors about *The Last Chance*? The Oscar talk?"

For a second it looks as though Frankie's brought up a negative rumor, something June would like to forget. But then she smiles widely. "I did. She couldn't believe it." Her eye twitches. "I don't think I've ever seen her so proud."

And then she's gone.

The crowd is cheering for Jack, louder, shouting his name in unison as if understanding it's their job to draw him out. More voices, more calls, and it must be irresistible to be wanted like this, to be loved like this, because in an almost clumsy move, he steps out of the car and slowly straightens to his full height, tall and sturdy and facing his fans. Frankie's heart pulls. Jack in a tuxedo. Handsome and refreshing and surprising. A rugged softness. But he turns and she sees a knot in his jaw and the set of his mouth. He's not happy. Soon he's swallowed into a throng of press, and when he smiles, it's with an almost vicious charm.

Then he's beelining toward her. Again, everyone's eyes are on her, and she wants to shake her head no, to make him turn around, but she recognizes this reckless determination, the way he gets when he no longer cares.

The second he's in front of her, he says, "Don't bother asking about what we read."

She smiles broadly. "I already talked to Nico, and it's fine. It was to protect you and not upset you and—"

"And you believe them?" A returned, gritted smile. "Don't forget who we're up against. They lie."

Without giving her a chance to respond, he leaves to join June, whose hand flutters to her forehead as if feeling for a fever. Already exhausted, Frankie follows the crowd into the lobby, where Ida immediately spots her.

"She's been bad the last week," Ida says. Demure in an unadorned navy-blue dress, she has the appearance of someone who doesn't believe in folly or fun, and something about the perfume she wears makes Frankie think of an Alpine lake, cold water and flowers. "She's barely spoken to me recently. I think she knows."

Ida's right; for someone who's supposed to be glowing, June looks pale and anxious.

But then Frankie hears what she said. "Knows what? Did you have a fight?"

Now Ida examines Frankie as if for the first time. Frankie realizes she's overstepped, and starts to backtrack, when Ida clears her throat.

"What I meant," she says, "is that I've got two people outside who don't have tickets."

"I'll take care of it." Frankie forces a smile. Then, trying to distract with something good, she adds, "What'd you think of June's news, about the rumor?"

A cloud passes over Ida's face.

Frankie clarifies. "The rumor that she's a shoo-in for an Oscar, for *The Last Chance*."

"Until a statue can pay the bills, does it matter?"

I don't think I've ever seen her so proud. The twitch in June's eyelid, her tic. The tell that she was lying. *Ida is the one person whose approval June needs,* Nico told Frankie when she first started working for him. *There's some older-sister reverence there, so tread carefully.* Ida's response must have broken June's heart.

Then Frankie sees Dede Domenico across the room, standing by Nico at the bar, wearing a red dress that looks painted on. Awkwardly, the girl pulls up on the strap, clearly uncomfortable, as the bartender mixes some powdered lemon-lime Kool-Ade into a glass of water.

Ida stares disapprovingly. "A fifteen-year-old shouldn't be wearing that dress. Who's looking out for her?"

When June was younger, Ida was reportedly the epitome of a protective older sister, taking drinks away and running interference when men got too close. "I think she's doing all right," Frankie tries.

Ida shakes her head. "Do you know what that girl said the other day? That she came to Hollywood because she loves acting. Little does she know that being talented is nothing more than admission to the battle. And no one should fight alone. Which is why I need to see to June. Excuse me."

Frankie leans against the wall.

"Got rid of Tank," Nico says when he joins her.

"I'm ready for this to be over."

"You're telling me. And Jack's got a flask in his pant leg. Mr. I Don't Drink is fixing to tie one on while standing in the spotlight."

"They need rest. Everything is too much right now."

"Agreed. Let's bow out of the party—no way I'm letting them drink in public in this state, and neither one of them wants to be there anyhow. Then sure, a couple days of rest."

Frankie remembers the twitch in June's eye when she spoke of how proud her sister was. "I think June needs a break from Ida. She was going home tonight, but maybe that's not good. Jack can be in Venice, but let's put June at the bungalows."

"As long as the press doesn't know where to look, I don't care where they are. Get O'Shea to take the decoy limousine to Malibu. Then have two other drivers separate our ticking time bombs. Malibu Protocol tonight."

Malibu Protocol. The studio's sleight of hand. A claim that both stars are at a beach house that the studio owns, and *the lovebirds request their privacy*. Witnesses will attest to spotting them in the windows, and the grocer will recognize the orders. Photographers wait at the corner of the driveway, and now and then a car will go in and out, curtained windows rolled all the way up, O'Shea, recognized and known, at the wheel. *The butcher drops off Jack's favorite cut of meat,* Nico long ago explained, *and even though he doesn't see Jack, he tells ten people Jack Sawyer's in Malibu by dinner.* The truth is the shapes in the window are just that—shapes, the silhouettes of Frankie or Betty or any longtime, trusted employee—but the power of suggestion goes a long way. A maid who's under orders to not disturb the couple in the master suite will bring in the groceries, and because she will find much of the food in the trash the next day and will take home what she can, she won't say a word. Shame, the great silencer, will keep that detail unknown. Witnesses, testifiers, corroborators. Soon, an entire army will back up the story of the lovebirds hiding out in Malibu together, belief like a snowball that builds as it goes, and Jack and June will have gotten rest elsewhere, undisturbed and alone.

At first, it felt strange to perpetuate the lie. But breaks are necessary, and the only way the stars can get them is with a little subterfuge. Or that's what Frankie told herself until she saw it differently: The public *wants* the lie. They don't *want* June without makeup, and they don't want Jack reading a script on the front porch of a cottage in Venice Beach. Though they love the humble beginnings for the proof that anything is possible—Clara Bow, after all, was born in a tenement, and Valentino was processed through Ellis Island and slept on the street before his big break—no one wants reality to intrude on the fantasy. They want the glamour, and they want a mansion. They want what they don't have, and the last thing they want is to see themselves within their stars, because they need the promise that life can be different. They need the dream.

"Malibu it is," Frankie says to Nico. "Ida wasn't so pleased with you talking to Dede."

Nico laughs. "Dede was on roller skates the other day. Can you imagine the powers that be finding out? Their next starlet flying around on wheels? God bless her. To be young and not afraid."

Jack and June stand side by side, and though Frankie can see only their backs, when June says something and laughs, Frankie notices Jack's grip, the way he squeezes her hand. A signal for her to stop whatever it is she's done. June yanks her hand from his grasp.

Nico must catch this as well. "We gotta get Jack away from her before he kills her."

It's only when they turn around that they see Dottie, the tabloid writer, standing with her back to them, studying a program in her hand. Or pretending to study a program. Did she hear?

Nico takes Frankie's arm and leads her away, shaking his head. "This night is gonna be the death of me."

CHAPTER 11

She Didn't Say Goodbye

The premiere feels like a near miss, like the breeze of a passing arrow. Somehow, both stars make it to the end without causing a stir, and the press buys the excuses for them leaving before the party. No one questions the couple as they get into the same limousine, driven by O'Shea, which then secretly meets up with two other cars a few blocks over so the lovebirds can go their separate ways.

Standing on the street corner, Frankie peers up at the sky, dark and ominous but behaving. Not even a drop of rain. A wash of light appears and fades as a car turns the corner, and sounds of the party grow louder when someone leaves the building.

The night's over, and they made it out alive, disaster avoided.

An ironic, fate-tempting thought.

Without the distraction of the premiere, this new life without Jack is already becoming real. He's getting married. June's having a baby. Every minute that passes is one closer to a life without him. Jack, who can't cook without doing the recipe's accompanying accent, and once backed against the counter in pure delight when they were making chicken cacciatore and Frankie launched into an Italian accent. Jack, who always uses a coaster, and who makes her take off her shoes the second she walks into the Venice cottage. Jack, who traces letters with his finger onto her back. *Close your eyes. What am I saying?*

Another blessing: At home, both roommates are gone. Frankie runs a bath, determined to soak in the silence while she can. Soon the white subway tiles bead with condensation, and the medicine cabinet's mirror fogs. Somewhere there's a bird calling in the night. She's never minded being alone, never cared about having a boyfriend, and she knows she'll fall right back into that. It's all for the best. She never worked in his world; she sees the confusion on people's faces when Jack is happy to see her. Her, of all people. The surprise. The last thing she'd want is the whole country questioning her worth; though Frankie's never had much, she's always had her pride. But there is pain to this, to this ending she didn't want. Leaning her head back, she sinks in further, her toes by the faucet, a steady drip of cool.

She only realizes she's fallen asleep when she wakes to what sounds like a rock hitting the window in the room next to the bathroom—her bedroom window. And then another. Someone must be standing by the garage behind the building, trying to get her or Susan's attention. Is Susan home? The bathwater's cold. Another tap.

Dripping water, she grabs her robe—a gift from Jack, parchment-colored silk with deep burgundy roses—and flips off the bathroom light so whoever is below won't see her. Another tap, this one harder. Heart beating, she feels her way to the window and twists open the clasp. "Hey! Police are on the way, so you—"

"Frankie."

Jack. She pushes her head against the screen, trying to see him in the dark, and then thinks of her neighbors—the three other units filled with people—and hurries through the apartment, grabbing her car keys so she can hide him. Barefoot, she rushes down the path. A rock pushes into the bottom of her foot, and pain flares.

He's standing behind her building by the garage, and his hair is wet. In his arms he's got a soaked brown paper bag that he holds to his chest. Everything is wet, she realizes. Her feet are muddy.

She points to her car. "Get in."

Even before he gets the door closed, she smells the bourbon on him. The top of a bottle sticks out of the brown bag. Quickly she starts the car, which rumbles to life, and throws the gear into reverse, the clutch grinding. Pulling out of the driveway, she searches the street.

"Where's your car?"

He's slouched, his head against the window. "Walked."

"From where?"

"You have roommates. I forgot." He says it accusingly, as if she's failed him in this regard.

Roommates. Were they home? Frankie left so quickly, she didn't check—but no, if anyone were home, they'd have knocked on the bathroom door. She pushes up Jack's coat sleeve to peer at his watch, and he jerks his hand away.

"I just want to know the time."

He holds up his arm, squinting at it. When he says nothing, she looks over. "After one a.m. Where were you?"

"A pool hall on Alvarado."

"You went to a *pool hall*? You were supposed to be in Venice. Was it the Lucky Break?" If she has cleanup to do, she needs to know where to start. Eyes closed, he nods. The Lucky Break. A small sign. A door that sticks and a floor that's stickier. A seedy place that's usually empty, but now and then finds a way to serve liquor and attracts a rough crowd. "How the hell did you get there?"

"Driver."

It wasn't O'Shea. O'Shea was driving the decoy to Malibu, since people recognize him. "The same man who was supposed to take you to Venice? I'll have him fired."

"No, you won't." He closes his eyes.

Scenarios scroll through her head: people seeing him in the car in the morning, someone spotting him now or catching her trying to drag a six-foot-three man outside. O'Shea can help her, but not if Jack's passed out. She needs to keep him awake, so she shakes his shoulder. His eyes fly open, his body tense. "Jack. Come on. It's me."

When he looks at what she's wearing, she realizes she's still in her robe.

"I've never even seen you . . ." he says, but his voice trails off.

She keeps the robe at her apartment. He's never seen her in it. Logistics scroll through her mind: Louis and O'Shea can't see her at this time in a robe, with nothing underneath, and there's the distance to get him home to Pasadena that she needs to factor in, a distance she doesn't want to drive while dressed like this. If she's pulled over, it would get back to Nico in a heartbeat. "I can't take you to your house. The bungalows are closer."

A headlight's beam smooths his face. Eyes closed, his features are relaxed. She looks away, gripping the steering wheel tighter as they hit a bump.

The bungalows, two white clapboard houses on the last lot of the street, are officially on Glenhollow, a small dead-end road with so much vegetation that parking means scratching up against a hedge or a bush. Bungalow one is close to the sidewalk, private and well kept, and bungalow two is far behind it, all the way back on the lot, existing in the shade of trees and through the clutch of spiderwebs. To get to that second bungalow, one takes the path just to the left of the first bungalow, a long brick walkway that dives deep into the property and all the way to the street behind the lot, Arlington Way, a narrow, tiny road where Frankie once got her car stuck for an hour as she tried to turn around. *If you value your paint job,* Nico likes to say, *don't park on Glenhollow. But if you value your life and time, don't even think about Arlington Way, because that was made for horses.*

So this, pulling in front of the driveway on Glenhollow, is the best option, even though it means that at any point June could look outside and see them. And getting him out of the car is just the beginning. From here, he has to make his way on the path all the way to the second bungalow, dodging spiderwebs while drunk and staying calm as the neighbor's dog on the other side of the fence makes a ruckus. *And why are you together?* June would ask if she woke and saw Frankie escorting Jack. What would Frankie say? *He needed me.* Plain, simple. Somehow, she knows June would respect that. But dressed like this, she can't take the chance.

She says his name, and his eyes open. "Why did you even come tonight?" she asks.

His eyes close again. "You're who I want to talk to. When I'm mad. Happy."

"Well, you can't talk like this, can you?"

One eye opens, just enough to glare at her.

Frankie looks past him, to the path that leads to June's front door. The porch light is off, the path shaded and dark. "Jack," she says.

He opens his eyes but doesn't move.

"You need to go. June's in number one, so go to two, in the far back. You remember where the key is, right? The key's on top of the doorframe. Jack, I need you to get inside."

Just as he opens his door, he leans back again, head against the seat and eyes shut tight as if to block something out. "I'm stuck."

She puts her hand on her door handle to get out and help, but he continues.

"They have me trapped. And they *knew* where she was. Is. Don't defend them." He starts to get out again, trying to stand.

"I'm not defending anybody."

Leaning as far forward as he can, as if needing the momentum, he remembers to close the door and loses his balance, falling forward and barely catching himself against the mailbox.

Something in her breaks. Patience, understanding. All her sympathy is gone, as sudden as a door slamming shut within her heart. Maybe it's harsh, but the sight of someone drunk—even if it doesn't happen often—hardens something within her. She grew up surrounded by the chaos that follows episodes like this, and her life has spiraled one too many times because of other people's messes. When all she wants is to control her life, it's someone like this who renders that impossible.

She doesn't care if he makes it to the bungalow, or if he finds the key. He can wake up June and sleep on the pathway, tangled in spiderwebs, for all she minds. But then she takes a deep breath. This is her job.

He turns to wave to her, and as he does, he notices the paper bag on the floor, the bottle of bourbon inside. "Forgot that," he says, and leans his hand against the doorframe while he strains to reach inside. Frankie, frustrated and disgusted and picturing him falling and bashing his head on the door, hands it to him. Another choice she will regret. Another marker on the path.

When he walks away, he veers slightly to the right. The back of his tuxedo is wrinkled, his hair unkempt. Bit by bit, her anger diminishes. Ever since her mother died, unexpectedly and fast, Frankie's found it hard to trust life enough to let someone walk away with anything left unsaid. But what does she need to say?

I'm sorry.

I don't know how to fix this.

Maybe we can still find a way.

"Jack," she says, in a loud whisper. He turns, off-balance, the brown bag with the bottle at his side, and once again she feels a wall inside her fortify, a pillar of self-reliance and control. Because of this, she doesn't say what she wanted to. "You'll make it all right?"

He gives her a salute and, once again, begins his slow shuffle down the path. A moment or two longer, and she hears the dog whose yard starts a bit past June's bungalow, the loud barking that announces Jack's at least made it that far. The barking continues, then stops. Just barely, just faintly, she sees part of the path brighten with a spill of light, and knows he's made it inside the bungalow. Relief.

Now, she thinks, the night's over. Finally, they've made it.

But as she pulls away, she thinks of her mother again, and how every person's existence is so fragile, like a thin pane of glass against the storm of life. What ends someone could be a shattering or could be a slow, destructive crack, but too often it comes out of nowhere. And for a second she pauses, eyes on the mirror, the place against the curb where they just were, where she didn't say goodbye.

CHAPTER 12

A Wordless Code for *I Love You*

Sunday, October 5, 1930

Death happens on normal days. It's but one of death's many injustices that it is, in fact, so unremarkable. The morning you die, Frankie's always thought, or the morning that someone you love dies, should start differently. But the same sun rises, the sky looks like a sky, and the truth is that the end makes no announcement. The day Frankie's mother died, Fiona woke up and got dressed and then went to work, and that was it. There was more to it, of course, but when the police lifted Fiona and spread her out on the ground and Frankie crawled alongside her, her head on her mother's still chest, it was Fiona's feet Frankie couldn't look away from, one foot without its shoe. There was the faint outline of her mother's toes through her socks. Her socks. Navy blue, a tear in the small toe, a bit of toenail showing through. Her mother had put on socks. Of course she had. Such a normal, heartbreaking thing to do, to put on socks only to die.

That day, there was a breeze. Nothing remarkable, nothing unusual. A few red maple leaves clung to branches, and now and then a gust picked up, and the rest swirled and skittered on the sidewalk, piling up in corners. The sky was blue but not incredibly so. The clouds full, but none in shapes worth noticing. A normal day.

Three times a week, they took the subway through the Joralemon Street Tunnel into Brooklyn. There, Fiona worked in a white mansion with a towering two-story portico and twenty-five-foot fluted columns that were better suited to ancient Greece than Prospect Park. The Hawthorne House. Mr. and Mrs. Hawthorne tended to spend time at their house in Connecticut but wanted their Brooklyn house spotless all the same, and since their eighteen-year-old daughter, Catherine, would be at home, they "required" Fiona's presence just to pick up the candy wrappers Catherine left on the counter or tables or sometimes on the long green chesterfield sofa where she liked to read.

That Sunday, Fiona wasn't feeling well. She was tired and moved slowly but made it to a restaurant four blocks from their apartment, where she pleaded with the owner to use his phone for a long-distance call she'd pay back. She called the Hawthornes in Connecticut, knowing that if she simply didn't show up, Catherine would tell on her. Catherine did that kind of thing—ran her finger along the tops of cabinets to check for dust, noted how long it took Fiona to clean each room. Though Mr. and Mrs. Hawthorne weren't in Brooklyn, weren't even in the same state, in fact, they still insisted she work, and since it was not the time to lose a job, Fiona agreed to go in, rubbing her left shoulder as if the decision itself had caused a pain.

At the Hawthorne House, Frankie was cleaning the bathroom when she heard a noise. Something slammed against a kitchen cupboard. Often, she would think of this moment, how she rinsed the sponge in the sink, how she swiped again at the toothpaste by the faucet. Still, it stuns her that she cleaned a sink as her mother lay dying.

Back in the kitchen, she scanned the room, looking for her mother to ask what next. But no one was there. It was when she was turning to leave that she saw her mother's foot, and then her body, slumped against the floor and the lower cupboard.

Frankie's scream drew the Hawthornes' daughter. The telephone was in the parlor, and Frankie yelled at her to tell the operator they needed help. Catherine disappeared, and Frankie held her mother's hand, pleading with her. Though it was faint, Frankie felt it, three taps in the center of her palm—the wordless code for *I love you*.

When Catherine returned, she said there was a fire in Flatbush, and it was only after she repeated it a third time that Frankie realized that what she was really saying was that there was no one to help them.

Then Frankie saw the burgundy Cadillac that the Hawthornes' driver used when they were in town. The keys hung by the door to the butler's pantry. "Get the keys."

Catherine studied a spot on the wall. "I'm not supposed to drive it."

Frankie looped her arms under her mother, pulling. "I will, then."

Still, Catherine stayed put.

"Help me. *Now.*" There was fury in Frankie's voice.

Catherine, not used to being yelled at, picked up Fiona's feet. One of Fiona's shoes came loose, and her leg hit the ground, hard. The shoe was still in Catherine's hand as she started to cry.

By pulling and prodding and lifting and dragging, Frankie got her mother into the back seat and crawled into the front but then didn't know what to do. She'd never even started a car, much less driven one. Catherine, meanwhile, was frozen by a boxwood hedge. How long were they there? Arguing on a perfectly normal Sunday, clouds drifting in the sky. Minutes? An hour? Time came loose, the last seconds with her mother gone, tumbled away, because at some point Fiona's face went still, peacefully still, and Frankie missed it. An entire life of smiles and dreams and barefoot dances on dirty floors, all the years of struggling to support a child who had no one and turning away from tables still hungry so that the child could eat, of nights being scared and mornings being happy, and slim, slender moments full of hope despite everything, all to die in the back seat of a car, alone.

When Frankie understood, her skin went tingly and she couldn't breathe properly, but it was the shaking in her legs that alarmed her.

Because they were trembling, almost violently, on their own. Shock, someone later told her.

When facts began to settle and solidify, when Frankie no longer felt as if her body were tingling like a foot that's gone to sleep, it came out that Catherine *was* allowed to drive but the clutch made her anxious. That, and her parents—the same people who'd insisted that Fiona come into work when she wasn't feeling well, to clean a house they weren't even at—preferred her not to. *Preferred.* The word, to Frankie, was rife with luxury and privilege. To have a life where you could *prefer* to not do something . . . It was as foreign to her as a distant sea.

In the long nights that followed her mother's death, Frankie realized that reliance, on anyone or anything, was no longer an option. So she learned how to drive, and returned to that white columned house and relocated the Hawthornes' Cadillac to a nearby pond. Dark water rose against the shining chrome grille, then spilled over the bloodred paint. Frankie faced the empty sky and wished she'd known on that Sunday that it was futile, so she could've crawled into the back seat and taken her mother's hand to do as Fiona had: three taps in the center of her palm. That's all she wanted. One last chance to say *I love you.*

CHAPTER 13

The Lie Is Smooth

Thursday, March 2, 1933

Now, on this day at the start of March, Frankie is buttoning her shirt when the phone rings. The radio is on in the living room, and she hears the announcer proclaim President Hoover's failure to stabilize the banks, and California and thirty-six other states' efforts to take matters into their own hands by declaring a bank holiday.

A bank holiday. Which means the banks are shutting down. Her heart races as she realizes her mistake. There wasn't much in her savings account, but with so much on her plate, she forgot to take out what she could.

"Folks," the announcer says, "we're talking no deposits, no withdrawals, nothing. For how long? Who can say?"

The ringing continues, and Frankie glances toward her jewelry box on the dresser. Under the lining, she's stashed eight dollars, enough to pay for food and gas for a while. But for how long? Again, the phone rings, and Frankie calls out Virginia's name, since she's closest.

The radio drones on. "Roosevelt's coming in in two days and is going to have his *hands full.* Will he take this solution nationwide? What will he do? Hopefully more than the Chief, I'll say that."

The phone rings again. Finally, Frankie runs down the hall to answer.

"Frankie? Something's happened."

~

She drives fast, painfully aware of a minute's importance. Over and over again, her mind returns to the day her mother died. Seconds more with her mother—what she would do for even seconds more.

On Glenhollow, she swerves to the curb, tires bumping. The car door slams behind her, shattering the silence. Carob pods crack under her feet, bricks wet from rain. Camellias grow by June's bungalow, dark-green leaves and bloodred blooms. She keeps going. The neighbors' stone wall is on her left, and beyond that a tree-filled lot, undeveloped. *They built a beautiful wall around their property, and then the Crash happened and they never built the house.*

Nico. As soon as she knows what she's up against, she'll call Nico.

There's June's back door. An old water fountain, velvet blooms of algae. Then the brick path splits off: the straight portion leading to Jack's bungalow and Arlington Way, while the portion that veers right travels smack between the two bungalows and disappears near the hill at the edge of the lot. For one second she pauses, thinking she heard something. A spiderweb glistens a warning.

Where the stone wall becomes a wooden fence is where a different neighbor's property begins, and in seconds their dog is there. A rush of noise. Furious barking. Bared teeth through the slats. It's only when she veers onto the smaller path that leads to Jack's bungalow that the dog stops, and her heart begins to settle.

Before she's raised her hand to knock, the door swings open. Jack. He reeks of bourbon but he's alive. Relief floods her—this means he can acknowledge that drinking shouldn't happen again, and maybe they can keep going, even in private, even at night, because nothing is ever too late if someone is alive. She's reaching out to him when she sees the blood on the white sleeve of his dress shirt. A lot of blood.

When he told her he needed her, there was urgency in his voice and he said to come alone. But she shouldn't have listened; he needs a doctor.

Already he's down the path, asking her to follow. She tells him to stop, demanding to know where he's hurt and how badly, but he won't listen.

Again, the dog hurls itself against the fence. The noise, the blood. Frankie's heart rate soars until they've passed the dog's yard and the creature silences. She pauses to clear her head, to take a breath, when she sees that Jack has swerved onto the short path that leads to June's back door.

Now she looks to him.

He faces her, and his voice is barely a whisper. "Please."

From deep within the carob tree, leaves rustle. The fact that Jack's standing there calmly tells her all she needs to know, because whatever has happened is over. It's too late.

And now she knows he called her not as his girlfriend, but as his fixer.

Inside, a clock ticks. The kitchen light is on, the curtains still closed, slices of light between fabric. There is a glass vase with old pink roses, necks wilted and heads hanging. It feels as though she's walked onto a set, everything carefully arranged and loaded with purpose. When Jack disappears through the kitchen door, she waits for the noise and scramble of the crew at the end of a take.

"Frankie," he calls.

This, she understands, is a set for a crime. Because the living room is struck with chaos. A chair is tipped over, and a lamp is knocked on its side, shade gaping. Sofa cushions are tousled, pillows missing. But the pillows are there, she sees, on the floor by the sofa, but then so is a stockinged foot and a leg, and now her heart pounds a remembrance of her mother, and Frankie's breath comes up short and she sees a dark-green satin dress stained above the abdomen, darker still at the chest.

Again, the safety of pretend: Makeup artists use chocolate syrup for blood. *Film is black and white,* a prop master once said, *but I tell you, you clip an artery, and the blood's* dark, *so we're not far off.* And this is dark but also red. Too red, really, all that wasted color for black-and-white film, and by the time Frankie looks up at June's face, she's feeling the pressing edge of reality, sharp like a blade.

She's seen June dead in films over and over, but it's the color of June's skin, ashy pale, that is beyond what they've achieved. "How did they do that?" she asks, taking a step forward.

Jack stops her. "Don't. You'll get it everywhere like I did."

The stillness of June's face is remarkable. *I think there was a struggle,* Jack is saying, *and she was shot*, but Frankie's watching June's lips, waiting for them to move.

"The makeup." But again, he's stopping her because she's stepped in blood, and the shoe print it leaves is red, bright red, and ultimately it's that color that clues her in because it's too red for syrup, just like June's face is too pale for makeup. Her skin is the same shade that Fiona's face was hours after she died, yet without a hint of powder. There is a scent that reminds Frankie of the carob tree outside, a strange, almost sweet decay.

All at once it hits her. Backing away, she trips. Jack grabs her arm.

"No." She presses her hand on her mouth. Sick. There's the sticky grab of red where she stepped.

"I had a dream I was in the war," Jack is saying. "Or I thought it was a dream. I must've heard the shot. I don't know. I woke up with an empty bottle of Old Stagg."

June's handbag is on the desk, open. Shoes toppled by the door. The details. Frankie knows she needs the details, but the second she notices something, it slips away. Over and over she scans the room. A champagne bottle on an end table, open. Empty. The cork on the ground. A juice glass beside the bottle with a small amount of liquid still inside. Another glass, clean, on the other end table. She feels as though she's struggling to get back inside herself. She needs to be present. "Start with what you remember."

"Jolting awake. Not long after I fell asleep, I think. I thought they were firing on us."

"Because you heard the shot."

His words are slow, as if he's wading through memory to find them. "I guess. I thought it was a dream. Then this morning, I wanted to talk to her. I wanted to get her on board with calling things off. And I found her, and everything got tangled. For an hour or so, I didn't know what was what." A pause. "It used to happen like that, time tangling up."

The long shadow of war. Its effect never truly over. "After you saw her, but before you called me—did you go back to your bungalow?"

He shakes his head. "I was still in her kitchen when everything started making sense."

Something scratches on the glass. A branch that's against the window.

"Go to the bedroom. Make sure the curtains are closed." She's getting back to herself, snapping to. When he shuts the door, she calls Nico. It's not yet eight a.m., the day after a premiere, which means he could be sleeping. Waiting, she faces the wall, feeling June like a presence at her back.

When Nico says *hello*, his voice is groggy.

"Hi," she says cheerfully, which she knows will alarm him. "Can you come to bungalow one? Now?"

To this, there is silence. And then he tells her he's on his way.

~

Time is stuck. It feels as though hours have passed, but it's still only morning. Frankie is alone in the kitchen, staring at pink roses that make no sense.

Ida. Though Frankie's never liked her, the woman will be destroyed. Nico will handle it. Like he has car accidents and fights and even an incident when a star was caught shoplifting. Everything will be fine. He just needs to get here.

The clock ticks. Light stretches on the table. A dust mote glitters in the air. Still, it is morning. Still, the unbelievable has only just happened.

Shock transitions to logic; there are things she needs to do. All the windows in the living room are covered, and the bedroom was dark. But it's hitting her that she should've made Jack leave and not just hide. If anyone sees him here, with blood on his shirt, they will think he did this.

Then, the sound of a car. When she hears it, she hurries through the living room. A speck of orange through the curtain: Nico's Bugatti. He's left his car in the middle of the road, facing the DEAD END sign at the end of the street as if the road is merely a driveway. Without looking back, he's storming up the pathway.

He pushes open the door and, in a second, sees June. As if punched in the stomach, he doubles over, whispering Italian—prayers or curses, Frankie's not sure. When he looks up again, there are tears in his eyes, and she can see the effort it takes to not look back at June. Because he loved her, Frankie knows. He protected her. He took care of her, above all else, and now he's failed.

As fast as she can, she starts to explain that Jack had a lot to drink and ended up in bungalow two, that he called her when he found June this morning, but she stops talking when Nico turns toward her. Slow and focused. Calm. "Jack was *here*?"

She motions to the bedroom.

"He's *still* here?"

When they push open the bedroom door, Jack is on his back, feet hanging over the end of the bed. His eyes are open, staring at the ceiling.

Then they are in the kitchen, and Jack is talking. In each pause, Frankie gathers the courage to come clean, to hand Nico every card—including the truth of her and Jack—and let him figure out a play. But she's too slow. Muddled. Jack fills the silences, telling the story of what happened as if she were never a part of it, then saying it must have been close to three a.m. when he jolted awake. Frankie knows he's right to omit her role; it would make everything ten times worse if Nico knew she was part of *why* Jack was here to begin with.

"And you got a ride from who at the pool hall?" Nico asks.

"Some guy. Barely talked to him, but he heard I needed a ride and volunteered, till I said *Pasadena*. Then he was set to leave me—so I told him to take me here. It was closer."

The lie is smooth. Though it shouldn't surprise her, since he's essentially trained in lying, it still throws her how convincing he is.

A sound. A bird. It's loud, a crow that must be on the branch outside the window, but Jack's reaction is disproportionate. He flinches as if someone slammed a door beside him.

Nico eyes him. "We just lost one star. If we're not careful, we'll lose another. Jack, tell me about the pool hall and the guy."

Jack looks around the room as if hunting for any further potential noise. "It was a dive. No one in there knew who I was. Or cared. I wouldn't know how to find that guy if I tried."

Nico nods. "We need to stick with Malibu, that you went straight there. We've got everything in place; pretty much already got alibis. Thank God. O'Shea, the champagne delivery, everything works in our favor right now, and *if* someone from the pool hall comes out of the woodwork, I'll deal with it."

Frankie glances at Jack, who blinks heavily, as if he has to clear his vision of something he doesn't want to see. "They were going to elope," she says. "That's why June wasn't with him. Last minute, she came here so they didn't see each other. Whatever that tradition is."

"That's good. Jack, you hear me? You were sick of the hysteria around the wedding, and you decided to elope."

Barely, Jack nods. Then he leans forward. "Who was the father?"

"What?"

"Motive."

Nico shakes his head. "She didn't tell me. She said she wanted part of her life to be just hers. I didn't press."

"The man finds out she's marrying me, he's furious, he kills her."

"She never said anything that made me think he was jealous or angry, or anything. But I guess nothing's off the table."

Frankie touches a pink rose petal. "Why would you kill someone if you *want* to be with them? Unless that love is unreciprocated. Unless you live in a fantasy world."

"Tank Adams," Nico says. Frankie nods.

Could Tank have done it? Years back, there was a scandal at the warehouse where he worked, and rumors made it to the papers that he stole money. There was more, Nico said. Plenty of reasons to keep him away, and plenty of damage he could do to her reputation. Frankie sees Tank following June, watching her from across streets. Once, he left a letter for her on a chair in the makeup department, and no one knew how he got in. When June read it, her face seemed to collapse with sadness like someone finally glimpsing an unfortunate truth.

Nico stands, heading to the phone. "Tank being jealous and shooting her because he couldn't have her—that I see. I need to call my guys and then Mickey." Mickey Mulroney. The chief of police, who also works for the studio.

In another world, the police would've already been here. But in this world, there is what they can do to save June—which is nothing—and what they can do to save Jack—which is everything.

Then Jack says something quietly, and Nico looks as though he's going to be sick. In a rush, he's hung up the phone before anyone answered, and stormed into the living room.

"What'd you say to him?" Frankie asks.

"I said the back door wasn't completely closed. It's hard to lock. It happened after the last rain."

In the other room, Nico's swearing.

"It sticks," Jack continues. "Maybe he didn't know. You think that's how the person who shot her got in? It's how I got in."

From the other room, Nico's voice goes loud. "The *necklace*. Where's the necklace?"

Just like that, what happened crystallizes. And though they know they won't find it, Frankie searches the house while Nico makes calls—the first to a few associates he ropes in only for the big jobs, and second to Mickey.

What they learn is that June must have been staying here for a while. In the closet, there are shirts and skirts and a few dresses, as well as high heels lined up along the floorboards. In the bathroom, there's Noxzema, pill bottles, even perfume. Jean Patou's Joy Parfum Luxe. Ten thousand jasmine flowers and twenty-eight dozen roses, just to make one ounce. Claimed to be the costliest perfume in the world. *They just gave it to me, Frankie,* June had said of the bottle, whose label even had June's name on it. *It makes me delirious, it's so beautiful.* Frankie picks up the flacon and twists the crystal stopper, bringing it to her nose: flowery green, a heart of rose, and a hint of the musk to come. Closing her eyes, she feels as if June stands beside her.

Off the phone, Nico leans forward in the wooden chair at the desk, elbows on his knees. June's eyes are still open. Once, not long enough ago, Frankie watched a stranger close her mother's eyes for the last time. Now, she goes to June and calls to Nico. When he understands what she's doing, he nods.

Against the wall, Jack watches, his face pale. "No one but us knew she was staying here."

Nico corrects him. "No one at the *outset*. Then we had a premiere with hundreds of people who saw her in that thing, and how hard would it be to follow the limo and catch her ducking into a different car? This day and age, that necklace would've tempted anyone."

June's gun. Her beaded handbag is on the table, but when Frankie goes to it, she sees the gun's not there. "I didn't see her gun *anywhere* when I looked for the necklace."

Nico eyes June's small handbag. "Doubt she'd take it to a premiere."

"No, she did."

Jack. They turn to him.

He continues. "She had it in there. On the way to the premiere, she got a mint from her bag and I saw it. Said she felt better with it."

"Those people," Nico says. "Goddamn those people who scared her."

"You think it was them?" Frankie asks.

But Nico's shaking his head. "No. No, they didn't know who she was. But they were the reason she started carrying that thing. And my guess is that the bullet that killed her is a .41, like her gun. My guess is her gun was turned against her."

"Maybe he had a knife," Frankie says. "Maybe she thought she could defend herself."

"And if he used her gun, he wouldn't leave it behind, because his prints were on it. So I see two possibilities. One, she went for it to defend herself, and he got it. Or two, he came in, knew where it was, and *he* went for it."

He knew where it was.

Jack narrows his eyes, staring at the floor. Because he just admitted he knew the gun was in her purse.

Light from the kitchen slips into the room, time a slow unravel. Now and then, understanding hits her. June is dead. This fact is there and then gone, a claw of grief that retracts as fast as it emerges. Because June is still there, in the stack of magazines in the corner, her name on a script on the desk, her voice in rooms across the country. She's larger than life, and so that she's dead makes no sense.

Suddenly Frankie's own words return to her, words she spoke at the premiere when she and Nico were talking about Harry Winston.

"*Without a security guard.* I said that. At the premiere. About June wearing the necklace. Remember? Nico, what—"

But he cuts her off. "No one heard that."

"There were people right next to us—"

"And you just *happened* to say it within earshot of the one person who would do something like this?"

"*This day and age, the necklace would've tempted anyone.* You *just* said that."

"Frankie." He's pleading. "Don't go down that road. Either it was Tank or a robbery because someone *saw* her there, with their own eyes, and followed her. Either way, it has nothing to do with you."

A knock on the door. Nico answers, assuming it's his men. In a beat, the neighbor woman from up the hill has her hands on her mouth, her eyes wide.

"Oh my God. Oh my God. I knew I heard—"

Nico's got her arm, saying, *"Shh, shh, shh,"* as he ushers her inside, passing Jack—whom the woman cranes her neck to look at—and straight into the kitchen.

It's the neighbor with the dog. Mid-fifties, a face that's on a slow slide away from beautiful, a blue paisley scarf wrapped on her hair and rollers bulging underneath. Uneven red lipstick as if she heard Nico's car and raced down here but first needed to look presentable. *Darlene Cleary,* she says to Frankie. *I live up the hill.* Her voice is crumbly, breaking apart. *The complainer,* Nico's called her. A staunch prohibitionist.

Unprompted, Darlene unleashes everything she knows. A bang around three a.m. She got up and out of bed and saw the dark shape of a man walking the path from the back of June's bungalow toward Arlington. Though she waited to hear the sound of a car starting or sirens, there was nothing. "A bang, and then silence. I figured someone got drunk and shot off a gun. That happens here, believe you me."

The words slide into one. *Believeyoume.* With barely a pause, she continues.

"And they want to bring it back, don't they? So the fools don't even need to sneak in booze, they just traipse it right in?" She turns to Frankie. "One man, a couple years back, he aimed at my weather vane. Missed and got the corner of my house—even worse! No point in calling the cops, Mr. Marconi told me. I have his personal number."

"I apologize, Darlene," Nico says. "You've been one of the best neighbors we've had. Truly."

Momentarily, Darlene looks flattered, but then she raises her hand to her mouth and bites her thumbnail before repeating the entire story again, her eyes jittery. Another one of life's ironies: The most important times to be present and make sound choices are when you're reeling and barely holding on.

Darlene lowers her hand. There's lipstick on her thumb. "I figured when I didn't hear a car start up or sirens or anything that someone's good time just got out of hand. I figured they were staying in that back house."

That back house. Nico glances at Frankie, and with his look, the implication hits home: A man took the path from the back of June's bungalow toward Arlington Way, which also happens to lead past Jack's door. If a car didn't start up, it means they either didn't leave by car or didn't leave at all. A sour feeling begins to gnaw at her stomach.

"But you don't *always* hear the cars, do you?" Frankie asks.

The woman gives a laugh. "No one drives on Arlington. Not if they're smart. You can bet if there's a car there, I hear it. Even people who use that tunnel—"

"The *tunnel*," Frankie says. The entrance is a barely concealed faux-brick wall behind the second bungalow.

"No," Nico says. "The tunnel also spits out on Arlington Way. Just up from Darlene's house. She'd have heard a car there too. And she's right. No one in their right mind would have a getaway car there, not unless they want to take an hour to turn around."

The woman's eyes well again. "June Finney never caused problems. You know that? I can't see much from up there, but I can see the part of the path at her back door, where that fountain is? One morning, I looked down and saw her setting camellia blooms on the water. I suppose because it was beautiful." A teardrop hangs on her chin. "I saw all her movies. She's from Iowa, like me."

Nico's nodding. "Everyone loved her, Darlene. So, I'm asking, as a favor to June, let us figure out the best way to tell people about this."

Using the tail end of her headscarf to wipe her cheek, Darlene nods solemnly. Standing, she glances toward the living room. "That was her fiancé, wasn't it?"

Nico takes a moment, either debating about coming clean or perhaps trying to impart the impression that this, too, is monumental information that he's trusting her with. Finally, he nods.

"You'll tell him I'm sorry?" Darlene asks.

Frankie leads the way to the back door, away from June's body. Outside, it's started to drizzle, haphazard drops that seem to match the buzzing in her mind.

CHAPTER 14

Perception Takes More Casualties

The morning continues, distant and unreal. Nico's other associates appear before the police. Men who don't say much as they attempt to preserve an ounce of privacy for a person who can no longer protect herself. Within minutes, they correct the scene. Anything that could mar June's reputation is gone. The empty champagne bottle gets replaced by an unopened bottle from the kitchen as if to cover that June drank alone while offering an ounce of truth that she drank at all. The pill bottles taken. Any undergarments deemed too risqué removed. What they leave behind is safe to list on a police report: makeup, a hairbrush, the perfume, aspirin, clothing. Jack, as well, is fixed up, given a new shirt and pants, and told to stay in the bedroom.

And then the police arrive. Black shoes and scuff marks. Bursts of flashbulbs. Statements given at the kitchen table. Nico watches the cops like children who've wandered into a candy store. Even Betty appears momentarily, leaving behind a platter of sandwiches and paper plates. The plates are from a Halloween party with thick orange borders and wispy black shapes of ghouls and goblins, arms outstretched. June, Frankie remembers, dressed as a monk in a long brown robe. *Oh, they're all having a fit,* she said about the studio heads, who'd expected their starlet to look like a starlet. *But they have the* best *cupcakes here.* A smile as she scooped up sugary orange swirls with her finger. *It catches you off guard sometimes, doesn't it? When you realize you're happy?*

An officer beside June works to lower her dress, covering more of her leg, and Nico nods approvingly.

"You can't be too careful," he tells Frankie, and then recounts the day Alexander Marquand, one of their stars, died from "tuberculosis"—the code word studios use for *overdose*. Voice low, he continues. "One of the cops wasn't with us. Wouldn't you know, a watch goes missing. A toothbrush. The water glass Alex drank from before he died—all of it, off with souvenir hunters. It devastated his wife. You can imagine. Maybe she would've kept that glass for the rest of her life, I don't know. But for someone else to have it? It's a line no one should cross. So I'm not taking chances. Not with her. She hated that her life became an open book. Hell if I let that happen with her death too." A beat as he looks toward the bathroom. "I want you to have that bottle of Joy."

"I can't."

"You want that perfume to end up broken in an evidence box? Or sold to the highest bidder? It was made special for her. It's got her name on it. Someone's gonna get their mitts on it. No, you need to take it."

"Maybe it should go to her sister."

Ida, whom Betty has been tasked with telling.

"Hey, you get any without mustard?" a man asks Frankie, motioning to the sandwiches. The district attorney. His face was on the cover of newspapers a few months back.

"This is my associate," Nico says. "Frankie Donnelly. Someone else got the sandwiches."

The man blinks, still waiting for an answer.

Though she doesn't know if it's true or not, Frankie says flatly, "They've all got mustard."

In the bedroom, Jack is wrapping up his statement: They were going to elope. This morning was their secret wedding. When June didn't show up at the courthouse, as planned, he came here. When he found her shot, he went to bungalow two, reeling, and called Frankie. Frankie says the same thing when she gives her statement, and reminds herself that she's not lying about the murder itself, just about Jack's timing.

Maybe Nico sees the doubt on her face, because after she's done, he leads her to the corner of the room. "Talk to me."

"It's the right thing, what we're doing."

He's nodding. "Anyone learns he was here last night, and he's the suspect. It's that simple. First thing they do is look to the husband or the boyfriend. Or the ex."

"They find Tank Adams?"

"Not yet. He's top on their list, though, so it's a matter of time. What *I* know is Jack had nothing to do with it, so anything we say about him makes no difference. Right? We could say he was wearing a cowboy hat, and what would that matter when it comes to June being shot?"

"It doesn't get in the way of the investigation?"

"Not unless you think he did it."

They've left me no way to prove how much I want to be with you.

The words slam into her, accompanied by a flush of guilt. Though Jack and June didn't get along, and the timing of him being here was less than ideal, he never would so much as wish her harm. Jack's got a temper and has ended up in fights, but he always had reasons: to defend someone, to put someone in their place, once even to end a fight so it didn't get worse. But what Frankie's realizing is that none of this matters, and what she knows or believes won't make a difference. The only thing that matters is just how far she'll go to protect him.

Around them, cops are pacing, talking, even leafing through a pile of scripts and magazines. Someone's left a plate by the phone, with a half-eaten sandwich. Someone else exits the bedroom, talking about a price tag still on a dress. The way they've handled this crime scene has been about protecting the victim's reputation, not about finding justice. Keeping her voice low, Frankie leans in to Nico. "With us trying to protect Jack and June—what if we've gotten in the way of the truth?"

Nico's ready for the question. "In a burning building, you save who you can; you don't stop to figure out who set the fire. The truth is important, yes, but if you have someone you can save, you save them. We have Jack. And it's all hands on deck for that, because, Frankie, he's had a rough but *charmed* life. Every scrape he got into, all the trouble he's gotten in, he's used to getting out of it. But this? This could go differently, because Jack being innocent is only part of the equation. And that's why we do what we do, because *perception takes more casualties than truth ever saves.* Remember that. If we go a little further than we should, there's a reason." He motions toward the porch. "That officer requested a word, so I'll be out there. Let's just get through this."

Frankie takes a seat by the front door. Fashion magazines are on the table by the window, June radiant on the top cover. One Lucky Gal, the headline announces. There's that pricking in her sinuses that tells her she's about to cry, and Frankie pinches the bridge of her nose just as she overhears Nico say that Jack left in the limo after the premiere to go to Malibu, with O'Shea driving. O'Shea, who dropped him off, safe and sound, at the beach house.

Suddenly, she sets down the magazine. Because Jack's here, but his car is not.

It's a glaring hole in their story, and Nico has no idea he could be walking into a trap. She can practically feel the officer peering down the street, looking for a car fancy enough to be driven by a star.

"So he wasn't driving?" the officer asks.

"My stars don't drive to premieres."

Right there. Nico's foot in the trap. Because if Jack didn't have his car, how did he get here?

Behind her, the medical examiner's assistant says, "Now she's immortal. If you got to go, this is how you do it. Truthfully, this is a good death."

Just slightly, Frankie turns to glare at the man.

But instead of backing down, he shrugs and gives Frankie a half smile. "Oh, come on. We all gotta die sometime. Might as well go out on a good note, when you're still young and loved. Hell, she's even dressed like a star."

"What would've been a good death," Frankie says, "would be when she's old and got a chance to say goodbye. Not young and in the prime—"

"In the prime of her life. Sure. But I guarantee she's been to more *countries* than I've been to states. More parties, had better food. In terms of living, she packed it in, and I got *a lot* of people I need to feel bad for, but she's not one of them. I mean, look at her. A stunner, even now. She didn't even take off her makeup. No, I'm telling you, this was a good death. A very good death."

Frankie's about to let him have it when she hears the officer on the porch say, "So this morning, Mr. Sawyer got here how early?"

Before Nico can reply, she's outside. "Nico, I have to go, but when you see Jack, tell him we put his car keys in the kitchen when we dropped it off, will you?"

Lies are like salting food, Nico once said. *Too much and it's no good.* She hopes what she said was vague enough to not raise more questions but enough to stop the officer's line of thinking. As he catches on, Nico's gaze shifts to the street—but his eyes widen at what he sees there: Ida, pale-faced, determined, and storming toward the house.

"Oh hell," Nico says. He's turning to Frankie when something in the living room catches his eye. His face contorts with anger. *"What are you doing? What are you doing?"*

When Frankie looks, her stomach drops. A police officer is smiling, kneeling by June's body as another camera clicks. In a flash, Nico's there and something hits the wall—a small Leica 50 mm, Frankie later learns. Mickey Mulroney grabs Nico's shoulders while Nico tries to pull free, arm swinging toward the person who held the camera—the medical examiner's assistant, Frankie realizes.

And then there is a scream that cuts through the room.

Ida, standing in the doorway.

Everyone freezes.

On the ground, the officer who smiled and posed beside June scrambles to his feet, and Frankie realizes what's about to happen before it does. Time seems to lengthen and spread, because there's the officer's black shoe, scuffed on the edge, and there's June's hand, her pale fingers frozen in a slight curl, nails painted light pink like little shells. Frankie opens her mouth to yell at the man, but everything is too late because, without looking, the man takes a hurried step back, away from Nico, and there's a sound that silences the room. Understanding what's happened, the cop jerks his leg back. June's fingers are askew and broken.

Silence. Even Ida is speechless, staring at her sister's hand.

Then everything breaks loose. Jack rushes into the room, face flushed with rage, arm drawn back and fist tight—a windup before he unleashes. The cop who stepped on June's hand flies backward, head whipping to the side, a streak of blood when he steadies and wipes his face. Every other cop descends upon Jack. Some hold him back while others shove him, everyone yelling and barking orders until suddenly their voices taper off.

Ida strides into the room. She passes her sister. Passes Frankie, and Nico. Her eyes don't leave Jack's face.

Placing her hand on top of his bloodied fist, she nods as if to thank him. Then she turns back to the room. "Everyone, get the hell out."

CHAPTER 15

However I Have To

A Shining Star Snuffed Out.
Hollywood's Unhappy Ending.
Heaven Just Got Brighter.
America's Depressed Heart Breaks.

The evening headlines vary, but one thing is clear: The world, already shattered, is broken. Fans have gathered in front of the studio, piling bouquets of roses by the gate. All over the country, vases of flowers dot theatre sidewalks, and sobbing girls and devastated men stand alongside posters with June's face. In the car that night, driving home, Frankie listens to the radio host announce that in France someone's painted a red heart around June's face on a billboard. *It's sick,* Nico told Frankie when she was leaving, *but I heard a costume jeweler's started copying that necklace.*

At home, Virginia is in tears. Tears that are a bit much, even for Virginia.

"She broke up with Fred," Susan whispers. "She said she would've done it anyhow, that she wanted someone who looked at her like Jack looked at June, but then June is dead and life ends without warning and she didn't want to wait. So, she ended it."

The one good thing to come out of all this, Frankie thinks.

All night, she vacillates between a general shock and sadness over June and worry over Jack. What this must've done, what it must have triggered. When she manages to call his house, O'Shea says he's sleeping. Frankie waits till the morning, and tries again.

Again, O'Shea answers, and when she asks him how Jack is, there is a long pause.

"I'll come by," she says.

"There's no point, miss. He'll be sleeping until the press conference."

"That's this afternoon."

"The studio doctor was here last night."

The implication being, of course, that the man left enough pills to help Jack sleep through the day, if necessary.

Driving to Pasadena, she passes through a lifting dark, her window down to try to clear her mind. Now and then there are a few remaining orange groves and the scent of early blooms, that sweetness of flowers and leaves, a decadent green freshness. By the time she reaches Jack's house, half the sky is dusted with pink while mist still hangs in the Arroyo.

A couple of older Model Ts are parked on the street, one with a homemade sign hanging out the window. WE LOVE YOU, JACK. If Frankie had to guess, the people are living in their cars, not just here early.

She stops at the closed gate, waiting for Louis. A young girl, maybe thirteen, gets out of the nearest car and approaches Frankie's window.

"Do you know him?"

The girl is thin. All angles and lines, a sharp chin and carved cheekbones. The sleeves on her dress are too short—a mark of a hand-me-down. By the fade of the fabric and varying thread in the seams, Frankie guesses at least three or four others have worn the dress. Frankie herself was almost twenty-four years old before she owned something that was brand new and only ever hers. A blouse and slacks. She kept the tags on for as long as possible, tucked just out of sight, until finally the paper softened and tore.

"I do know him," Frankie says. She peers over her shoulder at the car the girl got out of. Three other shapes are inside, one slumped in the seat, a pillow against the glass.

The girl gives a closed-mouth smile. "You know him, really know him?"

"I do."

"Do you know how he is?"

A girl who appears to be living in a car is concerned about a movie star. "Time always helps with these things, and it's worse now than it will be later." Then Frankie asks for her name—Agnes—and says she'll tell Jack she's thinking of him. She's about to pull through the gate when Agnes folds her arms across her chest and stares at the ground.

"How could she die?" the girl finally asks, looking up. "It didn't seem like she could."

Louis is waiting. The gate is open. "A lot of things happen that feel like they shouldn't. To everyone. Even to someone who lives in a house like that."

"I heard there's a ballroom."

"There's not a ballroom, but there *is* a pond, with catfish. And he goes fishing, and cooks what he catches."

Agnes smiles before thinking better of it, and Frankie catches sight of a hole where a front tooth is missing.

Inside the house, Jack sits in the chair by the living room window. Hair wet, just washed. When he turns, she sees his eyes are red, his gaze loose and slightly confused. Still, he gives a smile, and she can't help it, she's in his arms, hugging him. The palm of his hand presses against her back, and she hears him breathing, the soft fury of his heart.

Then she stands back, aware they're not alone in the house. "I thought you might be sleeping."

"Doc also gave me something to wake up."

"Jack."

"My only goal right now is to get through today. However I have to."

All she wants to do is hold him, to feel his comforting solidity, his presence that tells her everything will be okay. And from the way he's looking at her—with a sad sort of longing—she knows he feels the same. Purposefully, she takes a seat in the chair opposite him. "Today's conference. We control the questions, and if anything goes too far, you can signal us. We'll both be there."

Between them is a little table that's almost lost beneath an elaborate floral arrangement, dominated by white lilies. He wipes at a bit of pollen on the table, then looks at his skin, stained orange. "Someone told me she didn't suffer. That it was quick."

Death flowers, her mother used to call the lilies, back when she cleaned at a mortuary. *If sadness has a smell,* she once said, *that's it.* "People always say it was quick."

"You think the medical examiner was lying?"

She wants to say yes, that she knows he's capable of lying since he had certain directives. But the fact is she's tired of people claiming a fast death is a good death. "I just don't think that dying fast is better."

"You'd rather them be in pain? A long, drawn-out illness?"

"Of course not." A pause. "But at least there'd be a chance to say goodbye."

He nods, realizing whom she didn't say goodbye to. "You know June made me mad, but she wasn't supposed to die."

In the hall, a housekeeper passes by with another bouquet. "There's a girl in front of the house named Agnes. She's worried about you. And she said that she didn't think June *could* die."

But Jack is staring out the window, his gaze on the treetops, his lashes tipped in light. "I heard that the president doesn't eat in public so people can't photograph him eating. Eating would make him human. And what would that do to our image?"

"That can't be true. I saw a photo of Hoover eating a doughnut, I know I did."

"True or not, I wasn't allowed to be affected by war, and June's not supposed to die. Yet here we are." Again, he looks at the pollen stain on his finger, then scrapes at it with his nail. "O'Shea said I was yelling in my sleep. I did that when I got back from France. They say you can have years that are good, then something happens and it's bad again." He glances at her. "What if I was sober that night? Maybe you still would've taken me to the bungalows, but maybe I'd hear the shot. And see the person. Stopped them. Or gone to her and helped."

"If you'd intervened or stopped the person, you might've been shot too."

A half smile. "Two people who can't stand each other, trapped together in life and then joined in death too? At least it'd be fast."

"Don't say that. Not even as a joke."

He doesn't close his eyes as much as he lets them close. As if up till now he's forced himself awake. The morning light is soft on his face. "I wouldn't want that. I'd take the pain if it meant I got to say goodbye to you."

"Jack."

Surprised at her anger, he opens his eyes. But she turns toward the window; she won't let him see her cry. The bridge is in the distance, mist hanging at its sides. But then her eyes refocus, and in the reflection, she sees him reaching his hand toward her.

"Don't." He lowers his hand, and she wipes her cheek before turning back to him. "If anyone found out about us, it would call everything into question. If you lied about me, they'd think you could lie about anything. And they'd see *us* as motive. Tell me you understand this."

He puts his hands together, pressing his thumb into his palm as if to work out a pain. "When I woke up, there was this moment when I felt good. I *felt* that there was no wedding and no fake relationship, and I had this surge of happiness, because for one split second I knew I could have my life back—but I forgot *why*."

"Jack, did you hear me? *Nothing* can happen right now."

"I heard you."

She stands up. "You'll be all right?"

He looks up at her and gives her a slow, sad smile. "Do I have a choice?"

CHAPTER 16

Toss Him to the Wolves

At midday, the blue sky drains of color, then begins to deepen once more. White, almost whimsical clouds drift toward the horizon. The day is beautiful, and beauty at a horrible time has always infuriated Frankie, like a hard slap that life goes on even when it shouldn't.

Late in the afternoon, she's in Nico's car, about to leave the studio to return to Jack's house for the press conference. Though she lives closer and would've preferred to drive separately, Nico suggested that it might be a good time to talk, and when Nico makes suggestions, they're not suggestions.

Just outside the studio gates, there is a spot designated for flowers. Pink roses carpet the ground, some in bundles tied with twine, others stuffed in mason jars. Little lanes of loose stems and petals creep between everything as if someone sheared off a rose garden and turned it into a pathway. Last night, Betty told her, six studio janitors walked as carefully as they could, removing any wilted blooms in order to keep the grief fresh and pleasant.

Now, she and Nico pass a woman holding a sign. JUSTICE FOR JUNE. On the corner, three young boys have their shoeshine kits set up, their backs against a wall.

"Tell me how hungover he was when he called you yesterday."

Frankie knows what Nico's really asking, and she'll make him say it. "Why?"

"You believe he didn't do it, right?"

"Of course I believe he didn't do it. You believe he *did*?"

A sidelong glance at her. "Would I be doing what I'm doing if I believed that? The answer is no. If I thought someone killed my star, I would not hold back."

"Even if it's your *other* star."

He's quiet for a bit. Finally, he says, "You won't like this, but Jack killing June would be a story to end all stories."

She turns in her seat to look at him.

"Sure," he continues, "we'd fire him. And he'd be arrested—the works. But publicity alone would skyrocket June and all her films beyond anything we're experiencing now. Even *his* films. And I'm not saying this because I'd like it—it would kill me. It's a disgusting part of this business that I can even say these things, but I'm good at my job, and this is what the job demands. You get that, right? It's not me, it's what I'm supposed to do."

And she does get that. The second she chose to lie to Jack about the woman and child in the alleyway, in order to keep him in good form, she did the same. It was what the job demanded.

Continuing, Nico says, "Jack causes problems, but he's as down to earth as a star can be, and I respect that. Still, *in a heartbeat*, I'd throw him to the wolves if he did it. Not just for the job but for June. That's the truth. And here's another truth: The country needs Jack and June. And they will always, always be 'Jack and June,' even with her gone. Their rags-to-riches stories, their love, their success. In this world where everything's gone to hell, for two people to rise up like that? And find each other? I can't take that away. And can I tell you one more thing?"

"Do you really want an answer, or—"

"I had bungalow two searched. While we were all in number one with the cops, and while Jack was being interviewed. I had one of my guys go there to look for the gun and the necklace."

Frozen, she studies his profile.

"*And they weren't there.* What'd you think I was going to say? You think if we found the gun that killed June in with Jack's stuff, we'd even be having this conversation? Refer back to what I said earlier, please—I'd toss him to the *wolves* if I thought he did it. But here's what I'm saying now: It's not just that I *believe* he wouldn't do it, it's that I looked into it. You and I both know the only way he's *maybe* capable of doing something like that is if he's having one of his moments and is confused. Even then, it's a huge stretch. But let's think about it . . . In that state, you don't *also* remember where the gun is and then have the presence of mind to hide it and the necklace. To be messed up enough to kill someone means he'd be too messed up to cover it up."

The relief she feels is immediate and encompassing but worrisome—because she didn't realize how much she needed this assurance. She sees Jack in the alley with the shotgun, and reminds herself that he only intended to scare whomever it was. Even if she weren't there to stop him, nothing might've happened.

Nico continues. "Drunk people leave a trail. I *want* to believe he told us everything, but if you know otherwise, then I need to know too. You can't play your hand till you've looked at all your cards. Strategy relies on information."

Frankie sits with his words on the drive from the studio to Jack's house in Pasadena, which takes almost an hour. After a while, Nico tells her about Tank Adams, found hiding out in Westchester, a Los Angeles County city that's mostly rows and rows of bean plants and an airport called Mines Field.

"Why didn't you lead with this?" she asks. "This is *big*. They *found* him."

"Could be great, if he did it. Tank claims to have an alibi."

"But he was there. Outside the premiere, watching June."

"That was earlier. Story is he met up with friends later. But till the police talk to those friends, it's empty words. He's still our best bet. And we need something to stick, because I don't love how things look." He taps the steering wheel as if ticking off a list. "*Jack* found her. *Jack's* the last person she was with. *Jack* was in a relationship with her—and cops know that doesn't always mean bliss. God help us if they find out he didn't want to marry her. No, I don't care if Tank did it or not, he's the carrot I need dangled in front of the police so they *don't* look to Jack."

As they drive, small stretches of land become buildings and houses and jam-packed life. Soon they pass through the Figueroa Street tunnels, geometric patterns on the retaining walls and on the mouths of the portals. Beautiful designs that lead the way to a plunge through the hills. On the sidewalk alongside the roadway, a man, woman, and child walk together, the mother's hand over her mouth as she coughs.

"These tunnels saved me," Nico says, as they emerge back into the light. "Used to take me twice as long to get to him. But I do like him being out of the way. Less spying eyes, if you know what I mean." He takes in the view from his window. "Pasadena used to be where the tourists and rich snowbirds went. Then this Depression hit. One day, what's left of the orange groves will be gone. Every one of them. Orange Grove Boulevard will just be a name, and no one will know why. Fifty years from now, a hundred years, what survives? For June, what survives? That she was a mess? That she was knocked up and needed saving? They'll never know her. They'll just know the bottom line."

"That people remember her to begin with would be nice." Frankie's thinking of Fiona, gone as if she never was.

"True. What'd Oscar Wilde say? *There's only one thing worse than being talked about, and that's not being talked about.* Something like that."

The San Gabriel Mountains rise in the distance, bracing the valley. *Still growing,* Jack once told her about the range, a comment that, from that point on, made it impossible to look at mountains without imagining the force of the many earthquakes involved in their creation. *Isn't there something nice about that,* he asked, *that they're not done?*

When they round the corner to Jack's street, Nico taps on the brakes. "So much for people not wanting to journey to Pasadena."

The entire street is packed with people and cars, signs propped up on hoods and roofs as if with hopes Jack might spot them from his house. Nico noses his car into the chaos, and people step aside, craning their heads to look through the windows. Frankie searches the crowd for Agnes, at last spotting the girl picking a yellow flower from the clover. She places the stem in her mouth, and makes a face. "I could've told her it would be sour."

"What?" Nico asks.

Frankie nods toward the girl. The flower hangs from her mouth as she sucks on the stem. "We called it sour flower."

"It's wood sorrel. Betty said crowds are at June's too. Ida's afraid to go outside."

Ida, demanding and unsatisfied. The opposite of June in all ways—dark to June's light, silence to June's laughter. Yet Ida was also the one who set her own alarm earlier than anyone in the house so she could open June's door and slowly raise the shades, or bring the lights on one by one to ease June awake. *No one wants to wake up in the middle of a dream,* she once told Frankie. "I can't believe Ida's not signing autographs."

Nico gives her a sidelong glance. "I'm mad at her too, if it helps. I know she was hard on June. Impossibly hard, like a mother, really, ever since their own mother's mind started slipping."

"That was almost a *decade* ago. That's years and years of Ida bossing June around and making June prove herself. All June wanted was her approval. To make her proud."

"Never try to make sense of family." The iron gate swings open, and they start to wind up to the house. "And this probably won't help, but Ida didn't get to be Ida growing up. Ida was always *June's sister*. Everything was for June. Doesn't excuse anything, but I get the sense that Ida's not sure when her life begins. Maybe it's now, I don't know."

Bringing up something Nico's already dismissed can be tricky, but if Tank is cleared, there's another person who warrants examination.

"Nico, we need to look into the father of June's baby." He shakes his head. "If Tank's alibis check out, and it wasn't him, don't we—"

"I know who the father is. All right?" He parks the car, and glances at the mirrors before continuing. "I want to respect her privacy, but what I *will* say is that the guy's decent enough, but didn't want anything to do with a baby. That made me furious, if you want to know the truth. But he was fine with her having it, as long as he wasn't involved—which actually worked a hell of a lot better for us than if he *did* want to be in the picture. Still, he wasn't angry, or mad or jealous. He had nothing to gain or lose with her death. So, if I keep dismissing the guy, that's why—because it's a dead end, and would only cause problems and put *her* reputation at risk."

She leans against the car door, her head on the glass.

"Sometimes I don't tell you things," he continues. "Not because I don't trust you. But because I feel bad that our stars shouldn't trust *me*. Because I do what I gotta do to protect them from their secrets, and that means revealing those secrets at times. To you, for instance. And it doesn't make me feel the best. So I keep quiet when I can."

On the second floor, a light goes on. "Come on," Nico continues. "And it's not over with Tank. We all know how alibis can be bought."

Inside, cameramen are set up in Jack's living room, and reporters do their best to pretend they're not impressed with the surroundings. "This seems like a bad idea," Frankie says as a man runs his hand along the rim of a ceramic vase.

"Here, we need Jack up and presentable for thirty minutes. Anywhere else, there's travel time, there's talking to other people. This was our best bet."

Upstairs, they've just turned the corner when a man steps out of Jack's room. The studio doctor. Gray, thinning hair, wire-rimmed glasses, and an uneven gait. A man people either dread or look forward to seeing; there's no in-between.

Nico nods to him and knocks on Jack's door before pushing it open and disappearing inside. But Frankie waits to intercept the doctor. "He doesn't need more."

The man hitches up his bag on his shoulder. "Says who?"

Though Nico hates anything and everything to do with the doctor, the man works for Nico's boss, not Nico. Frankie certainly has no say.

The doctor smiles, sympathetic yet patronizing. "You want him asleep for the press? Because he's not snapping out of this. Not today. Hell, not even tomorrow."

"He just lost his fiancée. He needs time."

Now he raises an eyebrow as if to challenge Frankie's lie. Perhaps thinking better of it, he says, "I'm not that kind of doctor, but you ask me, it's not grief I'm seeing. It's guilt."

Frankie tries to be calm as the doctor continues.

"He wasn't there to protect her. Survivors of accidents too, they feel guilty it wasn't them."

A rush of relief. She thanks him for his insight, as patronizingly as she can, and opens Jack's bedroom door. The bed is unmade. The closet door open. There are pill bottles on his bedside table, stacks of scripts by a love seat that have spilled over, pages splayed. A soup bowl on a tray by the wall. Jack, standing at the window, turns when he hears her. Never has she seen him this sad, this deep in his own misery.

Nico picks a sweater off the floor. "I need to make sure the reporters are good girls and boys and stick to their questions. Frankie, get some concealer under his eyes, would you? It's radio, but people in Europe could see those circles."

Frankie waits till Nico's gone, and finds the concealer in a drawer, there to assist after late nights. Jack's still facing the window when she goes to him. Dabbing the makeup on her finger, she angles his face toward her. "You looked better this morning."

His eyes meet hers, that gut-wrenching blue gaze, but then he's looking lower, to her mouth. In the silence of the room, she can hear him breathing, and it feels like when they first met, when they were off-limits and not allowed.

"Frankie," he says, so quietly she wonders if maybe she imagined it. With two fingers, he touches her wrist, tentative, as if he's unsure. He's watching her. Steady.

"I'm worried about you," she says.

From the hall, Nico yells to someone downstairs. Jack drops his hand. "You have to let me be a mess."

"You can be a mess without that man and whatever he's giving you."

"I won't go down that road. I promise."

At last he looks up at the ceiling. Lightly, she touches the skin under his eyes, and even this touch she is grateful for.

"I'm worried," he says. "I've told myself not to be, but I have to face it. The possibility that . . ." He stops, unable to continue.

She lowers her hand but says nothing.

He registers her silence, and keeps going. "I blacked out the night with the coyotes and the shotgun. I don't drink much, but when I do, that's happened. So what if I'm just not remembering something? From when she was killed?"

Frankie glances at the door. They're alone, and for once she wishes someone would walk in. Would stop him from saying what he's about to say.

"It's like worrying you talked in your sleep," he continues. "Unless someone's there to say *no, I was beside you the whole night, I was listening*, there's always a chance."

All her instincts tell her to keep quiet. To let the rest remain unsaid.

In the hall, Nico calls for her.

This is her job.

Finally, she forces herself to speak. "Jack. I can't help you if I don't know what you're worried about."

To this, he smiles sadly. "I tell myself I wouldn't do something like that, but what if I did?"

~

Wondering is not the same thing as believing. This is what she tells herself as she readies for the press conference. He's nervous because he can't remember, but that doesn't mean there's actually something to remember. Just because you can't rule something out doesn't mean it happened.

Still, his fear lurks in her mind. Even as she places the members of the press into assigned seats—Magda in the front row, Dottie wedged into a corner—it's there. A pervasive apprehension.

Are there any leads on the whereabouts of June Finney's ex, Tank Adams? Have his alibis been verified? Why did you decide to elope? Are you getting any of the casseroles that your fans sent to the studio? What do you eat for dinner? The questions continue, and Jack's voice begins to slow. Maybe whatever the doctor gave him to wake up is fading, or maybe whatever the doctor gave him to settle down is finally kicking in; it could be anything. All Frankie knows is that he doesn't have much longer. Which, of course, is when one of the reporters goes off script.

"Who gets to take June's place as your love interest in the upcoming pictures?"

No one says a word. The question has thrown the crowd, jolted them awake. Nico steps forward, arm raised in a signal to Jack that he doesn't need to answer that.

For the first time, Jack looks present. He sits up, and the throng of reporters stills. Steadily, he says, "Her body's barely cold, and you're asking who gets the part?"

Pencils hover above pads. Microphones held aloft. Even the grandfather clock in the corner seems to pause longer than usual till it releases one frightful *tick*.

Nico steps in front of Jack as if to physically shield him. "He's saying it's a little soon."

Frankie searches for the reporter in the crowd. The man's new but undaunted.

"Reports are already out that Dede Domenico's taken June Finney's spot in *Moving Up*, that Milton Ewing project. Milton's your friend, right?"

"Dede's fifteen," Jack says. "She's a child. I don't do casting, and I only have a cameo in that film. How about a question that has to do with me?"

Almost under his breath, the man says, "It starts shooting in days, someone must know."

Now Jack starts to stand. The table before him wobbles, and Nico reaches for a glass of water before it spills, then quickly whispers something to Jack, whose eyes never leave the reporter. At last, Jack seems to make a decision, and sits.

But the reporter continues. "All right, then. Can you confirm or deny that two studio staffers were in the crowd outside Grauman's talking about the necklace and lack of security?"

With this, Frankie's heart begins to pound. It feels as though the room is filling with sediment, everything heavy and suffocating.

Now it's Nico who faces the man. "What was your name?"

"Jerry."

"Jerry, look, the necklace was stolen, so obviously something went wrong. Thankfully it was insured. But the very nature of eloping is to do it in secret—so the studio was not *aware* that Ms. Finney would be at the bungalow by herself, or arrangements would've been made. But, being in love and happy, June didn't see the danger. Are you going to fault her for that, Jerry?"

The twist is artful, and the shamer shamed. Jerry looks rattled as he sits back down, but Frankie's pulse won't settle, because this means her words about lack of security *were* heard at the premiere, and with this, she understands there is a very good chance that she's the one who set everything in motion.

CHAPTER 17

This Is What It's Come To

Saturday, March 4, 1933

After. That's how Frankie thinks of it; they are in the *after*, the time without June in the world, a time that has changed drastically from the golden *before*. Or maybe the delineation was the dread she saw in Jack's eyes, because for him to so much as entertain the idea that he'd be capable of hurting June has rattled Frankie and made her wish for the days of innocent certainty. Again, she hears his voice: *You have to let me be a mess.* Even that goes against her instincts, because all she wants to do is mend the tear, and yet she can't.

Though it's Saturday, both she and Nico are in the office. The one time she brings up the reporter, Jerry, and what he said, Nico tells her not to worry and promptly picks up the phone to make a call, swiveling his chair to face the window, an indication he wants privacy. Through the glass, she catches a studio gardener pause while mowing the lawn, a narrow path of light-green cut grass behind him. He lowers his head, then takes another step before stopping once more. Stooped over, he puts his hands on his knees, a reddened patch of exposed skin on the back of his neck. Frankie's seen this before; the man is about to pass out. In seconds she's at the window, her hand on the glass as, beside her,

Nico's forgotten about the phone and is watching as well, the operator's voice faint yet demanding through the line. At last the man raises his chin and trudges forward.

Back at her desk, she answers automatically when her phone rings, but is met with silence. She's about to hang up when she hears the steady intake of breath, and then a slow exhale. And even that is enough, because she's spent countless hours beside him, listening to him breathe.

Quietly, she says, "I was just thinking about you. I'll try to come to you tonight."

"Don't. There are still people outside. I just wanted to hear your voice. Tell me one thing."

"A good thing?"

"Do I need more bad?"

She glances toward the window. "A man I thought was about to faint didn't."

A small laugh. "So this is what it's come to."

Despite herself, she smiles. His laugh, she'd needed even that.

On the way home, she stops by the little house—*her* little house—for the reminder that a better day will come, soon. She's in the driveway, sitting in her car, when she worries that she shouldn't be here. It's as though she's treading the line between belonging to this place, and not belonging, perched before a future that feels unearned, as if she's skipped ahead in a book. Tucked in the green, the house is shaded by trees, quiet and peaceful. Fresh white trim against red. A pot of violets on the porch. This, she decides, is what she would show her mother, if she could. Not the spotlights and the cameras and the red carpets but a little house that is just hers, with a line to dry her wash that she never needs to keep an eye on, and a front path that will never be littered with cigarette butts or bottles. Again, she hears Jack's voice, telling her about the man who jumped, his insistence he could've helped. *It's not always about money,* she said to him. *You break my heart,* he replied.

She never told him about the house. This chance of hers, this correction to her life, to her mother's life, to everyone like her who's only thought of treading softly and staying out of the way, whose goals are to not take up much space or cause too much trouble or overstay their welcome. From that to this. A house that is hers and hers alone. She sees herself on the porch, reading a script, or in the window, drawing down the shade at night. This is the salve on a burn, the chance to sit after years of walking. It's everything she's worked for, and it disturbs her that she hasn't mentioned it to Jack, because he is the one she wants to tell everything to, and yet instinct tells her to protect this little house, to build a wall around it in her heart and keep it clear of all the sadness that fills their days.

And yet the happier she feels about it, the more the omission begins to sting like a lie. When at last she starts the car, she doesn't look back at the house, as if worried it might not look the same.

~

The next morning, there is a moment where everything is as it should be. Then it all floods back. Taking even breaths, she pulls back the covers.

In the other room, Susan and Virginia have taken books off shelves and emptied drawers, hunting for mementos or anything June related.

Virginia, cross-legged on the floor, presses a Kleenex to her eyes. "I had those stills. The ones the photographer wasn't using that I took. Did I throw them away? I wouldn't do that, would I?"

Susan shakes her head, and swipes a dustrag along a bare shelf. "You wouldn't do that." Then she sees Frankie. She stops, arm still extended. "You can cry. For us, it's strange, I know, because we didn't know her really, but you did. And you're not crying."

"I have to go to work. Now. I have to go."

Susan eyes the pajama bottoms Frankie's wearing. "On a Sunday?"

When the phone rings, Virginia doesn't bother looking up. "Speak of the devil."

It's Nico, telling her to stay home. "Rest," he says, and she waits for him to invite her to his house, to be with him and his family. "No dinner tonight either. This is Gabriella's first death. Angela's spending all her time with her so she doesn't have to go through it alone."

When Frankie's mother died, the family who shared the apartment with her had her over to their side for dinner. The parents cried and the children played and looked confused, and though the mother didn't speak English, she held Frankie's hand and didn't let go even as she ate. But it was one meal. Then Frankie returned to her side and an emptiness that never left.

"That's good—that she doesn't have to be alone."

There's silence on the other end as he must hear what she's not saying. Then he adds, "You could still come over. I didn't mean you should be alone. I'm just not good company."

Which is what she needs to remember; he lost someone he's known for years, someone he vowed to protect and care for. She wraps the phone cord around her finger, watching the skin turn white. "I'm not alone. I have my roommates."

"If you change your mind, you know where we are. Oh, tomorrow, I want you at the station. Be a fly on the wall. I gave Mickey a talking-to on Friday, but I want you listening for whispers, anything to do with Jack."

"Nico, I know you said not to worry, but that reporter? Jerry? What he mentioned in the press conference—"

"He's not invited back."

"It's true, then?" Off his silence, she adds, "People overheard my comment?"

"It's hard to talk now, right? But what he said is nothing crucial."

"How could it not be?"

"Listen to me. If I was in line at a movie and said I forgot to lock my front door, what are the odds that the very person next to me is going to act on that?"

What are the odds, what are the odds. Over and over, Frankie repeats this in her mind.

~

That night, a wind is blowing and everything feels cold. Drafts seep from under the doors and through the windows' gaps, Los Angeles not equipped for anything close to a real winter. In bed, each time she nears sleep, a chill wakes her with a shiver. When the phone rings, she races to get it, her bare feet hitting the cold hardwood floor.

"I can't sleep," Jack says.

"Me either. It's too cold."

"You're cold? Is your radiator not working?"

"Apparently not."

"I'll get someone to look at it."

"Don't do that. I can figure it out."

"It's not a weakness to let me take care of you."

With a glance over her shoulder, she says quietly, "Not to argue the point, but I think I'm the one taking care of you."

A laugh. "True."

"Why can't you sleep?"

"Well, there are the obvious reasons, but it's too windy. I don't like the sound. And I haven't taken anything."

"Good. Don't."

There is a pause, and he says, "You don't have to talk, but will you stay on the phone with me? I'll pay for it."

Frankie listens for her roommates. "Sure."

Curled into a curved green club chair, she holds the phone against her ear. And the strange thing is, it doesn't feel strange to sit with him like this. Saying nothing, just knowing he's there. The sound of his breathing. The steady rhythm. In her mind, she sees him in bed, the way he likes to have one arm thrown out across the mattress, palm up. After a while, his breathing slows, becoming softer. And when she wakes in the morning, the phone beside her is in its cradle—one of her roommates must have found her—and her back is sore from having slept in a chair, but it's the most she's slept since this began.

CHAPTER 18

Mountains Made of Clouds

Monday, March 6, 1933

Mist burns off fast, the week in a hurry to start. The police station is a two-story building, with stone on the bottom floor and brick on the top, as if the building itself has grown and shifted alongside the Los Angeles population. Palm trees flank either side, and a flagpole is off to the right, missing its flag. Frankie parks on the side street, in front of houses that are small but tidy. Before one of them, a man with a camera leads a pony up the path to a front door. Nico has a photo from one of these photographers, one that captures his daughter, Gabriella, in Western gear atop a horse with white splotches that look like paint. *I tried telling her I had an entire make-believe world at her disposal,* Nico explained, *but the sight of a pony at her front door was irresistible.*

Inside the station, there is noise. Phones ringing, shoes squeaking on the floor, and voices, so many voices. The station's switchboard—rows of operators concentrated on black panels with toggles and switches and cords—is off to the side. Through another door is reception, and a hall that leads to the interrogation rooms. *Pass reception*, Nico said. *Don't even look at them. Straight to the bullpen. Act like you know where you're going, and they won't stop you.*

Doing as told, Frankie doesn't even pause. She goes straight through the door on the right and into a large bullpen with detectives at their desks, cops crowded around an easel. *You'll always find reporters in a police station,* Nico warned her. *It's where they get their scoops. In exchange, they answer phones and even make coffee.*

And there, sitting on the corner of a desk, wearing a red dress as if determined to be seen, is Dottie. Frankie turns to the wall beside her, pretending to study a map of Los Angeles. Is Dottie here because it's something she does, or is she here to follow up on a hunch? *We gotta get Jack away from her before he kills her.* What Nico said the night of the premiere. Did Dottie hear?

Keeping her back to the bullpen, Frankie edges along the wall, pretending to be interested in whatever's pinned to bulletin boards while listening in on the conversations closest. Then there's the smell of coffee, and Frankie hears the clatter of a spoon against ceramic.

"I know you," a man says. "The writer. The one whose friend drove like a bat out of hell to that movie."

Frankie turns. A cop stirs a cup of coffee behind her. It's the officer they met outside the theatre, the man with no love for Hollywood, the perfect person to get the scoop from. If anyone's going to reveal the rumors or suspicion, it's someone not in the studio's pocket.

"I *thought* that was you," Frankie says. With a glance over her shoulder, she confirms that Dottie's still on the corner of the desk, and is actually now on the phone. "My article took a turn. Ever since the star of that movie died."

He gives a low whistle. "It's all anybody's talking about. She was young."

"Hollywood's taking a toll on young actresses."

"You're telling me. And her sister's calling here every ten minutes. *What are you doing? Are you trying to solve this?* Bet that actress got herself into something. The number of times I've broken up parties and seen starlets making fools of themselves, it's shameful."

Frankie keeps her voice steady. "But June Finney was killed in a robbery, right? She didn't bring that on herself."

"Wearing a necklace like that?" He takes off his hat to scratch his head, and his forehead shines under the lights. "You bet she did. Someone followed her home because they saw her flaunting diamonds. That's the truth of it."

"Or," Frankie forces herself to say, "because they overheard someone say there was no security following her home?"

Now he laughs. "Someone said that? That wasn't smart."

A wash of embarrassment—but then relief, because this was news to him, and Frankie wants to believe that's because it's not part of any of the working theories. If the police don't think it's important that someone said what she did, then she can let it go and try to find out what's being said about Jack, the real reason for her visit. "She was the fiancée of the costar. Jack Sawyer?"

But the man doesn't react to Jack's name. Absentmindedly, he takes the spoon from his mug and sets it on the desk beside him, on top of a newspaper. Coffee seeps and spreads, darkening the print. "I don't follow all that gossip. Though I did hear about the ex, a real creep."

Another glance over Frankie's shoulder. Across the room, Dottie places the receiver back on the phone just as an officer walks by and swats her butt playfully. She laughs, and takes her time getting off the desk.

"Nice chatting," Frankie says right as Dottie turns to wave to someone across the room—someone right in front of Frankie.

Without thinking, Frankie lowers her head and hurries in the other direction, deeper into the station. But in another hall, she pauses, trying to decide where to go, and realizes that she's standing directly in front of the chief's office, and the door is open.

He's watching her questioningly.

She smiles. "Nico wanted me to stop by."

Impatiently, he waves her inside. Then he's back to flipping through the contents of a folder, a black-and-white mug shot stapled to the cover.

"So," she says, trying to think of something, because the truth is Nico sent her to be a fly on the wall, and she has failed monumentally.

Without looking up, he says, "Let him know the ME's working on his report, but her reputation will be intact."

The pregnancy. Still, no one knows about it, and with this discretion, it will stay that way.

"Good. Nico will be happy." She smiles. "One other thing, that reporter, Dottie?"

He looks up, confused. "Who?"

"Never mind. I thought maybe you knew the reporters out there."

"Of course I know them. Don't let them tell you otherwise—letting them spend time at the station is a gift. From me to them. I vet each and every one of them."

Frankie digests this. Because if Dottie's not one of the regular reporters he's vetted, that means she's here for a specific reason, and could be chasing a story or a hunch.

When she leaves, Frankie veers off through the hall that takes her past the interrogation rooms, keeping her head down and walking quickly. Maybe it's his feet, the worn saddle brown of his shoes that she's seen when he's picked up Virginia, but something makes her look up to see Fred leaving the last room. Fred, a middle manager at the studio. *Middle managers are the perfect alibis,* Nico once explained. At the time, he was telling Frankie about the man who claimed *he* was the one who'd been speeding in one of their actors' cars, not the actor himself, when that car hit a truck on La Brea and left the scene. Frankie wanted to correct him, to tell him that the word he was looking for was *patsy*. But instead, she watched him write a check out to the man, who'd be employed forever . . . just as soon as he got out of jail. *They're high enough up that they're invested in their job and want to be in the studio's good graces,* Nico continued, *but they're not high enough to say no. When you gotta ask a favor, you have to find someone with* need. *Identify that need, and they're yours.*

Fred. Not moving up through the ranks, not in anyone's good graces, enduring the end of his engagement, and now leaving an interrogation room when Frankie knows he was nowhere near Jack or June the night of the murder. If Susan was right about him being a homosexual, the studio might know, and might be exploiting this. Frankie would put money on Fred suddenly being an alibi, and before she gets in trouble by not knowing this detail of the story, she needs to talk to Nico.

~

While Frankie waits, Betty eats her lunch, cries about June, and drops details about the funeral, which is set for Wednesday at Hollywood Memorial Park. Paramount Pictures sprang up on the original south side of the property, Betty tells her, so naturally the cemetery is where everyone wants to be. *Where everyone wants to be,* said as if she's referring to the latest nightclub. Stars from both behind and in front of the camera are laid to rest there, including Rudolph Valentino. Even Hobart Johnstone Whitley, the real estate developer known as the Father of Hollywood, and Hannah Chaplin, Charlie Chaplin's mother.

"Valentino lay in state in New York," Frankie says, "before they sent him to Los Angeles." She's sitting in a chair by the parrots' addition, her legs bent and on the seat. *Legs down like a lady,* she was always told. "There were a hundred thousand people in the street."

Fiona was a Valentino fan. She was the one who taught Frankie how to sneak in to see a film, instructing her to wait around the corner to the Bowery Theatre until a friend who worked the concession stand propped open the alley door with a brick. At night, she whispered about Hollywood, brightening Frankie's dreams with spotlights and tinsel. *When he first came to America,* Fiona said about Rudolph Valentino, *he couldn't find work and slept on the streets. From that to having an estate called Falcon Lair and four or five cars and horses for fun, just think of it!* As a distraction, when Frankie was scared, Fiona would repeat his full name—*Rodolfo Alfonso Raffaello Pierre Filibert Guglielmi di Valentina d'Antonguolla*—to the rhythm of the Lord's Prayer. Sometimes Frankie wonders if her mother was ever aware that Valentino was almost broke when he died. She likes to think Fiona never knew. "I was there," Frankie continues. "There were crowds for eleven blocks."

Betty sets her fork down. Her tears stopped. "You were *there*?"

"Valentino was at Frank Campbell's funeral home for *days*. There were riots, people smashing windows and fighting with police just to see him. And it was hot. Women killed themselves when he died."

"I *heard*. Two girls in Japan jumped into a volcano." Betty glances over her shoulder. "I know he was married, twice, but sometimes I'm not sure he even *liked* women." She lowers her voice. "Lavender marriages, that's my guess."

The term used for marriages that cover up homosexuality. "Could be."

"And Mussolini sent four fascists to guard the body? You saw them?"

"They were right there, giving the salute next to the body. But they were actors. Hired by Campbell's press agent."

"No, they weren't! Were they?"

Frankie lifts the window shade to peer out. The sun, Betty claims, gives her a headache, so now and then, she draws the shades down. "It was all an act. There were rumors that Valentino's body was in some back room and they put a wax replica in the casket."

Betty sets a glass paperweight on top of a stack of papers. Inside the glass, orange, pink, and yellow flowers bloom. "And people think Hollywood's the only one pulling stunts like that."

"The explorers who came to America lied to get people here. They called swampland *fertile soil*. And the Boston Tea Party was a publicity stunt. Needing good publicity's as old as time. Hollywood doesn't have a corner on that market, we just do it better."

"You've spent *far* too much time with Nico."

"You really don't know when he's back?"

"He said *later*. You could try him on stage four. Oh God, Frankie, I heard someone refer to the project as *the new Dede Domenico film*. How can anyone even *say* that before June's funeral?"

But Frankie doesn't stay to commiserate. Soon she's on her bike and whizzing past clusters of men in suits and costumed actors smoking and mouthing lines and one even sitting on a step, staring at the sky as if reading words. She passes the mill that's loud and choking with sawdust, and then Sound Alley, where musicians score films and Foley artists improve and replace everything from doors sighing open to screams to dogs barking to the sound of running through leaves. At last she's at the stages, and carefully creeps past the one where horses have been running, bolting, really, from inside to out so the camera can capture just one moment of a race. Next to that building is one with the number four at the top, faded in the bright sun. The red light flashes, which means they're filming. She waits patiently. When it's safe to enter, she carefully steps over the cords and wires and navigates equipment and people until she turns the corner to the set and finds herself in the midst of a tenement. She freezes.

A wall missing plaster. A floor, splintered and paint spattered. A tiny bathroom with a stained porcelain sink and a toilet with an aluminum pail beside it. Her heart has begun to pound. There's another room with stacks of old newspapers. Cardboard boxes as chairs and what looks like a wall made of nailed-together sheets of plywood and other wood scraps. A wave of nausea overcomes her, because she knows what's next.

Sure enough, the wall becomes a sheet. And at the end, there's a window that might as well be a glimpse straight into her heart, because around its frame is a string of plastic morning glory vine. When a man beside her angles a light just so, the windowsill flares with brightness, and there they are, hearts carved into the wood.

This is her life. Details she's only ever told Jack—not because she was ashamed but because she was protective. Her mother. All her mother's efforts at caring for her and keeping her safe. All of it, recreated by people who don't know, who don't care, whose only goal was to capture the look of being poor. They never considered the life behind these details.

Intense emotions can turn physical. It's something she first discovered when her mother died and Frankie's skin went cold and her legs wouldn't stop shaking. Now this happens again, only with heart-pounding nausea. Taking a few steps back, she looks for a place to sit—on the floor, a chair, anywhere—but then loses the energy to do even that. She crouches where she is, faint.

Feet race past her. Barely, she looks up, at a gaffer's legs and then his hands as he adjusts a light. "What project is this?"

"You didn't see the door? *Moving Up*."

Moving Up, the film Jack's friend, Milton Ewing, wrote. Since Jack's involvement was minimal—he's not starring in the film—and more a favor to his friend, Frankie never paid it much attention. "What's it about, in a nutshell?"

The guy looks at her as if suspecting she's pranking him, but then perhaps recognizes her. "A poor girl in New York marries a rich man on the Upper East Side. That's a rich area in Manhattan—"

She's up and turning away. She doesn't want to hear more.

It's never about money until it is. And it always is, Jack told her. *It's a quote I gave Milton.*

And here before her is what he truly gave Milton: her life.

Finding her way outside, she's just opened the stage door as the assistant director yells, *"Let's go again—places, everyone!"* There is a blast of light. A slap of daytime. It's a smash cut, harsh sunlight and truth. She sits on a step and lowers her head. Did he not care enough to understand that her memories and stories of her past are *her*, and worth protecting? He would be furious if she passed along the details of his life, if she relayed stories he'd told her in confidence. And though she tells herself it shouldn't be a big deal, that it was over anyhow, it somehow feels different from past letdowns. Bigger. Like someone who's only ever seen flat land learning that the first mountain they finally glimpse is made of clouds.

The worst thing is she knows he doesn't think she's with him for the money—she's made it clear she prefers the cottage in Venice to the mansion in Pasadena, and sandwiches in bed over steak on porcelain—but what is truly heartbreaking is that he thought so little of her that he'd reduce her to a story he heard, to details he passed along without thought. After everything she'd said about her mother, all that she'd revealed, he was careless. He allowed her childhood to be turned into a joke.

"Any news?" Nico. The soundstage door closes behind him. "You okay?"

The truth is, *she's* the one who handed over her life. She's the one who failed her mother and the reason her mother's attempt at beauty is now a sad display meant to evoke pity. Looking up at Nico, she squints hard against the sun. "I need to know about Fred."

Nico's eyes widen at her tone. "Sure, follow me."

The lot is busy, and they have to pause to let a tour group pass. A group of showgirls with pluming feathers rounds the corner. What else did Jack take? She's afraid to read the script. When they pass by the start of the New York City back lot, she tries not to look, but a trace of white catches her eye.

Nico notices her take in the scene. "In this movie, it's a week after a storm hit. They nailed it, that old-snow look. They really did."

Dirtied white cotton batting edges the sidewalks and stoops. All at once, she sees the glimmer of melting snow on a sun-warmed sidewalk, and her mother crouching down to point out the tiny rivulets that formed in the ice. *It's a miniature Alaska,* she said about a place she'd only ever seen on a map. *Big fields of ice and melting waterfalls. Everything shines. Can you imagine?*

"And lookee there," Nico says, pointing. The cat. The black-and-white one with six toes on each foot. It's perched on an apple crate, eating a bowl of tuna someone left out. "Told you it's fine. Not a better place in the world to be. So that night. Fred was with Jack, in Malibu. He's our alibi."

Frankie looks away from the cat, who actually looks as though it's put on weight. "He hasn't been accused, right?"

"Not out loud. But like I said, it's always the husband."

"You said the first thing they do is *look* to the husband or boyfriend. You didn't say it *is*."

"I'm not saying it is now either. Just that it's a matter of time till they come after him, and we need to be ready, because it's looking like Tank's alibis are checking out."

Frankie stops walking. "They are?"

He motions her forward, but she won't move. "Look, our alibi's also gonna hold, so what does that tell you about alibis? I'd bet my house that the person who shot her was either Tank or some jerk who had nothing to do with anything and just wanted the necklace. But we need to be ready for them to come after Jack. And we *are*. Readier than we thought. Already had reports of champagne brought in to Malibu and security by the road, the works. O'Shea saying he dropped him off. It was all in place. We just needed *one* person to say he was *with* Jack in Malibu. Playing cards."

"It couldn't be you?"

"I was at the premiere till late. People saw me. That's hours he'd be unaccounted for. I needed someone who could say they were *there* when Jack got in and can say that Jack stayed put. And Fred, I understand, just went through a breakup. A little guy time fit the bill."

"And you trust Fred that much?"

A man in the distance raises his hand, waving to Nico before he starts walking toward them. Nico lowers his voice. "What I trust is how much he wants what we're offering him."

"And what's that?"

But Nico just claps his hands together. "Let's get a move on. I stay here a second longer, there's gonna be a line to talk to me, and then why do I pay Betty the big bucks? Tell me what you learned at the station, but let's mosey."

The two of them walk in the shadows of the massive stages. "Mickey says the ME's working on his report and June's reputation will be fine."

"It's about time people behave."

"Well, not everyone's behaving. Dottie was there this morning."

"Where? At the station?" Off Frankie's nod, he continues. "She's there a lot? Because he's got reporters who practically work there."

"Mickey didn't know who she was."

Nico shakes his head. "Like sharks in the water."

Again, Frankie sees the set they just left, a visual betrayal. She shivers in the shade of a stage, rubbing her shoulders. "And Jack knows he was playing cards with Fred, his new best friend?"

"He knows. He's actually here. Jack." Maybe he registers her surprise, because he continues. "Fred's meeting him at the commissary. Soon."

A lunch for appearances. So people can honestly say they saw them together.

"You hungry?" Nico asks. "Because Jack said he wanted to talk to you—I don't know what about, but maybe go and make sure he gets settled in and see what he needs. I've got a one-thirty meeting with Iffy to discuss Wednesday." *Wednesday,* he calls it. Not *the funeral.* He takes a deep breath. "Everything we're doing, June would ask us to do if she were here. Her reputation was important to her."

When Frankie sees Jack, he's seated at a table, surrounded by a crowd that's keeping an eye on him like they would a stray penny. Anyone else would feel the scrutiny and examination and wither under its weight, but this is Jack's kingdom. People gravitate toward him like he's the sun. Leaned back, he nods, smiles, and makes eye contact. Frankie lets herself watch him a moment longer, always blown away by how relaxed he is under the gaze of hundreds of eyes.

But since it's clear they have an audience, he lifts one brow, surprised, when she takes a seat opposite him at the table. "Is this allowed?"

She's come prepared. From her bag she takes out a call sheet, and points to it as if she's going over information, times or locations. "Nico said you wanted to talk to me."

He nods, resigned. Perhaps disappointed. "I thought you'd find me later, but sure."

His voice is low enough that she has to lean in. As she does, she concentrates on the call sheet, doodling on it with a pen. For a second, she senses him smiling. When she doesn't return it, he asks if she's okay.

"There's no point in talking about it."

"Sounds like I did something wrong."

Her voice comes out stronger than she feels. "Tell me what you need."

For the first time she sees a crack in his composure. "No one's trying to solve this."

"We shouldn't talk about this here."

He laughs. "Then where, on the phone with the operator listening? At my house with caravans of fans outside, watching you pull in?"

"The police are trying to solve it."

"Are they?" His voice is so low, she must lean in even closer, and then try not to breathe in his soap-and-tobacco scent, that olfactory anchor to nights in his arms. She scoots back, and he continues. "What I see is that they're interested in what the studio's interested in—which is preserving her memory. The truth of what happened is *not* their goal. The truth of what happened is no one's goal. And I get that Nico's trying to save me here, but everything that's being done, isn't it mucking up the investigation?"

That's what worries Frankie, that what they've done to protect the living could come at the expense of the dead.

"The crime scene was a mess," he continues. "Everyone in and out and touching things they shouldn't. Nico's guys did their work before the cops even got there. What chance do the police have when everything's been tampered with like that?"

A pause as someone passes too close to their table and smiles in Jack's direction.

Jack gives a nod and a wave. "One more thing. June and Ida were fighting."

"You think *Ida* did it?"

He looks straight at her, his blue gaze steady. *A Ulysses,* she hears the boy long ago declare over the electric-blue butterfly.

"No," he says. "I think she was going to meet her, to apologize or something. Maybe June was waiting for her. There were two glasses, remember?"

"Ida doesn't know how to apologize. And the porch light wasn't on. It's dark there; she'd have left it on if she were expecting somebody."

"Maybe someone didn't show. Maybe she turned off the light before—" He stops talking, spotting Fred weaving through tables. "Wait," he quickly adds, "you're not going to tell me what's wrong?"

"I guess I didn't really learn the lessons I thought I did."

Then she's up and heading to the side exit. Pushing through the door, she gives one last glance over her shoulder. Fred and Jack are hugging, best friends who've only just now met.

CHAPTER 19

Words Don't Pull the Trigger

Tuesday, March 7, 1933

Everyone braces for the funeral the next day. Last-minute seating charts, flower arrangements plotted on a map, programs with June's face hot off a printing press. *Go to bed early,* Nico tells Frankie. *Tomorrow's a big day*. But at almost eleven p.m., her phone rings.

"I'm at the Tam O'Shanter," Nico says. "That's not far from you, is it?"

Fifteen minutes later, Frankie's got a long coat tied tight around navy silk pajamas and is parked in front of the storybook-style house. Stepping inside is like entering a Scottish hunting lodge, with coved timbered ceilings, dark wood walls, and yellow lighting that makes her feel as though she can't see properly. Coats of arms hang from the walls, and a diamond-shaped lattice window reflects the room's warmth. Actors and producers and directors alike all dine here, with the exception of Jack. Even when Mary Pickford asked him to join her, he made excuses, claiming he couldn't meet at the Tam O'Shanter because he wanted an excuse to visit Pickfair, the twenty-five-room mansion where Mary and Douglas Fairbanks famously canoe in their enormous pool. *A bit of a farther drive,* Jack told Frankie, *but if you can finagle an invite, you go. You better believe I'll pass up the Scottish place any day.* When she pressed him on his avoidance of the restaurant, he admitted that one night someone spilled a bottle and the restaurant reeked like the Highlands. *And how would you know?* she asked playfully, aware he'd never been to Scotland. *Because my dad was Scottish, and it smelled just like him, and now you know why I don't drink Scotch or even Irish whiskey.* Or, she understood, dined at a place that brought it all back.

Nico sits at a table by the fireplace, not far from Walt Disney's usual spot. Flames crackle and shift orange and yellow, breathing hot beneath a large portrait in a gilded frame, and Frankie imagines the paint bubbling and boiling, and a worker replacing the painting every night when the doors lock.

Nico takes in her navy-blue silk pant legs. "Dressed up for me, I see."

"You were the one who said to go to bed early. Just because I'm summoned doesn't mean I'm awake."

"You want an apple juice or something?"

"Just because I don't drink doesn't mean I'm twelve." She smiles, but there's a testiness pushing against her that wants out. A waiter stands off to the side. "Canada Dry ginger ale and lime, please," she says.

The bottom of Nico's glass flashes with light as he downs the dregs of his cocktail. "Ginger ale's only good to mask bootleg liquor." He slides his glass to the edge of the table.

The waiter appears to be waiting for Nico to approve her order. Frankie repeats herself, firmly, and catches Nico smiling. At last, the waiter taps his pencil on a pad of paper, takes Nico's glass, and disappears.

Sitting back in his chair, Nico says, "Bank holiday's about to be everywhere, not just here. You got money out in time?"

"A lot's been happening."

"Frankie." But then he nods. "Tell me what's going on."

"*You* asked me to come here. You tell me."

"I mean, you don't seem happy."

"There's the obvious fact, that—" But she stops, catching the look on his face. She doesn't need to remind him that someone they cared about is dead. Leaning forward, she says, "Everything we're doing feels wrong."

"There's no being perfect in an imperfect system."

"I don't know what that means, but it sounds like an excuse."

Now he smiles. "You know who was here all the time? Fatty Arbuckle."

The Keystone Studios turned Paramount star who was so popular and rich he had a twenty-room mansion with gold-leaf bathtubs. But then, in '21, he was arrested for rape and murder. Though he was eventually acquitted, the scandal ruined his career. The first big celebrity scandal, what he went through was a salacious story that the public lapped up. A moneymaking spectacle.

Nico continues. "I haven't stopped thinking about him since this started. He's the reason the studios came up with morality clauses in the first place. Universal first, mandating nonpayment to actors who 'forfeit the respect of the public.' *The respect of the public.* Could mean almost anything, right? But Fatty, he was either an innocent man destroyed, or justice was served, because he lost everything. Really, I don't know. What I do know is that the real sentence was determined in the court of public opinion, and *that* is the court where you and I work."

Frankie feels the heat from the fire, and shifts in her seat, uncomfortable. "Murder or rape, or a crime where somebody gets hurt, of course they should be punished. But human things, like a mistake? Nico, shouldn't they be able to do *that*? Because the public's standards of what's respectful—I don't think they'd hold their best friends to those standards."

Nico nods as the waiter sets down their drinks. "A painting is good or not good, and it has nothing to do with the artist going to church or cheating on his wife. That's the truth. But then the person behind it gets famous enough that the public takes credit for that fame. *We made them, we can unmake them.*"

"Doesn't mean it's right."

"Right or wrong, the public is necessary. That's why they get a say. Does it matter if you're talented in a room by yourself? No? Then you need the public. Simple."

The nature of celebrity centers on the stars' lives, Nico's said. Frankie takes a sip of her drink. "But it still might go too far."

Nico nods. "It still might go too far. And you and I are the ones who try to protect them from that."

"Them, or the studio?"

"You tell me."

With her finger, Frankie traces the edge of her glass. "Jack said the tide is going to turn."

"Already has."

She looks up sharply.

"That neighbor lady, Darlene Cleary. She went to the police and said Jack was there that night, in the second bungalow."

Somewhere, a glass spills. There is a tumble and rush of water, ice cubes hitting the ground as voices rise. "But Mickey puts a stop to that, right?"

"Usually he would, but she didn't give him a chance. She already called Dottie."

"So we get Dottie to bury it. What can we give her?"

"Frankie, we're having this conversation because it's too late for that. Dottie's got it in print tomorrow. First thing." He takes a sip of his drink and winces from the cold. "Been a busy night. Bottom line: Dottie wants to be in our good graces, but this is too big. You remember the night of the premiere, I made some stupid joke about how I swore Jack wanted to kill June?"

"Sure. A joke."

"And ill-timed, because Dottie heard. Combine that with Darlene saying Jack was there, and voilà, the story's got legs. At least as far as Dottie's concerned."

This is it. The words streak through her mind. All at once, she feels the shift, that Jack's been pushed straight into the path they wished to avoid. "But Darlene has no *proof.* She only suspected he was there."

"If she had proof, he'd be arrested by now. But does it matter? We know what an accusation can do."

Perception takes more casualties than truth ever saves.

Nico continues. "There's more. And this complicates things. I needed to know what Tank's alibis were gonna say so I know what the cops are gonna know. So my guys tracked them down. Every one of them. They're solid. They all corroborate Tank's story that he went to visit a friend at Loyola Marymount University after the premiere."

"They could be lying."

"Of course they could. But he's got *several* people saying this, including 'esteemed' professors, so it's a bit uphill from here. But they were drinking. All night." A pause, and he explains: "Jesuits."

"And Mickey doesn't know this yet?"

"Well, unfortunately for Mickey, we had some VIP passes at Agua Caliente—that casino and spa in Tijuana. They got a nice racetrack too. So, you know, those folks might be hard to reach. We've got a day, two maybe."

A loud snap from the fireplace. Both of them turn. A tendril of smoke curls into the air and disappears.

"They're burning wet wood," Nico says.

"Do we tell Mickey about the baby?"

His eyes widen. "So what, someone can make a pretty penny selling the story that she was knocked up? So we destroy her reputation needlessly?" He pauses as if to give her time to answer, though clearly he spoke rhetorically. "Just so you know, I had my guys look into the man to be sure, and they said it too; the father was harmless. Why drag her reputation through the mud?"

"Because they're going to look at Jack."

"Not with a little luck." A pause, and he says, "One of the main working theories is that someone overheard the bit about no security and followed her home."

The way he says it—clearly, concisely—is so logical that it seems impossible that's *not* it. This is really what happened. "The bit that I said, you mean. I did this."

"No. Come on. That's why I almost didn't tell you. But look at me, look at me—it's *one* theory of many. And it's the *start* of a theory. And ultimately it doesn't matter—you could say anything you want, words don't pull the trigger. But, Frankie, we *want* them to go that route, because it doesn't involve Jack. You understand? At this very moment, they're still thinking it's Tank, but when they check everything out, like my guys did, they'll decide it's not Tank, and we're going to *want* them to focus on the theory that someone in that crowd heard what you said—even if that wasn't it. All right? This is a good thing. I promise."

The room dims. A couple has stopped before the fireplace, warming their hands. She'd assured Jack that the police were trying to solve this when he worried that nothing was truly being done. But he was right. In fixating on what's very possibly a dead end, or on the dangled carrots only meant to distract, the only thing no one's looking at just might be the truth.

CHAPTER 20

Luck Has Nothing to Do with It

Wednesday, March 8, 1933

President Roosevelt—only thirty-six hours into his presidency—shut banks down nationwide. California, however, was already disrupted with a freeze of its own, and now people with already loose belts find themselves staring into a bleak future. As the radio announcer lists off markets that are willing to extend credit, Frankie reminds herself that she has Nico if she runs out of money, and that the studio covers her big expenses. It's a comforting thought that also leaves her uneasy.

Then she hears Jack's name from the radio.

"This, on the day of June Finney's funeral! A neighbor at the house where our starlet was murdered *saw* Jack Sawyer next to the body—wearing a bloody tux. Wearing a bloody tux! That's right, folks, I said *blood.* But here's the kicker: The woman says he was there *all* night. *Pee-yew*, are we beginning to catch the stench of a lie? It's all in today's paper, so be swift and find yourself a newsie."

Hair unbrushed, Frankie races to the nearest stand and reads the entire article while walking back to her car. Mist swims in the air, gathering on print that smudges and smears. The pull quote alone is damaging. Jack Sawyer was there. The article is conjecture and speculation, but the fact that he's linked in this way to the location and even the time of the murder is enough.

Less than an hour later, Frankie arrives at Hollywood Memorial Park. She's early, but craving the quiet. The walkways are empty, grass jeweled with dew. Bags of lawn clippings line the road, and in the far distance, a groundskeeper gathers leaves into yet another pile. Frankie readies the site, and tries to not picture Jack at home, a newspaper with Dottie's article outside his front door. *I gave him a warning,* Nico told her last night, *but I don't think he followed just how bad it could get.* Given today's news, Frankie's opted to rearrange the seating chart just slightly, tucking Jack off to the side so he's less visible to the press.

Slowly, the mist burns off. The bags of grass clippings are hauled away. When people start to arrive, they bring updates: A crowd has gathered outside the studio, demanding Jack be arrested.

Frankie stands close to Nico. "All from one article without any facts. The same people loved him just yesterday."

Nico nods a greeting to a man who walks with a cane, slow and plodding. "The only thing they'd love more than Jack being a victim is him being a killer."

Fans are penned up just beyond the arriving limousines, held back by barricades. In the very front are three young women Frankie recognizes from outside the studio gates, each holding WE LOVE YOU, JACK! signs. "Lucky they came here today."

Nico laughs. "Luck has nothing to do with it. But the studio tour I promised them might."

White lilies are everywhere, though the studio arranged to have what looks like a waterfall of pink roses cascade down the sides of the stone mausoleum.

"Where will you go?" a man off to Frankie's right asks his friend. Frankie thinks they're talking about dinner until the man answers.

"Forest Lawn. Double plot, me and the missus. Plunked down a pretty penny."

June has an entire building, it seems, while Frankie's own mother is on Hart Island, New York City's potter's field, a municipal burial ground where the unclaimed and poor are buried. Only a mile long, it's a remote stretch of sorrow and sadness, tucked off the edge of the Bronx. It never occurred to Frankie to wish for more.

"I hate lilies," she says to Nico.

"Good to know."

"She's got room for a family of four to live inside there. Furniture, the works."

"If you go missing, I know where to find you."

The procession of limos continues, curved around the road in a dark gleam of grief. Soon, everyone who's anyone is here, and the day becomes mockingly clear and beautiful. Knives of sunlight glint on the pond near the mausoleum. Now, more than ever, they need to draw attention away from Jack. *A robbery gone wrong,* Nico's been saying all morning. Each time she hears it, Frankie's thoughts spin with guilt. "Jack's still not here."

Nico doesn't look concerned. "I told him to play it safe and wait till after she's in place."

Frankie understands what Nico means when she spots a hearse in the distance, slowly beginning its approach. A hush falls, everyone silenced and waiting.

Pallbearers are in position. Fans push against barricades, ripples of grief overtaking them. With the first glimpse of the casket—a shock of white—there is a loud, solitary wail. Frankie turns in time to see Nico grasping Ida's arm, fighting to keep her steady. It's too much. The bright shine of the casket, the graves of all the people who no longer draw crowds, or who maybe never drew a crowd. All Frankie can bear to watch are the pallbearers' shoes. Black and shiny. One foot in front of the other.

That day in New York years ago, that afternoon when the sky split with color—that was it. No matter how she looks at it, *that* was the only path to California and working for Nico. Right there, right then.

Though she can examine and chide herself for much else, nothing would've happened if the sky didn't crack open that day. She never would've stood on a street in Hollywood and announced that a starlet would be by herself with a valuable necklace, nor would she have suggested she stay alone and unprotected. The more Frankie thinks about it, the further she digs herself into this hole: June might be alive if it weren't for her.

A murmur. People turn, leaning into each other with whispers, as Jack steps out of a limo. Without looking at anyone, he heads straight to the coffin while the world around him silences. Head down, his shoulders hunch like they do when he's holding too much in.

Nico's suddenly at her side. "Go see to him."

Just as she's stepped beyond another plot, she notices a tall man in the distance, his face in his hands. About to trip, she quickly looks down, narrowly avoiding a low marker, and it's then that she places who the man is: Tank.

She looks back up, but there's no one by the tree. Was it really Tank?

Quickly she waves Nico over, and within seconds he's gathered a few of his men. They spread out, long strides through the grass, while Jack stands by the coffin, a handkerchief hanging from his hand.

When she's beside him, he keeps his head down. "She's really in there?"

"You think it's empty?"

"Wouldn't surprise me."

The shaded reflection of clouds on the coffin's surface shift and spread. "Me either."

"There's an old sailor's tradition," he says quietly. "They wear earrings valuable enough to pay for a coffin, in case they die at sea and get washed to shore. Till the day he died, my father wore earrings that could've paid for a lot. Rent money so I didn't have to work as a kid. A new roof so I didn't need to sleep next to a pail that I had to wake up and empty. The hospital bill when my grandmother got sick. Before I shipped off to Europe, when he died? First thing I did was bury him in a box with those earrings still on him. A pine box at St. Roch Cemetery."

Frankie watches the shadowed reflection. "I don't know what my mom got buried in. I don't think anything."

The problem is, it feels good to talk to Jack. It feels right, and she's missed this. Missed it so much, she's almost forgotten the Milton Ewing project, the one in which Jack handed over the details of her life. But the mention of her mom brings it all back.

"Where is she?" he asks. "Your mom."

"Somewhere I can't visit."

Suddenly the crowd of mourners parts as Ida walks to the coffin. She looks unsteady, as if her heels are sinking into the earth with each step, despite the fact that she's walking on a red carpet. Black feathers on the top of her hat appear slick in the sun.

Frankie tells her how sorry she is, and as she does, Jack shifts in the other direction. It's a subtle slight, but Frankie sees Ida register it—right before the woman crumples to the ground.

Fans behind the barricade give a startled scream and every camera swings in their direction.

It takes seconds. Jack turns to see what the fuss is about and looks down at his fiancée's sister, and already Frankie knows the photo that will be plastered on covers everywhere, and the impression it will give: Jack, the cold and uncaring actor, looking down at Ida, the devastated and dedicated sister.

Frankie drops to Ida's side as Jack does the same, albeit more slowly. "Ida. Wake up."

Ida's eyelids quiver, right before she closes them even tighter. Is she faking it? This woman loved June undeniably but also rode the coattails of her success. She was the one at June's bedroom door at the crack of dawn to be sure she was awake to go to work but also the reason why June didn't get rest. She was the reason June never breached her contract but also the reason June struggled. Ida was the voice that told June to stay in line, and who ultimately cared more about box office receipts than anything June cared about.

Something in Frankie gives. "*Get up.* This is your sister's day. Not yours."

A crease forms on Ida's forehead, and when Frankie glances at Jack, she catches him watching her with a slight smile and a look that is so clear with adoration that her heart aches from longing and fear. Because if someone saw this look, they'd know.

Still, Ida pretends to be out cold. Sick of the charade, Frankie pinches her arm, and the woman's eyes fly open before focusing on Frankie. But then she must spot something through the crowd, because her eyes narrow.

Guests, mourners, fans, everyone has turned toward the road. Frankie watches, waiting as the crowd shifts, and suddenly there they are. Police officers. At least a dozen. Their black-and-white cars parked haphazardly, their eyes scanning the crowd. *They have news,* Frankie thinks, though later she isn't sure how this thought made sense.

Nico shoulders past a group of men in suits just as one of the police officers stops in front of Jack. First, the man apologizes. He takes off his hat, and there's remorse on his face.

And that's when everything comes together and Frankie understands.

They are here to arrest Jack.

CHAPTER 21

It Doesn't Get Better than This

June didn't get her funeral. That's what Frankie thinks as they rush from the cemetery and even as Nico storms into Mickey Mulroney's office—Mickey, who takes anxious pulls off his cigarette but offers only a half-hearted apology, like someone with a nagging worry they put money on the wrong fighter. All the while, June is alone, the world around her silent and green.

Mickey stays seated and Nico paces, his words furious. "You made a mistake here. A big one."

"There was gonna be a revolt," Mickey says. "You don't know the calls we've gotten. You don't know the pressure we're under to *lock him up*."

"At her funeral? At her funeral you do this? Because it's bad enough you're targeting the wrong guy, but at his *fiancée's funeral*?"

"We knew he'd be there."

"*Bullshit.* You knew every eye would be on you and it would make all the papers and make you look good."

"Your lawyers will get him out. What does it matter?"

"Perception! That's what matters. The accusation is everything. No one will care when you let him go or that his alibi *checked* out. Past tense. You already knew that about his alibi."

Now Mickey leans forward in his seat as if smelling a meal he's been cooking. "My issue is about what *you* already knew. That Tank Adams's alibis check out too. That's the problem."

"What, there are two men in the whole world? If it's not one, it has to be the other? Come on, I'm not a detective, but—"

"That's what I'm saying! You're not a detective, but your guys got to every alibi—"

"Because we're faster! Which is something I'm sure the good people of Los Angeles would love to know, that we're faster than the actual police—"

"Faster because you sent them to *Mexico*!"

"Now hold on, because, like I said, we've got two guys who are proven innocent by way of their alibis—*which means it's someone else.* But meanwhile you're chaining *my* star to a rumor he may never shake."

Mickey lines up some papers on his desk and punches his stapler. "When push comes to shove," he says, with another smack on the stapler, "it's about the public—not you. Even the studio works for the *public*. You think they don't? Their opinion is your paycheck. Their interest, their approval—that's what pays you, my friend. We're no different. Be furious if you want, but we *had* to do this, and you would've too."

"Sure." Nico nods. "Sure. I don't have to be understanding, but I am. And here's my offer: I give you this moment in the sun, so you can satisfy your public's thirst for blood, and we say that Jack's here cooperating and helping. All right? Give him books, give him clean sheets, make his stay better than the lousy motels I'm sure you've frequented, and maybe my temper settles. But that's not it. Because here's what's key: I need you to hold off on releasing the bit about Tank Adams and his alibis, just for now. *And*, to undo this spectacle you made today, I'm suggesting you bring Tank in while you figure it all out."

Mickey blinks. "Bring in the man whose alibis checked out?"

"Like you did Jack, whose alibi checked out."

"Nico."

"A day, two. Even things out. Take some of the spotlight off my guy. That's all I'm asking. In the past we've had words with Tank Adams, and he knows it's best to keep us happy, so I'm thinking he'll remember that. After the performance you put on today, you owe me this. Then maybe we forgive everything."

Mickey sighs. "I've got no cause, Nico. I want to—"

"No cause? You keep looking into it like we did, and you might see that one of those professors from the school has a bit of a card problem and owes Tank a bit of dough. That's already one alibi you should question. It's looking like another card player is Tank's relative. Bet you didn't know that, did you? You want me to keep going? Because I also noticed some cruisers out there that could be a bit rusted."

Mickey raises an eyebrow. At last, he nods. "A day, two at the most."

"That's all I'm asking. Jack goes home, Tank goes home."

Then, kinder, Mickey says, "You want to see him? We'll put you in a room without eyes or ears. You can talk privately."

~

Jack sits at a long table, still wearing the black suit he wore to the funeral. For all intents and purposes, it appears as though he's just visiting, perhaps doing research for a role. But the look on his face belies the truth.

"As much wrong as I've done in my life," he says when he sees Nico and Frankie, "I always kept myself out of jail."

Nico pauses to be sure no one's lingering in the hall, and shuts the door. "Mickey only did this to prove a point."

"Point proven."

"Was that true," Frankie says to Nico, "about one of the alibis being Tank's relative?"

Nico shrugs. "Could be. I thought they looked alike."

Jack leans back in his chair. "I'm over. You know that right? Even out of here, I might have my freedom, but I won't have a career. Not anymore."

Frankie tries to be calm, and takes a seat. "You haven't been charged. You're just being held—"

Bang. The noise is so loud that Frankie jumps and her heart goes wild before her mind latches on to what Nico is saying: "Jail door. It was a jail door."

Jack is up and backed against the wall. "That noise," he says angrily. "Fifty times a day here."

"Not much longer," Nico says. "You'll be out and we'll fix this."

"*There's no fixing this.* No one cares if I'm innocent. They just want the story, and *I'm* the story. Doesn't get better than this."

"*Now* you are," Nico says. "Yes. But something bigger and brighter always comes along, and people forget." Then he narrows his eyes. "You're still in your suit. I sent regular clothes. Give me a second."

The moment the door closes and Nico's gone, Jack takes a seat, leaning in across the table. "No one can hear us, right?"

"Right."

"Frankie, what happened in the alley?"

It takes her a second. "The alley at your house?"

"I need to know what happened."

"I told you—"

"No," he says, his voice turning into a furious whisper. "*I had a gun.* And I don't remember what happened."

She glances at the door, then makes a decision. "There was a noise. You thought it was press or a trophy hunter, I don't know. But you wanted to scare them. That was it."

He waits, and when she doesn't continue, he leans forward. "What happened next? *Tell me.*"

Finally, resigned, she says, "A woman and her child were looking for food."

In an instant, grief and repulsion cave his features.

Quickly, she says, "You didn't hurt them. They were fine. Scared, but that was all. I didn't tell you *because* they were fine and I didn't want to worry you."

"Do you see? *This* is why I need to know what happened with June. Because of what I did and don't remember. The fact that that's *possible.* And what if it were *you*? What if I did that with you?"

"You didn't. You *wouldn't.* And you didn't do anything in the alley or with June—"

"Until I know for sure"—he stops, glancing around the room as if trying to verify once more that no one is listening in—"my career is the *least* of my worries."

"You didn't do this."

"Then we need to prove that." He motions to the rest of the station. "What are they doing other than trying to cover their own asses? *They brought me in because the public made them.* They're doing what they need to for appearances—until the door closes and their allegiance shifts to the studio. They don't care. Please. I don't know what I did to make you mad—"

"You gave Milton Ewing my life."

She's said it without thinking, and watches the confusion on his face.

"What?"

"My life, Jack. My mother. All the details of where we lived. The morning glories."

He sits back, thrown. "You didn't like it?"

Incredulous, she says, "Didn't like a story about a poor girl who ends up with a rich man?"

"And saves him. She *saves* him."

Frankie says nothing, unsure.

"You didn't read it."

"I *saw* it. Everything I told you was right there, for everyone to laugh at. What I told you in confidence about the person who meant more to me than anything in the world."

Slowly, he nods. Understanding. Accepting. "It was a tribute. To you. Something only we'd recognize. No one knows where it came from or what it means."

"*I* know what it means. And I know where it came from, because I told *you*, and that's it, my whole life."

"Frankie, I'm sorry. I'm sorry a million times over, but I'm in jail at the moment—"

"*You are not.* This is for appearances. They're not going to touch you. This isn't real."

He narrows his eyes. "It sure feels real."

The week she spent in jail after taking the Hawthornes' car, that was real. Strangely, it was Catherine Hawthorne who convinced the judge that the time was punishment enough. Still, it was the longest week of her life. "You're being held in a break room, with a couch."

For a moment he says nothing. Then he relents. "All right." The chair creaks as he leans back. "But I can't live not knowing."

I can't live not knowing. Strangely, it's his fear over what he might have done that seems to seal it for her. "Maybe I have more faith in you than you have in yourself, but I *know* you didn't do this."

As if her words have made it worse, he looks to the wall, unable to meet her eyes. "I heard from someone else that June and Ida were fighting."

She's barely spoken to me recently, Ida said. *I think she knows.*

A knock, right as Nico pushes open the door. "You're getting other clothes."

"June and Ida were fighting at the premiere," Frankie says to him. "Ida said that June was barely speaking to her—"

"Not this again."

"Then Ida said *I think she knows.* Knows *what*? What if whatever she was talking about has to do with why June was shot?" She feels Jack watching her. "We need to tell Mickey."

Nico shakes his head. "It's not worth telling him."

Now Jack is up, pacing. "*Not worth telling him?* What if it has to do with whoever the father was or an affair or—was Ida stealing? Ida always seemed out for herself. And she's the sole beneficiary! The only one in June's will, the—" But then Jack stops talking, eyes steady on Nico. "You *know* what Ida was referring to. I can see it. You know exactly what it is that June found out. I'm in here, and you know something you're not saying."

Nico gives a sigh. "We'd been enlisting Ida's help. *We*, meaning the studio. That's all."

"Help with what?" Frankie asks.

"Keeping June in line."

Frankie watches Nico. "No. We already knew that. There's something more."

Exasperated, Nico shakes his head. "The *something more* was that we didn't just ask for her help, we were writing out checks for that help. To Ida."

It takes Frankie a second. *Lucky we've got Ida on our side, because just this morning June's telling me she can be a single mother and maybe she's done acting.* June, who always sought her older sister's approval. "You were paying Ida to make June do what you wanted."

"Nobody could make June do anything."

Frankie feels sick. "June listened to Ida. And you were worried because June was talking about having her baby without getting married and maybe quitting acting—"

"Jesus." Jack takes a seat and leans over, his elbows on his knees.

"Ida was helping," Nico says. "Helping June not make rash decisions. Helping her think things through, because I'm telling you, June wasn't herself. She stopped caring. About roles, about schedules, appearances, whether the public likes her or not. This was one of those times when she needed someone to talk *sense* into her before she threw it all away."

Now Jack looks up. "She finally got her priorities straight, and wanted to live her own life, and you put a stop to that. You had no right."

"I had *every* right! My job is to take care of you. Both of you. All of you. I'm not going to sit back and watch her destroy herself—the pills, the drinking, the decision to throw it all away. She wasn't going to listen to me, so I found someone she *would* listen to. It's that simple. How is that bad?"

"You bought her sister," Jack says, furious. "Which makes me wonder: What else did you buy?"

With that, his eyes shift to Frankie.

Frankie's breath lodges in her throat. Just barely, she registers Nico's observation, the way he takes both of them in.

Then Jack nods as if agreeing with something in his mind, and stands. "It's amazing, what you can justify. What you refuse to see."

"Nico, can you give us a minute?" Frankie asks, for once not caring, not giving a damn that her boss knows there's something between her and Jack, because she needs to explain. She needs to make Jack understand that, yes, the studio's done things they shouldn't have, and now she's seeing through those justifications and realizing that there was so much that was wrong—but *never* was she paid to be with him. That it was the opposite. Every time she was with him, she put her job at risk.

But Jack's heading toward the door. Without looking back, he knocks twice for the guard to come and get him.

"Don't bother, Frankie," he says. "I think we're done."

CHAPTER 22

Par for the Course

Thursday, March 9, 1933

I think we're done. As mad as she is at Jack for handing over the most private details of her life *for a script*, his fury over what the studio is capable of—and what he now thinks *she's* capable of—has put her on the defensive. And worse, it's made her question herself.

Every good they've done has come with a bad. Intertwined, the yin and the yang. They help their stars by invading their privacy. Boost a career or give someone much-needed rest and solitude by spreading lies and rumors. At times, Frankie's glimpsed that there's a nebulous, murky quality to what they do, but so far she's been able to justify their actions. Hiring Ida to portray the studio's agenda as her own, however, is beyond what Frankie can defend.

"Spare yourself and don't go into work," Nico tells her Thursday morning when he calls. An angry group is already outside the studio, calling for a boycott of any and all of the studio's films. "We'll work from my house today, let security figure out a way to clear them out."

But at Nico's house, his car is not there. She knocks on the door, wondering if she somehow heard his instructions wrong.

"He left to meet the big boss," Angela tells her. "When they beckon, you come. Give him about twenty minutes. And holler if you need coffee. I've got some percolating."

Inside Nico's office, there's dust on an oak table by the window, a full wastebasket by the door. She glances at the desk. Underneath is his safe. *It's amazing, what you can justify. What you refuse to see.* Is Jack right? Nico's said he keeps all the correspondence here, and with one move, she can verify that's the case and prove to Jack that at least everything Nico said in regard to Donna and Jack's life is true. Though it's not much, it would be a start.

The safe is bloodred with gold borders and a painting of a ship toward the top. Emergency money, files with sensitive information, a few photographs he doesn't want in the wrong hands; he's been open with what he keeps here as well as with the combination, which is his wedding anniversary. June 17, 1920. That's the day they married, and Frankie remembers this because he had an anniversary party when she first moved to California, and ever since she's helped him find restaurants to celebrate the occasion. But when she tries that combination, it doesn't work. She tries it again. Then once more, now leaving off the *19*. Nothing.

She sits back in his desk chair, confused.

And then she remembers him telling her about the safe combination: *You ever need to get in there, just ask Angela for our anniversary, and then let me know what it is, because I'm always a day off.*

Could he still have been a day off when he set the combination? She tries June 16, but the safe doesn't budge. Then she tries June 18, and the door swings open. A small laugh as she wonders whether Nico has any idea what his anniversary actually is.

Everything is organized. A large envelope with cash. Folders with different stars' names typed neatly on the front, letters and documents inside. Quickly, she flips open the one with Jack's name. Letters from Donna. Telegrams from Donna. Check receipts. Heart racing, Frankie reads everything—but it all confirms what she already knows, which is what Nico's told her. Nothing is out of place or alarming, and though she's relieved, she's not surprised; after all, he gave her the combination.

She's putting the file back when she sees June's folder. Listening for his car or for Angela, she flips through the contents. There are payment stubs to Ida, going back years. Then, below, another check stub for a staggering sum, paid out to someone whose name Frankie doesn't recognize. Below that, a copy of a police report that lists that same person, and an address on June's street. As fast as she can, Frankie scans the document, spotting Ida's name and the word *negligence*, but also *tragic accident* and *no indication of alcohol or drug use*. From what it looks like, the neighbor's two-year-old child drowned in the pool, almost a year before Frankie started working for Nico. Though he's told her he tries to keep some of their stars' secrets hidden, even from her, somehow this feels significant.

Because she is so engrossed in the report, she doesn't hear the footsteps till they're at the door.

She freezes, eyes on the door handle. Did she miss the sound of his car in the driveway? The front door opening?

But then, mercy. The steps continue, the sound disappearing down the hall. Frankie checks the driveway—empty. She has to do this fast.

On the other side of the folder is a letter, dated last year, from Tank to June, in which he professes his love and claims he can't live without her. How did Nico get it? *Keep everything,* he's told her. *You never know when something might come in handy.* She scans the letter, but though it's in line with Tank's obsession with June, it's not alarming. Then there's another note, underneath, in June's scribbled handwriting:

Nico, You always said to end strong, and know when to leave. I might not be ending strong, but I know it's time to leave.

Right behind that is another letter from Tank, begging June to stay. June needed Nico's help to get away from Tank, that much is clear.

And then, the sound of a car. Within seconds, she's got everything put back and is drawing the safe door shut, spinning it locked.

"Sorry about that," Nico says when he enters the room, tossing a stack of newspapers on his desk. "Jack was right. He's the story, and it doesn't get better than that."

Jack's face is on the cover of each paper. "They still have Tank?"

"Thankfully, yes. But every paper's got someone camped outside the station, and all they care about is that Jack's *still there*."

When they spoke yesterday, privately, about Nico's decision to hire Ida, it was brief. *Later,* he'd said. "Is now *later*?"

Nico sighs as if he expected this. "There's not much to say. June changed with the pregnancy. Hormones, maybe, I don't know, but she wasn't thinking straight. Even Ida knew she wasn't thinking straight."

"When did you start paying her?"

"Ages ago. Not to influence June, per se, but to be there and keep her safe and clean up her messes and be the angel on her shoulder. Basically, we paid Ida to babysit June."

"Her own sister."

"Who better? This was someone *with* June, who cared about her, who was already doing these things. Why not pay her so it's worth her time? Makes sense?"

And the worst thing is, it does make sense. "It doesn't matter what I think; June didn't think it made sense."

"*Of course* she didn't. You and I, we work in the background so our stars don't know the half of it. Then something like this happens, and they get up in arms. Par for the course. But we've got bigger problems." He picks up the newspaper on top of the stack and tosses it in her direction. "This is Magda. She's turned on us."

Frankie scans the article. Magda reports that Darlene Cleary is convinced Jack did it—more conjecture. "Again, it's hunches and rumors. There's no new information here. Nothing but Darlene's gut feeling."

"The point is *Magda's* reporting it. That's the problem. First Dottie, now Magda. We're losing them, and let me tell you, the powers that be at the studio are not happy. With us, or with Magda." He swivels in his chair, facing the window. "You know what? Get her on the phone for me."

Magda immediately knows she's in trouble. Frankie listens in as Nico castigates her, tossing out thinly veiled threats, accusing her of yellow journalism, that sensationalistic writing style that only serves to catch eyes rather than tell the truth. When he hangs up, he tells her that Magda has come to her senses and even gave him a heads-up on something so he could shut it down. "Size-twelve shoe prints on the neighbor's property," Nico says to Frankie. "This is the neighbor who never got around to building a house, the one with the empty lot and the stone wall. His wife told this to Magda. Size-twelve shoe prints in an area like someone was hiding out of sight but walking toward June's house. The husband wanted to stay out of it, but the wife plays bridge and has a big mouth."

"Jack's size twelve," Frankie says. "But you know that."

"I know that, and so does Magda, because Magda did a profile on him and even remembers what size tie he wears. So her penance, to us, is that she won't repeat that to anyone. Yet. *Yet,* she said."

"But the man with the stone wall doesn't even live there. How would he know about prints?"

"Claims he went over right away and saw them."

"That could be anyone. Cops, even."

"I know that, you know that, but that's not how it'll show up in the press. *Shoe Prints Matching Jack Sawyer's Found in Neighbor's Yard.* That's the headline."

"But if Jack was staying there, like Darlene claimed, then why would he be sneaking around in the neighbor's yard?"

"Doesn't matter. Magda's asking questions, and that should scare us." He pauses, running his hand through his hair. "It's not always *what* you're asking but the fact that you're asking it in the first place that's the problem. In Magda's mind, there's a chance Jack did it, or she wouldn't be pursuing any of this."

No one's trying to solve this. "Nico. The shoe prints *could* be from the person who did it. Maybe they *should* look into—"

"*Any* other size, I agree with you. An eleven, thirteen—but twelve? That opens a can of worms, and why? These prints have nothing to do with anything. If they were left in mud, there would've been mud at the scene, right? Do you remember mud? Even on the porch?"

"No."

"Right. So why stir things up for nothing? What it is, is someone looking for attention and excitement. But listen, you can't win if you don't play the game, so here's what I want you to do: Meet with Magda, tell her you think there *were* muddy prints at the scene, but the whole morning was a blur. Tell her to ask Mickey what size they found inside, if there were any. She won't be able to resist. And when she asks Mickey, he's gonna want to do me a favor, and he's gonna pick up the phone to report back that she's there, sniffing around. And I'll have that on her. It won't hurt to keep her occupied—and in my debt."

Lying to Magda in an attempt to throw her off Jack—Frankie owes that to Jack, but lies compounding lies has hurled them into such hazy territory that she no longer knows how to extricate right from wrong. "You just threatened Magda. She won't go against you."

"She will if you tell her I said she was just a tabloid writer. That'll do it. Trust me."

So Frankie does. She meets with Magda at a coffee shop in Hollywood. Ivy covers the white wood shingles on the exterior, and though there's a chill in the air, they sit at a table outside, alone.

"Thing is," Magda says, "if these prints were Jack's, if they match his shoes, that means he was there when it rained, when the ground was soft. Which means he wasn't in Malibu, as reported. Which means he was there while someone killed her."

Magda stops just short of suggesting that the someone could've been Jack. "My dad has size twelve shoes," Frankie lies. "So do countless men in Los Angeles. But the person who did this—these could be their prints, and *I* need to know about them." That last part is, at least, the truth.

"So not Jack."

"*Of course* not Jack. Jack wandering around the neighbor's property makes no sense. June would just let him in. He wouldn't need to hide or break in. Why would he do that?"

"To throw people off? Or not be seen?"

"So he throws people off with his *own* shoe prints? Here's what I'm thinking. If the shoe prints had *anything* to do with June, there should've been mud inside or on the porch." Now she leans in. "I'm only telling you this because I want this person caught. That morning, I think I was in shock, but I heard one of the cops making a note about mud. At least I think I did. Which now makes sense, with the shoe prints in the mud next door."

Magda glances behind her, then back at Frankie. "You heard that?"

Frankie watches her write down the word *porch* on her steno pad just as a truck rumbles past, loud, like a clap of thunder. "Don't quote me on it because I'm not certain, but I'm certain enough to want to look into it. But I can't. For obvious reasons."

Magda closes her notepad, lips pursed as if considering Frankie's words. "Nico told me to leave the investigation to the professionals."

"Well, he thinks you're just a tabloid writer."

Now Magda looks up sharply, and Frankie stands to gather her things, both relieved and unnerved that it went exactly as Nico planned.

CHAPTER 23

Loud Enough to Wake the Dead

A sign outside the corner market informs people they can extend their credit, and a line of people creeps along the block. On the other side of the street, bougainvillea climbs up and off a stone wall, blaring against a darkening sky, and a woman reaches to catch her hat when it lifts in a breeze.

It's futile to think of what she might have done differently, but Frankie's mind revisits certain spots, like a tooth that draws your attention because it hurts. The night with the gun and the woman and child in the alley, what would've happened if she'd told the truth? If her priority had been *Jack*, and not just appearances? Giving him the ugly truth about his behavior would've meant he'd most likely have been sober the night of the premiere, and maybe nowhere near June or this mess.

It's early evening when she arrives at the bungalows to explore the vacant lot. The air is crisp, and there is the scent of crushed leaves and overturned earth. She's looking for prints when the barking begins next door. In seconds the dog's snout is straining against the space between the fence's slats.

"I recognize you," a voice says. Darlene, the neighbor. She's trying to silence her dog and see what Frankie's doing at the same time. "We've had some rubberneckers over there, but they're mostly at the windows. Looking for what, I don't know."

Saliva drips from the dog's mouth. "I was trying to find shoe prints."

"Louise Foster and her big mouth. I play bridge too. I was there when she blabbed to that tabloid reporter. Hold on, let me get this dog out of here."

Waiting, Frankie studies the ground. If there were prints near the wall, they're long gone. The ground is clean, raked of leaves, the soil smooth and undisturbed.

When she returns, Darlene says, "Cliff Foster never went anywhere near the property the next day. He and Louise were in San Diego. They came three days later, and by that time, people had been crawling all over everywhere."

"He just made it up?"

"You work in Hollywood. You're shocked by a lie?"

A reaction she's used to. She's found people either love Hollywood and are curious about it, or hate it and are somehow resentful of it. *It's like people think we're cheating by having stars that look flawless and glamorous and are rich and loved,* Nico once said, and Frankie resisted the urge to remind him that, yes, it was cheating in some regard. "But who'd want that kind of attention? Why would you want people to think that a killer was on your property?"

Darlene laughs. "Why would someone who'd been trying to unload a property because he can't afford to build a house want free press? People are obsessed with this murder. They've been driving by and calling him to ask about price and parcel size, and I actually think he's even got someone interested."

"And what about you? Your claim that Jack was there that night. That's not for attention?"

Now Darlene straightens, clearly offended. "He *was* there. I heard it when someone walked to that back bungalow after midnight. Probably more like one a.m., actually. I know he was there."

Or just after one a.m., Frankie thinks. She remembers the dog barking when Jack hit the midway part of the path, just past June's bungalow. "Darlene, if your dog was barking, that means the person was already *past* June's house. Why would Jack go past his own fiancée's house?"

Though Darlene doesn't say anything, Frankie catches her looking toward the bungalows as if searching for an explanation.

Off her silence, Frankie continues. "What that says to me is it could've been *anyone*. You didn't get up to look, right?"

"Moving around wakes me up. I'm a troubled sleeper. But I got up when I heard the bang hours later because I was mad—I thought someone was shooting at my house again. The weather vane, I told you about that."

Something occurs to Frankie. "And you heard barking in the morning."

"Right. When he must've gone back to her bungalow so he could *pretend* to discover the body. I saw him, you know. Inside the house, in his tux. Covered in blood."

"I did too. Because he tried to *save* her," Frankie says, irritated. "You think someone finds their fiancée shot and doesn't touch her? Of course he had blood on him. But this is what *I* want to know: Did you, or a husband maybe, did anyone let the dog inside after the person walked down the path around one a.m.? After the barking woke you up?"

Darlene laughs, confused. "Now it's about my dog?"

Frankie says nothing, and Darlene finally continues.

"An indoor dog is not a guard dog. No, if he's bothersome, like now, we tie him up to the tree up there. But my husband could sleep through a bomb. *I'm* the one who wakes up and has a hard time going back to bed. So no, *I* stayed in bed so I didn't wake up even more. And the dog stayed outside."

"But hours later, it was the gunshot that woke you up—*not* more barking? Even though the dog was outside?"

There is silence as Darlene must be piecing this together.

Frankie keeps going. "That tells me that whomever you heard walking toward Arlington Way around one a.m.—"

"Or not all the way to Arlington Way, but to the second bungalow."

"Fine, *if* what you heard was someone walking to the second bungalow around one a.m., then they'd also have to walk *back* to June's bungalow to kill her, and that would've started your dog barking all over again. Right? But you didn't hear that. There was silence, and then a gunshot." Frankie pauses, waiting for protest, but Darlene says nothing. "So *no one* walked on the path by the second bungalow, immediately before or after the shot."

Which, she thinks, means that Jack stayed put in his bungalow the rest of the night. It's not definitive, but it's something, and though she knew in her heart Jack didn't do it, the relief she feels is still immense, like someone who didn't realize they were hot until they felt the shade. Her instinct is to find a phone and tell Jack, but then she remembers she can't.

Darlene shakes her head. "No, a person definitely went that way after the shot. I *saw* it. I got up after the bang, and I saw it."

"But then *he must have turned around*, or your dog would've had a fit."

Now Darlene sighs. "I don't know. Maybe."

"You were tired. Who knows what you saw."

"I was awake enough to get up and see what I saw and then make the phone call and—"

"Wait." Frankie stops. "You said you didn't call the police."

"I didn't. Remember, Mr. Marconi told me not to. He said not to bother them, that he'd take care of things. So I called *Mr. Marconi* when I heard the shot."

It feels as though something's lodged in her throat.

"I told you this," Darlene continues. "He gave me his card and his personal number so that he could handle any party or star that got out of hand. That's what I thought it was. Someone drunk."

Almost in a whisper, Frankie asks, "And what did he say?"

"He didn't. It rang and rang."

It rang and rang. The phone in Nico's house that's loud enough to wake the dead, as his wife says. How late did Nico stay at the party? He never said specifically when he left. All he said was he was at the party late enough that he couldn't claim to have been in Malibu.

"You'll be all right in this dark?" Darlene asks.

It's only now that Frankie looks behind her. At some point, the sun went down, the trees black against the sky.

CHAPTER 24

People in the Know

Later that evening, Frankie sits at the kitchen table with a bowl of tomato soup and saltine crackers on a plate. Steam has already tapered off and disappeared; the soup must be cool, but she just moves the spoon around, not hungry.

A door slams; her roommates are home. Virginia heads straight to a bottle of wine that she got from a friend, who got it from a friend. "So if it was another man," she says, "then she *wasn't* in love with Jack?"

Frankie looks up. "Another man?"

Susan takes two juice cups off the drying rack. "You didn't hear? It got back to my boss. *June didn't love Jack, and he knew it.*" She turns to Virginia. "You're exactly right, it's *just* like their movie. Jack killed her because he couldn't have her. Because he couldn't live with someone else having her."

Frankie lets go of her spoon. "*That's* what people are saying?"

Susan nods. "People in the know."

"But then where's the necklace?" Virginia asks.

"Exactly," Susan says. "Where's the necklace? They searched Jack's house."

"They searched his house?" Frankie's question comes out too loud, and both turn to her, surprised. "When?"

"It was on the radio," Susan says, pouring the wine. "Out of all of us, *you're* the one who should know this."

Virginia takes her glass, and grimaces with a sip. "To think, I broke up with Fred because of Jack, but he might have actually *killed* her. At least Fred wouldn't do *that*."

Frankie's losing patience. "First, Jack didn't kill her. Second, what do you mean you broke up *because* of Jack?"

Virginia shrugs. "I'm partially kidding. But I suppose when I looked at them, I saw a whole lot of what I was missing."

"Is this regret I'm hearing?" Susan asks.

"I'm back and forth."

Frankie pushes her soup bowl away. "What changed? Him being friends with Jack Sawyer?"

She's said it before thinking. The kitchen goes quiet, and Susan suddenly takes interest in a speck of something on the counter.

At last, Virginia says evenly, "I'm *angry* about that. It hasn't made me change my mind, it's made me more mad. Fred could've told me that's who he was with on certain nights, and I would've kept it to myself, but he didn't trust me. So no, Frankie, that's actually made it worse."

Frankie starts to apologize, but Virginia won't let her.

"I know my relationship wasn't perfect, I know that. And sure, I might've ended it regardless, but it didn't help comparing it to what looked like the greatest love story ever. When you think that's even *possible*, it's hard to be happy with what you have."

Frankie, of course, knows that Fred was never out with Jack on the nights in question. "Maybe the lie did you a favor."

"Frankie," Susan says, shocked. "What's gotten into you?"

But Virginia doesn't let her answer. "Fred made me laugh and was my best friend and would've given me a very nice life. Maybe you think I was settling because of whatever *you* think is important, and maybe I'm wrong or weak or stupid—"

"No, I *never* said that."

"But the way I see it is people look up and see a big, grand story, and all it does is make them question their own lives. How does it help if I spend my whole life thinking I could've had it better, because of a lie? Because I believed in some"—her hand flutters in the air as she searches for the word—"impossible perfection? And what if I decide to leave something that was actually pretty good because of a lie? My relationship *might've* actually been pretty good if I gave it a chance, if I wasn't comparing it to a lie."

Frankie breaks a cracker in half, salt gritty on her fingertips.

"The question is," Susan says, swirling the wine in her glass, "what he did with the necklace. Jack doesn't need the money."

Now Frankie stands up, wiping her hand on her leg. "Jack didn't kill June because Jack didn't kill June. End of sentence."

When neither roommate says anything, Frankie sets her bowl in the sink. Tomorrow she'll return to the bungalows. Maybe she missed something. If the person who killed June didn't take the back path toward Arlington Way, then they left via Glenhollow. At this point she needs to find anything she can, because the damage to Jack's reputation is snowballing.

Ducking into her bedroom, she shuts the door. Her roommates' silence in the other room tells her they're whispering. Worried about her, most likely. Wondering why she'd take an accusation against Jack so personally before chalking it up to their usual complaint that she takes her job too seriously.

Lined up against the wall are five sad boxes, all the possessions Frankie has in the world. Her whole life amounts to boxes that barely get in the way. She stares at them. There's so much she doesn't have—dishes, a phone, even.

A phone.

It's possible Nico just didn't tell her that Darlene called him. Like he didn't tell her about the Jack-and-Donna situation until much later. An omission is not the same as a lie, but the worry that he's hiding something has settled beneath her skin like a splinter. Tomorrow, she'll find a way to ask him about it.

Lying down, she draws her quilt around her, the lights still on. In less than a week, she'll have her little house, the independence and the privacy and silence she's always dreamed of. The thought, though, leaves her apprehensive—not excited. She never told Jack about the house, because she didn't want him to think she was going along with enforcing the studio's wishes *in exchange* for the house, and now she wonders if, in fact, that's what she did. Somewhere along the line, she lost her conviction that what she's done was right. Or that *why* she did it was right.

Her roommates' voices peal in laughter, and even though she's not in the room with them, there is comfort from their presence. Suddenly Frankie doesn't want to leave, doesn't know how she'll sleep when there are too many noises in the night and a killer who walks the streets and blends in and could be anyone. Why did she think being alone was the goal? Was it simply that the noise of her childhood taught her to dream of silence?

Maybe she can stay. Tell Nico that since June's death, she no longer wants to live alone. But then she remembers Virginia telling Susan about someone who won a "caption this" contest for Coca-Cola—a competition to see who could come up with the best caption to go along with an image of a man pretending to toast the Empire State Building with a soda. *Being creative is great, sure, but let's hope she's got enough muscle to clean the kitchen sink*, Susan replied, *because I have a recollection that it used to be white.* The "caption this" winner—that must be the new secretary the studio's arranged to move in. Just like that, Frankie will be replaced, something she brought on herself.

It's too much. Jack is in custody as a murder suspect, and something is off with Nico—the two people she trusts most in life. She has no one she can talk to about any of this, and she's somehow alienating her roommates, who are her closest friends. She eyes the boxes against the wall. All this time, she's thought that the goal was to work hard in order to not need anyone, but never once did she consider what it would mean to be truly alone.

CHAPTER 25

A World That Won't Stand Still

Friday, March 10, 1933

Early morning is when the studio and all its facades feel real. There are no yelling directors or frantic script supervisors, no makeup artists chasing after actors, no producers in fancy cars, no one at all to interject reality into this world of pretend. Empty, the lot is acres and acres of magical playground, the perfect setting for an imagination to run wild. *Anything that can be built can be believed,* Nico used to tell her.

It's not often that Frankie arrives before Betty, but today she's determined to be the first in the office. Outside the gates, security's cleared a wide area so protesters can't set up, and in front of their building, a man sweeps the sidewalk, pausing to let Frankie pass, then pulling on the brim of his hat in a greeting. Another man washes windows, old newspapers stacked at his feet. Somewhere in the trees, a bird calls, the sound like Romeo and Juliet, and Frankie wonders whether it could be the parrot Betty claimed she saw.

Right as she opens the door, she spots a poster of Jack and June on a wall, one of the ads for *Desert Son*. Beside it is an even larger image of Dede Domenico, the poster three times the size of Jack and June's. Dede. Fifteen years old. Innocent enough to want to fly through the world on roller skates, and young enough to not be afraid. Once Frankie found the girl in the prop house playing a Steinway with a sword hanging from her belt. To be a kid and have access to this world would be amazing. But how much longer will Dede have that innocence? Maybe it's gone already. Frankie sees Dede in her skintight dress at the premiere, teetering into a new world, dressed to the nines while sipping on a kid's drink.

Inside the office, Frankie opens Romeo and Juliet's curtain. The birds eye her and stretch their wings, neck feathers ruffling. She's riffling through messages at her desk when Betty arrives, spots Frankie and stops short, then gives the birds a dirty look. On cue, they start their chatter. Slowly other people trickle in. Frankie keeps an eye on the office door till she sees Nico enter, and then barges into his office, closing the door behind her.

"We have a problem," she says.

Nico's still hanging up his coat. "I figured we did when Betty called to tell me you were here before she was. Also, before I forget, Angela hates our couch, so it's yours if you want it. Which means she gets to buy a new one."

"Great, all right. I'll take it. But there's a rumor that June was in love with someone else and Jack killed her because he couldn't have her, like in *The Last Chance*."

For a second he says nothing, and then he breaks into a laugh. "You've got to be kidding."

"It's too ridiculous for me to make up."

"So, he was inspired by his own role? Should we see if June left a Christmas present somewhere that implicates him, like her character did with Charles?"

"People are convinced it was him." She watches him sit at his desk and swivel his chair as he flips through messages. She needs to bring up Darlene and the phone call. The words are there, weighing on her chest. At last: "Darlene said she called you. After the gunshot."

He nods. "That's what she says, but my phone never rang. And you know that thing rings loud. Next time you see her, ask her what number she called, because I asked Angela, and she heard nothing. I was hoping she *did* hear it, because at least that would give us the time it happened. And you know Angela wakes up if the neighbor sneezes. It was late, though—mistakes happen."

Frankie considers this. "And your number's not listed."

"Right. I don't get people calling me at all times, but it does have its downside."

She hadn't thought of it being a mistake. But late at night, it's conceivable.

Nico indicates a message on his desk. "*Neighbor says she's no longer sure what direction the man went in after the shot.* Guessing that had to do with you, since it sounds like you spoke to Darlene?" She nods. "Good work. That helps. A little kink in the *Jack shot her and hid in bungalow two till the morning* theory."

Frankie looks out the window, at a man who's pulling a dolly with a tree on it.

"But here's the real good news," Nico continues. "He's getting out today."

She knows Nico's essentially thrown flowers at bees and distracted her with something good, but she doesn't care. Jack is getting out. "He is?"

"I was on the phone with Mickey till late. Fred's sticking to his word." He laughs. "You might want to tell your roommate to reconsider the breakup—with what we owe him, he'll be running the studio soon. But Tank's getting out too—right about now, unfortunately. I'm not too happy that he's out before Jack, but not much I can do."

"Jack didn't leave his bungalow that night. I wanted you to know. The dog didn't bark. Darlene's dog, the one that makes all the noise? It didn't wake her up before the shot. If someone came from the second bungalow and walked past his fence, that dog would've had a fit and she would've been awake before the shot, not because of it."

Nico nods, his attention back to his messages. "Good. From here on out, though, let's steer clear and let the police do their job."

"Are they, though?"

But he just stares at a message in his hand. Then he shakes the note. "This has to do with you. My friend in records. Looks like he learned something about your birth certificate."

"I had one?"

"Says right here he found an original."

"And it would list my parents' names?"

"At least your biological mother's, I would think."

She feels as though she's been caught with empty pockets, staring at a pie case, and tries to put any eagerness she feels into perspective. "They aren't family. After what they did, there's no way they'd be family. But I don't need that. This is just for me to fill in the blanks and get answers. Don't worry."

He smiles. "Well, *now* I'm worried. And I'm hoping it's only me you're lying to. Because it might not work out, that's true. And it might just be more hurt. But I can't imagine living in a world where there's nothing—or no one—worth wanting."

~

When Betty pulls down the shade to block the late-afternoon light, Frankie makes up an errand so she can leave. All day her mind has circled back to her birth family, drawn to what feels like an off-limits topic. What she's always told herself is that she wants answers. That's it. Not another family, not another chance. Just answers as to why they'd give her up at age five. But is Nico right? Has she been lying to herself?

When she gathers her bag, Romeo and Juliet turn their heads, watching. Waiting. "All right, all right," she says, and finds a carrot that she breaks in two. She's just given them the pieces when the phone at her desk rings.

"Is this Frankie?"

A man. A voice she doesn't know. He doesn't give her a chance to respond.

"Don't hang up. This is Tank."

Her eyes widen. She's never spoken to him directly. She angles herself so Betty can't see her face. "Why are you calling me?"

Through the phone, she hears Tank take a sip of a drink. Ice cubes rattle and chime. He just got out today, she remembers, and from the sound of it, he immediately found a bottle of booze.

When he speaks, his voice is deep and his words heavy, as if each is being dropped from a high place. "She said she liked you." Silence as the words land. "Maybe *you'll* tell me. Because *he* said she didn't love me."

There is distress in his voice. A loose sort of agony.

In a whisper, she says, "Tell you what? That she loved you?"

"You hate me too. I hear it. Don't blame you. I messed up."

Now her heart races. *I messed up.* This is the unhinged man people warned her about. "What did you do?"

There's fumbling as if he's dropped the phone. Then: "She loved me, right?"

Plaintive. Desperate.

"I've stayed quiet," he continues. "I did my part. At least tell me."

Did my part.

Frankie doesn't know what to do. Most likely the operator's listening, so prodding him for more isn't safe. Best to hang up and let Nico handle things. And she's about to do this, but something stops her. Some feeling that he's on the verge. She settles on the truth. "I don't know how to help you."

But she must have said the wrong thing, because when he speaks, he's angry. Resigned. Someone told they'll never have what they want. "All right. If that's my lot in life, then all right."

Then he's gone.

"Who was that?" Betty asks casually.

For a bit, Frankie'd forgotten about her. Betty, who knows when to be quiet and is always listening. Will the operator say anything? Report back to Nico? "Someone who thinks they know me, asking for a favor."

Betty laughs, flipping through papers on her desk. "People sure come out of the woodwork when they hear you work in Hollywood, don't they?"

What did Tank agree to?

I did my part.

She glances at her watch. She needs to tell Nico about this, to see what he thinks. Right about now, he should be picking Jack up at the station. Jack, who will be free, but not free. He was right—the shadow of this accusation will follow him. Until someone else is convicted, it will always be Jack. And now, even though Tank's alibis have checked out, Frankie *knows* he had something to do with it, because what she heard wasn't just the voice of an unstable man but that of a man filled with remorse. A man who regrets something he did.

By the time she gets to the bungalows, early evening seeps in like a bruise, gray and purple. Lights turn on in living rooms, and shapes move through kitchen windows. Families readying for dinner. Frankie parks beneath a carob tree, and a diamond of faint sun spreads on the hood of her car. Again, her mind returns to her parents—the slim glimpse she's held on to of them—and she wonders if there's even a point in looking for them. What could possibly excuse their actions? What would it take to believe that their giving her up was for any reason beyond her own likability? Her own lovability?

Bungalow number one is dark, and the absence of light feels poignant, a reminder of an end. Inside, Frankie remembers the other glass for champagne. Was Jack right? Was June waiting for someone? Did the person not show up? Frankie stops walking in the hall, a chill on her shoulder.

Then, a noise outside the window. Heart racing, Frankie approaches the glass from the side so no one can see her right as a squirrel's tail lifts up only to shoot back down into the hedge below the window. She wants to laugh and cry. Her nerves are shot.

Standing in the middle of the main room, Frankie recreates the scene in her mind. June's bag was on the desk, she remembers. Her gun missing. The report came back indicating that she was killed by the same caliber bullet that her gun shot, and given that it's missing, it's assumed to be the murder weapon. Then Frankie thinks of Tank. Why would Tank want the woman he was obsessed with dead? Did someone tell Tank that June didn't love him, and did that send him over the edge? Was the fact of the child she was carrying too much for him, evidence that she'd moved on and no longer loved him? Betrayal in a physical, undeniable form. Reason enough to make him snap.

Looking around the room, Frankie lets it play out. Tank arrives, angry. June, feeling threatened, pulls the gun for self-defense—but he's big and strong, and in a step or two, he's there, yanking the gun away from her. A flash. White heat. And noise.

Actual noise.

There is actual noise. Not just in her mind but around her—loud and terrifying—and she wants to run from this noise, but she can't because it's fast and growing, and she bursts into the kitchen just as the shaking begins.

Earthquake. The word slips into her mind, useless.

She tries to get to the door, but her knees are buckling over and over, and with her arms out, she stumbles toward the wall. The sound should be impossible: the fury of the earth, the separation and pulverizing grind of land. The breaking of rocks and glass and streets and cities. Tectonic plates, angry and ancient and lurching. All of it comes together in a single sound that is like nothing she's ever known. And then she hears glass shattering nearby and sees the cupboards beside her swinging open and the ceramic plates rattling with such intensity that they appear blurred.

Ten seconds. That's the time frame that people will cite later, one that doesn't correspond to any second she's ever experienced. These are new seconds. Long and vicious.

Finally it stops, and there is nothing but silence. A pure, horrifying silence. No ticking. No humming. No cars. Just complete, shocked quiet.

Frankie stumbles outside, looking for someone, anyone. She needs to know the world still exists. Jack—that's who she wants, and thinking of him fills her with an anxious pain, because she doesn't know where he was when the quake hit, and she doesn't know if he's all right, and what if it was worse where he is? What if he was driving? Or is trapped? She knows he was released today, but when? Was it long enough ago that he was able to get home by the time the quake struck?

The fountain by June's back door is split, one half dropped on the brick path, algae exposed and the ground wet. A glance up—roof shingles are missing like teeth knocked loose. Behind her, bungalow two has a broken window. She turns. Bungalow one's chimney is gone.

Desperate to see other people, she starts to walk, heading toward the front, toward Glenhollow Street, but there are bricks on the path from the chimney. A look up reveals more on the roof, precarious and on the edge. One more bout of shaking could send them right onto her, so she turns, going back toward bungalow two and Arlington Way, but something catches her eye off to the right. Something else is wrong. An absence where usually there is not.

She blinks in the falling dark and tries to focus on the lush yard between the bungalows. At the far edge of the property is a hill. It's there that something is different. The stone retaining wall against the hill is broken, one spot gaping black. With a glance over her shoulder, she approaches, wary. Tall weeds scrape at her legs. Thistles stick to her pants. Closer, she sees that there is stone, but in one spot, the stone has fallen away. But no, what's fallen was *fake* stone that covered a door, painted to look just like the rest of the wall. Now the thin door hangs by a hinge, cracked and revealing a dark entrance to what looks like a cellar.

Another, smaller shaking. A flock of birds startles into the sky.

As fast as she can, she navigates the pile of bricks on the path and hurries to her car, swiping a small branch off the hood before getting the flashlight she always keeps inside. Up the block, a woman stands in the middle of the street, arms out as if to maintain balance. Frankie watches her a moment longer to make sure she's okay until a man approaches the woman and draws her to him. Then Frankie rushes back to where she found the hidden entrance.

Aiming the light into the dark, she sees old stone steps that lead down and under the hill. This isn't a cellar at all, she sees. It's a tunnel, with wood beams for support and dusty bottles near the entrance that spell out the purpose: This is one of the old bootlegging tunnels.

And then she understands. Someone could've exited June's back door and started walking toward bungalow two and Arlington Way, just as Darlene reported, but then veered off the path and come here. And doing that, leaving the brick path before reaching the border of Darlene's property, means her dog wouldn't have had a fit. This tunnel is how someone could kill June and disappear.

She needs to see where it leads. If it leads to a road, that could be where the killer either left his car or escaped to. But the tunnel is pure dark. Unknown and terrifying. Are the walls sturdy? Or would one more shake be too much? No one would know where to look for her. She'd be buried in the earth.

With a deep breath, she steadies the light, takes a few steps inside, and is hit with cold, dank air. All she can see is what the flashlight's beam illuminates. Rough-hewn stone. Chiseled rock. A turn, and there are spiderwebs and an old wooden crate. Dark-green wine bottles on their sides, uncorked. She keeps walking, praying to make it to the other side without another bout of shaking.

When she finally gets to the end, there's a closed wooden door without a handle. Panic is closing in. There has to be a way out. There has to be. Frantically, she pats down the door, feeling for any way to get leverage enough to pull. But there's nothing. Suddenly, the stories Jack told of the trenches in the war return to her. Belowground mazes that were hell itself: rats and disease and decomposing bodies, ceilings and walls that caved in, trapping people in a suffocating soup of horror. Her heart rate soars, and her breaths come up shorter. Frantic, she hurls herself at the door—once, twice, the third time, the flashlight blinks off, and there is a moment of pure dark before a blast of evening light. She wants to laugh and cry—the door just needed a hard push.

After such dark, even the fading light hurts her eyes. Then she thinks of Jack. If she experienced what she did from only his secondhand memories, what might he be going through?

Having passed through the hill, she's now at the base of another retaining wall, this one made of old railroad ties that disguise the door from the outside. To the right, there are only trees. But to the left, there's a house, all the windows dark, save for one on the first floor with a bright lantern on a table. At the side of the house, a man closes a gate. When he sees her, he approaches, concerned. "You all right there?"

"I'm fine. Just didn't know where this ended up."

"You're on Washburn."

She looks around, trying to get her bearings. "Right."

"All good with that earthquake?"

"Good as can be."

"Are you with that man? I don't see his car."

Now she turns to him. He's wearing brown suspenders and a light-blue button-down shirt, his brown tweed hat on at an angle. Even as she asks the question, she knows the answer. "What car?"

"Don't know what you call it, but it's orange and black. Fancy. He's the only one I ever see use that tunnel. Claims the parking on this street is better. My wife and I won't go near that thing."

Nico's Bugatti. *If you value your paint job,* she hears Nico say, *don't park on Glenhollow. But if you value your life and time, don't even think about Arlington Way, because that was made for horses.* She didn't realize there was a third option.

"I'm with him, but he's not here now." And then, a feeling. "When did you last see him?"

"Oh, I wouldn't know. Been a while."

The premiere was nine days ago. Nico knowing about this tunnel and using it to help keep his prized car safe is one thing, but add in

Darlene's assertion that she called him the night of the murder and his claim that his phone never rang, and it feels like there's something at her back, something she doesn't want to turn around to see. "It's been a while, like, months?" She hears the hope in her voice.

"Maybe. I don't spend all my time looking out the window." He laughs, then turns serious. "Why, he do something?"

"No," she says, too firmly. In her mind, she hears Nico's excuses about Darlene's call. "We just couldn't remember when he was last this way." In one last effort, she adds, leadingly, "He thought it might've been a couple weeks ago. Or a week and a half."

The man shrugs. "Can't help you. But listen, I've got a nervous wife I gotta get back to. Maybe you should take the streets, though. That tunnel looks anything but safe, and seems this world is ready to be done with us."

Frankie thanks him and watches him disappear inside the house. She glances back at the tunnel. Though he's right, and she has no business going through a possibly unstable tunnel right now, she also has no idea how to get back to her car if she takes the streets. While she's sure she could find her way, the tunnel is the straight shot.

Taking a deep breath, she pushes the door open, turns on her light, and almost walks smack into a spiderweb she somehow managed to avoid before. She studies the strands, trying to see where they go so she doesn't walk into them. Carefully, she ducks, training the beam of light on the path before her, afraid to shine it anywhere else for fear of what might lurk in the dark.

Suddenly she stops walking. Dust sifts through the light.

Looping in others helps sell a story.

Nico told Frankie he asked Angela if the phone rang. He said there were too many people who saw him late at the party for him to have posed as Jack's alibi. Was that on purpose, so Frankie would hear the mention of others and not question the story?

She makes herself keep going, glass crunching under her shoes. *Imagine loving someone so much that you can't let anyone else have them.*

You'd rather they be dead than with someone else. Her roommate's words about Jack and June's movie.

Nico loved June. But was he *in love* with June?

Tank was obsessed with June, but Nico was the one who used this tunnel. Unless he told Tank about it as well. But why? Was Nico a part of Tank killing June? It makes no sense.

And then, for one second, an idea flashes: *Nico paid Tank to kill June, to bump the studio's ticket sales.*

It's so ridiculous, so far-fetched, that Frankie stops walking and actually laughs in the tunnel. The rock walls immediately swallow the sound, the world stifling. Nico wouldn't hurt June, ever. And besides, she also knows he would turn on Tank in a heartbeat to save Jack. Callous and vile, but that's the truth. He would never lose two stars.

No, the simple explanation is that what Tank regretted was his trouble with the law, because that's what led to him losing June. And at the studio's urging, he's keeping quiet about what they once shared.

Almost toward the end of the tunnel, the temperature seems to dip. There's a chill like a breeze, though, of course, there can't be one, not inside like this. Frankie rubs her arms as she keeps walking, and is mere feet from the closed exit door when there is that noise again—the rumble and shake of anything and everything.

Panic. She scrambles, arms out, the flashlight's beam jumping and faltering, and for a second she is lost in a shuddering black tunnel that could be collapsing. Her hand scrapes the wall. Her breath comes up short. When the shaking stops, she stumbles to the door and pushes it open. Light is a smack of relief.

Outside, she stands in the weeds, trying to catch her breath, worn out from worrying that the person she most trusted might have lied, and exhausted from trying to make sense of a world that won't stand still.

CHAPTER 26

Something Nice About a Disaster

Night falls fast, and no one wants to be alone. Groups gather on sidewalks, weary eyes taking in collapsed roofs and buildings left in heaps. At one corner, a little girl sits cross-legged on a steamer trunk, her dog in her lap. To her left, a long balcony's crushed three cars, and a man stands in the street, staring at the remains, a ring of keys hanging from his hand.

There is no electricity. Streets are dark, windows black. Entire blocks look abandoned, but now and then there is the orange glow of bonfires and clusters of people gathered around the light, afraid to be inside or alone. Above, the moon and stars form a velvet bowl pinpricked with ancient light. Without the competition of the city lights, the stars are center stage at last, and it feels like something blooming, as if this whole time, the sky needed pure dark to grow and to radiate and to shine.

But below, it's different. A world of shadows, landmarks darkened. A thrumming hint of danger. She pulls onto a road she doesn't know, trying to get her bearings. There are only two people on the planet she wants to be with now, and neither is truly an option. Not now, not after Jack hurled his accusation, and not after her questions about Nico have spiraled. *It's not always what you're asking but the fact that you're asking it in the first place that's the problem.*

Never has she felt this alone. What she would do for her mother right now, or even just some proof that she still exists somehow, that all the love Frankie had for her and all the love Fiona gave remain somewhere, pulsing and beautiful despite this feeling of empty solitude. But there's nothing. Just distant sirens through the window and moonlight on the hood of her car. No voice comes to her. No magic or sign. No hope. How can a life, magnificent and monumental, just disappear?

She's crying when she pulls through a darkened intersection, the Pacific Electric Railway switches crisscrossing in the air above her. The only light comes from her headlights. Passing a shuttered bank, she barely makes out the shape of a man pacing outside.

Suddenly, a couple of kids are running alongside her car, trying to flag her down. She slows, pulling to the curb, but then glances at her side mirror in time to see two men step out from behind a broken wall. They're heading toward her, and they've got what look like pipes in their hands. She slams her foot down on the gas, screeching away from the kids and the men. Still, they follow. Quickly, she takes the next turn, and catches sight of the men in her mirror, running toward another car. That driver slows—either a saint or a victim.

Another few turns, and she's back on a familiar road, but it's congested. Car after car after car in a slow crawl. No matter, there's comfort in being with so many people, everyone trying to go anywhere that's not here—until she hears a noise. A chugging sound. Her car. Her eyes find the gas gauge. It's close to zero.

There is a gas station in the distance. Hoping to avoid the main thoroughfare, she pulls onto a different street, barely pausing at a stop sign. With one hand, she opens her coin purse but only finds thirty-five cents. Just enough, she thinks, remembering the shuttered bank. How much does she have at home? As long as she can get there, she should make it through the week. She thinks.

But up close, the station is dark. Not believing it, she pulls beside the one other car there. A man, the owner of the car, she presumes, stands at the teller's window, trying to see through the glass.

"No one's there?" Frankie calls to him. Her car's engine has started to falter.

The man turns to observe her. "No, ma'am. You should use whatever gas you have left to get someplace safe."

But then he must hear her car, must understand that she's out of gas, because he looks at his car and back at the line of traffic before deciding something. He motions to her to shut off her car, which she does—and that's when she realizes that he could do anything. No one would even notice. Scenarios scroll through her mind as her heart hammers, but then she sees that what he's doing is siphoning gas out of his own car and putting it in hers.

"This wasn't gonna get me to Utah, so it might as well help you get where you're going."

How does one thank a perfect stranger for coming into their life at the exact right time? For returning a bit of faith she didn't think she could get back? Without thinking, she hugs him, and instantly remembers the woman from the restaurant long ago who let her cut in line. Like her, the man stiffens at first, surprised, but then hugs her back.

It's not much, but it gets her home. As she approaches her neighborhood, the damage seems less—a lot of chimneys and broken windows. Then she thinks of the little house that's supposed to be hers, and wonders how it is. She imagines being there alone when the quake struck, and knows the solitude she loves would turn on her.

When she pulls onto her block, the road is packed. Everyone is outside and in the street, clustered around multiple bonfires.

"Thank God, thank God, thank God," Susan says when she finds her. A few feet away, a family of five sits on dining room chairs, blankets over their legs.

"What about our apartment?" Frankie asks, peering down the street.

Virginia rubs her hands together. "It's fine, from what we can see. But who knows about foundations or gas pipes or if it'll happen again. I'll sleep out here if I have to."

"Me too," Susan adds.

Frankie knows they won't. They don't know what it's like to really be cold, because if they did, they would know there is almost nothing worse. You can't sleep, you can't think—but though you cannot concentrate on much of anything, your mind becomes consumed with the body's state. A hyperfocus of misery. Los Angeles, for all its palm tree postcards and sunny beaches, gets cold at night. Frankie bets almost everyone here will be inside by one a.m. But now it's still early enough, and people go from bonfire to bonfire, warming their hands, faces lit orange from the glow. Kids play in the street. Someone has a guitar, and more than a few people can really sing.

"Look at all those stars," Virginia says, holding a cup of hot coffee someone made over a fire.

Susan tilts her head to the sky. "For once, Hollywood can't compete."

Virginia laughs. "There's something nice about a disaster, isn't there?"

And that's when Frankie sees Nico. Hands in his coat pockets, he searches the faces on the street. He's cast in the bonfire's glow and smiles at a kid before handing him an orange from his pocket.

All it takes is raising her arm, and he sees her. Immediately, he smiles, and her heart lurches because she misses him and she misses Jack and she misses how everything used to be and what she thought it would become.

"Whew," he says once he's made his way to her. "That was some shaker. Your building all right?"

"Supposedly," she says. That he could've been involved somehow with Tank weighs down her words, making her response less than friendly.

But Nico doesn't appear to notice. "Good. Us too. But the phone lines are down, and everything's a mess. Imagine if this happened even a couple hours before it did—all the kids still in school. Hundreds of schools collapsed, you hear that? Thank God it was at night. Dinner plans shot to hell, but at least people were together."

"I almost ran out of gas." She gives a hesitant smile, knowing she's in for a lecture.

"*Kid.* What have I told you? Fill it up at half tank. Never trust the gauge." When she doesn't say anything, he shakes his head. "You didn't have money."

"I left it at home."

He's digging in his pocket, then opening his wallet.

"Nico, I'm home now. Honestly, I have plenty of money."

"What'd I say about leading with the word *honestly*? And you already told me you didn't go to the bank before they shut down, so I'm onto you. Though I heard California banks are defying the government and opening, because of the emergency, but I wouldn't *bank* on that." He stops to laugh, then peels off a five-dollar bill. "Take this. Don't argue. Fill up tomorrow and keep it full. There's a problem? You need gas in your car. Always be prepared for a fire to break out—how you gonna outrun it if you run out of gas? You saw the lines of people today. You'll burn fuel just sitting there."

She promises to fill up, and then, almost hesitantly, says, "Have you heard how others are?"

"Got some crazy reports in, some sticky situations we'll have to clean up—but everyone's alive." He pauses, then adds offhandedly, "Jack got out in the nick of time. Pretty sure that house of his barely trembled."

She nods, thankful. "And Angela and Gabriella?"

"Fine. Scared but fine. You're the one I couldn't get through to, so a drive was in order."

She flushes with guilt. She's never had this. Fiona, as protective as she was, had so much to worry about and so little control over their lives that Frankie never felt *truly* taken care of. After all, how can you offer help when you're stuck in the struggle yourself?

"Tank Adams called me," she says before she can think better of it. "He said he shouldn't have done what he did and wanted to know if June loved him. He said someone told him she didn't."

“Yeah, *me*. I told him that a thousand times. Including when I scared him away from the premiere. You were there, don’t you remember?”

She does. When Nico saw Tank across the street, he took care of it. “But what did he mean? What did he do that he regretted?”

“How do *I* know? You gotta ask him. If I had to *guess*, it would be that he regrets being a law-breaking sap who drove his woman away. That’s what almost destroyed June years ago. That’s what made her hate him. I know he regrets all that.”

“You don’t think he meant that he killed her, or arranged to kill her?”

Nico’s brows lift in surprise. “I haven’t ruled out that he did it, or was involved, despite what alibis are saying—because we know how that goes. But *if* he did, you think he’s going to call you and admit it? Nah. He probably just regrets what he did that turned their relationship.”

“He also said he was keeping quiet. Something like that. That he was doing his part.”

“Good. Can’t have him trying to make a buck on her death. I’d say I’m proud that he’s acting honorably there, but let’s be honest—we’ve got enough on him that we could destroy him if he so much as tries to sell an old hairbrush of hers, much less a love letter.”

Everything makes sense but for a nagging worry that Nico could have been involved with June romantically, and the knowledge that he’s used that tunnel, which is the next order of business. She’s about to bring it up when she catches him squinting at something behind her. A fig tree, its branches still dormant. “Nico, at a time like this?”

“You know if it fruits? Because my money’s on that being a volunteer. And before it leafs out is the best time to get a cutting.”

“I’ll ask. But I haven’t seen the guy tonight.”

“Great. Thanks. So, we’ve got lighting equipment headed to Long Beach. That’s where the quake was centered, I guess. It’s a mess. But RCO’s sending lights for the tents where the doctors are set up.”

“That’s good. I wanted to ask you something, though.”

One eyebrow raises. “More? Shoot.”

With a deep breath, she says, "You loved June."

He nods and waits for her to continue.

"No, I mean, you *loved* her." Quickly, before she can stop herself, and to catch him off guard, she asks, "Was it your baby?"

"Frankie." Now he takes her arm, leading her farther from the crowd. "I loved her like I love you, like a daughter. And no, it was not mine. I don't know how you've missed this, but I love my wife. I've never, not once, cheated. Nor do I want to."

She observes him for any tricks of the trade, any sign he's lying. As far as she can tell, he's being truthful.

He shakes his head. "June, God love her. She was like a ray of sun when she was feeling good, but when she tilted to the other side? Watch out. There was nothing happy about her, and she was hell-bent on self-destruction. I know she really wanted to be a mother. That's what I know. And then there was the one-night stand that ended up, well, you know. Was that on purpose? To have the kid she's always wanted? I've wondered. But no. It wasn't mine."

Below their feet, a tremble. Frankie has her arms out as if to steady herself, and though everyone looks to each other—as if to gauge whether their reactions are correct—they take it in stride. When it stops, she makes herself bring up the one other thing that's weighing heavily on her. "I found the tunnel. The one off to the side of the bungalows, at the end of the side yard."

He's looking at the nearby bonfire, and his face is cast in orange. "The other bootlegging tunnel. That's what I use when I go there."

"You do?"

Now he turns to her, surprised she didn't know. "I'm not going to scratch up my car. I told you; parallel parking on Glenhollow next to rosebushes and trees is like setting a tiger loose on your paint job."

"The night June was killed, after the shot, Darlene saw someone who went toward bungalow two but then for all intents and purposes disappeared. But that tunnel. You'd turn toward two and—"

"Go to the tunnel instead. I'll tell Mickey, have it searched. Did you go inside?"

"I did, but I wasn't searching for anything. I just wanted to see where it went. There were bottles and spiderwebs. A lot of spiderwebs."

He laughs. "That's where we send the booze through, because you can unload it easy on Washburn. But with those webs, we keep the guests out of there. Now you know why. Just got the one neighbor to keep quiet."

Carefully, she says, "I met him. He said you park there and use the tunnel."

"Yeah, him and his wife like fancy chocolate, that's . . ." But then he stops talking. His eyes narrow as if he's not sure he's seeing something right. "You were wondering if I was there that night. You thought *I* did it."

The look on his face: It's sad, stunned, but worse, it's *hurt*. To have suspected the one person who's been a solid and good force in her life, to have kept going with her accusation even after he so readily admitted that he used the tunnel—what was she thinking? "The tunnel, the phone ringing at your house—"

"Not at my house. At someone's house, but not mine."

"Right, but knowing you used the tunnel and that's the direction the killer most likely went in." She can't keep talking. She's making it worse. "I'm sorry."

But strangely, he smiles. "Frankie, good for you. Don't get me wrong, I'm not glad you thought I could do it—or that you thought I could cheat on Angela, even—but I *am* glad you're *thinking*. You're a critical thinker. And you're not sentimental enough to let anything cloud your judgment, and that's good. Never let someone you love get in the way of doing what's right."

She wants to cry with relief. "Nothing makes sense right now."

"Truer words have never been spoken." He surveys the people in the street. "But listen, I'm gonna add to that. It's another reason I came out here."

At first, she doesn't know what he means, and then she remembers—he was going to talk to his friend who found her birth certificate. The man must have had bad news. In her mind, she sees smeared print. "He couldn't read it?"

"He read it."

"And?"

"Frankie, you can't *unknow* something. The truth—sometimes it just sets loose a lot of unanswerable questions."

"Nico. Tell me."

"No father was mentioned. But a mother was."

Frankie waits.

"Fiona Donnelly."

She stares at him, confused. "That must be my adoption certificate. Fiona was my adoptive mother."

"No, you don't have an adoption certificate. You have a *birth* certificate, which lists your biological mother. Frankie, it's right there on the paper. Your biological mother was Fiona."

CHAPTER 27

Everything to Do with You

There are sporadic, soft murmurings from the earth. If even one of these aftershocks happened yesterday, she'd have flown from her bed, terrified, but already this is a new reality with new thresholds of fear, and so, late at night, she rides out the temblors while keeping her covers in place.

Fiona was her mother. *Is* her mother. Fiona, with her dark-red hair and light eyes and freckles, her *Irish freckles,* as she called them. Did they look alike? Their coloring was almost opposite, but in hindsight, Frankie sees it in their eyes. Different shades of blue—arctic light blue versus Atlantic dark blue—though the same shape. *Your father must have been Italian,* Nico said. *His genes would've been dominant. She named you Francesca, too. A tribute to his side, I'd say.*

The moon brightens half the ceiling, and she notices a crack that spreads from the light fixture. *She told you she adopted you because she must've thought it would help.* Frankie feels a slight tremble, and turns over in bed, thinking of Nico's words. Does a lie matter if its outcome helps? Or is the truth always better even if it does harm? If someone's told they're taking medicine, and they feel better, does it matter if it's made of sugar?

A movie. People sit in a theatre and look up at a world that captivates them and lifts them above their own life, that gives them escape and allows them experiences they otherwise would never have, and it's about the *feeling* that's created. The thrill, the aching, the gratification, the fear or sadness. And those feelings have nothing to do with truth or fiction, and everything to do with *belief.* She lived with a mother whom she deemed a rescuer, a savior. Years and years of happy belief in someone during which the truth of the situation had no impact on the experience, because she believed the lie.

But if experience trumps reality, then does the truth even matter?

Needing a distraction, Frankie gets out of bed. From the kitchen, she sees Virginia and Susan, asleep on a mattress they dragged into the living room as if needing to be closer to the exit. Though they'd asked her to join them, in Frankie's heart, she was already one step out the door, and so she made up an excuse and retreated to her room, alone.

"She wasn't even sixteen years old," Nico said earlier tonight, about Frankie's mother, as a neighbor splashed water on the nearest bonfire and announced he was going inside. "It's admirable, really. She must have planned on getting you back the second she could, the second she was on her feet."

"She was never on her feet. We were always behind and barely hanging on."

"And yet she never looked back. Like I said, admirable. You know people leave, all the time, because of whatever they're going through, and it has nothing to do with you. But more often than not, when they come back, it has *everything* to do with you."

Loss was threading around her, a touch here and there—a wisp she suddenly identified. "It's like I just lost the family I might've had."

"I thought that might be the case—despite your protests. But you still have family. They're just not the kind you're related to, that's all." A pause, and he added, "She told you she adopted you, because she must've thought it would help. We do that every day, try to angle things in just the right way. Try to change the way something's perceived."

"No. It's different. She painted herself as the *rescuer*. She sold a lie so she'd look good. She spun the story of my *birth*."

Suddenly, Nico seemed angry. "No. She fixed it so she'd look good in *your* eyes, Frankie. She didn't want her daughter to think ill of her, to question her love. What's wrong with that? Think of what it would've done, living with the woman who gave you up. Always doubting if she was going to come home at night. Never trusting her. She did you a favor."

Did she? A lifetime of mystery. A cascade of doubt. All the years spent wondering what was wrong with her that would cause her family to give her up. They kept her siblings but not her, and that first abandonment drove home an important lesson: People come and go, and you're never enough to make them stay if they really want to leave. On top of this, her mother left behind a puzzle box of questions. Was Fiona related to the man or the woman who cared for her? Could they have been an aunt or an uncle, perhaps? If that was the case, why would Fiona never see them again? Behind each inquiry is another, and the only person who could answer them is gone. *We'll keep looking for them if you want,* Nico said. *You can decide later.*

Now is the chance to appreciate the silence outside, this full and complete darkness and the dusting of stars, now that all her neighbors have gone back to their houses. Quietly, she tiptoes past her roommates and out the front door. Pine needles and rocks press into her bare feet, the damp grass cold. Then the sidewalk, rough. The street has cleared out, faint embers all that's left of the bonfires. Everyone's gone but one older couple who dragged a mattress to their driveway. They've got a fire going in a steel drum, and their shoes are lined up in a row. Even from here, Frankie can see they're awake, speaking in whispers and pointing to the stars.

Frankie breathes in the beauty. This, she thinks, is the closest she'll ever come to understanding eternity.

When she looks down, she spots a familiar car: O'Shea's Ford Roadster pickup. The one Jack drives when he doesn't want to draw attention to himself.

Inside, slumped across the tan seat, is one of the country's biggest stars. Asleep in an average car on an average street. Unshaven, his hair slightly bent as if he's had his head at an angle for a while. She hasn't been able to watch him since everything began, or ended, rather, and asleep, he's a captivating combination of rugged vulnerability. Strong but gentle. She watches his eyelashes till he twitches as if feeling her gaze, and so, gently, she taps on the window. Waking up, he seems confused, and then sees her and smiles before catching himself.

Smile gone, he unlocks the door so she can get in the passenger side. All she wants to do is touch him, to lean against him and let him hold her and tell her that not everything is a lie.

Instead, she says, too forcefully, "Why'd you come if you're still mad?"

"Hello to you too." He glances at her robe and pajamas, then back down the street, at the couple sleeping in their driveway. "Just because I'm mad doesn't mean I want you hurt. I thought if I saw you leave in the morning, I'd know you were all right. And for what it's worth, you still seem mad too." With that, he reaches into the back seat. "Which is why I brought this."

Moving Up, the script by Milton Ewing.

He sets it in her lap. "If you disagree with what I've done after you read it, I will personally pay for them to reshoot those scenes with a different set."

The fact that he's willing to do this, and confident enough that she will understand once she reads the script, immediately and almost frustratingly takes the edge off her anger. What's actually in the script remains to be seen, but the effort he's going to already runs contrary to what she'd seen as thoughtless behavior. "Then I guess I'll read it."

"I guess you will." He gives her a hesitant smile.

"Are you doing all right?"

He moves his hand, indicating fifty-fifty. "Being back in my house is already nice. Hopefully the nightmares stop."

"You're having nightmares?" It kills her that she didn't know this. But then she thinks of something that will hopefully help him—that the dog wasn't barking before the gunshot, so it's unlikely he walked back and past that point again after she dropped him off. She tells him this, and he smiles.

"A dog, Frankie? I like that you're trying, but you know I need more than that."

"But now we have *more* reason to think you just went to sleep, and *no* reason to think you left and saw June before she was shot. When you got to your bungalow, you stayed there."

He taps his thumb on the door. "There's something I found out that I wanted you to know."

"I don't know if I can handle finding out more tonight."

"Why? What'd you find out?"

She can't look at him. If she does, and if she tells him about her mother, she will cry. What she needs is to be strong. Instead, she tells him about the tunnel.

When she's finished, Jack is incredulous. "And Nico knew about it? He's used it?"

"I don't know *when* he last—"

"Frankie."

"I can't believe I even have to say this, but Nico didn't kill her, Jack. I know he didn't."

"Of course he didn't."

Now it's Frankie's turn to look surprised. Jack, who's always critical of Nico, agrees.

"But just because I don't think he killed her doesn't mean I like this. Doesn't mean you should look away when something's off. Because something *is* off. You know it is. And you're making excuses like you did with the telegrams and him knowing where Donna was—"

"I didn't look away. I got into his safe at his house when he wasn't there. Everything is as he said it was."

"You broke into Nico's safe?"

"I didn't break in. He gave me the combination a long time ago. There's emergency money in there, there's—"

"He *gave* you the combination? Then *of course* you didn't find anything."

"Maybe I didn't find anything *because there's nothing to find*." She thinks of the police report involving Ida and the boy who drowned, as well as the letters Frankie had never read. Just because she didn't know about those things doesn't mean he was *hiding* them. On the contrary, if he was, he wouldn't have put them where he knew she could look.

"He *bought* June's sister," Jack says.

"And me? He bought me too?" She glares at him.

"You know I didn't really think that."

She stays silent, stewing.

"Come on," he finally says. "Neither one of us is perfect right now, but you have to admit, what Nico did is bad."

"He did something wrong but for the right reason."

Jack's mouth opens before he finds his words. "For the right reason? You mean because she was realizing there was more to life than just this?"

"That's what *you* wanted her to realize."

"No. She *never* cared about acting. She did it because her family wanted her to and because Ida gave up everything for her, and she felt like she had to."

"She told you that?"

"Frankie, we had time together. Lots of time. I saw her at her best and her worst, and yes, her not liking acting but being *famous* for it was the problem. Think about it—what if you're really good at something that makes the people you love happy but isn't something *you* enjoy? How long do you keep at a job just because you're good at it? She was a natural, but *she* never had a love for it. Me, I have a love for it. Acting, I mean, not the fame."

Outside, someone calls for their dog. Frankie slinks down in her seat, cautious.

Quickly, Jack continues. "Here's what I wanted to tell you: The reporter, that new reporter at my house the day of the conference, the one asking the questions I didn't like? Jerry. He's the one who brought up the staffers outside the premiere talking about the necklace."

Can you confirm or deny that two studio staffers were in the crowd outside Grauman's talking about the necklace and lack of security? "I remember."

"Nico *paid* him to ask that."

"No, he didn't." An immediate denial. Even she hears how quickly she jumped to Nico's defense.

"Frankie, he *did*. I met the guy today. He thought I was in on it. He's an actor."

"*In* on it." She's trying to understand. "In on what he was asking you? As in—"

"As in Nico told Jerry what to ask. Exactly what to ask. Like a script. In exchange for a part in—"

"But *I* was the staffer who said there was no security. And I said it to *Nico*. Why would he want anyone to know that? He was a part of that conversation. That doesn't make sense."

"I don't know. But Nico doesn't make mistakes. So there *was* a reason."

"Do you hear how sinister that sounds?"

"You didn't know the truth about Donna. Or the tunnel. What else has he kept from you?"

"*Not telling me everything isn't the same as lying.* And for everything you just brought up, he had reasons!"

"And you don't think that's suspicious?"

She stares at him, incredulous. "You've *never* liked him. You hate him because he represents the studio and what you have to do for them, and that's colored your judgment."

"*Of course it has!* Don't be fooled—they *want* me to be a mess. They want me to need them so I do what they want me to do. So how do I know Nico's telling the truth?"

"I saw them! I saw the letters; I told you. And yet you're still doubting him. You're still trying to make me choose between him and you." Her heart is racing, anger surging. "He came here tonight to check on me. It was his kid, his wife, and then *me* that he cared about. I've never had that. But *he* came to make sure I was all right, while you came to *be* right."

With that, she opens her door, letting in the cold.

"Frankie, just because you don't want to see something—"

"The same goes for you, Jack," she says, stepping onto the sidewalk. "You don't want to see your own part in your own life. Much easier to sit back and blame others and do nothing, isn't it?"

Though he was about to say something, he clamps his mouth shut. Script under her arm, she tightens her robe as she steps onto the curb, and tries not to listen as his car pulls away.

CHAPTER 28

When, Not If

Saturday, March 11, 1933

When Frankie wakes, it's early. There, on the nightstand beside her, is the script. She reaches for it and rolls over in bed, eyes adjusting to the print. The truth is she wants it to make her angry, just so she won't regret how things ended last night with Jack. Still, she's not prepared to be immediately irritated, but by page three, she's mad. The woman is the man's maid. Now Frankie sits up in bed and turns on the light, trying to be calm. The character lives in a tenement, destitute though morally grounded and strong, and though the man she works for is rich and people describe him as blessed, he's lost all sense of right and wrong. To add to the situation, he's a single father and raising his son all on his own, a child who seemingly has everything but is craving the one thing he doesn't have: a mother. And indeed, the woman does the saving—both of the child and the man, who realizes what it is to truly be happy. It's trite, but Frankie knows audiences are going to love it. They will relate, and they might even feel better about their lot in life. As Frankie turns the last page, she knows that it's true—this was a tribute to both Frankie and her mother, one that only she'd recognize.

She puts the script back on the nightstand. In an alternate version of her own story, she would've seen this play out in a theatre. June and Jack would be in the front row, and behind them would be an entire audience watching their every reaction. Frankie would be rows behind, off in a corner maybe, but close enough to see Jack turn. And she would know he was looking for her, and know who he really meant was saved.

"They're saying it was Los Angeles's biggest known earthquake," Virginia says, still in pajamas.

The floor is cold, and Frankie searches for her slippers as her roommate continues.

"John, from across the street, he said that the farther south you go, the more like a war zone it is. And he was at Verdun, so he knows. Oh, and that production assistant with the red hair was here this morning and said they need you at work."

"He was here?" Frankie looks at the clock. It's barely nine a.m.

"Our phone lines are still down. Sorry, I thought you were sleeping."

Getting to work is a challenge, both from the fact that many streets are a mess but also from the fact that Frankie wants to slow down to look at the damage. The quake was centered in Long Beach, a small community now reeling with the most extensive destruction: collapsed houses and destroyed schools and fire-gutted neighborhoods and broken families. *Let this be a reminder,* the man on the radio says, *no matter how fancy we think we are, Mother Nature can and will put us in check.*

Houses thrown off their foundations. Walls crumbled. Sidewalks split. Wrecking crews are scattered throughout the city, there to finish the job, like putting animals out of their misery. Friends and neighbors and strangers, everyone is outside, sweeping glass and shoveling concrete and uncovering cars from beneath bricks. At a park, food stations are set up alongside long tables as if the city is preparing for a massive picnic.

Once she gets to work, the talk is endless. Everyone has a story to tell. *Where were you? What were you doing?* Betty looks as though she hasn't slept in a week, even though the quake was only yesterday.

"You hear about the prop room? All the china and crystal, gone. And that big chandelier fell. It's just glass in there."

"It could've been worse," Frankie says, the mantra everyone repeats in a disaster.

Betty hands her a stack of messages. "Now we circle the wagons. Damage-control time, literally and figuratively. Nico's already out handling the big messes."

Frankie gathers reports on all their stars and sends off a cleaning crew to remove what sounds like a roomful of broken liquor bottles from an actor's house before then concocting a cover-up story to hide the fact that another one of their stars was trapped in his pool house with the pool boy. It's lying, yes, but it's a lie she endorses, because why should the public crucify the actor for his own choice in his own life? If lying is what protects him and his desire to be with the pool boy, then she will lie. The whole day, Nico's gone, and his absence only prolongs a sort of limbo, some uncertain territory where he could still be upset at her accusation. The only way she can gauge whether things have gone back to normal is when she sees him. *Putting out fires*, he told her about his tasks for the afternoon. *Thankfully not real ones.*

On the way home, she stops at a local market and joins the line for food.

"There's the reminder, isn't it? And that's just the part we see."

A man stands on the sidewalk, gesturing to a giant sheer rock wall behind the parking lot. The layers of earth are exposed like a slice of cake, but the layers aren't straight—they're ruffled like a bedsheet. Countless times, she's walked past this and wondered at the sight but never stopped to appreciate the force involved in actually bending the earth like this. Within seconds, another woman stops and stares.

"When did *that* happen?" she asks, eyes wide.

The man replies, with a laugh, "Not yesterday."

Offended, the woman shakes her head as she walks away, finally calling back, "They need a tree to block that. No one needs to see that."

Now the man smiles at Frankie. "A tree's not going to make it go away." He laughs. "Out of sight, out of mind, I suppose. Which works till you realize it's been under your feet the whole damn time."

~

Candles and canned food and heavy blankets and a battery-operated "farm radio" that Susan finds in the small storage basement. The power's still off all through the night, and it's cold, colder than before, and Sunday morning, Frankie wakes up to the phone ringing, which at least tells her that's back on and gives her hope. She clicks the light switch, but there's nothing.

"Frankie," Virginia yells down the hall.

For a fleeting moment, Frankie waits for her to tell her it's Grant. Grant, whom her roommates haven't even asked about, as if suspecting that the man they've never met would naturally disappear at the first sign of trouble. Frankie thinks of Jack's visit after the quake, there to check on her, sure, but with the goal of getting her to turn on Nico.

"My suspicion," Nico says when she picks up the phone, "is that you're not eating properly and everything in your refrigerator needs to go in the trash."

"All true."

"Well, we've got more power than we know what to do with and food coming out of our ears, so six p.m. dinner is on. We've canceled enough. If this earthquake taught us anything, it's that if you're lucky enough to be alive, you better live."

Relief. He was telling the truth; he *was* proud she was thinking critically, and she didn't ruin anything with her accusation.

When she's about to leave, she spots the neighbor with the fig tree locking his front door behind him. Quickly, she grabs the garden clippers that her downstairs neighbor keeps in a basket by the hose and crosses the street. The man listens with confusion as she explains herself and why she's holding clippers. Wary but in a hurry, he waves his hand toward the tree before shutting his car door. Frankie finds a branch and does as Nico's taught her, making a clean cut at a forty-five-degree angle. Ultimately, she takes the tips of four branches. *The more, the better,* he's told her, *in case some fail.*

It's ten to six when Frankie rings the bell. Angela's wearing the same apron she always does, and the familiar sight—a vestige of the past—makes Frankie hopeful that things can return to normal.

"He's teaching Gabriella soccer out back. So far, he claims she's better than anyone ever was at that age, ever, in the history of the world, and I've lost two flowerpots. They're blaming the earthquake, but I know."

Frankie holds out the fig cuttings, wrapped in damp newspaper, and Angela sighs.

"You too? We'll be out of yard soon." Then, as she heads back to the kitchen, she adds, "Be sure to score the bottoms."

The little bathroom attached to his office is filled with cuttings in pots, many with bright-green leaves that angle toward the window. Frankie had never even tasted a fig till she met Nico, but he could charm a snake by describing them, listing off flavors and profiles like wine: dark blackberry or bright strawberry, notes of floral honey or sweet melon.

Along the wall are shelves, each with cuttings in various stages, and one with soil-filled pots, ready with the special mix he uses. She takes four prefilled plastic pots to the little potting table. Working in the dimming light, she scores the bottom of each section of branch, scraping away the bark, then inserts one into the first pot, another into the second, and is working on planting the third cutting when it meets resistance. Something hard is mixed in with the potting soil. Digging her hand in, she freezes when her finger touches something smooth.

Even as she pulls it out, she understands she will not come back from this. This solid truth in her hand will change everything, forever. But it's as if her body has chosen to learn what her heart's not ready for, because her hand works on its own. She shakes the item loose.

There, covered in dirt, is June's necklace.

Flecks of green blaze through the dirt. Even now, the giant emerald is radiant, desperate to be seen. With the tip of her finger, she brushes the smooth facet, and color bursts through. Suddenly, it feels heavy in her hand. Hot, as if she's touched something she shouldn't have.

If he didn't walk in now, as the necklace dangles from her open hand, would she have put it back? She will wonder this later. If she had the chance, would she simply reach for a different pot and act as though all is normal and well and she didn't just find something that swings like a hammer into her heart? What lengths would she go to, to preserve what's left of her life? Put the necklace back. Let its existence swirl like a fury in her mind over dinner. She'd mull it over at home and have time to decide what to do, and then she'd act. She'd turn him in. She'd confront him. She'd do *something*. Of course she would. Wouldn't she?

But the decision is made for her. There is a loud exhalation of breath, as if this evening is nothing more than an inevitability, a necessary bridge that must be crossed but could never bear the weight. When, not if.

Silently, she turns to him, the necklace still in her hand. All her words are gone, and in their place is a mounting horror, because of course this necklace went missing the moment June was murdered, and yet here it is.

Nico nods as if affirming her thoughts. "Well, it's not good, but it's not what you think. Come sit."

In shock, she leaves the necklace on the potting table, abandoned in a filthy coil. Nico's office door is closed, and Frankie sits across from him at the desk when she realizes that she's not afraid, but maybe she should be.

"I didn't kill her," he says, and she's relieved and then angry because it's what she wants to hear, but at this point, her heart is flying against all logic.

"I didn't," he says again. "She'd threatened herself before. Twice. Never did anything, just made me come running."

"Threatened herself," Frankie says, lowering her voice, "as in to *kill* herself?"

He cringes. "She never meant it. Never did anything other than cry when I got there. But she knew I'd do almost anything to fix whatever upset her. I don't know when June found out about Ida. Or how. But the night of the premiere, June told me I'd been playing God with her life. That's what she said. That the studio was playing God and she was a puppet. She felt betrayed. And don't point it out—I get why. So, I got a call, right around two a.m. Little after, maybe. I'd just gotten home, I was tired, but I answered, and she said, *He didn't even show up*, and she wasn't making sense, but then she's telling me she's ending it. So, I did what I always do, and I dropped everything to get to her."

A pause, and Frankie notices his hand on his desk, curled into a fist. As if he feels her watching, he sets it in his lap. When he looks up, his eyes shine.

"I parked on Washburn. I was thinking about my car, keeping it safe. It's what I do when I go there. But that extra time to get through the tunnel—" He breaks off, then nods, affirming something in his mind. "This was different. I saw it the second I arrived. I went around the front like I always do, and the porch light was off. The door locked. I had to look for the spare key, in the dark. She meant it. I knew it, then and there. And when I saw the empty pill bottle—she was gone."

An empty pill bottle. June gone. The meanings hover above Frankie; she can't make sense of them yet.

"It wasn't like other times," Nico repeats.

And then what he's saying seems to split in two. Release for Jack, that he'll know without a doubt that he didn't do it. But also the pain that June must have been in, to have done this. It hits Frankie at once: Jack didn't do it—June did. A brutal relief. A cruel absolution. A reality that makes no sense.

"She killed herself?" A tear hits her wrist—she didn't realize she was crying. She's known people who've ended this way; everyone does since the stock market crash. But June? That June reached this point? June, who had everything, even the love of strangers?

"She had struggles," Nico says, and his voice catches. "Real struggles. Hard to see when they happen inside a mansion, but they're real all the same. But I'm the one who could've seen it, and I didn't. I failed her."

"We," she starts to say but stops when he holds his hand up.

But he doesn't stay anything, just studies the ceiling for a moment. She watches his eyes, tracing a crack. Then he takes a deep breath. "She left a note." He reaches under his desk, turning the dial to his safe, but Frankie already knows which note it is.

Nico, You always said to end strong, and know when to leave. I might not be ending strong, but I know it's time to leave.

She wasn't asking for help with Tank. She was saying goodbye.

"I kept it in case Jack or anyone else really got up a creek. I don't know how I'd explain finding it later, but I wasn't thinking when I took it." He gives a small laugh. "Apparently I don't make good decisions when I find someone I love like that. All I knew was I couldn't let anyone go down for a murder they didn't commit, so I took it."

Frankie is still trying to understand how June got to this point, but more so how she missed that June was there. How all of them missed it.

Though he sets the note on his desk, he doesn't look at it. "My car. If I'd parked closer, would she still be here? It can't come down to that, can it?" With his thumb, he moves the note to the side as if he can't bear it so close. "She probably took enough pills where it wouldn't have mattered when I got there, but a minute, two, would she still be here?"

Frankie shakes her head, something finally occurring to her. "No. That's not right. She was *shot*. In the chest—"

And then it clicks.

"You shot her."

Slowly, he meets her eyes. "She was gone. She was gone, and it was my fault for not getting there. The one thing I *could* do was save her reputation. I couldn't have people thinking she did this to herself. Not June. Not their June."

"You shot a pregnant woman."

But he shakes his head, adamant. "No. No, she wasn't pregnant. Not anymore."

"What?"

"You didn't notice how sick she was the day before the premiere? She had a miscarriage. She held it together, God bless her, but it was rough. She wanted that baby, more than I knew."

The day of interviews, June looked bad. Ida was there, practically holding her up. "But the wedding was still happening. Even after that, we were still planning—"

"Frankie, the miscarriage had *just* happened. What was I going to do, put out a release saying, *Whoops, our stars changed their minds*? No. She can't go through all that *and* be the butt of a joke about a flash-in-the-pan engagement. We had time to get out of it, but not before the premiere."

Not before the premiere. Everything bent to the needs of the studio. Including Jack, sitting in jail as Nico withheld the truth that would've absolved him. "People think Jack did it, and you could've changed that. You let him sit in jail. You let him think he did this."

Frustration thickens his words. "*He wasn't supposed to be at the bungalows.* I didn't know he was *there* till it was all said and done. And what do you mean, *think he did this*? When did he think he did this?"

"You could've cleared up *everything* in a heartbeat!"

"*You want me to ruin her?* That's what you want?"

Now Frankie's standing, pacing. "It doesn't matter that he's out of jail—people will *always* think he did it. Always. And you *know* that."

"Come on, I wasn't going to let him go down for it. If things went south, I would *arrange* for the necklace to show up somewhere else."

She turns to him. "You mean frame someone else."

"Not necessarily."

"And the gun?"

"Also somewhere safe. Should I need it."

Everything is too much. That June felt this was the only way, that Nico felt this was the only way, and that Frankie's involved in something that makes her feel as if the floor has dropped from beneath her feet. Trying to be steady, she takes a seat. "This is wrong."

"It was right *for her*. I did it for her. It broke my heart to do it, but it was *the right thing to do for her.*"

Never let someone you love get in the way of doing what's right.

He's watching her, imploring. "Tell me you understand that."

And he really wants to know. Her opinion matters. "You let me think this was *my* fault, because of what I said outside the premiere. That someone heard me—"

"No, no, you thought that all on your own."

Did she? She no longer remembers. "It worked for you, me thinking that. You paid that reporter—"

"No, Frankie, it worked for the *press* to think that. That's why we needed that to happen. So they'd take their claws out of Jack. But I never wanted *you* to feel guilt. I just couldn't explain it without dragging you in deeper. But come on, if this were Jack, wouldn't you have done the same thing? You go out on a limb for the people you care about. Wouldn't you do what's best for him?"

What's best for him. She thinks of all the times she thought she knew what was best. How she dissuaded him from risk to keep him safe.

Nico must take her silence as understanding. "Exactly. And I'd do it again. Because of me, America's sweetheart can stay America's sweetheart. Everything she did to uphold her reputation; it was for her. She *wanted* to be loved."

But Frankie's not sure. "Did she?"

"Thing is, I think you and I are on the same page. I wish she'd never let the studio doctor in the room. I wish she had no pressure. I wish no one was relying on her. But that wasn't how it was. She sacrificed to keep her reputation, to be who people thought she was. How can I let that be for nothing? She didn't leave a note for America. She left it for *me*, because I'd find it, and I'd understand. No. I'm not giving her death to the public. It's *hers*." Off her silence, he adds, "All those flowers, all those grieving fans outside the studio, you think they would've shown up for a suicide?"

Suicide. The word feels like a punch. But Frankie knows he's right. A nation, already struggling, would be gutted. The dream they needed shattered. And there'd be no sympathy, no empathy, because no one was privy to her struggle. To them, someone with a perfect life did the unthinkable.

"For ten years," Nico continues, "she worked and didn't get to live life how she wanted. But people would only remember her last ten minutes. It's not right, but it's true: You're only as good as your worst moment."

And though it pains her, Frankie realizes it's true: Turning June into a victim was the right move. It was the fix.

CHAPTER 29

Undoing This Is Not an Option

Monday, March 13, 1933

It's not a lie when Frankie calls in sick. It feels as though a ruthless hand is pressing on her stomach and her heart can't settle on a pace. She can't eat. She can't think. There's no getting around it: She was a part of what killed June.

"I felt queasy yesterday," Betty says when Frankie calls to let them know she's staying home. A laugh. "Not that that's stopping me from making Nico bring me back a French dip from lunch today. He's gonna be furious if it gets all over his car, but c'est la vie."

Back in bed, restless with anxiety and tired from lack of sleep, Frankie pulls the covers on before kicking them off again right as Susan pops her head in. She eyes the boxes along the wall. In days, Frankie is supposed to be gone, but the new girl, they told her, is no longer coming. The earthquake was enough to wreck her Hollywood dreams.

"Do you need soup?" Susan asks, pulling on her coat.

The house. This apartment. Her car. Everything belongs to the studio.

"I'm good," Frankie manages, and Susan tells her about the muffins she hid in the oven so Virginia wouldn't find them.

Jack. Frankie wants to go to him, to ask him what to do. She wants to curl against him, his hand tracing circles on her back. Somehow, she needs to tell him he had nothing to do with June's death without getting into details that would surely send him over the edge. She needs to find a way to get him *out* of this, not further involve him, and she needs to do right by him and by June and by herself, though she no longer knows what any of that entails. Everything she's done feels like a mistake.

After ten minutes of lying in the dark, Frankie gets up and grabs her car keys. Within the hour, she's pulling into Hollywood Memorial Park and parking beside a boy who's got a makeshift flower stand. Mason jars of various sizes are all filled with blooms, clusters that look as though they were snapped from someone's yard only moments prior. She hands the kid a nickel for a jam jar of yellow daffodils, and sets out toward June's mausoleum.

The grass is wet with dew, and the pond holds the slate sky's reflection, a white cloud drifting toward the edge of the water. On the ground, there are traces of rose petals, as if several bouquets have recently been removed. A simple twig wreath with white and yellow daisies rests against the mausoleum door. Frankie smiles. That's the one June would love.

June's name, carved in stone. A name. After everything, that's all that's left, mere letters. And yet Fiona doesn't have even that. In the distance, dark mountain peaks bleed into the sky like ink. She wishes for a sign from June, and waits. Somewhere a dog barks, and Frankie feels her eyes stinging with tears. She looks back at June's name. "I'm sorry. I don't know what to do."

A shadow moves against the white stone. Frankie turns.

Ida. Blouse and trousers ironed, hat on at the perfect angle. She takes in the clothes Frankie's wearing—the shirt and pants she fell asleep in last night—and her unbrushed hair. "No one taught you to dress for a cemetery? You should show respect." Ida doesn't smile, doesn't hug Frankie, just turns around. "Come on, then. Let's walk."

They leave June as if preferring not to talk with her there. The truth of her death weighs on Frankie, and suddenly she wants to stop and hide and let Ida keep going. Because she needs to tell Ida what actually happened, but what will that do? Mystery solved; regrets unleashed.

They cut across the grass toward the ribbon of road, the hems of their pants dampening. Still, Ida says nothing. Just squints into the morning sun.

"You visit her often?" Frankie finally asks, for something to say.

"Every day. You're not the only one who's sorry." A pause. "They won't solve this, will they?"

Wordlessly, Frankie shakes her head.

Ida stops walking and faces her. "I don't want to know."

"You don't?"

It appears as if Ida's weighing her words, searching for ones that will land right. Eventually, she keeps walking, slow and defeated. "The truth won't bring her back."

Frankie folds her arms around herself, suddenly cold.

"I never hated her, you know," Ida says.

"Of course I know that."

"It was hard not to resent her, though. Our parents did everything for her. Everything. She was the hope. The one with the pretty eyes."

Frankie wants to tell Ida no, that her eyes are pretty too—but it's true, they don't compare to June's. Though she's looking straight ahead, Ida smiles as if reading her thoughts. Then she loses her smile.

"There was somebody I loved, you know. His wife died after their son was born. I didn't think I ever wanted children, but this kid was . . ." She stops talking and looks up again at the sun as if needing the toughening burn. "I won't get into what happened, but it was the *one time* I thought I could have something good for myself. I asked for June's help, and she fell asleep on the job. Actually fell asleep." Casually, almost too casually, she turns her head to observe Frankie, perhaps checking whether this information is familiar.

The police report from Nico's safe. "The boy who drowned."

Ida nods. "It was my fault. Ultimately. I shouldn't have asked her to watch him. They didn't wrap till late the night before, or early that morning, I don't remember. But I shouldn't have asked." She starts walking again, aimlessly, watching the grass. "When we got home that day, she was asleep. And then we found him. Nico took care of things, as Nico does. And my name went onto the police report, to keep her out of it." She stops at a grave where a vase with dried flowers lies on its side. Righting it, she nestles it against the headstone. "Understandably, the man, the father, never spoke to me again. Grief, of course, but I chose her over the truth."

In a burning building, you save who you can; you don't stop to figure out who set the fire. Yes, the truth is important, but if you have someone you can save, you save them. "Putting her on the report wouldn't have brought him back."

"That's what I told myself. I'll never be sorry I protected her. But she paid; she built a prison in her mind."

Frankie stops walking. When Ida notices, she stops as well, turning hesitantly, braced.

"You didn't need to explain any of this," Frankie says. "I know you love her."

Now Ida smiles. "I'm not explaining it so you know I loved her. I'm saying that I lost a lot, for her sake and for her reputation. I think I've earned what's coming to me. And I don't want that to change because of the public's change of heart, so to speak."

Frankie tries to digest this. That Ida might suspect the truth but wants it kept from the public. At last, all she says is "I wish we'd done things differently."

To that, Ida laughs. "The story of our lives would always be better with a rewrite."

Along the road, a car has pulled up. A man and a woman, each carefully holding several mason jars of flowers. They must've bought the kid out.

"I should've let her elope," Ida says. "That's what I should've done."

Trying not to betray surprise, Frankie nods and then says, leadingly, "Let her elope with . . ."

But Ida doesn't seem to hear. Her gaze has drifted to the couple, to the woman who is now lowering herself to lie on the grass alongside a small headstone. Nearby, the man stands, watching as a sparrow lands on the grave marker closest to them. His face widens in a smile, before he quickly looks down at his feet. Everybody, Frankie thinks, can't help but search for the signs they need.

Continuing, Ida finally says, "Telling Nico that was her plan will always be my cross to bear. I knew she was unhappy with acting lately. I just thought we could fix that. I thought there'd be time. I guess that's what we all think."

~

The fixes. Ida thought her sister was about to make a mistake and tried to fix it. Nico heard June was unwed and with child and tried to fix it. Jack wanted out of a marriage and lied about his past and let the studio fix it. So many fixes for what Frankie is now seeing is simply life. Messy and untamed and inconvenient. But just because something entails struggle and needs work doesn't mean it's broken.

Betty and her French dip sandwich. Frankie knows exactly where Nico's having lunch, and drives straight to Cole's. Outside the Pacific Electric building, she leans down to look through one of the low windows into the restaurant on the bottom floor. The lunch rush is over. The booths empty. But then there's Nico in a corner.

When she slides across from him, he looks up, surprised, and smiles before seeing the state of her appearance.

"I'm fine," she says.

"If you say so." He opens his wallet. "Betty needed the French dip hot, and I ordered too late. So you're in luck. Looks like I've got time for whatever this is."

"She wanted to *elope*. And you stopped them."

Though only one couple remains at the bar, he still glances around, cautious. "Who'd you talk to? Ida, I'm assuming. No one else knew. She was about to throw away her whole life, everything she'd worked for."

"To be with the person she wanted to be with. The father? You told me it was a one-night stand. You told me the man didn't care an iota."

Nico unfolds a five-dollar bill and sets it on the table near his glass of water. "Because he *didn't*. And because I hate all of this. She's gone, and I hate saying things bad about her. So I told you it was a one-night thing because *I didn't want to get into it*. And all you need to know is that the guy *didn't* want anything to do with her, or the kid, until she convinced him or whatever happened that took him from *have a nice life* to *I'll meet you at the courthouse*. So, of course, I put an end to it. Wouldn't you? You trust that about-face? Because I don't. A split-second decision, an impulse, and her career would've been *over*. America's sweetheart pregnant by someone who wasn't her long-term boyfriend?"

"But if she wanted—"

"*What she wanted changed from minute to minute*. But if she eloped with a guy who changed his mind about her the next day, then she blew up her life *for what*? A whim that it would be nice to play house with the—" He stops talking as the waiter approaches.

Frankie lifts her hand. "Apple pie with vanilla sauce, please. Add it to his check."

Nico waits for the man to disappear into the kitchen. When he leans forward, his voice is a whisper, and the gold of his wristwatch flashes in the low light. "Undoing this is *not an option*. The pills aren't even a part of the report. I said, *Value her privacy when you do this*, and they did, so there's no Pandora's box of secrets, nothing that gets us or her in trouble. Because, believe me, the powers that be *will take us down with them* if they have to. Don't think for a second they won't hurl us out the window just so they have a softer landing. And June? She's gonna be Hollywood lore. Forever loved. You want to take that from her? Jack's *safe*. They will *never* be able to prove anything. Not if I'm watching out for him. So why destroy her?"

"Safe? Until this is *solved*, he can't do what he loves. Does it matter if he's safe?"

"You're not thinking logically. An engagement announcement followed by a breakup announcement a week later? The marriage was good for them."

She studies him. "The marriage? You said they could've gotten out of the *engagement*, that they just needed to get through the premiere."

He's nodding. "Right. Honestly, a couple weeks more, and they could've done what they wanted."

Never lead with the word honestly. *I'll always know you're lying.*

"You were going to make them get married. You weren't letting them out of it. She knew that, didn't she?"

When he says nothing, Frankie understands. June knew.

He takes a sip of his water, then sits back. "Hollywood is the land of dreams, and people *need* the dream. They need the idea of happiness and success, and to think they can rise up from the ashes into something great. You tell them June hated her life and couldn't get through a day without pills, and who does that help? Not the people who need to believe it's possible. Because if June didn't like her life, what does that say about everyone else?"

In the kitchen, plates crash and someone curses. Frankie knows she should just agree so she can decide later what to do.

"Do you understand what I'm saying?" Nico asks.

This could be over if she just looks the other way. She could go back to her job, her life. "You know something, Nico? It does makes sense."

"Good." He nods. "Good. Glad you understand."

"Really, I do," she says, once again thankful no one can tell when she's lying.

CHAPTER 30

Strategy Relies on Information

Nothing that gets us or her in trouble.

Frankie needs to get to the medical examiner's office before Nico fully questions her loyalty. He referred to whatever *wasn't* listed on the medical examiner's report as *Pandora's box*, which means something significant and troublesome was omitted. If June was no longer pregnant, then a pregnancy wasn't what he meant. What did he intend to hide? The pills, Frankie guesses, but right now she doesn't feel safe assuming anything. Repeatedly Nico's lied to cover things up, and so the best shot she has at determining the truth might just be finding out what was so problematic that it had to be left off the report. Strategy, after all, relies on information.

Not only that, but she now understands what else is at stake: Nico's own culpability.

The Los Angeles County Department of Medical Examiner is east of the Los Angeles River, in a large brick building decorated with tan concrete cornices and embellishments. Frankie takes the stairs two at a time and bypasses the front desk, finding the ME's office at the end of the hall. As she knocks, she pushes the door open, and the man, Cyrus Ekhdahl—as the nameplate on his desk announces—looks up.

"Cyrus," Frankie says. "I'm sure you remember me. Frankie. I work with Nico."

He glances behind her as if expecting Nico himself, then nods. "Sure."

"We have a slight situation. Nothing to worry about, but there's a reporter who's doing her due diligence and then some. So he sent me to talk about the report in a way we couldn't over the phone."

Cyrus doesn't look worried. "Nothing's in there that shouldn't be."

She says *good* a few times and then gets to the point. "The pills. That's our only real concern."

"No mention of the pills." Then he corrects himself. "Other than the one. We wrote down the number *one* but omitted the *two*."

Frankie hazards a guess, and forces a laugh. "One pill or twenty-one, what's the difference?"

He gives a lopsided smile. "Exactly."

Relief—that many pills means Nico wasn't lying. A thought rips through her mind: *This really could be over.* Maybe the last curveball was thrown.

But then the man continues.

"Not that it matters, anyhow. You got a gunshot victim, nobody's asking for a list of what was undigested or partially digested. We're fine."

It takes her a second. *Undigested. Partially digested.* All the relief she felt is gone. If the pills weren't totally digested, does that mean they didn't kill her? "You mean not everything was absorbed?"

"Of what we found, not entirely, but no way to be sure without looking into it more thoroughly."

"And you didn't do that?"

Now he looks at her, curious. "We were told to respect her privacy. She'd just been shot. Why get into that baloney?"

Just then, someone knocks on his door and pushes it open. His secretary, with a coffee. She notices Frankie. "I'm sorry, I didn't see you there. Can I get you one?"

Rattled, Frankie manages to say no, and only remembers to thank her as the secretary closes the door. If June was alive, it means her heart was still pumping. Frankie turns to Cyrus. "I'm so sorry. I'm not good at this. But if someone's shot when they're already dead, there's not *that* much blood, is there?"

Cyrus takes a sip of coffee, then pats the corner of his mouth with a napkin. "Why would someone shoot a dead person?"

She laughs. "Oh, I know. I'm just making sure, because in this case, there was *a lot* of blood listed on the police report, and we were there. It sure looked like a lot. At least I thought it was a lot, but that's why I'm checking. Did you see that report?"

"'Course I saw it. Heart pumps five liters of blood per minute at rest, so yes, a lot of blood is to be expected. And yes, there was a lot of it."

"Right. So what was listed on the report, that was *actually* what was there, right?"

"From what I remember."

"And what was there made sense for someone who'd been killed by a gunshot?"

Now he's getting annoyed, "Of course it did. I told you already."

She wipes her forehead, hoping he doesn't notice. "Good. Because there'd have been a lot *less* blood if she was already dead, if her heart wasn't beating."

As she knew it would be, it's too much. "*Yes, yes.* For the last time, yes. Anyone reads the reports, and all of it works together because it's all true, and no, it doesn't look like a dead person was shot, which would make *no sense anyhow*."

Frankie feels sick. She needs to get out of here.

But now he's watching her. "Why the third degree?"

"It's this reporter. Like I said. She's got doctors she's asking. I had to make sure it's consistent with being killed by a bullet."

"It's consistent."

Forcing a smile, she stands and thanks him, still reeling.

Was June's death a fix that went horribly wrong?

Maybe she was dying, maybe she was seconds away from being completely gone, but June was *alive* when Nico shot her.

CHAPTER 31

Get Ahead of It

Tuesday, March 14, 1933

Her mother would know what to do. Maybe it's being thoroughly alone at a time like this, but Frankie has finally realized that she needs someone, that being *able* to be alone isn't the same thing as wanting to be alone. She would forgive a thousand well-intentioned lies just to lean against her mother's shoulder or hear her voice. Or Jack. She thinks of going to him to tell him she's in over her head, that Nico might have shot June when she was alive, but Jack warned her, and she still chose to believe Nico over him. The only way she might redeem herself is if she helps to untangle Jack from June's death. Somehow.

One thing she knows is if she doesn't go to work today, Nico will notice and register the threat. And Nico does not respond well to threats.

On the drive, she rehearses what she'll say. She'll get ahead of it by telling Nico that she visited Cyrus, that she went to be sure the story was airtight, because she's heard rumors that a reporter's looking into things. If he questions who the rumors came from, she'll say one of her roommates; after all, both are secretaries who spend all day on the phone and are frequently on the receiving end of gossip. What's important is that she tells him this *before* Cyrus gets to him.

Meanwhile, the city seems to have gotten worse, not better. More and more buildings are demolished, with messy timbered piles left on the sides of roads. Dust and debris are everywhere. The car radio requires a key to unlock, and at a stop sign, she does this, turning up the volume on the news show. All over the country, the host says, banks have reopened, though President Roosevelt's pleading with the American people to leave their money be. *But good news, folks,* he continues, *because our prezzie's also recommending to Congress that they modify the Volstead Act in order to legalize the sale and transportation of liquor.* Laughter as the man catches his breath. *They need the revenue! I tell ya, we could get out of the Depression if they tax my booze alone, because I will cel-e-brate!*

People cross the street to join a line at the bank. Every second feels like another in which Nico's phone rings and Cyrus gets to him first. Right as she's about to accelerate, a family steps off the curb. Frankie slams on the brakes just in time, and a girl peers at Frankie's car as the mother pulls on her arm, eyes impatient, taking in the line. *People need the dream. They need the idea of happiness and success, and to think they can rise up from the ashes into something great. You tell them June hated her life and couldn't get through a day without pills, and who does that help?* Frankie wishes she could pull over and ask these people if it helps to think that anything is possible, or if the more important lesson is that struggle is a part of everyone's life, and there is no such thing as perfection. What has more impact, the value of a dream or the cost of a lie?

Every light turns red. Every car in front of her slows. It's the longest drive of her life, but at last she's outside the studio gates and pulling in. Along the wall, a tall woman holds a single pink rose, stepping carefully among the dried flowers as she reads notes that fans left behind.

"He's in a mood," Betty says the second Frankie walks in. "Got on a call and slammed the door."

Calmly, Frankie forces herself to drop her bag on her chair as she usually does, then go to the parrots. "Do you know who called?" she asks Betty.

"The ME."

The medical examiner. Frankie turns, eyeing the door behind her. If she goes home now, he will take it as confirmation of her guilt. Her only choice is to stay and try to play things off.

Through the window, she spots a crew filming two actors on bikes, kids who pedal as fast as they can, then stand up as the wind lifts their hair. To the left of their building are the Statue of Liberty and the Eiffel Tower. And somewhere behind her, like a memory never far off, is New York, those blocks that yank her through the years. All of it part of a magic that can save and an illusion that can destroy.

"Betty, does it help people to think the dream is possible?"

After a moment, the woman says, "Guess it depends on *what* dream. But we all need something to want, right? And it would be horrible to think you could just want and want and never get. So the possibility seems essential."

Nico's voice goes loud in the other room. Directly below the window, a group of people follow a tour guide. In unison, their faces angle toward Frankie's window.

So many movies, so many stories they've sold and worlds they've created. But threaded alongside are the stars themselves, actors whose names roll off tongues the same as if someone were referring to a friend. The movies are escape and entertainment, but what is the rest? The fascination that makes it not just about acting or stories? "Can you love someone's art and not them? That's the problem, isn't it? Celebrity has made it so the two go together."

"Do they?"

"What made June a great actress is what she couldn't show to the public because they wouldn't like it, but it made her real and it made her who she was, but they don't want that. Same with Jack, same with—"

"Frankie," Betty says. Her face is unreadable. She waits to be sure she has Frankie's attention, and then, under her breath, she continues: *"Careful."*

Through the wall, Nico yells Frankie's name. Already, Betty's back to her typewriter, a moment of silence before she unleashes a storm of clacking. Heart racing, Frankie goes to Nico's office and knocks on the door.

"I called you, didn't I?" Nico says when she enters. "Why'd you need to knock?"

Closing the door behind her, Frankie catches Betty watching before quickly looking down.

She forces a smile and takes a seat. "Everything good?"

The line between his brow deepens as if he's trying to figure something out. "Cyrus, the medical examiner, called to say a reporter is sniffing around."

Get ahead of it. "That's what I told him."

"When you were there."

"Right. Yesterday. I went to talk to him because I'm worried."

"About a reporter?"

"About *all* the reporters, but yes. I heard some rumors that someone's looking into the crime scene."

He taps his pen on the desk, and she sees that he wants to believe her, just as she wants to believe him. "Any idea who?"

She shakes her head. "It was vague. But I thought if I went there, maybe I'd run into someone. I hoped." *All believable,* she thinks.

"Mickey told me Magda was at the station trying to get information."

Magda. They sent her to the police station on a wild-goose chase to look into muddy shoe prints, and they did it so the chief of police would call Nico and tell him she was there, and so Magda would learn she was told on and be beholden to Nico. That is exactly what happened. Did he forget, or is he beginning to suspect everyone? "*We* sent her there," she says, not wanting Magda to get in trouble.

"Right, but what else has she stumbled on? With that article she printed, all conjecture and speculation—she's not on our side. I bet it was her."

From the other room, one of the parrots lets out a loud squawk. *Never let someone you love get in the way of doing what's right.* What is she doing? She can't live like this. Suddenly she's speaking, with no plan. "I think I'm going to leave."

He says nothing, confused.

"I can't do this anymore."

Now it hits him what she means. He studies her as if she's grown smaller. "Frankie, this is a tough time, I'll grant you that. But it's almost over."

She shakes her head. "It's not almost over. I don't think it ends."

He scratches his forehead, a red mark left behind, then looks to the door to make sure it's shut. "Cyrus said you were asking questions."

Always catch a person off guard, before they can rehearse.

Calmly, she says, "You shot her when she was still alive."

There is genuine confusion on his face. He's thrown, and almost starts to laugh, before realizing she's serious. "No, she wasn't. How could you say that?" He glances at the door as if it might have opened, then back to Frankie, waiting for her to respond.

"You did, Nico."

"I don't know why you're saying this."

"Because it's true."

"No. She was *gone*. Empty bottle of pills, I couldn't wake her up. A note. I told you—"

"She was *passed out*. From that bottle of champagne and who knows what she took earlier—but not twenty-one pills that weren't absorbed and were still *whole enough to be counted*."

There is fear on his face, but he doesn't fidget. He doesn't look away. He doesn't wring his hands or clear his throat. He's steady when he speaks, and his voice comes out strong and genuine. "What are you saying? You're saying that it wasn't the pills?"

"I'm saying her heart was still beating. That's why there was so much blood."

"No, I didn't feel a pulse. She was gone."

He believes what he's saying. But she also knows that he will double down, and at this point, he's gone way too far to back out. All that makes for a man who is very, very dangerous.

"Twenty-one pills, Nico. She might have *just* taken them."

He lowers his head. "She had the lights off. And the door locked. She didn't leave it open because she didn't *want* me to find her. Because she meant it. And she left a note," he says again, as if reading from a list he's compiled at night, all the ways he's reassured himself. "There was no pulse, nothing I could—" He stops. "She meant it."

Later she will wonder if she was cruel. Later she will remember that the medical examiner said *undissolved* and *partially dissolved pills*, and that without a real autopsy whose purpose was to find the truth—rather than scratch the surface for appearances—there's no way to know what impact the pills truly had, or what she might have taken prior. *Was* she as good as gone? Or was she gone? All Frankie knows for sure is Nico's done enough, and forcing June and Jack to marry could've been the final straw. The bottom line is that, for years, June was made to lead a life that wasn't her own, and now he's trying to take away the truth of her death as well.

Calmly, Frankie replies, "Maybe she did mean it. And maybe it *was* too late. But we'll never know, because you cared more about saving the studio than you did about saving her."

The second she says it, he nods as if a new understanding is taking hold. And though his eyes are red and shine as if he's holding back tears, his gaze is steady.

"The house is ours. The apartment is ours. The car is ours."

He'll take everything. It's as if the moment has finally arrived. As if all her life she's been running toward an edge, closer and closer, and here, right now, her feet have found the air. She will be alone and she will have nothing. Somehow, though, she's not afraid. Because she had what she thought was right and told herself she didn't need anyone and that the goal was a house on a hill and silence, and she had all that within reach. The steady check and the safety net that Nico affords her. But now she sees what it truly amounts to.

"If you make this choice," he continues, "it's a big one. You don't come back from it. And don't think the tides won't turn on Jack. I'm the one who's keeping him safe, for now."

The necklace. The gun. He has the means to frame Jack, anytime. And maybe this ruthlessness drives it home: If she embraces her long-held idea of success by turning her back on what's truly right, *that's* when she'll fail. That's when the ground beneath her feet will disappear.

So she stands. He looks at her only for a moment before angling the lampshade on his desk as if the light has grown too much, and doesn't watch as she walks out the door.

~

She doesn't tell Betty what happened, but from the way Betty looks down, the way she fills the silence with typing, she knows. What all did she hear? Betty, whose desk fills with flowers on her birthday and who's invited to every premiere and party. How much does she keep quiet about? One last time, Frankie goes to Romeo and Juliet, whispering a goodbye, then gathers her belongings at her desk: a photo of her and Nico in front of the New York restaurant facade, a Bayer aspirin tin, and the script of *The Last Chance* that the cast signed. *Frankie, It's always a good day for a beach day! —Jack*

Venice. The little house.

With her back to Betty, she picks up the phone and asks to be put through to Jack's Pasadena residence, where O'Shea answers. Quietly, she says, "Tell him Frankie needs a beach day and is going there. Tell him that I need to do this, and I hope that's all right with him."

O'Shea knows what she's referring to, and must know she doesn't want the studio operator to hear. She can hear the concern in his voice. "Of course, but are you—"

"I'm fine. I will be fine. Right now, I just need a beach day."

When she hangs up, Betty is standing at a plant nearby, slowly pouring in water. "They loved each other. You should know that."

Frankie glances at Nico's closed door. "Who did?"

"June and Tank."

Does Betty know that Tank called her? It's not far-fetched to think she checked in with the studio operator after overhearing a call that seemed suspicious. "I was still in New York then."

Betty gives a short laugh. "*Then?* You mean a few weeks ago you were in New York?"

Frankie tries to play it off with a laugh of her own. "I just mean I wasn't always sure it *was* love. Real love, I mean."

"You weren't? Seemed clear to me. I blame Iffy," she says about June's sister, "if you want to know the truth. If she didn't run her big mouth to Nico the second June told her they were eloping, everything might've been different."

Frankie tries to keep the surprise from her face as Betty continues. "I think about it, sometimes. How different it all would've been. The two of them married, and not one thing we could do. Not one thing." She pulls a dead leaf off the plant, and then another one, crumpling them in her hand. "Husband and wife happy and together, at last. Call me old-fashioned, but I think a man should at least have the *option* of raising his own child."

Words stick in Frankie's throat. She wants to throw the phone against the wall, to slam open the window and scream across the lot. Because *Tank* was the father, and Tank and June were in love. They *wanted* to be together. *June was trying to fix her own life* when the studio stopped her.

All she manages to say, quietly, is, "You're right. It would've been so different."

That one moment, the moment Ida heard the plan. If she congratulated her sister. If she forced a smile. If she turned away and let the rest unfold.

Betty tests the soil in another pot. "I know Iffy thought she knew what was best for June, everyone did. But I'm not forgiving her. No way. And I *know* Tank wasn't perfect, but he's *still* doing right by June's reputation. The way I see it, *that's* love."

Tank, who the studio most likely strong-armed into not talking about his relationship with June or the truth of their feelings or the child that they'd wanted, because it would damage her reputation. Tank, who behaved, even when the police dragged him in and kept him for questioning, because he genuinely wanted what was best for June.

Tank, who just wanted to know that June really loved him.

A bit of water splashes onto the floor, and Betty uses her shoe to spread it out till it's almost gone. What did Nico tell Frankie? That in that last call June made, she said *he didn't even show up.* June meant Tank. *He* was who the other glass was for. But June didn't know that Nico made him leave that night, that Nico had enough on Tank to ensure he listened. Did he pay him? Threaten him? Or just lie?

She doesn't want to be with you, and you will destroy her. Did Nico say that?

If you love her, you will let her go.

Frankie can almost hear him saying those words.

I messed up, Tank told Frankie. Because he listened to Nico, because he didn't go to June that night.

Softly, Frankie says, "If only Tank didn't buy the lies, hook, line, and sinker."

"People are so vulnerable when it comes to love. I guess I see why. Love is pretty unbelievable, so maybe it just makes more sense to think it can't be real."

"It's *easier* to think it's not real."

Through this new lens, everything with Tank and June looks different. June never wanted to be rid of him. And he was never stalking her or invading her privacy—they were simply caught trying to have a forbidden relationship. When he showed up at nearby hotels when she was on location, it would've been because June told him where to go.

When he was at the premiere, it was because he was proud and wanted to be close by, any way he could. And at the funeral, he was only trying to grieve.

"The whole Jack-and-June thing was a mess," Betty says. "I love a good romance, but some things are just cruel. And really, it gives me *hope* that an even better love story could be the one without an audience. Bodes well for the rest of us, doesn't it?" Looking straight at Frankie, Betty adds, "Still, it might be nice for him to know it *was* real. That she did really love him."

"You're right." Frankie glances toward Nico's office door. "Love is hard enough without other people making it impossible."

"Well, I expect you might know a bit about that too." Betty gives a small smile, and then, as if she never spoke, she turns to a palm tree in the corner and pours in the rest of the water.

Betty. Sometimes forgotten, but always listening.

Frankie needs to get out of here. But for the first time in years, she has no direction and no plan. And worse, she's walking away from the best thing she's ever had.

Silently, she puts *The Last Chance* script in her bag when she sees the corner where June signed her name:

Frankie, don't worry, it's not your last chance . . . it's all just beginning! ❤ *June*

CHAPTER 32

You Can't Win if You Don't Play the Game

Palm trees line the path to the parking lot, fronds splayed against the blue dome of sky. The box of Frankie's belongings is under her arm, an announcement to the world that she's now unemployed. Even the word sparks fear into her heart, because it's the state she's sworn to avoid, the beginning of the end. But somehow it doesn't feel that way. Somehow it feels as though she already reached the end and is about to keep going.

At the parking lot, a group of executives avoids her eyes, sensing devastation. But then there's one person, leaned against a car, smoking, who looks hard at Frankie and doesn't look away.

"*No,*" Magda says. A cloudy wisp escapes her mouth, a smoky tendril. "I don't believe it."

Frankie hoists the box up on her hip. At the corner, a man in a Ford De Luxe Roadster pulls to the side to let out his passenger, a woman dressed in a ball gown. With one gloved hand, the woman holds up her jeweled hem as she hurries toward the path.

Frankie looks away. "Magda, don't you know that anything is possible."

Not a question but a statement. A slightly angry, sarcastic statement.

A laugh. "We didn't always see eye to eye, but I respect you, Frankie. I do wish you the best."

Instead of leaving, Frankie sets the box on the hood of Magda's car. "Why?"

Surprise widens Magda's face. "Why what? Why do I wish you the best, or why do I respect you?"

"The respect. What have I done to deserve it?"

"Oh, well. You work hard. You're determined. I can tell you're smart. Women don't have an easy road here, so you must've done something right." She glances at the box on the hood. "I'd venture to say you're *still* doing something right, and it wasn't taken kindly."

Right; Frankie thought she'd been right, and was helping people. She saw the relief when she or Nico swooped in. She witnessed the happiness when she fixed things. "I don't know what's right anymore."

Magda drops her cigarette on the ground. Grinding it with her heel, she says, "Good grief. Do I need to worry about you now?"

"No. Worry about all the people that you don't . . ." She stops, searching for the words. "Worry about your part in this."

Immediately Magda's brows rise. "Boy, Frankie, I was trying to be nice."

Behind Magda are the studio gates, the giant arches that dwarf the street. A flock of birds twists and turns above, slipping like rope through the sky. "I'm not trying to insult you. It's that the stories you write, they're *stories*. And you see what's wrong. You must. The studios own the actors, and they own the stories that come out about them, and everyone lives in fear of not being loved, and it's *impossible* and it's not real."

"Slow down, Frankie, the whole world's not—"

"You, me, Nico, we're all complicit. We've turned entertainment into reality and reality into entertainment, and somehow it's all become a lie."

"I write about movies. You're saying you don't like movies?"

"Are you kidding? I *love* movies. Movies saved me, more than once. What we do *is* important, but there's more alongside it, isn't there? How many articles do you really write about the *actual* movies?"

Magda purses her lips, defensive. Still, she considers her words before saying, "I give people what they want. If they want a gossip story, that's what I give them. I don't *tell* people what to want. I'm not good at making people want something. I'm good at figuring out *what* they want."

In a way, Frankie agrees. But it's more than what the people want. It's filtering what they believe is *possible*. It's pressure to be perfect. It's thinking that perfection exists and should be aspired to. She thinks of Virginia. *How does it help if I spend my whole life thinking I could've had it better, because of a lie? Because I believed in some impossible perfection?* Maybe it boils down to the fact that the dream can be great, but it's a temporary fix. The lie, however, can lead to a lifetime of heartbreak. And if it's up to people to sort through what's what, then they need to have a chance at true understanding.

At last, she says, "Strategy relies on information. People need truth."

Magda laughs. "You try your hand at a paper that only tells the truth. See how far you get."

"That's why you stopped, because it wasn't easy. Isn't that what you said?"

Magda sighs. "Right now, I'm trying to figure out how to get back on Nico's good side, and from the looks of things, you know how important that is. So, let's leave it at this: I respect you, and I wish you the best."

With that, Magda walks onto the studio lot.

~

Leaving her life is easy. The five boxes are already packed, and Frankie loads them into her car, which she'll ask O'Shea to return tomorrow. Tonight, she just needs to get to Venice. Someplace safe, a house that might be small and worn but reminds her of better times and all that's right in the world.

She'll talk to her roommates later, explain as much as she can. For now, she's got what she needs and is readying to leave the apartment when the radio host follows up an advertisement with an excited trill and whistle.

"Folks, have I got a juicy rumor for you. I've just been handed the scoop of the century or, at least, the scoop of the week, because Hollywood's moving fast these days. But dare I say, one of Hollywood's *preeminent* tabloid reporters just let me in on the possibility that RCO Studios *may* be admitting that Jack Sawyer's alibi is suddenly *not sure* if he's remembering things correctly."

Frankie stares at the radio, her car keys hanging in her hand, forgotten.

"You heard me. *Not sure.* How can this guy be confused? Don't you remember if you play cards with someone like Jack Sawyer in a fancy Malibu house? All I know is things could get very interesting in the next few days."

A song starts up, and Frankie switches off the radio, reeling. Heavily, she sits in the nearby chair, weighted with fear, because she knows this is Nico. Magda's caved to his pressure, and he's telling Frankie to back off. What she just heard was a warning shot.

Without thinking, she sets her keys on the table, picks up the phone, and calls Magda's office.

The second the woman answers, Frankie says, "How *could* you?"

There is a beat of silence before Magda says, "Frankie. That wasn't me."

"The *preeminent* Hollywood tabloid reporter? After you *just* told me you were trying to get back on his good side? I thought you understood what I meant when I said we were *all* complicit. I thought you were listening and maybe even agreed, but then you went and—"

"Stop. Frankie, stop. *It wasn't me.*" There is a loud sigh, and Magda continues. "I think they meant Dottie."

Dottie. Of course. Nico's playing the reporters against each other, and no doubt made Dottie promises in exchange for this favor. *The truth means nothing?* Once upon a time, Dottie asked Frankie this question as they walked through the parking lot at the Ambassador Hotel. It wasn't even that long ago, but it feels like a different lifetime.

Worse, Nico's sending the message that he can take down Jack, just like that.

You can't win if you don't play the game.

An idea is forming. A plan. But she can't spell it out with the operator listening. "Magda. I can't say much now. And you might hate me, and I don't blame you. I hate me too right now. But somewhere deep down, you know things aren't right."

There's no response, and Frankie glances at the clock on the wall. She wants to get to Venice before it gets dark. Maybe nothing she does will make a difference, but she thinks of Dede, who's already hailed as the next June, and all the actresses who will follow, and of Jack, who will never be free from the studio's grasp. "If you want a chance to do what's right, and you want to know more about that night, then I'll tell you."

Magda's voice emerges in a whisper. "*That* night? As in—"

"Yes. That one."

"And *you* know more?"

Frankie thinks of the operator possibly listening in, and knows there's no way the person would know which night she's referring to, at least not definitively. "I know everything. Call O'Shea, Jack's valet. Tell him Frankie wants you to join her beach day, and he'll tell you where to go."

It's an extra step, but a different operator will connect that call, and that will ensure nothing could be pieced together.

Frankie picks up her keys. "Maybe you were right, and we only give people what they want. But I have to do something, because I'm not sure I want to live in a world where what's real doesn't matter."

CHAPTER 33

The Big Picture

Dusk is falling, the world lilac-tinged and furtive. *Dusk is the time things disappear,* her mother used to say when cautioning her to be careful crossing streets in the evening. Frankie thinks of Fiona, can practically hear her urging her to act, to do something. Her mother was no stranger to mistakes, but she lived life fully. Fear never factored into her decisions.

Jack keeps a spare key under a pot near the back fence, but on her way to Venice, Frankie realizes he might have removed it. Maybe he didn't want to risk her dropping in. Then she thinks of the quake, of the damage the house might have endured since it's closer to Long Beach. She didn't think any of this through, but she tightens her grip on the steering wheel all the same, determined to keep going.

Venice High School has been destroyed, and the ruins look almost Greek or Roman, with only columns and statues left standing. Already, there is a tent city for classrooms, and Frankie pauses to let two teachers cross the street, textbooks in their hands. Elsewhere, the damage is sporadic: a row of hotels with signs that hang askew and a bank of windows boarded up, while a block over, a stretch of houses looks untouched. When she reaches Menotti's, the market, she thinks about a night Jack wore a hat and glasses, and together they went through

Cesar Menotti's trapdoor by the crates of apples and down into a secret speakeasy—not to drink but to be a part of pulse-spiking fun. No one recognized him, or maybe no one cared, and he and Frankie sat in a corner together with a script on the table should they need to pretend the visit was work-related. The one time they were out, just the two of them. He'd asked the waiter about his accent and ended up getting the man's life story, including the fact that his mother just died and he was working to afford the trip back to Sorrento. When they left, Jack slid a tip under the menu that was more than enough for the journey home.

Oil rigs are off to the right, an ominous sight. Then, through the window, there's the scent of still water and algae and sea, a murky green comfort. At the end of the street is the Abbott Kinney Pier, which Jack has told her is crucial in moving liquor from three miles out—just past the territorial waters of the United Sates—and into Venice.

There is a small alley behind the cottage, and a narrow garage. Inside it, her car's headlights catch on spiderwebs, shining intricacies. So, she's not the only one who hasn't been here, she sees. Maybe it was too much for him as well, this physical reminder of an easier time.

The backyard is no bigger than a postage stamp, but neat and tidy. She tips back the third clay pot by the fence and holds her breath. The key is there. A relief. The windows are dark, and when she jiggles the knob and opens the back door, there's the scent of old wood and pipe tobacco. She flips on the light, surveying the kitchen. There are chipped mixing bowls in the corner, ones they used to mix pancake batter in the middle of the night. Pot holders, still hanging from a hook on the wall, stained red from a day when Frankie made cherry pie and the filling boiled over. And on the counter are dog-eared cookbooks, just waiting for hungry hands. Holding them in place is an orange enamel pitcher that's weighted down with sand.

And then she sees the trash can and the glimmer of broken glass. Someone *has* been here. Her heart races as she thinks of Nico, one of the few who knows about this house. Could he be here? Waiting?

"Frankie."

She startles. There, looking as though he's just woken up, is Jack. In one second, without thought or worry, she's in his arms, her cheek against the cotton of his shirt. "You're all right," he says.

"I didn't see your car."

"I didn't tell you? A tree branch got it. I've been either borrowing O'Shea's or he's driving me in his. But he said you were coming here and you needed me, so I had him drop me off."

She feels his fingers trace a circle on her back, and closes her eyes. "I'm sorry," she says. "Well, really, *you* should be sorry you didn't ask me to use those details in the movie, because you're not *entitled* to my life, but I'm sorry I didn't read the script before getting mad."

She feels a laugh build in his chest. "I *am* sorry," he says. "I told you I'd have them reshoot if you want. I mean it."

"No. I might like it the way it is."

He pulls back to look her in the eye. "You too, you know. You're not entitled to my life. I know it's your job to fix things, but if it's my mess and *I* want to fix it, you have to let me. I can't be with someone who doesn't trust me with my own life."

"Agreed."

He raises a brow, surprised. "Good."

"Though it's not really my job either. Not anymore."

A pause as he takes this in. He pulls out a chair for her, from the kitchen table, and then takes a seat.

When Jack hears that without a doubt he did *not* cause June's death, his relief is enormous but temporary, because Frankie continues and tells him the rest. The house grows quiet, the kitchen light throwing shadows. Any solace he must have felt is gone, because he gets up, pacing and frustrated, until she tells him her plan.

~

Close to nine p.m., there's a knock on the front door. Jack peers behind the curtain and then signals to Frankie that it's okay. Though Frankie wasn't sure that Magda would come, she had a hunch that the promise of learning about that night would be too great a lure.

Jack opens the door, motioning to the living room as Magda steps inside, her eyes wide at the sight of him. Frankie, sitting in an old armchair with a plate of spaghetti, stands to greet her.

"Spaghetti?" Frankie asks as she sets the plate on the coffee table.

Magda just shakes her head, surveying the room. "Whose house is this?"

Jack raises his hand, and Magda turns, taking in the pile of scripts, a fishing pole leaned in the corner of the room, the brown tweed coat and hat that he uses when he tries to leave the house with a slight disguise, and a NuGrape soda bottle on the coffee table. "Of course," she repeats a few times as if everyone has a secret house that is *them*, a place like an essence that's left behind after everything unnecessary is boiled away.

Now she must register that Frankie's barefoot and comfortable. She looks to Jack, also barefoot and comfortable. "Well, you two are full of secrets."

Frankie smiles. "You have no idea."

Jack's already looking for wine. "I'm going to say you might need a beverage for this. I'm sticking to soda from here on out, but I've got a bottle hidden somewhere."

So as Magda takes sips that soon increase in speed, Frankie tells her the version that she and Jack agreed upon, which involves the truth about the studio and its pressures, its vise grip on those under contract, as well as June and her problems, the doctor who gave her "medicine" that helped her meet deadlines and obligations but hurt her health, the secret baby she lost, the one she couldn't have with the man she loved, the truth about her and Tank, and of course the truth about Frankie and Jack.

"Good Lord," Magda says.

And then Frankie tells her about the call June made to Nico before she swallowed a bottle of pills.

In the pause, Frankie waits for Magda to make the connection.

"But she was *shot*," Magda says, refilling her glass. And then her hand shakes, and she spills. She sets the bottle down.

Frankie nods. "Right."

"He shot her."

"Only when she was already dead." That, Frankie will stick to. Medically, she's murky on what really happened, and fairly convinced that at this point no one could ever learn the truth, but the bottom line is Magda knowing what Nico did could only put her in danger. "He did it to save her reputation. He knew people would still love her if she was a victim."

"I need air."

"There are chairs out back," Jack says.

Outside, Frankie takes a seat in one of the wicker rockers, and Magda sits heavily beside her, head lowered. The moon is partially shaded but so clear that the curvature is obvious in a way it's normally not. With the dimension, it feels real, and for the first time, Frankie grasps just the edge of life's enormity, that she is one little person, on one little planet. And whereas, any other day, that might make her feel small and insignificant, now it is a comfort, because it means she belongs to something bigger, something she could never fully see. But just because you don't see it, doesn't mean it's not there.

She thinks of her mother. Of all the signs she's asked for, all the times she's craved to hear her mother's voice or feel her presence, anything to prove that something so monumental as a life hasn't completely disappeared. Could the signs have been there the whole time, unseen? She thinks of the man at the gas station. The colors in the sky. The woman who let her take her place in line. The list could go on, she realizes. So many moments like the grasp of a hand that helped her up. And maybe it's all just coincidence and luck, existence a tangled and beautiful confusion, but she wants to believe that it's true: Her mother *has* been here the whole time.

This, she thinks, looking up, is what they are all a part of. A stunningly vast and endless fabric, limitless and constant and full of possibilities. A big picture that is composed of all that is small, and all those who worry they won't matter.

Magda still has her head lowered, trying to take deep breaths. "Keep going."

Frankie looks away from the moon. "I thought I was helping. Spelling it out like tonight makes it seem black and white. But it wasn't. At least it didn't feel like it was. I think I was afraid to see the parts that were wrong; I guess that's the bottom line."

Head still lowered, Magda nods. "You and me both." At last, she looks up. She touches the corner of her eye as if to press a tear in place. "And you didn't mind losing him?"

At first Frankie thinks she means Nico. Then she sees that she's glancing back at the window, where Jack stands at the sink, washing the plates. "I told myself I couldn't lose what I didn't have."

"You didn't believe he loved you."

"I didn't believe I was worth loving."

Neither says anything more, the steady pulse of crickets and frogs the only sound. Then Magda leans back in the chair, tilting her head to take in the moon. "I'm familiar with that song and dance too, by the way. But the matter at hand. I'm assuming you have a plan?"

Frankie nods. "There are two problems. The first one is June. Because I hate to admit it, but Nico was right: We reveal she did this to herself, and it hurts her all over again. It destroys her reputation, needlessly. And she's not here to defend herself. I don't want to victimize her again. But there might be a way we can honor her by exposing the studio, just enough that maybe something changes."

"I'm all ears."

"But the second problem is Nico. We push him too far, and he pushes back—and he *will* push harder. What he did by having Dottie leak this alibi rumor, that was a message."

"I figured."

"He can frame Jack. Easily. But if we get ahead of it, if we're fast, we have the element of surprise. We can take what he put out there and spin it."

"Even though he's got the necklace? And the cops in his pocket?"

"Yes."

Magda laughs. "He's got all the evidence. What exactly do we have?"

"We have you. The power of the press."

CHAPTER 34

The Last Lie

Wednesday, March 15, 1933

The first day of trading after the closure of Wall Street, the world wakes with an excited start. Already, the country is looking at a gaining Dow Jones Industrial Average, and hope is in the air—a new feeling, invigorated and motivated. On the radio, the announcer talks about new starts and new beginnings, and for the first time ever, Frankie wakes to languid late-morning sun through the window, and Jack's arm around her. No longer is she worried they'll be caught. No longer are they trying to hide.

"I won't move in," she says.

"Ah, see, I like to start the day with *good morning*."

"I'm here while I figure things out and get another job, but I'm not making the same mistakes my mom—" She stops. For as long as she can remember, she saw her mother's life as a warning: a woman weak enough to constantly be overpowered by a man's lure, to always hope that the next time would be different. Suddenly, she wonders if she's been seeing it wrong, if her mother's strength was actually the *ability* to hope, the bravery to hope, in the face of everything. To try again. Or maybe not. Maybe it's a bit of everything, because that's how life is. The one thing she knows is being brave enough to love, or even being open to love, is also a kind of strength. She remembers Nico telling her to tread carefully, that *fearless people take too many risks*. But Frankie wasn't fearless. She held anything that could've really hurt her at arm's length. Where was the bravery in that?

"I don't know what I'm doing," Frankie finally says.

"I think you're in bed, in Venice."

"I don't have a plan, past today." She stares at the ceiling.

"You know what that says to me? That you have a whole lot of options."

~

Later, O'Shea calls to report that he did as instructed and returned the car to the studio. Officially, Frankie has broken free.

Then they wait. An entire day of nothing but each other. Luxurious in its mundanity. They make pancakes for lunch, they take a bath, they organize the bookshelf, searching for a four-leaf clover Frankie once pressed between the pages of one of the novels. And later they sit on the porch, watching shifting reflections on the canal. Algae and settled water and a whiff of sea in the air, an ocean promise. She thinks of going to the beach tonight, to sit on the sand and dig her toes into the cold, to take in a view that speaks of the past and the future, of here and distant lands, because it won't matter if people see them together. Not after tonight.

"A picnic," she says.

"On the beach. It's a date."

But tension starts to creep in. They're waiting for the evening edition of Magda's paper to be delivered, and for the chaos her article will unleash. Working to their advantage is the fact that it will be too late for Nico to do anything to counter, though, still, Frankie watches the clock on the kitchen wall, and every noise sounds like the thwack of a newspaper and the repercussions it will bring.

"A watched clock doesn't deliver a newspaper," Jack says. "You feel like sandwiches?"

There's no bread, so they do peanut butter and strawberry jelly on saltine crackers, dozens and dozens of surprisingly delicious little sandwiches.

Jack watches her. "You were wrong, by the way."

Frankie, chewing, looks up.

"You told me I had people fixing things and cleaning up my messes, so I didn't know repercussions. But I was *living* the repercussion. And I did it, willingly, for years. I went along with everything, because I figured I was lucky, and I'd reached the goal. Big house, money, fame. That's the pinnacle, right? The be-all end-all?"

"Supposedly." A pause. "I figured you weren't *really* willing to risk it all."

"You're wrong there too. Because how lucky could I be if I can't do what I love, or be with who I—" He stops, and smiles.

Wiping jelly from the corner of her mouth, she says, "I think I like being wrong."

Then there's a knock on the front door.

They freeze. Glance at each other. They arranged to have a special messenger deliver a paper to Nico at his house, which should be happening right about now, so there's no way it's Nico at the door. "The paper," Jack says.

Halfway on the Welcome Mat is the evening edition, the words We Lied in big capital letters on the front page. They take it to the kitchen, where Frankie reads aloud. The article is written from Magda, directly to her readers.

> Excuse the interruption of your evening, but a development in the death of June Finney has just come to light, and I promise it deserves your attention. RCO Studios, in a brave and bold move, has disclosed to yours truly that the facts of June Finney's final days were different than they'd reported.

Here is what is still true: June was killed in a robbery gone wrong, and Jack Sawyer had *nothing* to do with her death.

Other than that, the studio admits that much of the June-and-Jack lore was just that: fiction, a tale, a myth, an invention to make the public happy . . . a lie. Though their supposed romance captivated fans all over the world, June and Jack did not, in fact, have a love to end all ages . . . at least not with each other. In fact, June Finney was desperately in love with someone whom she wanted to spend the rest of her life with, a man who was not Jack. Jack, similarly, was in a relationship with a woman who was not June. While the public, at times, feels as though it's their right to know the details of their favorite stars' personal to-dos, this reporter will opt to respect their privacy and only say this: They found love. And that's all that needs saying.

Sources close to the couple claim they'd planned on publicly calling off their engagement so they could be with the people of their choosing when June's life was cut short. You may have caught wind of the swirling rumor that Jack was not with a friend in Malibu on the night in question, and that his alibi couldn't hold a drop of water. That's because Jack was with the woman he was seeing, a woman who, for obvious reasons, couldn't be mentioned without opening Pandora's box.

"We made a choice to keep up the charade of their relationship," studio publicist Frankie Donnelly said. "After all, the American people had just lost their favorite star. We didn't want to destroy their favorite love story as well."

But now RCO is taking the world by storm with this rare and gutsy mea culpa.

"What we realized is we chose wrong," Ms. Donnelly continued. "It wasn't fair to anyone, including the man June loved unquestioningly and unwaveringly right up until the end. And though we are respecting his privacy, he deserves to know how much he meant to her. Just as the American people deserve to know that what was presented to them wasn't always truth. The ability to dream and imagine a life that's different than your own is no small thing. Films are extraordinary and important and have been a gift to the world during these hard times. But though people deserve the ability to dream, they also need the truth that makes dreams attainable. Perfect is not possible. June Finney had flaws. She struggled and made mistakes. But instead of letting her be true to herself, faults and all, we tried to make her into what we thought the public would want, even going so far as to deny her real love. This was wrong, and it's time for a rewrite. It's time for us to be more truthful and accepting of our very human celebrities. The public deserves this, the many talented actors and actresses at RCO and every studio deserve this, and certainly June Finney deserved this. Hollywood's stars are earthbound, after all, and nothing is perfect, including us. We will try to do better."

How's that for a Wednesday-night revelation? I don't know about you, but I wish June could've been with the person she loved, and I certainly hope Jack and others will get that chance. In fact, stay tuned, because Jack Sawyer has told me something else he wants to come clean about. It takes a big man—or woman, or studio—to admit they're wrong, and I, for one, think even more highly about RCO because they

> love their stars enough to let them be who they are. I certainly hope my fine readers feel the same.

Frankie and Jack debated about taking it further, about revealing more, but ultimately decided against it. Was that right? Or wrong? Could Nico have saved June in the first place? Without a true medical inquiry—and one not determined to protect the studio's interests—how could anyone know? And though even Frankie understands that this line of thinking could be nothing more than a feeble and final way to protect someone she feels conflicted about, the truth is there was no way to reveal Nico's involvement without betraying June and revealing her private life in a way she would've hated.

For now, this was the best they could do. For June, and for everyone. Including Tank. Frankie pictures him reading these words, knowing definitively that June *did* love him. Soon, she will reach out to him as well, but in the meantime, she hopes this reconstructs a bit of the world he once believed in.

"The article's good," Jack says, wrapping two bottles of NuGrape soda with a kitchen towel and setting them in the basket. "Remind me I said that later, when Magda's next story comes out." Then a pause. "But I'm glad, for June. Even though it's not perfect."

"There's no being perfect in an imperfect world," Frankie says. "But at least it's something."

~

They are about to leave for their picnic when the phone rings. Frankie knew he'd call her apartment first, then track her down with Jack. Again, the phone rings, and she pictures Nico answering the door, the messenger handing over the paper with the note she paper-clipped to the front: *For June . . . the last lie.*

She picks up the phone. "Hi."

"You have no idea what you've done."

"I think I do."

Silence. From across the room, Jack watches her, then leaves to give her privacy.

"This is going to affect other studios, not just us," Nico says.

"I hope it does."

"It's not gonna go over well."

"Didn't think it would."

There is a long silence, and then he gives a small laugh. "You got ahead of it, I'll give you that." Another pause, and he continues. "Timed it so I couldn't get a response out till tomorrow. Spun what I planted. Recalled that I used the words *Pandora's box* and put that line in there as a reminder of all you know, a message I'd receive loud and clear. *And* made it so somehow the studio looks good enough that I can't undo this."

"You're saying I did well?"

"For someone intent on blowing up their place of work, yes, you did amazing."

Despite herself, she smiles.

"Jack too," Nico adds. "Donna—that story's gonna be a doozy. And his agent already called. The powers that be will *not* love him doing plays."

An addendum to his contract. A correction, a chance to get back to the core of what he loves.

"I think he's earned the chance to do what he wants." Then she adds, "But, Nico, I tried to tread carefully."

When he says nothing, she presses the phone closer. She thinks she hears him breathing.

Finally, voice jagged, he says, "I appreciate it. More than you know." A pause. Again, she hears a wavering breath. "I didn't *know*, if that helps. That she was—well, I didn't know."

She says nothing.

"I tried, but I couldn't wake—"

"Nico." Now she stops him before he admits too much with an operator listening. "Aren't you the one who told me you'd be a rich man if intentions counted?"

Barely, she thinks she hears him pushing the phone away, as though he doesn't want her to hear him cry.

"I should go," she finally says.

"Wait." He clears his throat. "Are you behind what happened with Romeo and Juliet?"

It takes Frankie a second to understand he's talking about the parrots. "No. Why? What happened?"

"Someone left the door to their addition *and* a window open."

Immediately she's hit with worry but then remembers that Nico once told her that Los Angeles would make a good home for them, with all the tropical fruits and berries people insist on planting.

Now he continues. "They were last seen enjoying their freedom at the rainforest set before taking off. Just strange that one of the windows was open at the same time that door was open, so I thought you might've known something about it."

"No," Frankie says, but then she pictures Betty with her hands on the latch. Betty, who told Frankie about the wild parrot she saw outside the window. "Actually, it might've been me."

"Really?" Nico says, but she hears the doubt in his voice. "And you're only now remembering this?"

"It's been a busy few days."

"I guess at least Betty will be happy."

Betty, who told her that the studio kept June and Tank apart so they could enforce their own version of romance. *I love a good love story, but some things are just cruel.*

CHAPTER 35

This Golden Age

There is a stripe of blazing, brilliant orange above the horizon and a wide golden reflection that shoots like a ray across the water, glinting and bright. The weather is still cool, so the beach is empty. They've weighted down a blanket on all corners with their belongings, and two pillows prop up their heads so they can see the sunset.

Frankie tells Jack about the birds.

"Betty talked about seeing one outside," Jack says. "Did she tell you?"

Frankie nods. "They'd find each other, right?"

"I think it's the first thing they'll do."

In her mind, a whole future unravels for Los Angeles, and she imagines that in a hundred years there will be flocks and flocks of lime-green parrots—drifting in the sky, peering from between palm fronds, brightening the world with improbability. In a city that's growing bigger every day, with boulevards that get fatter and wider and buildings that get taller and taller, the birds will be tropical and exotic and illogical. A touch of fantasy. A child will look up, entranced. *It doesn't make sense,* people will say, and they will never know. Stories will be invented, theories tossed about. But it will be nothing more than lore.

Lore. Myth. Legend. The fascination with stars and their lives has grown right alongside the rise of movies, but where will it go? She thinks about the article, the impact it might have. That she *hopes* it has. This same city in a hundred years, this same country, this same world—what will they think about this time, this golden age? Will they look back and see anything other than the glitz and glamour? Will they know the truth and see the scars and blemishes? She thinks of the ugly beauty that Jack once spoke of, and hopes that people see the truth, because despite any faults or imperfections, the truth is always more meaningful than the best of lies.

They eat their cracker sandwiches, fingers sticky with strawberry jelly. They drink their NuGrape soda, sand clinging to the bottles. Then they lie back on their simple blanket, facing a sky that's losing brightness and seeping into violet and steel blue, then indigo and navy.

At one point, Jack rolls over and breathes his words into her ear. "Do you still not want me to say it?"

She smiles to the darkened sky. This is her Jack.

"I don't *need* you to," she says, "but I might want you to."

Before he can speak, something catches her eye, and she sits up. Light fills the water as if a spotlight shines from deep within the earth. The waves are electric blue with glowing white that brightens with each tumult and crash.

Beside her, Jack stares, speechless. Then they're walking, feet sinking into the sand until their ankles are covered with water that looks normal until agitated with a wave or a kick. Then, with even the slightest disturbance, it flares with glow.

Jack is saying the word *bioluminescence*, claiming he's heard this happens here but has never seen it in person. Frankie, however, is barely listening, too consumed with simply enjoying what's before her, feeling the tug and pull of waves. It's as though they're at the border of magic and reality, of fantasy and truth—a hem in the fabric of both worlds. Maybe where the edges meet, anything is possible.

Above her, the stars are a dusting of brightness. Before her, a tide of impossible beauty. She wants to cry at the wonder of it all. How easily they could've missed this night. So many ways and so many paths they might've taken away from each other, so many moments that might've led somewhere else, into other arms or cities or hearts. But like everything that is too big to understand or too vast to fully glimpse, there is something comforting in that this would've been here, even on an empty beach, just waiting to be seen.

Acknowledgments

Los Angeles is my home, and I would first like to thank the city itself for being a place where one can journey from sand to snow in an afternoon, but also for being the birthplace of so many stories, so much cinematic history, and so much wild and inspiring creativity. Stories, in book or film format, have always been my cherished form of escape. And though this novel takes place in the past, this world is still very much around us, from Grauman's Theatre to the Tam O'Shanter, from Hollywood Forever Cemetery (once known as Hollywood Memorial Park) to Venice Beach, where the Townhouse serves drinks in Cesar Menotti's former underground speakeasy. The Colorado Street Bridge is still hauntingly beautiful, curving alongside the 134, and Cole's in downtown Los Angeles still serves the original French dip sandwich (though, at the time of writing this, I'm told that Cole's end is near, which breaks my heart). Everyone sees the alluring beauty of the Hollywood sign, but don't forget the small clapboard bungalows in Silver Lake and Echo Park (formally the Edendale district), where unknown actors dreamed of a different day. Always, the past is present.

Though this novel is a work of fiction and I took some creative liberties, the truth of these years and this city provided ample material, from the Long Beach earthquake (a 6.4) to the parrots (yes, we have parrots!). And of course there are the lives and scandals of Hollywood legends. An article about Loretta Young, written by Anne Helen Petersen, as well as her book *Scandals of Classic Hollywood*, and the book *The Fixers* by E. J. Fleming, sparked the interest I had in the time period and the focus. In addition, books such as *Hollywood Horrors* by Andrea Van Landingham, *The Hollywood Studios* by Ethan Mordden, *How We Worked, How We Played: Herman Schultheis and Los Angeles in the 1930s* by Christina Rice, and the Images of America books were all amazing ways to glimpse early Hollywood and even Pasadena. Pasadena, you get a special thanks for being the setting of my childhood.

The bottom line is this book is possible because of others. A writer's mind can be a lonely, dark place, and to have people around you who tell you they believe in you, that you can do it, that you should trust in yourself, makes all the difference. Because everyone needs encouragement and help, and my writing has been made infinitely stronger by my army of trusted friends/readers, people whom I turn to for notes and words of support. In no particular order, I need to thank the following . . . Nika Serras, Rebekah Faubion, and Liz Parker, not only for notes that helped improve this book but also for adventures to speakeasies and studio lots, and for being my lifeline in a pretty wacky world. Nika, you would've had every right to end our friendship when I asked you to read this novel a seventh or eighth (or fourteenth?) time, but instead you dropped everything and came to my rescue. Thank you. For your generous time and multiple reads and cherished input, I also need to thank Tara Hall (you graciously read a seventy-page "outline"), Stephanie Stephens, Becarren Schultz, Laura Logsdon, Dianne Schwehr, and my brother Kamaron Sardar. I also always, always, *always* need to thank my mother, Addi Sardar. Mom, you would most likely call a shopping list I wrote "brilliant," but we all need that unconditional support, don't we? Thank you, for everything.

To my incredible editor Nancy Taylor Holmes, and to Krista Stroever—*thank you.* You made this book what it is. To everyone at Lake Union: I am so grateful to have such an amazing publisher. As well, I want to thank Alicia Clancy and my agent, Lucy Carson. Lucy, you are not only a brilliant agent but a story-whisperer, and everything I write is better because of your wisdom.

I have too many friends to mention, all of whom make a difference daily, but you know who you are. And, of course, to my family. To my incredible, kind, caring, and brilliant boy, Max (see above about unconditional love—but, in your case, you've earned it), as well as to my creative and supportive husband, Joe. None of this would be possible without you both. Oh, and I must mention our dog. Onyx, thank you for being such a good writing partner, and running to the couch every time I said, "Okay, let's go to work!"

And last but not least . . . Dad. I ask for signs. I listen for your voice. Always, I look for you. One thing I know for sure is you *are* still here, in myself and Kam, and in your grandsons, Max and Kayan. But I'd also like to think you're here in other, unseen ways, all around us. All those moments that are like a hand when we need help, or hope when we need faith. Yes, I'm pretty sure you're still here. Even in the sky because it's beautiful.

About the Author

Photo © 2023 Max Schwehr

Gian Sardar is the author of the novels *When the World Goes Quiet*, *Take What You Can Carry*, and *You Were Here*, and is the coauthor of the memoir *Psychic Junkie*. She studied creative writing at Loyola Marymount University, and her work has appeared in the *New York Times* and *Confrontation Magazine* and on Salon.com, among other places. Gian was born in Los Angeles, California. Her father was from Kurdistan of Iraq, and her mother is Belgian American and from Minnesota. She lives in Los Angeles with her husband, son, and dog, where she enjoys gardening, cooking, and other forms of procrastination. For more information, visit www.giansardar.com.